Praise
Be Still M

"The rugged charm of Appalachia is the perfect backdrop to the hardship and beauty of Joanne Bischof's tender, heart-tugging debut. The author's lyrical voice drew me in; the rich detail and authentic emotion kept me turning the pages. Lovers of historical fiction and topsy-turvy romance will find much to rejoice about in this lovely story. *Be Still My Soul* is a delight from start to finish!"

—CARLA STEWART, award-winning author of *Chasing Lilacs* and *Stardust*

"*Be Still My Soul* is a rare gem: a powerful and compelling story for every woman who's known love's real ups and downs. Author Joanne Bischof draws a poignant picture of a forced marriage and its challenges and heartache, followed by the healing and joy of transformative love. A refreshingly honest new voice makes a memorable debut!"

—ROSSLYN ELLIOTT, award-winning author of *Fairer than Morning* and *Sweeter than Birdsong*

"*Be Still My Soul* is a wonderful debut from newcomer Joanne Bischof. If you grew up loving Janette Oke, you'll want to read this tender tale of grace, forgiveness, and redemption."

—SUSAN MEISSNER, author of *A Sound Among the Trees*

"Beautifully set in the Appalachian Mountains, Joanne Bischof's debut novel is one of those rare finds that will keep you up burning the midnight oil. I literally couldn't put it down! Her characters are engaging from the moment they walk onto the stage of your heart and so real you'll remember them long after you turn the last page. As an author of two historical novels set in the Appalachian Mountains, I was enchanted by the setting and Joanne's deft descriptions. I can't wait to read book two of the series."

—DIANE NOBLE, best-selling author

"*Be Still My Soul* gives readers a refreshing dip into nineteenth-century American Appalachian life, with a story that bubbles into the heart like a clear mountain spring. Ms. Bischof's uplifting tale hits the palate as sweetly as the pancakes and honey her characters enjoy for breakfast. You'll leave the book feeling you've made new friends you won't want to forget."

—LINORE ROSE BURKARD, author of *Before the Season Ends* and *The Country House Courtship*

"A moving debut! More than just a love story, *Be Still My Soul* takes compelling characters on a journey of redemption in the dangerous beauty of the Blue Ridge Mountains. Joanne Bischof's masterful and compassionate insight into human nature won me over. I can't wait for the second book in the Cadence of Grace series!"

—SARAH SUNDIN, award-winning author of the Wings of Glory series

"Joanne Bischof offers a heartrending tale set in the beautiful Blue Ridge Mountains, where two young souls must put away their past and accept life together as man and wife. The story is sometimes gut-wrenching, as the young couple must endure difficult trials that lead them to seek and find answers in the everlasting arms of Jesus. *Be Still My Soul* will stir your soul and will leave you thinking about the characters long after you've turned the last page."

—DEBORAH VOGTS, author of *Snow Melts in Spring* and *Seeds of Summer*

BE
STILL
MY
Soul

BE
STILL
MY
Soul

A NOVEL

JOANNE
BISCHOF

MULTNOMAH
BOOKS

Be Still My Soul
Published by Multnomah Books
12265 Oracle Boulevard, Suite 200
Colorado Springs, Colorado 80921

The characters and events in this book are fictional, and any resemblance to actual persons or events is coincidental.

ISBN 978-1-60142-421-1
ISBN 978-1-60142-422-8 (electronic)

Cover design by Kristopher K. Orr; cover photograph by Mike Heath, Magnus Creative

Published in the United States by WaterBrook Multnomah, an imprint of the Crown Publishing Group, a division of Random House Inc., New York.

Multnomah and its mountain colophon are registered trademarks of Random House Inc.

Library of Congress Cataloging-in-Publication Data
Bischof, Joanne.
   Be still my soul : a novel / Joanne Bischof. — 1st ed.
      p. cm.
   ISBN 978-1-60142-421-1 — ISBN 978-1-60142-422-8 (electronic)
   1. Marital conflict—Fiction. 2. Life change events—Fiction. 3. Blue Ridge Mountains—Fiction. I. Title.
   PS3602.I75B47 2012
   813'.6—dc23

                                        2012014168

Printed in the United States of America
2012—First Edition

10 9 8 7 6 5 4 3 2 1

To my parents, Mike and Janette Soffes.

Weeping may endure for a night,
but joy cometh in the morning.

PSALM 30:5

One

The night air brushed her arms, and Lonnie prayed autumn's cool breath could whisper her off—carry her into another life. *Lord, help me.* She looked up at her pa and forced a tight smile. With his broad back to the moonlit sky, his scruffy face was hidden beneath the shadow of a floppy hat. Chestnut hair swirled against her cheeks, and she blinked, willing the breeze to calm her nerves.

Joel Sawyer arched a bushy eyebrow. "Don't see what's gotten ya so shaken up all a sudden."

She lifted her chin. "I ain't shaken." Her eyes dared him to say otherwise. "I just don't see why…" She bit her tongue at the tremble in her voice. Her thumb traced the fresh bruises on her wrist, each small dent the same size as her pa's fingers.

"Because your ma's got a headache." Her pa's growl was for her ears alone. His eyes bored into hers, even through the lie. "Can't go lettin' Samson down." Sour breath hit her face. "Now get on up there and sing for these people."

Lonnie swallowed and eyed the crowd that had gathered for an evening of dancing. With the first autumn leaves blanketing the forest floor, it was sure to be the last of the summer. She'd never sung for a crowd before and, at seventeen, felt foolish when her heart pounded in her ears and her skin tingled with fear. If only Samson hadn't asked that her ma sing this night.

Her pa had made it clear. No wife of his was gonna *snuggle up* that close to Samson Brown. Over his dead body, or so he'd said. Lonnie watched her pa descend the steps, shoulders hunched.

"Sorry about your mama's headache," Samson whispered. He smiled and his eyes crinkled.

Lonnie nodded, certain he knew the truth, yet fighting the urge to make a liar out of the man who'd just deposited her at the stage as if she were no more than a pawn.

Lonnie glanced to the sky, and even as night's chill crept past her faded gingham dress, she prayed for a peace from the One who could help her through this. Her ma was the songbird. Not her. Folks were always going on about how Maggie Sawyer had the prettiest voice on any Sunday morning.

A gray-spotted dog tipped his ears when Lonnie stepped over him onto the makeshift stage. Her bare feet skirted around a pair of lanterns at the stage edge. Samson Brown, eyes twinkling, raised a banjo onto his lap. Lonnie took her place beside the trio's mandolin player, Gideon O'Riley, and when their shoulders touched, she stepped sideways, nearly tripping as she did.

Gideon glanced at her, his expression unreadable until amusement flitted through his green eyes. Lonnie chided herself for blushing so easily. The fiddler tilted his instrument to his chin. The creases in his blacksmith hands were stained dark as coal. He nodded and waited, bow poised. Reluctantly, Lonnie returned the nod.

The hollow sound of his tapping boot echoed through the cracks of the porch. The bow slid across the strings slower than a cat stretching after a good, long nap. Gideon struck the strings of his mandolin, and Samson's banjo twanged, rambling as free as a holler. Lonnie watched in awe, bewildered by their confidence.

She clung to the shadows from the eaves overhead, but when her pa motioned for her to step into the moonlight, she scooted forward. Her bare toes reached the edge of the porch, and she glanced away from her pa's smug stare. When the fiddle's strings thickened in harmonies, Lonnie sang out the words. Her heart quickened, stunned by the sound of her own voice belting out a song she'd learned at her ma's knee. She stared into the blur of faces as feet stomped and calico skirts swirled, revealing dozens of homemade petticoats and faded stockings. She forced her foot to tap in rhythm as men spun their girls around. Those without girls jigged up enough dust to make a body need a good bath.

As they were about to round into the third verse, the words snagged in her throat. She blinked, her mind suddenly blank. *Lonnie, you know this!* With his shoulders hunched, Gideon's hands flew over the fret board, and the fiddler played louder than ever. After clearing her throat, Lonnie readied herself for the last verse.

But Gideon sped up, leaving the rest of the band behind.

When the crowd bellowed and cheered, Lonnie bit her lip. Gideon played faster, an impish grin lighting his face. She clapped trembling hands and glanced to the musician beside her. Shaking his head, Samson rose slowly from his chair and, still plucking the strings of his banjo, crossed the porch. He flashed a twisted smile.

Cheers swarmed from the crowd. With slow movements, Samson reached out his boot and kicked Gideon's stool so hard it flew out from under him. Gideon stumbled but did not fall. His hand fell from the fret board, and after throwing a glare at Samson, he grabbed the stool and sat.

"C'mon, Gid! Lighten up a bit, would ya?" Samson yelled over the noise.

Gideon rushed in with a few last strums until only his vibrations remained, bouncing through the woods. Folks whistled and cheered so loudly Lonnie could no longer hear the pounding of her heart. Clapping along, she stepped back. Never again would her pa talk her into singing in front of folks. No sir. Her place was in the back of the crowd.

Gideon held his mandolin over his head and bowed. As cocky as he was, Lonnie couldn't help but smile. He walked toward her and, without hesitation, draped an arm over her shoulders. He smelled of smoke and cedar. Heat grew in the back of her neck and tingled into her cheeks. She needn't look down to see the flame in her pa's face as well—she knew it was there.

When the applause mellowed, she slid away and scurried down the steps, her legs weak and head light with relief. She brushed past a nuzzling couple and ducked under a thick arm that clutched a pint of cider, finally spotting her aunt Sarah beneath a scarlet maple. Enough moonlight danced through the leaves to make the woman's ginger bun shine. Rushing over, Lonnie clasped her cool hands, the rough skin worn and familiar.

"Why, you're tremblin' som'n awful." Sarah squeezed her hand. "Don't think for one moment you don't belong up there. You'da made your ma proud."

Lonnie fought to catch her breath. "That was the most terrifying thing I've ever done in my life."

She felt a shadow behind her. Lonnie didn't need to glance over her shoulder when rough fingertips clutched her elbow. "We'll be leaving now." Her pa's voice was gruff.

She glanced at her aunt, then peered up at him. "Mind if I stay a bit longer?"

His eyes flinched, but then he sighed. The smell of moonshine hung thick. "Walk home with Oliver. He's stayin' too."

"Yessir. Thank you, Pa." Her words seemed to fall on nothing but the breeze as he strode from the clearing. Lonnie knew her ma would be up waiting, the littlest ones already tucked into bed. With a sigh, she let the last of her worry melt into the cool night air and turned to her aunt, pleased to have her company for at least a little while longer.

"So…" Sarah's whimsical voice nearly sang the single word.

"Don't say it." Lonnie wagged a finger with little authority, knowing full well what her aunt was itching to say.

Sarah sobered, the lines around her eyes smoothing.

But Lonnie knew her mother's sister well. "I blush too easily," she blurted.

A smile lifted her aunt's round cheeks. Twice Lonnie's age and with skin a shade paler, she was as dear a friend as Lonnie had ever had. When Sarah's gaze moved past her, Lonnie tossed a glance over her shoulder and saw the blacksmith run a cloth over his fiddle. Samson lowered his banjo into a sack. Gideon had moved on. His shoulder was pressed to the bark of a hundred-year-old chestnut, and his arms lay folded over his chest. The girl he was wooing looked more than willing to have his undivided attention.

"Seems like every girl in Rocky Knob wants to steal that boy's heart." Sarah shook her head. "Don't you pay it no never mind."

Forcing a shrug, Lonnie tugged at a pinch of her faded dress. The fabric, different shades of blue, had seen better days. She suddenly wished she hadn't been so eager to stay behind.

"There you are!" Oliver bounded up to them, his voice stuck between a man's and a child's. Lonnie peered up into his thin face.

"Heard you were still here," he panted.

The crowd milled around them. A child's boot grazed her bare ankle, and Lonnie moved closer to her brother.

"I meant to come find you. Please, don't leave without me." She fought a yawn.

"Leave?" His voice cracked on the single word. "The night's just begun!"

A broad hand clapped Oliver on the shoulder. "Indeed it has."

Lonnie looked up to see Gideon passing by.

"Gid!" Oliver squeaked. "Just the man I wanted to see." He grabbed Gideon's arm, halting him. Then, with scarcely a breath, Oliver began pelting him with questions about playing.

Gideon chuckled, but his eyes drifted to where he had been headed, his lack of interest in Oliver clear.

"And when you hit that solo…" Oliver swallowed loudly. His chest heaved with enthusiasm. "It was…amazing!"

"You're my kinda fella." Gideon tousled the boy's hair, nearly bumping Lonnie with his elbow. She stepped back, embarrassed by how invisible she must seem. She thought back to his behavior on stage and the way he'd made her blush. When a girl had Gideon O'Riley's attention, she didn't have it for long.

"Say, Gid," Oliver said as Gideon turned to go, "I've been wanting to learn myself. What key was…?"

Lonnie didn't hear the rest of her brother's words.

Gideon's body shifted, and his demeanor changed when Cassie Allan strode by. Only a few years older than Lonnie and quite pretty, Cassie gave Gideon a sorrowful glance. He tugged off his hat and ran fingers through his hair. His hand lingered, arm up, as if to shield himself. He cleared his throat, suddenly showing interest in Oliver's ramblings.

"Evenin', Gideon," Cassie said softly.

Lonnie studied her and saw heartache in Cassie's blue eyes.

"Evenin'," Gideon replied without looking at her.

Several moments of silence passed, and Cassie's fingers grazed his elbow. "Would you mind if we talk—"

"Say, Oliver," Gideon blurted. "That song was in G."

Lowering her eyelashes, Cassie glanced at Lonnie and strode off.

Lonnie's heart ached for the girl. She chewed the inside of her cheek.

When Cassie moved on, Gideon's gaze followed her. His green eyes were troubled.

"Perhaps you should let Gideon get back to what he was doing," Lonnie said softly. "The night is still young."

Gideon turned to her, his eyes meeting hers for the first time. Lonnie fought a yawn, and his amusement was clear. "Not for you, I see." Though the words teased, his tone was soft.

Her sharp intake of breath cut the yawn short, and she glanced away, embarrassed.

"I'm off myself. Good night, Lonnie." Sarah flashed a carefully disguised wink. "Oliver." Then Sarah nodded to the man who stood head and shoulders above her. "Good night, Gideon."

"Miss Sarah." He pressed his hat to his chest as she strode off. His autumn-colored hair stood on end, and he slid the hat back in place.

Lonnie watched as her aunt disappeared, thick skirts swaying. "We should start for home, Oliver."

"Home? I'm just gettin' started. Ain't even had a chance to talk to Samson yet." Oliver moved toward the makeshift stage, dodging a rowdy crowd, leaving Lonnie alone with Gideon. Oliver glanced back over his shoulder. "Say, Lonnie, why don't you just ask Gid to walk you home?" He vanished in a sea of shadowed faces.

Mortified, Lonnie stared at her feet. Her heart pulsed beneath her shimmy as she searched for some way to remedy her brother's remark.

Gideon stood silent, as if he too were embarrassed. His shoulder was so near that she felt the warmth through his plaid shirt. A strap crossed his broad chest, his mandolin tucked safely against his back. When he didn't speak, she braved a peek at his face. His expression was torn, gaze pinned on a pair of young women giggling a few paces away. His dark lashes grazed his cheeks, and he thrust his hands into his pockets. He kicked at a clump of dirt.

The banjo sounded in the distance, and Lonnie knew Oliver would soon be immersed in a midnight lesson.

"You must have somewhere to be. I'm sorry." The words felt inadequate. Before she could muddle the situation further, Lonnie turned and hurried toward the dark edge of the clearing. The sound of music and laughter faded. Her pa would not be pleased. And she had more than a few words to say to her brother come morning. To think of passing her off to Gideon O'Riley like she was a burden to be carted home. She braved a glance back to see Gideon standing there, indecision thick in his expression. He'd made it more than clear he had better things to do. She hurried on, eager to be home. A lump rose in her throat as she rushed forward. How she wished she could crawl under the nearest wagon and disappear from sight.

Muted footfalls thumped against the hard-packed earth, and Lonnie spun to see Gideon jogging toward her.

He caught up to her and peered down. "You walking home alone," he panted, running a palm over the back of his neck, "just doesn't seem right."

"Please, don't think you have to—"

"I insist." For the first time that night, his smile was for her alone.

His eyes bored into hers. As if his gaze could read into her heart, she glanced away.

Before Lonnie had time to think, Gideon whisked her away from the noise and lantern light. Laughter drifted away behind them, and he led her toward the cool, still quiet.

Two

A full moon lit the trail home. Gideon pushed a laurel branch out of the pathway, and careful not to bump against him, Lonnie ducked under the glossy green leaves.

"Thank you," she whispered.

Gideon nodded, and when she hesitated, he took the lead on the narrow path. She followed close behind, and although they walked in silence, more than one critter sprang from its snug bed in a rustle of brittle leaves.

The path widened, and their shoulders touched. Gideon glanced sideways at her. Lonnie stepped away.

"You all right?"

She felt him studying her. "Yes, thank you." She peered at him in the dark and tried to make out the curves of his face in the moonlight. A face she had always known from afar was suddenly clearer. Only a few years younger than him, she'd often seen him in passing but never once had spoken to him. It was rumored around Rocky Knob that only the girls looking for trouble sought out Gideon O'Riley. *Is that what Cassie was doing? Looking for trouble?* Lonnie shook off the thought. Cassie had always been a sensible girl from what she knew of her.

And what about you, Lonnie? Here she was, walking the path alone with him. Her mouth suddenly dry, Lonnie blurted out the first thing that came to mind. "I'm sorry my brother made you feel like you had to do this."

"It's my pleasure." Gideon offered a smile. "Besides"—he stepped over a rock and held out his hand—"you never know who you could bump into out here alone."

She grasped his fingers, and he helped her over. They came around the bend, and she saw the rutted surface of a makeshift bridge jutting over a small creek. She'd crossed this bridge countless times, but when Gideon's unfamiliar hand cupped her elbow, Lonnie feared her wobbly knees might send her into the dark trickle below.

Once they were safely on the other bank, he released her. Night's chill tickled her skin. Lonnie pressed her hands together and glanced up. He was even more handsome up close. Having grown up the shy, awkward daughter of Joel Sawyer, she'd hardly spoken to any boy, let alone the one who had mothers whispering warnings in their daughters' ears and fathers loading shotguns.

Lonnie gulped, suddenly realizing how alone they were.

Even in the moonlight she could see the smattering of freckles across his nose and the curl of hair against the nape of his neck. When he looked at her, Lonnie dropped her gaze and studied her trudging feet. She'd never admit it to her aunt Sarah, but she suddenly understood what all the fuss was about. It seemed all her girlfriends were silly over Gideon O'Riley. When his steady hand pressed to the small of her back, she began to see why. Lonnie climbed over a stubborn stone embedded in the path. His hand fell away, and she fought the urge to look at him.

Lonnie quickened her pace, grateful he could not hear her thoughts.

The path narrowed, and he fell in step behind her. She pointed out where a fork in the trail led to her aunt's cabin. Her refuge. "I'll be livin' there soon, I suppose," she blurted, not liking the silence. "Aunt Sarah's a soap maker. She's gonna teach me the trade. Just the two of us." Lonnie lifted her shoulders in a contented sigh. "I've gotta turn eighteen first, Pa says." She wrinkled her nose at the thought of waiting all those months.

"Is that so?"

"Then I'll be free."

"Free?"

"Of my pa. Though I don't know why he makes me wait. It's not like he wants me around. I'm surprised he didn't ship me off long ago." She screwed her mouth to the side, realizing she may have said too much. If her pa got wind of her true feelings, there'd be hell to pay. Yet she could not catch her words and take them back. She wouldn't, even if she could. It was no more than the truth. "I hope that doesn't make me sound ungrateful."

"Your secret's safe with me." He winked.

They walked on.

"Almost there." Her heavy breathing slowed her words, but she wanted to change the subject. "Home's not far."

Digging her toes into the hard-packed dirt, Lonnie trudged upward. More than once, she heard Gideon slip behind her. Her pa's cabin was higher than most folks', but having lived there her whole life, Lonnie had no more trouble climbing the steepest parts of the Blue Ridge than a mountain mule.

"Couldn't your pa find any better land than this?" A smile carried on his voice.

"C'mon," Lonnie teased. "I thought you were a mountain boy. Are you saying this little hill is too hard to climb?"

"Yes," Gideon chuckled between breaths. His laughter fell to a mumble. "Better be worth it."

The air cooled as they rose. Lonnie rubbed her arms.

Gideon hurried to catch up with her, walking closer than necessary now that the path had opened. "So where is the top of this mountain of yours?" The back of his hand grazed hers.

"Right there." Lonnie paused and pointed. "That's as far as I go." Breathless, her chest heaved.

A small cabin stood quiet and humble on the hillside. Its rough timber and warped windowsills told of a harsh life. A candle flickered in the window, giving off the only light to be seen. Lonnie knew her ma had placed it there so she could see when she got home. She remembered just how late it was. Surely her family had long gone to bed.

A night owl hooted.

Gideon shoved his hands in his pockets. "I suppose this is where we part ways."

Lonnie studied him. It struck her how far he had come. Here she was worried that she had arrived home too late, and he had another hour of walking yet to do.

"Gideon." She turned toward her house, then paused, uncertain. "Thank you for walking me home. It was awful nice. You better hurry on if you want to beat the sunrise."

He tilted his head toward the stars.

Lonnie shook her head at the thought of the early morning glow lighting his way home. "I'm sorry I live so far. You shouldn't have walked me."

As if the pull of her words had tied a string to his heart, he looked at her. He stepped forward, confidence squaring his jaw. "It wasn't as much trouble as you might think."

Lonnie rubbed her palms together. "I better get inside. Ma will be worried."

Gideon didn't look at her as he spoke. "Don't a fella get a good-night kiss? I mean...you do live pretty far."

Her breath caught. She had never kissed a boy before. Her ma always said kissing was for married folk. "Well, I don't know." She turned away and stared at the lone flame that beckoned, and she wished someone would wake and call her inside. Her hesitation spoke what she could not.

"I see. Good night, Lonnie." He looked at her cabin before turning. He started back down the path.

Torn, Lonnie glanced back at the man who'd come so far—just for her. She'd always disappeared in a crowd, but not this night, not with Gideon at her side, smiling down on her as no man ever had. "Gideon, wait." She ran to catch up with him.

One kiss might not be so bad. Not for the man who'd promised to keep her secret.

Lonnie blurted out the words before she could change her mind. "You can kiss me good night. If you want to."

Gideon stepped toward her, closing the gap in three long strides. Her heart jumped, and she feared he would hear. She smoothed her dress and folded her hands, as if a nice appearance would affect his answer.

He leaned forward, and cool lips touched hers. Like the brush of a feather, Lonnie could feel his wide-brimmed hat covering her face, hiding their kiss from the stars.

A few moments passed, and she tried to pull away, but Gideon slipped his hand behind her and drew her closer. The taste of corn liquor was bitter on his lips. With his other hand, he clutched at her dress, lifting it above her knee. His fingers traced her flesh like a spider's spindly legs. Lonnie gripped his hand, but the strength there was impossible.

"Stop." She ground out the word.

A groan, like the sound of an old bear, came from the back of his throat, striking a chord of fear in her unlike any she had ever known.

When he nestled his mouth in the crook of her neck, chills shot through her. Lonnie squirmed. She pushed against him with one hand and kept the other locked around his, lest it go where it wanted. If she screamed, her pa would stumble onto the porch in two heartbeats— shotgun in hand.

But her innocence would be hard to prove.

Gideon leaned into her, nearly crushing her with his hold. Fear sped her breath and her head spun. Desperate, Lonnie did the only thing she could think of.

"Gid, stop!" she yelled as loudly as she dared. With all her strength behind it, her fist crashed against his jaw. Gideon stumbled back, his eyes unfocused, as if still stuck in a dream. Lonnie snatched up a mound of dirt and hurled it at him. It shattered against his chest.

Still panting, his eyes narrowed into slits. "What'd ya go and do that for?" Turning his head, he spat a few drops of blood. He rubbed his jaw and glared at her.

With a wave of fiery tears building inside her, Lonnie turned and ran up the pathway to the steps. She brushed a wrist over her eyes before she halted and turned. "If I didn't know any better…" Her vision blurred and she shook her head. "I trusted you." She climbed the steps and slipped inside the door without making a sound. How could she have been so foolish?

She stepped to the window, the glass cold in the snug room. Cupping the flame with her palm, she puffed it out. From the darkened room, she watched Gideon straighten the strap over his chest and felt his gaze on the window. He turned and disappeared into the trees.

"Is that you, Lonnie?"

Lonnie dropped the curtain, shutting out the moonlight. A set of small, shining eyes looked up at her.

"Go back to sleep, Addie, baby. It's just me." Lonnie hung her sweater over the chair, then slipped out of her dress. The wood floor was smooth beneath her bare feet as she stepped toward the bed. She slipped beneath the covers with her little sister and pulled up the worn quilt. She slid as close to Addie as she could, draped her arm over her sister, and closed her eyes.

Still on the edge of slumber, the four-year-old mumbled, "You're cold."

"I know. I'm sorry. Go back to sleep, baby." But Lonnie lay there wide-eyed.

Images assaulted her.

She could still feel Gideon's jaw beneath her hand, see his bloody lip. She could still feel his fingers crawling on her skin. Cold lips touching her flesh. Lonnie shivered. Her ma had told her to never lead the boys to thinking things. Lonnie's eyebrows pulled together, but she shook her head. She hadn't led him on. But she certainly never should have kissed him.

With Sid snoring like a bear in the lean-to, her parents nestled behind their closed door, and Oliver yet to come home, gratitude coursed through her that her family hadn't seen what happened. Lonnie buried her face in her sister's hair and forced her eyes closed.

She felt violated. Worse. She felt sinful. Her chin trembled. God knew the truth. Lonnie stared at the mantel clock, ticking away the late hour. If only turning back time were as easy as cranking the key. Her stomach dropped and churned. The grabbing and the touching—a shudder passed through her.

Lonnie pulled her pillow close, sank her face into the feathers, and let out a shaky breath. The back of her throat burned. She looked at Addie's baby-soft cheeks, so full and plump. Such innocence. A tear slipped down Lonnie's cheek and onto her pillow. If only she could turn back time and be as naive as Addie. As naive as she had been yesterday.

Three

Gideon lifted his head when sunlight glinted through the glass above his bed. With one eye cracked open, he glanced around. The room was a blur of light, and he saw that his brothers were already up. Dropping his head to the mattress, he moaned. His head hurt. Or was it his jaw? He hadn't had that much to drink the night before.

Images moved through his mind as memories unfolded. He rolled onto his side and ran a hot hand over his eyes. Something about Cassie. In his mind, he could see her full cheeks and rosebud lips. She was there last night. Wasn't she? Or was it Lonnie? The one with the freckled nose. The one who never seemed to meet his gaze. Joel Sawyer's oldest girl. Gideon blinked his eyes open. He stared up at the ceiling.

That's right. It was Lonnie.

He rubbed his jaw and winced when the skin beneath his fingers throbbed. No girl had ever hit him. Gideon licked his lips. The taste of blood on his tongue was more than a memory. He sat up, his head spinning, and lumbered to the mirror that hung at an odd angle on the far wall. He peered into the dust-streaked glass and saw a split in his lower lip where a smear of crimson blood had long since dried. He licked his thumb and rubbed it away. The pain intensified.

"Why, that little…" Gideon shook his head even as he stumbled back to bed. He wasn't ready to face the day. "Hadn't even been worth it," he mumbled into the mattress when he collapsed. His frame was too long for the rickety bed.

He knew he should get up and get to work. He had a rocking chair to finish for Old Man Tate, but his head was pulsing and he'd probably just end up cutting off a finger or doing something stupid. His stomach grumbled, and although the smell of bacon wafted heavy from the other side of the door, the sun was warm on his back, and he gave in to the pull of sleep.

Lonnie stepped over a pair of rocks and knelt at the water's edge, being careful not to slip on the wet maple leaves gathered there. She tipped her bucket, breaking the surface of the sleeping pool, and cool liquid rushed over galvanized metal. After heaving the bucket onto the bank, she climbed out of the creek bed, her bare knees sinking into the moist earth. With a day's worth of chores yet to be done, there was no time to dawdle.

She dashed across the yard, and with a glance over her shoulder, she spotted her younger brothers in the distance just as she reached the bottom step. Their hammers split the silence of the quiet mountain morning. Backs hunched, Sid and Oliver pieced together the fragments of a busted fence.

Her bucket sloshed as she trudged up the stairs, and when she slipped inside, the warm air, infused with the smell of fresh-baked bread, greeted her. Before she could set down the bucket, her ma handed her a clump of lye soap.

Her ma wiped her hands on her apron. "Addie, run outside and fetch your sister some sand." With a busy day of work ahead, she panted out the order.

Lips pushed into a pout, the four-year-old slid off the rocking chair and went to the door.

"Take this." Maggie handed her a cracked pie pan.

When she heard her sister lumbering down the steps, Lonnie glanced at her ma. Did she suspect anything? Her ma's weathered complexion revealed nothing but a focus on the day ahead.

Lonnie sank to the floor. Her gingham work dress barely reached past her knees, but she pulled it up to keep water from soaking the dark gray hem. She dipped a rough brush in the water, and soon the scratchy sound of bristles on planks filled the cabin. When Addie returned with the creek sand, Lonnie sprinkled it over the floor, careful to get under the table. Addie watched from the rocker, her grubby feet dangling high off the floor.

Lonnie wiped away beads of sweat along her hairline. As she worked, the door opened and slammed more times than she cared to count. Each time one of her brothers tried to come inside, Lonnie was quick to stop him. Their dramatic groans were enough to make her chuckle, but she cringed at the thought of muddy boots tramping across the wet, clean floor.

A song kept her spirits up and her arms in quick rhythm. Her ma didn't like scrubbing floors. She disliked making soap even more. Every few weeks, Aunt Sarah sent Lonnie home with a new bundle. As Lonnie scrubbed, the suds were clean and fragrant. After giving the floor a good rinse, she set the scrub brush aside. She swabbed up what sand she could and swept away the rest. Sitting back, she admired her work, then stretched her neck from side to side.

Her satisfaction fled behind familiar storm clouds when the sound of heavy boots thundered up the porch steps. The door flew open, and her pa plodded into the cabin. Lonnie glanced to the floor as mucky footprints circled the table, and she rose. She brushed her dress smooth. His glare pierced her, and Lonnie's heart sank.

He tugged a chair out, scraping it across the wood planks. Her ma snatched a tin mug from the counter and hurried to the coffeepot. Lonnie backed toward the door.

"Where do you think you're going, young lady?" His tone was a brick wall. She froze. Her hand clutched the latch.

He knows.

"Where were you last night?"

She forced her voice steady. "Gideon walked me home."

Her pa scratched his hairy jaw. "That's what Oliver said." Yellowed eyes narrowed. "What took so long?"

Lonnie opened her mouth. "I…uh." She shot a needy look to her ma, but Maggie's shoulders sagged. "Gideon's a slow walker." It was mostly true. "He could hardly keep up."

The chair crashed into the wall behind him.

Addie shrieked and Lonnie jumped.

"Don't you tell lies to me, girl!" He stumbled around the table and grabbed Lonnie's arm.

"I didn't do—"

"You're a liar." The condemnation reeked of moonshine and coffee.

When Maggie sank against the wall, Lonnie fought back tears lest they spring up to betray her.

"You were with that boy. I seen ya out there." His grip tightened. Grimy fingernails dug into her flesh. "You disgust me."

A single tear trickled past her resolve.

"You're seventeen years old…and out there with that boy like that." He yanked her arm, and Lonnie fought a yelp. "I saw him crawlin' all over you." His lips quivered. "I knew you was good for nothing." He tossed a glare in Maggie's direction. "I know right where you got it from."

"Pa," Lonnie cried, finally finding her voice even as tears came. With a gasp, she twisted her wrist. "I didn't do anything."

"Did you know this, Mama?" Joel turned to his wife. "Your oldest girl was out there last night…bein' *friendly* with the *O'Riley* boy." His eyes stabbed Lonnie's. "I'm sure it wasn't the first time."

"What boy?" her ma asked, her tone cool, meant to pacify.

"The oldest." His voice dripped with disdain. "The troublemaker."

Lonnie managed to pull free and dove toward the door. Before she could reach the latch, a hand grabbed the end of her hair. With a scream, she fell to her knees. Addie burst into tears.

Her pa stepped around the table and crouched behind Lonnie. He grasped her stomach and clenched the flesh with his fingernails.

"Joel, please," Maggie cried as she stepped forward. Her hand trembled when it touched his shoulder.

He batted her away but released Lonnie. "Your daughter's soiled, Maggie. I'd bet my life on it." He spat as he spoke.

"Should I hold you to that?" Lonnie mumbled, almost soundlessly.

"Don't sass me, girl!" He pulled her to her feet.

The smell of day-old moonshine made her stomach turn. He pushed her aside, and Lonnie slipped on the wet floor as she tried to stand. Muddy streaks marked his trail out, and he slammed the door behind him.

Addie's crying faded into a whimper.

"I'm so sorry, Lonnie." Her ma stepped toward her. "Your pa…he didn't mean it."

Lonnie stared at her feet, a wave of disappointment rising inside her. *What did you expect?* Her ma had never stood up to her pa. Lonnie forced herself to glance up. *Why would she start now?*

"I know how you feel, baby doll. Your pa, he ain't got a lot of patience sometimes."

Lonnie wanted to plug her ears and shut out her mother's words. She wanted to shut it all out. Even Addie's crying tugged at her nerves. Still trembling, Lonnie glanced out the window. Everyone in her life had let her down. All except for one.

Her mother's hand was soft on her shoulder. "Lonnie." Her brown eyes held a sorrow, a regret that Lonnie couldn't begin to fathom. "I wish it wasn't this way." A broken heart spilled into her voice.

Lonnie walked over to Addie and flung her little sister up on her hip even as she willed her words to be calm. "We're going to Sarah's."

Four

Lonnie hurried down the front steps and strode behind the house. She glanced around the farm for signs of her pa and hugged Addie tighter as she hurried out of sight.

"Where we going?" Addie wrapped her little arms around Lonnie's neck.

"We're going to see Aunt Sarah. Won't that be fun?"

Addie's soft nod held none of its usual cheer as she pressed her cheek to Lonnie's shoulder. Lonnie bounced her sister higher up on her hip. She was four now and almost too big to carry, but it was a long walk and Addie hadn't asked to come. Lonnie could no more leave her sister home alone than she could toss a chickadee toward a rising storm.

Lonnie stepped lightly through the fallen leaves. Neither of them spoke. She'd walked this path countless times. Ever since the day her pa had slapped the first bruise onto her cheek. She had only been six. Sarah had held her on her lap, both of them weeping. That night, by the light of the fire, Sarah had read from the psalms. Two weeks later when Lonnie returned, Sarah had read another. They'd gone through the book once already and were now on their second time around. Lonnie could almost mark the days of her life by those verses. And with each passing year, she continued to cling to the hope that the end was in sight.

When her arms ached, Lonnie set her sister down.

"Can you walk for a while, baby?"

With her thumb in her mouth, Addie lifted her other hand. Lonnie took her sister's tiny fingers and held them as they followed the path to their aunt's cabin. The sight of rising smoke warmed her.

She pointed. "We're almost there. See?"

Soon enough, their bare feet padded lightly on the porch. The scent of nutmeg carried on the air.

Sarah looked through the window. "Come on in, girls."

Careful to tuck her aching wrist behind her back, Lonnie opened the door and led her sister in. "We weren't plannin' on coming. Just seemed like a good day for a visit."

Addie took her thumb out and started to protest, but Lonnie shook her head. Sarah watched the exchange, her face soft. Lonnie supposed there was no point in trying to conceal the matter from her.

"Your pa?" Sarah mouthed the words.

When a fresh tear betrayed her, Lonnie dragged her sleeve across her cheeks. Sarah's eyes widened, and Lonnie lowered her wrist, tugging her sleeve down as she did.

Anger flicked through Sarah's expression, then faded. "I was just about to make up some biscuits. And I've got honey and jam. Won't that be a nice dinner?" Sarah pulled a jar of preserves from the cupboard and watched with warm eyes as Addie took the offering.

Lonnie smiled.

A hymn lifted from her lips as Sarah beat milk into a flour mixture with a large whisk. Lonnie formed the biscuits, snuggling them together in a greased cast-iron pan. She always liked hearing her aunt sing. It sounded so much like her ma. But apart from Sunday mornings, Maggie Sawyer didn't sing much these days. Never at home. Lonnie knew why. Singing was for showing joy.

And that was scarce these days.

Lonnie slid the biscuits into the oven. She sank into the maple rocker that had once belonged to her grandmother and read Addie a story. Sarah bustled around the kitchen, stepping out long enough to tote away the slop bucket before returning with a satisfied sigh.

They ate their sticky dinner on the front porch with the late-afternoon breeze soothing fingers too impatient to wait for cool biscuits. As Lonnie stacked plates, Sarah brought out a tin of cards and, insisting the dishes could wait, dealt out a game. They let Addie win every time even though she never understood the rules.

When the light faded, they went inside and Sarah lit an oil lamp. "You girls are spending the night, right?"

Lonnie's heart lightened at the invitation. "I think we're gonna have to." She glanced out the window. Her ma would not want her walking the dark path alone with her sister. Sarah moved to the cupboard and pulled out a stack of familiar quilts. Lonnie moved about, helping her aunt make up the trundle.

"Ma knows where we are." Lonnie stacked her cards together as Sarah bustled about putting supper together. Addie slid out of her chair only to send a waterfall of cards to the floor.

Lonnie accepted the tin of fragrant tea Sarah handed her. She tapped two spoonfuls into the bottom of a chipped teapot and filled the vessel with steaming water from the kettle. The stove door creaked when Sarah opened it. Coals popped in complaint to her metal poker. Lonnie cleaned up the cards and stacked them in a neat pile. Sarah pulled a chair close to the stove, helped Addie up, and handed the little girl a spoon for stirring. When Addie grew bored, Lonnie took over, and by the time supper was ready, the little girl was curled up on Sarah's bed, her thumb pressed to her sleeping pout.

The smell of cooking pork filled the little cabin. Sarah set the skillet on the table and put the kettle on. She looked at Addie and smiled. "She must be so tired."

"It's been a long day." Lonnie plunked down in her chair.

"I want to hear all about it." Sarah took hold of Lonnie's hand and whispered a quick prayer before picking up the wooden spoon. "Now, what happened?" Sarah cleared her throat, then took a bite, all the while keeping her gaze on Lonnie.

Tears welled in Lonnie's eyes, and she blinked them back.

Sarah took Lonnie's hand in hers. "Oh, my darling. What's happened?"

When her throat thickened, Lonnie shook her head. "Gideon." The word trembled on her lips.

Sarah's wide eyes searched hers.

"He walked me home last night. And he…" Unable to find the words, Lonnie lowered her face into her hands. "It was awful," she wept.

Sarah's grip tightened. "Are you saying…" She let out a groan. "If I had stuck around longer, if I had waited until…"

Lonnie lifted her face and sniffed. "Nothing happened." She glanced to the door, uncomfortable at the emotion in her aunt's face. "But he tried."

"Oh, my dear, dear girl." Sarah hung her head. "I'm so sorry."

"That wasn't the worst of it." Lonnie smoothed her finger over a knot in the table. "It was my pa."

Sarah leaned forward, waiting. "What did he do?" The words were sharp.

Lonnie poked food around with her fork and spoke without looking up. "He said I was soiled."

A shadow crossed Sarah's face. "I'd like to give that man a piece of my…" A tear slid down Lonnie's cheek, and Sarah rose to surround her in a warm embrace.

Lonnie held on to her aunt's sleeve and wept. For the first time that day, she allowed the memory of what really happened to wash through her.

"Don't you let those lies stay inside you. The only opinion that matters is God's, and He knows the truth."

Nodding fiercely, Lonnie looked up. With the hem of her apron, Sarah smoothed Lonnie's cheeks dry.

"Pa…he said something about my ma. Said she was where I *got it* from."

Fire flashed in Sarah's eyes, but just as quickly, she composed her features. "Don't you mind a word he said about you or your ma." She rose and moved to the stove, where she whisked dirty dishes into the washbasin. She worked without speaking, her shoulders stiff.

"There's something you're not telling me," Lonnie followed. "Aunt Sarah, I'm not a little girl."

Sarah scrubbed a wooden spoon harder than necessary, and when she didn't respond, Lonnie touched her arm.

"Please."

With a sigh, Sarah let the spoon sink to the bottom of the basin. She pressed her palms to the work surface and leaned her weight on them. The sigh she breathed bespoke years of frustration.

"What is it?" Lonnie circled to her side. "Nothing you can say will upset me. Not after what happened."

"I never thought the day would come that you would need to know this." Sarah brushed a strand of Lonnie's hair behind her ear. "But I see it has." She motioned for her to sit on the trundle bed, and Lonnie perched on the edge, careful not to wake Addie.

Sarah lifted the lid of a heavy chest and pulled out a nightgown. Her fingers lingered on the oiled wood before she spoke. "There was a time your pa made a horrible assumption about my sister." She turned, and the sheen in her eyes caught the firelight. "I can see his mind is still made up." She rose and gently laid the nightgown in Lonnie's lap.

Lonnie fingered the lace at the edge of the sleeve.

"He's still not convinced. Even after all these years." Sarah tilted her face up. "But you're his daughter, whether he believes it's so or not."

Swallowing, Lonnie fought to keep her emotions in check. She took several breaths, allowing her aunt's words to sink in.

"Your ma was innocent." Sarah touched the center of her blouse. "I know it in my gut. She never loved any man but your pa."

Lonnie clung to that peace, believing with all her might that her ma was as loyal a wife as a man ever had.

"I'll never forget the way your ma stood up to him." Sarah smiled. "And she's paid the price for it ever since." She shook her head, shadows playing on her features.

Uncomfortable, Lonnie shifted. When Sarah didn't speak, Lonnie touched her arm. "There's something else."

Sarah pulled a pin from her hair. "It's just rumors." Her voice was grave. She pulled another pin free with jerky movements.

"I still want to know."

Sarah tugged the last pin, and her bun fell in a twist that unraveled against her neck. She looked down at Addie for several heartbeats, and when she spoke, her voice was nearly inaudible. "The man...you wouldn't know him by name"—Sarah pulled her knees to her chest and smoothed her skirt down her ankles—"never saw the light of day again."

Lonnie's feet turned cold.

"Looked like an accident, but there are those who've whispered how a grown man couldn't drown in two feet of water." She shook her head, tossing the shadows off. She forced a tight smile. "But enough of that hearsay."

"What do you believe?" Lonnie felt Addie's warm breath against her arm.

Sarah tipped her chin. "That your mother loves you. She may not be showin' it as well as she could, but know that she does."

Lonnie couldn't speak.

"As for your pa…I'd like to give him a good spankin'." Her shoulders rose and fell. "It can be easy to hold on to something just for a reason to be angry. But bitterness will never satisfy that man. It's my constant prayer he'll realize that before it's too late." Sarah clasped Lonnie's hand. "There may come a time he grieves his deeds—all of them. I hope one day he'll grieve for the time he wasted with you." Sarah's eyes lifted to the window, to the direction Lonnie had come. "With all of you." She cupped Lonnie's cheek and, without speaking, pulled the heavy Bible from its shelf.

"Now then. Where did we leave off?"

Lonnie clutched the nightgown in her lap. "Twenty-three."

Sarah read softly, the candlelight playing games with her features. By the time she finished, Lonnie's eyelids were heavy and a peace had settled over her. Sarah pulled the quilt snugly over Lonnie's shoulders, then set about extinguishing candles. "Now all I want you to do is get a good night's sleep. Heaven knows you deserve it." She kissed the top of Lonnie's head, lingering as a mother would.

"Wake up, sleepyhead." Lonnie brushed a curl from her sister's pale forehead. Addie stirred and opened her eyes, then glanced around the cabin. "I want Ma." Her chubby cheeks drooped against the pillow.

"Me too."

"I'm getting some porridge started for you, little one." Sarah stood at the stove, where a pot of water steamed.

Addie slid out of bed and climbed onto a chair as if breakfast were already ready. A scraping sound came from the other side of the door, and she jumped up.

A rush of cool air filled the room, and Addie bent over. "Polly!"

The gray cat rubbed her bushy tail on the girl's bare leg.

"I wondered where you were." Addie picked up the oversized critter and carried the armful of gray fluff back to the table. She sat with a grin.

Breakfast was quiet except for the sound of spoons striking bowls. After, while Addie chased Polly around the cabin, Lonnie helped with the dishes.

Sarah scrubbed at her large pot. "When are you planning on going home?"

"When Addie is ready. She misses Ma."

"You're a good sister to that little girl. She sure is lucky to have you."

Lonnie stepped aside as Addie scrambled past. On her knees, the little girl chased the cat.

"You've got a good head on your shoulders. Just gotta hang on a little bit longer." Sarah blew a lock of hair out of her face and, with dripping hands, reached for the stack of bowls Lonnie handed her. "I'm looking forward to bein' bunkmates." She scrunched up her nose playfully. But a knock at the door made their heads turn.

Addie's squeals tapered off, and Polly escaped beneath the bed. Addie ran to the window. Her tiny toes sprang her an inch taller. "It's Oliver!"

Lonnie shook out her damp apron. The door opened, and eyes the same color as her pa's stared at her. Oliver stepped forward, his fourteen-year-old frame filling the slanted doorway.

She couldn't hide forever.

He tugged off his floppy hat and turned it in his hands. "Mornin', Aunt Sarah."

"Good to see ya, Oliver. Won't you come in?"

"I'd like to, but I just come to fetch Lonnie. Pa wants her."

Sarah dropped her wooden spoon with a *clang,* and Lonnie saw the flush in her aunt's cheeks.

Pursing her lips, Lonnie tugged the bow at her waist, and the apron slid free. "Come on, Addie. We're going home."

Oliver stepped outside. Sarah reached for Lonnie and surrounded her in a warm embrace.

"You remember what I told you. Chin up. You are loved." She pointed a finger heavenward, and Lonnie felt a peace at her aunt's reminder.

Knowing she could delay no longer, Lonnie followed her brother out the door. Addie ran ahead, skipping through the forest toward home. *If only I could forget as easily.* "Don't get too far ahead, Addie, baby."

Addie picked up a handful of leaves and tossed them into the morning breeze. With his head down, Oliver strode in lengthy, swift strides. Lonnie quickened her pace to match his.

They walked in silence, and Lonnie was in no mood to try to break the awkward strain.

The knot in her stomach tightened when they came around the bend. A wagon and a pair of mules stood in the shadow of the cabin that loomed in the clearing. One of the mules lowered its matted face and sniffed at the ground. When Lonnie drew closer, the animals tilted their ears.

"Who's here?" Lonnie looked to her brother.

Oliver stared at the wagon for a moment, the fuzz on his chin catching the morning light. "Mr. O'Riley."

Her lips parted, and Oliver arched a brow. "What's the matter? It's just Gid O'Riley and his pa. They're inside talking." Shrugging, he thrust his hands in his pockets. "That's why Pa wanted me to come and fetch ya."

Five

Lonnie's legs went numb. She glanced at the windows but saw only streaked glass glinting in the sunrise. For an instant, she considered running. She could leave. Run away and never be found. With a grin that brought out her dimples, Addie skipped off and crawled beneath the porch. Her dolls were already lined up in their hideout.

"You all right?" Oliver squinted at her.

When Lonnie simply swallowed, he rolled his eyes. She placed one foot on the bottom step and touched her cheek with a hand that shook worse than the rickety rail. There was nothing to do now but go inside. It was time to face her pa. She thought back to her aunt's words and clung to the truth she heard in them. God was with her.

The sunlight faded. Lonnie peered up at a gray veil of clouds. Oliver hurried up the steps and swung open the door. Lonnie just stared at a darkening sky draped over the hills and valleys below. A drop of rain struck her arm. Then another, and another. A shot of lightning danced among the clouds.

Her pa called her name. Thunder followed a heartbeat later.

Lonnie started up the steps and heard men's voices. Her ma offered another round of coffee. The door was open, and after tilting up her chin, she entered the dim room. Mr. O'Riley sat beside her pa, their voices low, expressions serious. Glancing around, Lonnie spotted Gideon in the corner, arms folded over his chest, his eyes pained. An untouched cup of coffee sat beside him. He glanced up, and his green eyes flashed with anger. *Good.* She hoped her pa had scared him out of his wits. The men fell quiet. Aware of how close she was to Gideon, Lonnie slid forward, closing the door with a soft *thud.*

Bill rose from his seat and nodded politely. Her pa didn't move. Lonnie felt Gideon watching her, and she wished she could escape his gaze.

When she didn't speak, her pa cleared his throat.

Lonnie moistened her lips. "Afternoon, Mr. O'Riley." She nodded and tucked her hands behind her back. "Gideon." His name tasted bitter on her tongue. She locked her fingers together to keep them from shaking.

"Afternoon." Bill tugged at an invisible hat. When silence fell, he darted a glare at his oldest son.

Gideon wiped his palms on his pants. A crooked necktie bounced against his chest. "Good to see you, Lonnie." He didn't look up.

Still standing near the door, she searched for a reason to head back outside. Anything to flee this crowded room and leave the men to go about their business. There was no need for her to remain.

"Have a seat, Lonnie." Her pa's voice was rigid.

She knew that tone. More sober than he'd been in a month, his eyes were clear, his speech smooth. Had her pa brought Gideon to scold him? Judging by the beads of sweat on Gideon's brow, she guessed he already had. Before Lonnie could savor the notion, thunder crashed in the distance and she jumped. Her cheeks warmed when she was the only one startled.

Knowing she best obey her pa, Lonnie sat and faced the men in their chairs. She crossed her ankles tightly and rested her hands in her lap.

Her pa spoke. "Oliver, go help Sid with the chores."

"Yessir." Oliver placed his hat on his head and left quickly, nearly tripping over his feet as he did.

Lonnie watched her brother, heart aching to see him disappear behind the rough-hewn door. When silence lingered, she stared at the window. Rain misted against the glass.

Finally, her pa rose. "Now, Bill, like I told you before, Lonnie is my sweet girl and I hate the thought of losing her."

Lonnie stared at him in disbelief.

"As you well know"—his dry palms swished together—"I aim to keep my daughter's honor intact." His hands continued circling, like a bidder pondering his auction price. "And I'm ready to strike this deal if you are."

Deal?

Leaning forward, Gideon cleared his throat and busied himself with his necktie. Judging by the fierce set of his jaw, Lonnie was glad she could not read his thoughts.

"What deal?" she asked.

Her pa gave her a cool smile. "Like we talked about earlier, *dear.*"

Dear? Lonnie stared at him. "Pa, I don't—"

"Do I have to spell it out for you, girl?" He laughed and looked at the others, obviously waiting for them to join him. Bill offered a half smile. Lonnie's cheeks burned.

"Let's not be shy, Lonnie," he continued, his calm demeanor fading. "We have already discussed the, uh, events that happened. There's nothin' to hide now."

Lonnie stood and forced the words out slowly. "Nothing happened." Despite her determination, her voice wavered.

Her pa's eyes dimmed, and she stepped back. "I saw this boy all over you. And you," he spat, "lettin' him like you was nothin' better than trash."

Lonnie turned to Gideon. Sweat glistened along his brow.

"You tell them exactly what happened, Gideon O'Riley."

When Gideon finally looked up at her, the regret in his eyes nearly strangled her. "I tried." His voice came out thin, and his eyes flicked to the shotgun hanging over the door. "Your pa's convinced—"

"Shut your mouth, boy." Joel followed Gideon's gaze to the gun, the hardness in his expression clear.

Although her heart stampeded in her chest, her head suddenly felt light. Lonnie blinked, trying to keep the room in focus.

Her pa raised his hand—a signal of peace. "Now. There is only one thing to be done in a situation like this."

No.

He flashed Lonnie a warning as he took in a slow breath, then turned to his guests. "Now that my daughter is no longer…desirable for a bride"—he looked at Lonnie—"I have spoken with Gideon, and he has agreed to do right by you."

"Now wait just a minute." Gideon rose.

"Son." Bill's voice boomed. "Enough. You will do what needs to be done."

Lonnie's voice slipped out in a faint whisper. "Right by me?" Her hands shook at her side.

Fire flashed in her pa's eyes. "This is the end of the discussion, Lonnie. You will marry this young man. If there is a child, it will be born in wedlock." He cut the last word off sharp. Rain clicked against the roof.

So he wanted to get rid of her after all. And it couldn't be by her own plans and dreams. She should have known.

"There is no child." Still standing, Gideon ground out each word.

Joel stomped forward, any thread of patience gone. He thrust a stubby finger in Gideon's face. "Sit down and shut up." His nostrils flared. "Before I show you what we do to men like you."

Slowly, but with his eyes filled with a silent dare, Gideon sank back on the bench.

Lonnie didn't wait to hear more. She dashed from the cabin without so much as a word. Warm droplets of rain struck her skin, as if the sky were crying.

In one quick motion, Gideon burst past the door and pounded down the stairs. He'd left his coat and hat behind, and the air nipped beneath his flannel shirt. He spotted Lonnie on the edge of the creek, sitting on a boulder, her head to her knees. He marched forward, not caring if he startled her.

"You know your pa better than I do."

She rose and moved closer to the water as if he hadn't spoken.

He followed her. "Is there nothing"—shame tinged the edges of his conscience at the words he was about to say—"that can be done to... prevent this?"

She spun. "You'd like that, wouldn't you?"

"And what of you?" He stepped closer, no longer caring to try and be a gentleman. "Do you want to get married?"

Lonnie flinched, then composed herself. Without speaking, she simply ran fingertips over her eyes and shook her head.

When he moved closer, she held up her hand and he froze. "How could you do this?" Her hand shook, but her face was a storm cloud.

"Me?" His voice almost squeaked. Gideon forced his tone to soften. "Talk to your pa. Surely you can reason with him."

"You don't know him." She kicked a clump of dirt, and it smacked his shoe. She picked up another, and he ducked when it hurtled past his shoulder. Her eyes flew heavenward before she sank to the ground. She buried her face in the skirts that billowed above her knees.

With slow steps, Gideon moved closer. He knew all too well the moody ways of women. *Smooth her feathers.* Then just maybe he could squeak out of this situation unscathed.

He crouched beside her, and she grimaced. He scooted back and rested his forearm on his knee. "What can you say that will change his mind? Surely there's something."

She mumbled something about how she should have known this day would come. Resting her chin against her shoulder, she peered at him, brown eyes as wide as a doe's. "It's as good as done now. There will be no reasoning with him."

Gideon's shoulders sank. He picked up a stick, rose, and snapped it in two. Didn't he have a choice? He studied her a moment and glanced back at the house. What Lonnie said was true. He knew it by the way Oliver had called on them that morning. Gideon had hardly taken a bite of breakfast when the boy had darkened their doorway. By the time Oliver had stumbled through a message from his pa, Gideon had known there was nothing to do but try to smooth things over. But now his hope was as thin as Lonnie's.

Crazy Joel Sawyer. Gideon could have picked any girl to walk home that night. But like a fool, he'd chosen Lonnie.

He looked down on her bowed head. One stupid decision, and he was going to pay. It wasn't a matter of desire. Just that he'd rather attend his wedding than his hanging.

Lonnie's abrupt words were no louder than a whisper. "Go away, Gideon."

He rose but studied her small form. She hardly seemed older than a child, but he knew better. She was seventeen and more than able to marry. "Tomorrow, then."

"Tomorrow?" She lifted her head. Her eyes were red.

"That's what your pa decided on."

The color drained from her cheeks.

Good. Perhaps a healthy dose of fear would get her to reason with the lunatic she called a father. "Unless you can get him to change his mind. If not, I have to do right by you. Is that what you really want?"

Lonnie rose and smoothed her dress. She started past him, then paused. Her shoulder nearly brushed against his. The scent of hickory and nutmeg lifted from her dress.

"It's never mattered what I want." She strode away, her ankles pale beneath her hemline.

Gideon did not follow her. He turned, picked up a grainy rock, and hurled it at a tree. The clump shattered.

He heard his pa call him, and Gideon wasted no time climbing into the wagon. He hardly gave his pa a chance to do the same before he slapped the reins against the mules' backs.

His pa cleared his throat, and Gideon looked at him.

"I can't believe this is happening," Gideon blurted. "I don't know what I'm gonna do."

His pa worked his jaw and leaned back against the wagon seat. "You're gonna bring that little gal home tomorrow and start making this right." He ran his knuckles over his knee.

"Is that so? And what about Ma?"

"I'll see to your mother."

"Sure you will." Gideon slapped the reins again. If there was one person who ruled the O'Riley roost, it certainly wasn't his pa.

When they pulled in front of their house, Gideon left the beasts in his pa's care and stormed toward the barn. He was in no mood for questions and curiosities from his siblings. He unloosened his necktie and yanked it off.

He closed the barn door tight, wishing he could lock it. He threw his necktie into the corner, then grabbed a pitchfork and got to work scraping old hay from the unoccupied stalls.

The events from the last few days turned over and over like a millstone in his mind, grinding his actions into his conscience. But there was nothing to be done.

He could not step back in time and erase it all. He certainly could not waltz over to the Sawyer farm and tell Joel that he would not marry his daughter. That would only land him on the receiving end of Joel's shotgun.

Gideon clenched his hands around the handle of the pitchfork until the splintered wood dug into his callused skin. Nothing in his past suggested he had the makings of a husband. In fact, he had more than enough evidence to prove that he wasn't. He, as well as the rest of Rocky Knob, knew that he was the last thing a young woman needed. And he hated the thought of being shackled to one woman. Despised it, in fact.

With a grunt, he threw the tool against the wall. It clanged to the floor, and he kicked it aside. A goat stumbled around in her stall. With all his strength, he hooked his left arm, and his fist struck the wall. Pain seared through his knuckles and into his arm, but he pulled back and struck the solid wall again.

A shot belted through him. Pulling his arm back, he stumbled away from the wall and stared at his battered hand.

His ma called from the house.

Gideon tucked his fist in his shirt and hurried off toward the cabin. He slipped in the door. His littlest brother and sister sat at the table. He kept to the shadow on the far wall as he walked toward the bedroom in search of his sister.

His mother gasped when she saw his fist. "What happened to you?"

The frown that wrinkled her lips told Gideon she was not amused. The flour that covered her hands and the pot boiling on the stove told him she had no time for his predicament.

"Oh." He shook out his hand as casually as he could lest she see the damage. He was already embarrassed enough. "It was an accident. It's not that bad."

His ma clicked her tongue. "Well, go and wash up. Mae'll see to your hand." She dipped a slice of rabbit meat into a pan of flour before dropping it in the frying pan. "I've got hungry kids waitin' for their food, and I ain't got time for your foolishness." Her tone indicated that she meant more than a battered hand. For a moment, Gideon wanted her to know that he hadn't done what they had already judged him for. But the thought passed quickly. There was no point. And he was too tired to care. *Let 'em think what they want.*

He grabbed the kettle and moved to the far end of the room. With his back to the children crowded around the table, Gideon dipped his hand into the washbasin. The hot water stung.

His sister stepped from the bedroom and leaned over his shoulder. She clutched a pair of crumpled sheets beneath her arm. "What on earth did you do?" she whispered.

He let out a heavy sigh but didn't respond.

"Pa told me what happened." Mae pursed her lips, making her cheeks dimple. She took Gideon's hand and spoke with motherly concern far beyond her fourteen years. A trait she'd developed with four rowdy brothers to look after. "Let me see that."

Gideon let her take his hand. "What else did he say?"

Mae dabbed at the dried blood with a damp rag. "He said you were going to marry Lonnie Sawyer." She glanced up. "He said her pa is *makin'* you."

He grimaced at the shameful truth in her words. Gideon exhaled and lowered his voice. "Did he tell you why?"

"Didn't have to. It's obvious, and Ma isn't too happy about it."

Gideon winced when Mae squeezed his hand too tight. She rinsed her rag and dabbed at the wound. "'Sides, you know how Ma feels about the Sawyers. She hasn't liked them for as long as I can remember." She glanced over her shoulder and continued in a quiet voice. "Granny used to say it was because Joel Sawyer picked Maggie over Ma and Ma never got over it." Mae's chestnut eyes glistened as they narrowed under the weight of her words.

His eyes flicked to his ma's back. "I remember her saying that."

He held up his hand as Mae dried it off. She wrapped a scrap of old fabric around his torn flesh as a makeshift bandage.

A muscle twitched in his jaw when she knotted it tightly. "Well, Ma's gonna have to learn to live with it."

And so would he.

"We'll see." Mae dropped the rag in the dingy water. "But Ma didn't take too kindly to the news. It seems you've gotten yourself into more trouble than you're used to, Gideon. I don't know what's gonna happen."

Across the room, their ma dropped a spoonful of grits in front of

Billie and Sadie. Their bare feet were streaked with dirt and dangled just below the oversize chair they shared. Ruth's hip knocked the table as she skirted the rough corner, finally lowering steaming bowls in front of John and Charlie, who stuffed food in their mouths as fast as they could scoop it.

Gideon nodded toward the food. "We better eat"—he watched as his ma brought the frying pan to the table and set it in front of her lanky sons—"before those two hogs get it all."

"Well, that oughta hold it for now." Mae fiddled with the loose end of Gideon's bandage. "Just don't go and do something as foolish as that next time."

"I'll try."

Gideon sat at the end of the bench and speared himself a piece of fried rabbit. He thought of another supper taking place on the other side of the hill. He rubbed his sore wrist as his ma spooned grits onto the plate in front of him.

"Thanks," he mumbled, then took a hearty bite. He was too worn out to worry about anything else for the night.

Six

Droplets fell here and there, striking the muslin shawl on Lonnie's shoulders. She wanted to pull it tighter, but it would have been no use. If only she had her coat. But brides didn't wear coats. Or so her ma had mumbled as she had knotted the white fabric gently, her eyes awash with unshed tears.

The gray light dimmed, the landscape no more than a blur of fog and mist. Lonnie held tight to Addie's hand as they made their way down the path. With baby Charlotte swaddled in a threadbare quilt, her ma and pa strode a holler ahead. Dressed in matching white shirts, Sid and Oliver trailed behind, their black ties slightly askew.

Lonnie stepped carefully in her polished boots. Clasping her gingham skirt, she held it away from the mud. She remembered her ma the day before—on her knees, pins stuck between her lips as she hurriedly lowered the sky-blue hem of Lonnie's best dress. Lonnie stepped over a rock and skirted a small puddle. She'd walked this path every Sunday of her life. If only today weren't so different.

Sure it's worth the effort, Maggie? Her pa's words stung as much today as they had only hours ago. He'd circled her, his boots hollow and menacing on the wood floor as he eyed her. Lonnie had also studied him, the air thick and silent between them. She waited for some flicker of emotion to show that his soul wasn't as black as his burnished boots. Recalling the rumors that surrounded his past, she searched his face for a fragment of the truth. She held his gaze until he finally gave up and walked away. A surge of satisfaction had warmed her belly. She was almost out from under his grip.

Lonnie clutched the hem of her dress in one hand and held Addie's small fingers in the other. She tried to focus on the path in front of her. *Lord, be my strength.* The day ahead seemed impossible, the months and years even more so.

Heads lifted and eyes probed as her family stepped into the churchyard. Familiar faces turned.

"Folk in these parts never miss a wedding," her pa mumbled under his breath. He smoothed his hand across a freshly shaven jaw. "They could care less who was gettin' hitched, long as they get a free meal and a drink of whiskey."

Her eyes roved the churchyard that would have held tables and a spot for dancing had the wedding been planned. Wanted. With a flick of his head, her pa led the family closer to the church. He smoothed the damp strings of his hair, streaked with silver and still wet from a bath, and tucked them behind his ears.

A few familiar faces smiled and offered a friendly wave. Yet others, their mouths covered and eyes averted, whispered among themselves.

Her pa glanced over his shoulder and smirked.

Lonnie tilted up her chin. A few more hours and she would no longer be his. If it took a wedding to sever his hold on her, so be it. He glanced away from her pointed look and hooked a thumb into his belt. His grip on her was fading. Her freedom was so close.

No. It was slipping away. Lonnie glanced around for signs of Gideon.

Her ma straightened Addie's bonnet. "Doesn't look like Gideon's family is here yet…" Her voice trailed off.

Lonnie surveyed the faces, seeing no sign of the O'Rileys. Hope tickled her senses. *Might he not show?* She knew how his ma disliked her family. Had the woman poisoned Gideon's mind against her? Hope budded inside her. If Gideon had indeed changed his mind, she would be free. The whispers continued. Some took no care to hide their heated opinions. Ignoring them, Lonnie flicked a piece of lint from her dress. If Gideon changed his mind, she would not become his wife today— but with her tainted reputation, she may never be anyone's wife. Lonnie tipped her chin. That was just fine with her. She could live with Aunt Sarah, and they could spend their days on the porch making soap and laughing about the bright future ahead. Lonnie nearly smiled until her pa's sour voice brought her from her thoughts. "I'd like to see that boy try and skip on outa here." His jaw flexed.

"Would he do that?" Oliver stepped forward, tightening the circle. His slicked-back hair made him seem years older.

"I certainly hope not." Her ma folded her arms and cast a worrisome glance in the direction of the O'Riley home.

Tiny raindrops fell, but not enough to drive them indoors. Her lanky brothers stood on each side of her, and Lonnie felt out of place in the freshly pressed gown and boots that shone.

Voices fell quiet. Conversations clipped to an end.

Tall, slender men walked silently into the churchyard. Mr. O'Riley led the way, flanked by his sons Charlie and John. Lonnie released Addie's small fist and pressed her hands together to keep them from shaking. Gideon's head bobbed behind his brothers', his face grave. They slowed their pace until the oldest O'Riley sons walked side by side. Each of them was the same height, a head taller than most men in town. But Gideon stood out as being broader than his younger brothers.

His hair was shorter, slicked back, and mostly straight until it reached the nape of his neck, where it curled around his ears. He looked like a soldier surrounded by his fellow men. Lonnie glanced up at the sky, wishing to see the face of the only One who loved her this day. *God, are You there?*

"Lonnie!"

Turning, she spotted her aunt Sarah hurrying toward them. She wore her usual ginger bun and her best dress. A delicate lace shawl draped over her soft shoulders, and the black fringe danced against her arms as she nearly ran. She reached for Lonnie's hand. Her skin was ice cold.

Sarah's eyes glistened as she searched Lonnie's. "I'm so sorry," she whispered.

Lonnie couldn't speak, so tight was her throat.

Her aunt's grip tightened, knuckles white. "Know that I love you. Know that." Her fervent whispers were spoken for Lonnie's ears alone. "And God loves you. His eye is on the sparrow." She pressed Lonnie's hand to her lips as a single tear slipped down her cheek. "Oh, my sweet girl. His eye is on you this day."

Lonnie nodded eagerly, clinging to the hope her aunt offered even as Sarah lowered her hand. Sniffing, her aunt looked up, and a shadow crossed her face.

"Good day, Bill," Lonnie's pa said, his words as crisp as the autumn morning.

"Fine day for a wedding." Bill's cheerful tone was a sharp contrast to Joel's sour mood. "Lonnie." He nodded in admiration. "You look right pretty."

She couldn't make a smile form.

Her ma adjusted baby Charlotte in the crook of her arm and pulled Addie along. She called the rest of the children, leaving Lonnie outside with her pa. Lonnie watched as Gideon's family passed and climbed the church steps. She didn't bother smiling. It would have only come out as empty as she felt.

Each of them glanced at her. All except Ruth. Lonnie's heart thudded against her chest in slow, heavy beats. Gideon's sister Mae squeezed his hand and started up the steps, leaving Gideon lingering outside.

She leaned toward Lonnie. "I'm looking forward to being sisters," she whispered. Her short lashes framed a pair of honest eyes.

Unable to speak, Lonnie simply nodded, and Mae disappeared into the packed building. When Gideon passed by without so much as a glance in her direction, Lonnie gazed at the sky and clung to her aunt's words.

It felt strange hanging on to her pa's arm as they made their way to the front of the church. Every face turned toward her. While some smiled, others frowned, wrinkles draping their angry pouts. Lonnie was grateful she could not hear their thoughts.

With her arm over her pa's, she forced her feet forward. Still, she could not match his pace, and her pa gave her a little tug. Lonnie turned to see her ma's smiling face and tear-stained cheeks.

Then her pa halted.

Lonnie looked into his eyes as he released her arm from his. He met her gaze and blinked quickly, his eyes wider than she'd ever seen. Was that regret she saw?

But just as quick, the brown depths hardened and he looked away. His stone face revealed nothing.

Her body seemed to move of its own accord as Lonnie slid her arm from his. Rain pattered on the roof, muting the thundering of her heart. So this was what her pa felt like all the time. Soon to be trapped in a loveless marriage, she feared that bitterness would take hold of her as well.

When her pa turned his back, nothing separated her from Gideon's outstretched hand. She stared at her pa's shoulder, silently willing him to turn around. Whisk her away. But he sat, pressed his spine against the pew, and took her ma's hand in his. His eyes never lifted from the floor.

Cold fingers grazed hers, and Lonnie turned, fighting the urge to pull away. Stale air pressed against her lungs. She scarcely heard the preacher begin. Gideon's grip was gentle, and Lonnie felt the soft brush of cotton from a thin strip of cloth wrapped around his knuckles. She studied their hands, finally glancing up at his face. He simply stared at the preacher, and as if he felt her watching him, a muscle flexed in his jaw.

When the time came, she repeated the vows she was told to say. She shifted her feet, which refused to stand still, and heaved in a shaky breath.

A man coughed.

A woman quieted a fussy baby.

Hot chills climbed her spine and spread up into her cheeks. She could hear them. Hear the lies and the rumors in her head. Lonnie knew every eye bored into her back, and she heard their thoughts.

She's lucky that boy's marrying her now.

She tried to shake away the lies. She had heard them spoken too many times in her mind over the last two days. God knew the truth, and it was all that mattered. Lonnie straightened and tilted her gaze to the window. The preacher droned on.

Lord, is this what You expect of me? No reply came. Slowly, she blinked up at the gray light. Had He forsaken her?

She lifted her eyes to the ceiling and tried to keep the tears from finding their way past her lashes. She was drowning. In the middle of a crowded room, she was sinking, and no one would stand up and save her. Not her pa. Not her ma. Lowering her head, Lonnie stared at the broad hand wrapped around hers, the fingers and lines unfamiliar.

The preacher cleared his throat. "Do you have rings?"

Lonnie withdrew a handkerchief from the lace at her sleeve. Inside lay her grandfather's ring. A keepsake she'd had since she was a girl. And she was about to give it to Gideon O'Riley, with his greedy hands and heart. She turned to her groom. A pain started low in her gut as she held out the treasured token.

Gideon thrust his hand into his pants pocket, and his cheeks flushed as he switched to the other. A pair of earnest eyes met hers. The crowd chuckled. Lonnie watched as his ears tinted red.

"Here," he said, finally retrieving a small tin circle.

Lonnie studied the lines of his face. His hair was tidy and his jaw cleanly shaven. He hardly looked like the same man. His lips creased, matching the pensive brow that furrowed in concentration as he slid the thin ring over her fingertip. Lonnie found his eyes. They were focused on her. But his face held no joy. She moistened her lips as the cool band settled into place.

The reverend was closing the ceremony, and not caring if it was proper, Lonnie scanned the crowd until she spotted her aunt. She swallowed the lump that threatened to choke her. Sarah nodded once. The slow motion was a reminder of the words she had spoken outside. Lonnie's vision blurred, and when tears fell she no longer cared what others thought. No one had saved her. Her ma, her pa—they were all silent. They had abandoned her. She looked at Gideon.

The preacher spoke, his words final. Lonnie's heart threatened to break in two. She and Gideon were bound together.

"I now pronounce you husband and wife. You may kiss yer bride."

Her breath quickened as Gideon swallowed visibly. With a motion perfected by experience, he leaned in and kissed her. The act was so swift it sent a few chuckles through the pews. When the clapping began, Lonnie wiped a bead of sweat from her forehead.

Suddenly, she felt Gideon's mouth near her ear. "Let's go outside," he murmured. She weaved through the milling crowd. Gideon's hand gripped her elbow, helping her forward.

The clouds had parted, and the sun was bright and warm. Lonnie glanced around the churchyard decorated only with dried summer grasses and early autumn leaves. She'd always imagined her wedding would have peach cobbler and plenty of waltzes. Her friends would have toasted to the happy couple, and she would want this day to last as long as possible. She would have danced into the night with her new husband, until the stars lighted their path home. But when Gideon's shoulder brushed against hers, she knew that dream was gone.

Seven

Her pack swung back and forth, plump with most everything she needed—all except comfort and a bit of courage. Those she stored in the depths of her heart, placed there by the One who would hear her prayers. Lonnie followed Gideon up the path to the unfamiliar cabin and clung to that fragile reminder, hoping it would be enough to get her through.

Gideon glanced over his shoulder, his gaze dropping to the sack in her hand. It was the third time he'd looked back on the walk home. Finally, he slowed, letting her catch up. "I can carry that for you."

"I'm all right," Lonnie said, though the sack was heavy.

When she stumbled on her hem, his hand caught hold of her elbow, and just as quickly, he released her. She hoisted the hem away from the mud and let out a frustrated breath. She'd just have to scrub it out later.

"We're almost home," he said.

Home. Lonnie slowed. "To your pa's cabin," she blurted out.

"For the time being."

What did it matter? Wherever she lived, it would be away from her ma and her beloved brothers and sisters. Would she see them often?

Lonnie gripped her sack tighter. She doubted her family would be very welcome in the O'Riley home.

Like her own home, the cabin was tucked into the hillside. Charlie and John stood on the porch, leaning casually against the railing, smug grins lighting their faces. They'd beaten the wedding couple home. With so many guests offering warm wishes in the churchyard, Lonnie and Gideon had been among the last to leave.

Charlie and John disappeared inside the house, and voices drifted out, rising and falling with excitement. Gideon caught hold of the front door and held it for Lonnie. She froze in the doorway, his shoulder bumping hers. The room fell silent, and she glanced around at half a dozen faces that were all staring at her.

Gideon spoke first, his voice flat. "Y'all know Lonnie. Lonnie, this is Billie and Sadie." He pointed to a pair of children sitting side by side in an oversize rocker. "They're the little'ns." He motioned with his thumb toward the young woman at the stove. "You know Mae."

Mae flashed a warm smile as she moved a pot of coffee to the table.

"And you know my brothers John and Charlie."

The O'Riley boys smirked.

"It's nice to see you all again," Lonnie forced.

When Gideon stepped around her, she suddenly felt cold. "You know my pa and ma. And that's little Sue." He spoke without looking at Lonnie.

Ruth smiled weakly and bounced the baby in her arms. When she didn't say anything, Bill spoke up. "It's a right mighty pleasure to have you with us, Lonnie."

Lonnie shifted her feet.

"Bet you two are hungry." Bill looked at his wife, who handed the baby to him.

"I'll get supper together right away." Ruth moved to the stove, muddy hems swaying.

Before turning back to the stove, Mae offered Lonnie another smile.

"Is there anything I can do to help?" Lonnie asked weakly, rubbing her palms together.

Ruth let out a single, harsh laugh. "What are you plannin' on doing in that dress of yours? Get bacon grease all over it?"

Lonnie's breath caught. She looked to Gideon in time to see him take a slow breath. Mae pursed her lips. Ruth puffed her chest and glanced away.

"Well," Lonnie stammered. "I just thought I would make myself useful."

"You can put your things in here." Mae spoke up, her voice tender. She stepped toward a door and waved for Lonnie to follow. "I put hot water in the washbasin when I got home." The door creaked as she pulled it nearly closed. "It might be cold now, but—"

"It's perfect." Lonnie yanked her striped apron from the rough sack and did her best to shake out the wrinkles. The worn-out fabric felt good as she secured it around her waist.

Mae cracked the door just far enough to squeeze through, then closed it behind her. In no hurry to leave the solitary room, Lonnie removed the shawl from her shoulders. She folded it gently before setting it on a chair.

Her wedding ring glinted. Lonnie turned the ring around on her finger. She held it up to the window, studying it in the dusky light of evening. It was only made of tin, but it was pretty all the same.

The air was warmer when she stepped from the bedroom and accepted the stack of plates Mae handed her. The littlest children watched in silence as Lonnie set the table around their poky elbows and curious stares.

Lonnie saw little of Ruth other than her slumped shoulders and wrinkled mouth pasted in a frown, but Mae was always quick to answer Lonnie's questions and even offered her a cup of tea from the steaming kettle on the back of the stove. When Ruth called everyone to the table, Lonnie sat beside Gideon, his arm pressed to hers on the crowded bench. She wanted to slide away, but with the youngest children on her other side, she was smashed into place.

Bill bowed his head for prayer, and the family clasped hands. Bill eyed Gideon, who hesitated before cupping Lonnie's fingers in his wide palm. He held them loosely.

She tried to swallow a swell of emotions.

When Bill finished, Ruth scooped food onto each tin plate, finishing with Lonnie. Her lips taut, Ruth glanced to her son. "Y'all will be on your own soon, I reckon."

Gideon cleared his throat. "Yes ma'am." He failed to mask the surprise in his voice.

"Well"—Ruth sweetened her tone as the wooden spoon *thunked* inside the empty pot—"I know you will." She waved a hand in the air. "Not like you had much time to plan."

Lonnie glanced down at her portion, and guilt soured her appetite. She couldn't look at Gideon's ma for the rest of the meal, and when she finally managed to finish her supper, Charlie and John had already complained about still being hungry.

When dishwater littered the yard and a stack of scrubbed plates was tucked away, the family sat around the fire and Bill read a chapter from the Bible. His voice echoed off the walls, strong and clear. Never once did he stumble over the easy words as her pa would have done. Lonnie sat in the rocking chair, her feet firmly planted on the floor, determined to keep the squeaky wood from drawing attention to her. Despite her efforts, she felt Gideon watching her.

When the coals in the fire were all that remained, Bill stretched and yawned. "Well, that's that." He stood, beat the back of his tobacco pipe against his palm, and set it on the mantle. "Time to turn in." He nodded his good-night to the others and disappeared into his bedroom. Ruth ordered Mae to tuck the little ones in before she followed her husband. A sleeping baby Sue nestled in her arms.

Mae drew her siblings over to the washbasin, where they each stood on tiptoe to rinse their hands and faces.

"Well, good night," John mumbled to no one in particular. He stood and stretched thin arms overhead.

Lonnie's heart leaped into her throat. *Stay. Please stay.* She watched as John blew out all but one of the few remaining candles. The room dimmed.

Don't leave me alone.

But Lonnie held her tongue. "Good night," she said softly.

John and Charlie headed for their bedroom. The room Lonnie had changed in. The room where all her belongings lay. Gideon reached out his foot. Charlie tripped and stumbled forward, catching himself before he fell. He spun around and stepped forward, eyes narrow. "What's the idea, Gid?"

Gideon crossed his arms over his chest. "Where do you think you're goin'?" His voice was low.

"Well, to bed!" Charlie hollered, his face inches from his older brother's.

"I know that. But you ain't sleepin' in there." He tossed his thumb in Lonnie's direction. His unspoken words made her stomach churn.

Her cheeks grew hotter than the coals in the fire. She lowered her eyes and suddenly found great interest in Charlie's worn-out boots.

Charlie put hands to hips. "You trying to tell us that we're gettin' kicked out of our own room?"

Gideon nodded slowly.

"Well, where we supposed to sleep?" John pitched in.

"On the floor. By the fire, where it's warm." Gideon rose and, without another word to Lonnie, disappeared into the bedroom.

She didn't move. Perhaps he intended for her to sleep somewhere else? A tiny warmth of hope grew in her, but before it could bloom, he stepped into the doorway.

"Come on, Lonnie, you can sleep in here." He held the door open, and as the room swallowed her up, she heard Charlie mutter under his breath.

"Guess I need to get me a wife."

"Who'd have you?" John countered.

Gideon shut the door, muting their scuffle.

Lonnie looked around the room, lit only by the candle Gideon held in his hand. Her gaze traveled across the furnishings. She tugged a comb and brush from her sack and set them neatly on the dresser to occupy herself. With that done, she turned around. The room was so small, it seemed impossible not to absorb in one blink. A bed with a swayed mattress huddled in the corner. Blankets lay scattered about. Shirts and pants hung over the bedframe in disarray, and Lonnie couldn't begin to guess which boy they belonged to. She glanced around the rest of the room, and it wasn't until her chest burned that she realized she was holding her breath.

As if he sensed her discomfort, Gideon pulled the clothes from the frame and tossed them in a heap on the floor. He tugged the blankets, barely straightening them. "We left in a hurry." Gideon fell silent as he moved two pillows to the head of the bed. "Hadn't thought this far ahead." Their gazes locked, and Gideon smeared his palms on his pants.

After the way he'd acted three nights before, Lonnie found that hard to believe.

He sat on the bed with a grunt and yanked off his shoes. Each boot thudded to the floor, and Lonnie thought of listening ears in the rest of the house. She cringed. Gideon tugged at his neatly tucked shirt, loosening it from his pants. With quick fingers, he started on the buttons. Lonnie stared at the floor and pressed her hands to her cheeks.

His fingers stilled. "You all right?"

If she spoke she would cry, so Lonnie just nodded.

"I'm gonna get a drink of water." The bedframe creaked when he stood.

Lonnie stepped aside, letting him pass. When he was gone, she undressed down to her shimmy and slid into her nightgown before climbing onto the straw tick mattress. She drew the covers up to her chin and scooted toward the wall until the rough logs jabbed at her back.

His eye is on the sparrow.

Lonnie prayed God could not see her now, not like this. Even so, she needed His strength.

When Gideon returned a few moments later, he shut the door silently. His every movement was slow and drawn out. Tortured, Lonnie closed her eyes. Finally, she heard him blow out the candle. When the weight of his body sank the straw tick, she grabbed at the homemade mattress to keep from rolling into him. He stilled, and she pulled her arms into her chest so as not to touch him.

She scarcely heard him swallow over the thundering of her heart. His pillow rustled when he turned to look at her. Then without a word, he rolled toward the wall. His shoulders rose and fell slowly. Lonnie stared at the ceiling as relief washed through her.

Eight

"I don't like her." Ruth's voice grated.

Gideon finished the last of his eggs. "Sorry to hear that." He'd woken to an empty bed and was in no mood for his ma's choice of topic.

"You gonna stand there and act like you don't care?"

"I don't see what can be done about it." He sipped his cold coffee. "'Cept to say that we'll be outa here soon anyway."

"Think that'll solve your problems?"

"Some of them." He pushed his empty plate away and threw back the last of his coffee. "I have work to do."

His ma poured boiling water from the kettle into the washbasin. "Is that what you call it? Just whittlin', if you ask me." Her eyes moved to a half-finished walking stick that should soon boast an intricate top. "It's not like you ever get paid with money."

When his irritation heightened, Gideon tapped his thumb on the table. "You didn't complain about the pair of rabbits I brought home last week."

Her face softened, but not by much. She shook her head. "Gideon." She moved the porridge pot from the table. It had long since been picked clean by hungry mouths. "You know I hate to see you go."

"Then that makes one of us." He looked his ma in the eye, not caring if his words would hurt. She was as tough as they came; she'd be over it before the dishes were done.

She waved a hand at his words. "It's not you, Gid." She lowered her voice, the wrinkles around her mouth deepening. "It's that girl."

Gideon ignored her comment as he reached for his coat.

"All I'm sayin' is that you could have done better—"

The slamming door drowned out the rest of her words as Gideon strode from the house.

"Little late for that." But his conscience told him otherwise.

If there was one thing he'd learned about Lonnie, it was that she was as brave a creature as he'd ever met. It didn't take him long with the candle snuffed out to realize that. Gideon chewed the inside of his cheek. What did she think he was going to do to her? He might have been a fool once, but he wasn't cruel.

Thinking of the half-finished rocker, he headed toward his woodshop. He spent the better part of an hour oiling the new wood before he spotted Charlie hauling water from the well. His younger brother's wiry arms were taut from the load. Knowing the oil would need to soak in, Gideon walked that way.

"Up for an outing?" he asked, taking the bucket.

Charlie fell in step beside him as they strode toward the house. "What do you have in mind?"

Gideon suggested they stroll down to their secret spot in the meadow. Charlie grinned. Gideon deposited the water by the door where his ma would find it.

"Where's Lonnie?" Charlie asked.

"Mae invited her berry pickin'."

"Oh. So when do I get my room back?"

A handful of years younger than Gideon, Charlie cared little of the ways of women. Gideon didn't blame him.

"Probably sooner than you think." With hardly any money to his name, Gideon's best bet was building a shanty on his pa's land. But his ma had made it clear how she felt having Lonnie around. Something inside Gideon told him a little distance would be better. With Joel no longer breathing down his neck, Gideon knew he had nothing to fear from Lonnie's pa. Still, the notion to distance himself from it all was growing more appealing by the hour.

"Should we see if Hollis is around?" Charlie asked, interrupting his thoughts.

Gideon pulled his hand from his pocket, and when they neared their friend's cabin, he picked up a small stone and tossed it at the loft window. A few moments passed and then a ruddy face appeared behind the glass. Charlie waved the young man down. They kept to the path without slowing. A bend brought them into a small hollow surrounded by thick trees and bordered on one side by a faint creek. The hollow opened to a meadow, the autumn grasses unfolding toward the hills in a dry, crisp blanket.

Gideon picked up a pebble and threw it with enough force to startle a pair of crows hopping along the water's edge. His younger brother grabbed a stick and did the same. They tried to see who could get their rock closest to an X in the rough bark of a gnarled oak. Gideon had carved the target a few summers before.

"What are you two sissies up to now?" a raspy voice croaked.

Gideon turned to see Hollis step past a tree. "I wondered if you'd be able to sneak away."

"When have I ever failed you?" Hollis held up a newspaper and a quart jar filled with clear liquid. The sun danced across the glass, piercing Gideon's soul as much as his eyes.

"That a boy."

"How many times have I told you to get your own paper?"

"I lost count."

"And yet I save them for you." Hollis slapped the paper against Gideon's chest.

Gideon grinned. He took the wrinkled newspaper and tucked it under his arm.

"Done stole this from my pa's still." Hollis tipped the jar to his lips. "Taste's rough." He grimaced, then swallowed. "But the kick's quick." He stepped in front of the mark, bringing the game to a halt. "He'll tan my hide if he finds out." He took a long chug, then wiped his mouth with the back of his hand before holding out the jar. "Look atcha. An old married man."

Gideon grunted and clutched the moonshine to his chest. "So it seems."

"Bet it's treatin' ya good." Hollis wagged bushy eyebrows.

Gideon shrugged. He put the glass to his lips. The sting of alcohol hit his throat, and in an instant, he pictured Lonnie's face. He swallowed the poor man's liquor and wiped his mouth. He wasn't much of a spiritual man, but if he were, he'd liken the feeling to guilt.

Shaking his head to dislodge the image, he lowered the jar. He knew his emotions had betrayed him when Hollis smirked. Throwing shame to the wind, Gideon took another swig and let the liquid burn its way down his throat until his eyes watered. Passing off the jar, he leaned his shoulder against a tree and shook open the newspaper. "Anything interestin'?"

"Not much." Hollis stepped closer and tapped the center of the second page. "But says here they're lookin' for workers in Stuart. Towns growin' ever since they ran the railroad through there. Stores, banks. That's what holds folks'—"

"I know what a bank is."

"Been thinkin' about takin' myself down there. See more of the world. Pays good too."

"That so?" Gideon studied the small printing and struggled to read half the words.

Hollis nodded and folded his hands behind his head. Still standing, he tilted his face toward the sun and closed his eyes.

Beside him, Charlie threw pebbles at the tree.

Finally, Hollis looked at him. "Say, Gid. Sorry I missed the weddin'."

"Were you waiting for a formal invitation or did you just sleep too late?"

Hollis grinned. "Sure would've liked to have seen the look on yer face." He flicked up the collar of his coat. "My pa says Joel Sawyer's crazy." His eyes sparkled with mischief. "You've heard what folks say about him."

Gideon sat and rested his forearms on his knees. "Yes." He cast Hollis a sideways glance. "And I'd rather not think about it."

Hollis guffawed, his ruddy face turning a shade redder. "You done messed with the wrong daughter!"

Gideon snatched up a stick and hurled it at him.

Still laughing, Hollis ducked, but it clattered against his shoulder. "Not so big for yer britches now, eh?"

Gideon made a face. "You talk too much." He took another swig of moonshine.

"Watch yourself there, Gid." Charlie snatched the quart from him. "Save some for me."

"Aw, hush, Charlie." Gideon leaned back against a tree, the liquor warming him. "You ain't never had a drink in your life and you know it."

Charlie set his jaw, and with a brave glint in his eyes, the sixteen-year-old took a sip. He choked and coughed but managed to swallow. "I have now," he said, eyes tearing.

"Give me that." Hollis yanked the jar from Charlie and plunked it down on a rock. He settled the drink between his boots and shook his head. "Sissy."

Charlie shoved his hands into his coat pockets, his face still screwed up from the taste.

"So tell me…," Hollis began.

"I don't want to talk about it if that's what you're getting at." Gideon stared straight ahead.

"Aw, c'mon. You're the first one to get married."

Gideon tossed a leaf toward the creek. "Yeah, so why am I hangin' out with two ugly bachelors?"

"Good question," Hollis murmured before taking another sip. He handed it to Charlie. "I've seen that Lonnie Sawyer." The whistle that slipped past his teeth sent a wave of irritation through Gideon.

"It's O'Riley now," Charlie blurted as he swallowed and passed the jar back.

"Shame. Shame." Hollis shook his head and traced his finger along the mouth of the jar. "Pretty thing."

"Watch it," Gideon said flatly. But Hollis's implication bothered him more than he liked. He crossed one boot over the other.

Hollis plunked the moonshine at his feet. He lifted his hands palms up, his freckled face the picture of innocence. "I'm as saintly as they come."

"Sure." Gideon tried to push Lonnie out of his mind.

"Oh, I see." Hollis dragged out the words slowly. "And here I thought you was just bein' a gentleman." He grinned. A snaggle tooth caught the afternoon sun. "I see what's gotten ya all moody." With the tip of his finger, he poked his hat back. "Nothin' happened." He leaned forward. "Did it?"

Gideon's eyebrows clamped together. "What makes you think I'd tell you?"

Hollis seemed to study him. "And all these years I had you pinned as some ladies' man."

"Shut up." Gideon stood.

"Aw, don't get your socks in a twist." Hollis screwed the lid on the jar.

"It's none of your business." Gideon motioned for his brother to stand.

"Well, I sure won't be gettin' the cold shoulder on *my* weddin' night." Hollis's laugh grated.

Gideon waved off the comment and tucked the paper beneath his arm before striding down the path. Charlie followed behind, his steps uneven. Gideon grasped his brother's arm and led him toward home.

"The moon looks mighty fine from up here," Charlie said, tipping back. He fell with a thud on the seat of his pants.

With a groan, Gideon retraced his steps. "First of all..." He crouched down. "You're not up there, you're down here." He flung Charlie's arm over his shoulder and, setting his jaw, heaved his brother to his feet with a grunt. " 'Sides. That's the sun." His ma would skin him alive if she saw Charlie in this state.

He helped his brother stumble up to the farm and left a near-snoozing Charlie leaning against a tree to sleep off the moonshine. Judging by the sky, there were still a few hours left before supper. Gideon studied the chimney with its thin trail of smoke. The door opened, and he watched as Lonnie walked toward the chicken coop, a basket in the crook of her arm. Hollis's taunt came to mind, and Gideon ran a hand over the back of his neck.

He'd never been rejected before. Not once.

Until the night Lonnie had socked him in the jaw.

He ran knuckles over the spot, remembering the ache that had lingered there for two days. He'd felt the same dejected feeling the night before. It wasn't that he liked her, but he knew a scared girl when he saw one, and last night, Lonnie had clearly wanted nothing to do with him. He couldn't have cared less when it was just between Lonnie and him, but after what Hollis had said, a fresh bruise was forming on his ego.

Gideon fiddled with the top button of his shirt until his collar was straight. He smoothed his hand through his hair and strode toward the chicken coop that nestled against his woodshop. He had no idea what he was going to do or say, but he had a mind to prove Hollis wrong. The sooner, the better.

Nine

"G ideon?" Lonnie looked up when Gideon pushed the small door
open. A dozen brown eggs filled her basket, and she clutched
another in her hand.

He leaned against the jamb as casually as he could manage.
"Thought I might find you here." He knew his voice was too smooth
when she arched an eyebrow. He cleared his throat, knowing he'd better try a different approach. "I was hoping you might have a few minutes to spare." He kept his tone light, friendly.

Girls liked that.

He motioned with his head toward his woodshop. She followed the
movement, her face still uncertain. And why shouldn't she be confused?
When had he ever proven that she could trust him? Gideon swallowed.
He hadn't so much as touched her last night. He hoped he might have
earned a tiny bit of her trust with that. All he needed was a little.

"I wanted to show you something."

"Me?" Her eyebrows pinched together.

"Yeah. I thought I might show you what I do." He straightened and
held the door ajar. "C'mon."

Her face was shadowed in confusion, but she set the basket down and followed him into the late afternoon sun. They walked without speaking. Gideon tugged the heavy door open, then pressed his hand to the small of her back. The fabric was soft to his fingers. Lonnie stepped into the darkness. He followed her in, turned the knob on the kerosene lamp, and when a yellow light pooled over his work surface, he closed the door tight.

Tilting her chin up, Lonnie glanced around. He heard her soft gasp.

He fought to keep his smile in check.

Unfinished furniture covered every surface. The tangy scent of fresh-cut wood hung thick in the air. Her mouth formed a small O. Gideon gripped the bottom of the rocking chair that stood in the center of the workbench. The oil had soaked in to a rich sheen, and it shone even in the weak light. Lonnie reached up and touched the curved seat. Her thumb followed the speckled grain of the precious bird's-eye maple. Gideon had spent hours shaping the seat. He reached up and, with one hand, pulled a child's stool down from the overhead shelf. He tilted it toward Lonnie. Her gaze roved the intricately carved legs, the delicate spindles that had taken him hours.

"You made all this?" she said softly.

"In my spare time." He leaned against the workbench and studied her, but she didn't blush as other girls did.

Her face was soft, as if taking it all in. Good. Gideon folded his arms, giving her time. No sense scaring her off again. Lonnie moved slowly around the workbench, her bare feet leaving small prints in the sawdust-covered floor. Gideon didn't move. He simply watched her. He'd seen the type before. He knew the kind of girl she was. The kind who just wanted to be loved. The kind who had no idea what that looked like.

He was just the man to swoop in and show her.

She seemed to notice a crock full of wooden spoons. She lifted one out and turned it in her hand.

"No. This one." He gently took the spoon from her and pulled out a smaller one. It was the perfect fit for her palm.

She felt the oak handle, and Gideon knew it was as soft as silk. He'd spent a lot of time on that one. Like his ma said, it wouldn't fetch much, and he was no doubt a fool to spend all his time in this dusty old shop, but he couldn't pass by a piece of wood without thinking what he might make it into.

"It's beautiful," Lonnie said softly. She went to put it back.

"Keep it." Gideon folded her fingers closed around the handle. "It's yours." He looked at the floor. "Consider it a wedding present." He straightened his collar again. "At least until I can make you something finer. Maybe a rocker. Whatever you want." He sounded too eager, so he reined himself in. "You can think about it for a while."

She studied the spoon in silence, and when she braved a glance up, he saw that her expression was torn. He laid his hand on the worktable so his fingers lay close to hers. Her eyes followed the movement. Her mouth parted as if to speak.

"Please," he said. "I know it won't make up for what's happened." His pinkie grazed hers.

When Lonnie looked up at him and he saw the hope in those brown eyes, something stopped him from saying more. He couldn't. Anything more would be a lie. But why should he care? It had never stopped him before. His confidence wavering, he gulped. *Pull yourself together.* He cleared his throat. It was now or never. Besides, she was his wife.

He tipped her chin, letting his finger linger. "I know it won't come close, but I'd like to try." He ducked his head until he met her eye level.

She swallowed visibly.

Gideon straightened and let his hand slide down until he cupped the side of her neck. Her heart pulsed against his palm as he moved toward her, slowly. Those doe eyes looked up at him. He kissed her forehead, then pulled back to gauge her reaction. She blinked several times. Her eyes searched his face. He was glad she couldn't read his thoughts. Glad she didn't know what had him so determined. When guilt pricked at the edges of his mind, he shoved it off. Slowly, he lifted the spoon from her grasp and set it on the workbench. He filled his hands with hers. When she didn't pull away, he moved closer.

The first star blinked from a purple sky as Lonnie ran toward the house, her throat on fire. She half expected Gideon to call her name, but he didn't. She should have known. *Oh, Lonnie, you fool.* Tears burned the backs of her eyes, but she didn't let one fall until she was safely behind the bedroom door.

She sank onto the lumpy mattress. She lay on her side, facing the window, and pulled her knees into her chest. Her heart thundered. She pressed a palm there, willing it to slow. When emotion welled in her throat, she slammed her eyes closed. What had she been thinking? Trusting Gideon. She felt his wedding shirt against her face and, with a whimper, shoved it to the floor in a heap.

He knew all the right words. Said sweet things at the right time. He'd made her feel safe. Loved almost. And she had believed he was sorry. Sorry enough to give her a gift. Sorry enough to prove he cared.

He'd shown her, all right. Shown her that he was as selfish a man as he'd ever been.

And in the frame of his arms, she'd given him everything.

Sniffling, she pressed her face into her arm but only smelled him on her skin. Her shoulders shook with sobs. She'd hardly had time to pull the straw from her hair by the time he'd stepped into the sunlight, mumbling something about needing to get back to work. She'd sat there, a pain blooming in her chest. Surrounded by that very work, she knew it was the best lie he could throw together. It had been clear in the way his eyes didn't meet hers. He'd wanted to get away from her. He didn't waste one moment in doing that. *Oh, what have I done?*

With early evening light spilling gray across the bed, Lonnie pressed her fist to the ache in her gut and wept.

Ten

Lonnie watched Ruth spoon thin broth into two bowls, then cup one bowl and disappear into the far bedroom where Bill lay resting. He'd fallen ill three days ago and was now on the mend, but John had started complaining of an ache in his stomach as well. Since then, both men had been given nothing but broth and brought cool compresses every few hours.

Muted voices floated from the bedroom, and Lonnie, not wanting to eavesdrop, turned back to her chore. She herself had hardly eaten breakfast. She wiped at the moisture along her temple.

"You all right?" Gideon asked from where he sat at the kitchen table, greasing traps.

"Just a little tired." She spoke without looking at him. She formed another dumpling and set it to the edge of the thick wooden board.

Mae sat in the rocker near the window, reading to the little ones from a book of fables.

Ruth stepped from the bedroom and closed the door quietly.

"How is he faring?" Lonnie asked, shaking flour from her fingers.

"A little better." Ruth reached for the second bowl.

"Is there anything I can do?"

When Ruth said nothing, Lonnie simply watched her carry the broth into the lean-to where John slept on the makeshift cot, as ill as his father. Whether Ruth spoke it aloud or not, Lonnie knew what she could do.

She could give poor John his bedroom back.

Surely a warmer place to sleep would help set him to rights. Ease the aches in his joints and stomach. Besides, this wasn't her home. She scarcely belonged here. But there was no sense in thinking that way. This *was* her home, whether she liked it or not.

Lonnie forced herself to focus on her task. She moved the dumplings to the soup pot and gently lowered them in. She quick-rinsed her hands and watched the dumplings float along the bubbling surface.

She felt Gideon watching her. The trap rattled against the table when he set it down.

She needed air. Lonnie moved to the front door and slipped out. The wind pulled the handle from her grip, and it slammed shut behind her. Her hair whipped, stinging her cheeks. She sank on the top step, not caring if supper overcooked. Ruth had managed her kitchen this long without Lonnie's help; one more meal would make no difference.

Lonnie pushed the toes of her boots together and held herself when the cold crept through her dress. She was tired. All she wanted to do was sleep. What she wouldn't give for her aunt Sarah's trundle. Lonnie closed her eyes and let her mind wander to the sound of her aunt's voice reading the psalms. Twenty-four. That's where they left off. Lonnie knew where Bill kept the family Bible. Perhaps after dinner she could borrow it for a while. She was in need of a heavy dose of comfort.

The door flung open, and Ruth poked her head out. "Not you too?" she asked flatly.

Lonnie rose. "I'm fine. Just needed a little air." Lonnie ducked back inside. She smoothed a hand over her hair and, knowing it was a mess, yanked a piece of cloth from the rag basket. With quick fingers, she wove the unruly strands into a quick braid and tied it securely. She started back toward the stove, but Ruth's stern look stopped her.

"Perhaps you should lie down."

Lonnie didn't want to be trouble, but the thought of laying her head down drew her feet to the small bedroom. She closed the door behind her. Lying in the dim room, she listened to the silent house breathe. She stared at the wall and listened to the sounds Gideon made just on the other side.

Finally Gideon spoke, his voice low. "It's high time to be movin' on."

Her heart tripped in her chest.

"Where do you plan on goin'?" Ruth asked.

Lonnie rolled to her side and pulled the blanket up to her shoulders, nestling her head deeper into the pillow. She stared at the rough-hewn door and imagined Gideon on the other side. The thought sent a jumble of emotions through her.

"Thinkin' about heading to Stuart. I'd like to leave soon."

A small pair of bare feet hustled past the bedroom, and a pot clanged onto the stove. "Why so far? The Allans have that small cabin on their farm. Bet you could—"

"No." Gideon cut her off in a tone that made Lonnie lift her head in surprise.

Chains clinked together as Gideon moved a trap about. Lonnie listened for several moments as no one spoke. Finally, a chair scraped across the floor, as if Ruth now sat at the table as well. "It's hard to imagine you gone." Ruth sounded almost sad.

When Gideon's voice didn't filter past the door, Lonnie wondered what silent response he had given her. With her hands folded beneath her cheek, she let her eyes close and gave in to the pull of sleep.

At a cool touch on her hand, Lonnie opened her eyes. Gideon was crouched in front of her, his face so near she could make out the freckles smattered across his nose. When she met his gaze, he stood.

"It's all settled."

"Settled?" she sat up slowly, her head spinning.

"High time I moved on from here."

She blinked up at him, unable to respond.

"From Rocky Knob. I can't stay here anymore. There's too much…" He tilted his face to the setting sun that shone orange in the small window. "Too much I'd like to forget."

Lonnie smoothed her unruly hair away from her face. "What do you mean?"

She twirled the cold tin ring around her finger, and when he didn't respond, she sighed loudly. Apparently he only spoke when he had something to gain.

Gideon reached under the bed, pulled out a pack, and blew off the dust. Without hesitating, he moved to the dresser and yanked open a drawer. He stuffed a pair of socks into the pack and then another. He shoved the drawer closed and opened the one below it.

"I take it I'm staying here?" she blurted. She felt a sense of satisfaction when he stopped and looked at her. Surprise leaked into his stony features. Good. It was high time he stopped looking past her as if she didn't exist.

He pulled out a white shirt and rolled the wrinkled fabric into a ball. He spoke without looking at her. "You're my wife." His voice held a sorrow that made her feel hollow inside. "Better pack your things."

Eleven

I'm gonna miss you, son."

Gideon felt the truth in his pa's words with his firm handshake.

"You take care of yourself now. And take care of that little lady." Bill's eyes drifted to Lonnie, his meaning clear.

Gideon studied the ground. Dew clung to the wilted grass beneath his feet. The cold chill of morning crept along his bare hands, and he pulled up the oilcloth collar of his outer coat. Lonnie stood beside him, her breathing surprisingly heavy despite the early hour. He glanced at her and, for a single moment, wondered if she was well enough to travel. Bill stepped back, shoulders hunched, cheeks thin from days of illness and weak broth.

Gideon glanced past his pa to the porch where his ma stood. The dim, gray light of dawn made her look years older.

"Safe travels." Her voice, though gritty as ever, trembled slightly.

"Thank you for your hospitality," Lonnie said.

Ruth nodded, though she said nothing.

The night before, after his pa had read from the Scriptures and laid the heavy family Bible aside, Gideon had bid each of his brothers and sisters farewell. Sound asleep now in their beds, they would wake to find him gone. Lonnie shifted her weight, silent as a field mouse. She reached up with a thin hand and brushed the wisps of chestnut hair away from her face.

Lifting his gaze to the dark windows of the cabin, Gideon slid his floppy hat over unruly hair. It was better this way. He wasn't much for good-byes, and another round was more than he had in him. A bedroll was strapped to his pack, and he hoisted both off the ground. He flung the pack over his shoulder and palmed the smooth wood of his rifle. His mandolin rested snug in its sack, the strap taut across his chest. He turned and headed up the path that would carry him from his pa's farm. The home of his childhood. *Toward what?*

To a life of his own. To freedom. Gideon fingered the newspaper cutting in his coat pocket. But when Lonnie fell in step beside him, he realized he was as far from freedom as he'd ever been.

Good-bye, Lonnie whispered in her heart, though her family would not hear the words.

She would not hold Addie one last time or bid farewell to Aunt Sarah. Sorrow stung the back of her throat. Surely she'd see them again. *Please, Lord, let it be so.* She'd left a note with Ruth, clinging to the promise that Gideon's ma would see it safely delivered. Again, Lonnie lifted up a prayer that it would be so.

"Where are we headed?"

Gideon drew in a slow breath. He strode on several more steps.

"If you keep actin' like it's none of my business, I'm going to perch myself right here and not budge." She folded her arms across her chest and leaned against a boulder.

He rolled his eyes and then planted them on her.

She didn't blink.

Finally, his resolve visibly crumbled and he yanked a piece of paper from his pocket. He thrust it toward her. Lonnie took it and read the headline. Her lips moved silently as she read the paragraph that followed.

"So this is where we're going? Stuart?"

He nodded once.

She screwed her mouth to the side and studied the paper that had been torn out carelessly.

He ducked beneath a maple branch and paused to hold it out of her way. "Are you coming or not?"

She looked at him, then back at the fragment of paper in her hand. Sticking her tongue in the side of her cheek, she weighed her options. With Gideon's ring on her finger, there weren't many.

"What if I say no?"

His eyebrows wedged together. "Would you?"

"Maybe." She pressed her wrist to her stomach when memories from the woodshop assaulted her.

He drew in a slow sigh. "Is this about last week?"

When emotion flooded her face, she shifted her stance and knew her heart had found its way to her sleeve.

His face lost its hard edge. "Don't worry." The words came out soft. "I won't come near you again."

Still leaning against the boulder, she bounced her heel. She didn't like the idea of living in the city. But then…she could learn a trade, perhaps. She glanced at Gideon from beneath her lashes. She wouldn't go home to her pa. Of that she was certain. As she balanced between the two men in her life who could make her miserable, a trade might one day come in handy.

He waited.

With a slow, shaky sigh, she folded the paper. "So." She held it out to him. "Tell me about your plan."

He lifted the branch again, and she ducked beneath it. "I figured we'd head there," he began. "It says Stuart's growin', so there's plenty of work. It wouldn't be forever." He stepped over a fallen log, then hesitated, as if deciding. "Maybe eventually we could get a few acres. I could do carpentry or something to make ends meet." He turned back and helped her over.

He released her hand. Her skin cooled instantly. Lonnie breathed in the early morning air, filling herself with hope.

They walked in silence. With the sun rising through the trees, Lonnie had no trouble seeing the trail. She stole around rocks and stepped nimbly over gnarled roots. The sound of their shoes crunching on dry leaves broke the stillness of the sleeping forest.

"Are you sure we're headed in the right direction?" Having lived along the Blue Ridge her whole life, she could find her way just about anywhere, but this was a new direction. She had never headed south, not with the intention of walking all the way to Stuart.

Gideon dropped his pack. With a few long strides, he bounded to the top of a low boulder. He scanned the land. "I think that's the Shaws' place. So we're heading in the right direction." He spoke as if she weren't there. He jumped to the ground, and his gun caught a glint of sunlight across the barrel.

"How you doing?" he asked, his eyes focused on the trail. Anywhere but on her, it seemed.

"Oh, I'm all right. Just a little tired."

He walked on as if she hadn't spoken. Lonnie blinked up at the morning light, suddenly feeling very small. Did God still see her? A strange sensation came over her as they walked away from Rocky Knob. They passed by the Shaw cabin, and Lonnie smelled a hot breakfast. She wanted her ma. She wanted to say good-bye. She wanted to hold Addie. Tears stung the backs of her eyes.

His eye is on the sparrow.

The promise brought a glimmer of peace, but not enough to keep her chin from trembling. Her feet froze on the path.

Gideon turned, his mandolin thumping against his back. "What's the matter?"

Lonnie touched shaky fingertips to her throat that was so tight a single word could not slip through. She wanted to cry.

"Nothing." She swallowed. "I just had to catch my breath for a second."

"We better be movin' or the day'll waste away."

When he turned, Lonnie hurried to catch up. Glancing toward the valley below, she found herself bewitched by the endless shadows as a thick layer of clouds retreated. It opened and rays of light touched the hills. Black land lit into a smoky gray. Trees came alive, their leaf-laced branches entwining with mists of fog that tucked itself into every nook and hollow. She spotted familiar farms and knew that just over that crest was her family's home. She drew in a chestful of cool air. A smile tipped her lips. She could almost hear Addie's laughter bouncing off the walls. Sid and Oliver would wrestle their way out of the lean-to, their hair askew. Lonnie's smile faded. Her pa would come out of his bedroom and shush them all. He always ate his breakfast in silence. Best way to work off his drinking headaches. Lonnie pulled her gaze away and suddenly wondered what the future held.

The fog circled around shallow peaks that lay before them, like a warm breath from heaven. Closing her eyes, Lonnie enjoyed the sun's warmth on her face. Felt the Lord's promise burn afresh in her heart.

Perhaps she could have a joyful life.

But when Gideon called her name, she opened her eyes and the peace that had surrounded her floated away on the breeze.

Twelve

A warbler jibber-jabbered from overhead, sending an echo of life through the sleeping forest. Knees digging into the soft dirt, Gideon tied up the tattered bedroll. His neck was stiff and his back ached. All night long, unease gnawed at him and his ears perked to every creak and moan of the forest. He'd spent many a night sleeping beneath the trees. Gideon glanced at Lonnie, who seemed so small in the vast forest. With all his possessions by his side, an unsettled feeling pressed in on him. Gideon yanked the strap tight around the bedroll until the fabric puckered in surrender.

Lonnie worked beside him, folding the blanket. Finished, she threw back the flap of her pack and pulled out two stale biscuits wrapped in a square of cloth. Without speaking, she handed him one. He felt her watching him and, wanting to move on, shoved the biscuit into his mouth, not caring for manners. It was dry and difficult to chew—nothing a strong cup of coffee wouldn't cure. If, of course, he had packed any. He cleared his throat and reached for the jug of water. He took a few gulps and heard her speak. He swiped his hand over his mouth. "Did you say somethin'?"

She pursed her lips the way his ma did when his pa didn't listen. "I asked you how long it will take to get to Stuart."

"'Bout a week, I s'pose." He handed her the water.

She sipped, and he found himself watching her. He'd never admit it to her, but he'd always thought her pretty enough. But now, with the morning light glinting off her braid, he found himself unable to glance away. A pale row of freckles passed from one cheek to the other, dusting her nose in the process, and her eyes, a rich shade of brown, were too big for her face.

She glanced at him, and Gideon cleared his throat before turning. He ran a hand over the back of his neck. The air was humid and strangely warm. His skin was already sticky, despite the early hour. "Stupid weather."

With an eye roll, Lonnie yanked open the pack and pulled out a wadded handkerchief. She threw it at him, and at the look on her face, Gideon was glad it wasn't a rock.

He looked skyward, wondering if the clouds on the horizon were headed their way.

Gideon shook dust from his pants leg and nodded toward the creek. "I'll go fill this up." He tucked the jug beneath his arm and strode down to the water's edge. He let a weary sigh wash through him as he dropped to his knees and, leaning forward, pushed the jug beneath the water's surface. He lifted the dripping container and screwed the lid on, then soaked the handkerchief and ran it over his face.

He strode back to their camp, his thoughts jumbled. And when he glanced down at Lonnie, who sat perched on the bedroll, the faint shadows beneath her eyes made him reconsider moving on so quickly. They could rest longer.

Yet the storm still chased them.

"Best to be gettin' on our way now." He slid the pack over his shoulder and tried not to notice when she followed a step behind.

Thunder crashed as Lonnie forced herself to put one tired foot in front of the other. They had been moving at a rapid pace for two days now. She fanned herself with her hand but found no relief from the stifling humidity. She drew in thick, moist air, and when a cold drop struck her skin, she peered up at the sky.

Gideon nodded toward charcoal-gray clouds. "Likely to be a lightnin' storm. It'll be pourin' before long." When a rustling came from nearby bushes, he switched his gun to his other hand and pressed the wooden stock to his shoulder. A small rabbit darted forward.

Lonnie's hands flew to her ears, but not before he pulled the trigger. The sound of the shot ricocheted between the trees. Slowly, Gideon walked over to his kill and shook his head. "That didn't turn out well."

Lonnie snorted. "What did you think was gonna happen? Large gun, small rabbit." Her brows furrowed. "Maybe next time you should use a slingshot."

He flashed her an annoyed look. She laughed, then hiccupped.

Gideon shook his head. "It's not funny."

"Depends on who you ask."

Shadows disappeared from the forest floor, replaced with a cool cover of gray light. As if startled by the coming storm, a pile of red and gold leaves stirred from their resting place, twirling in a dizzy circle. Several cartwheeled away, settling at her feet as Lonnie passed over them.

"Come on." He tossed his head in the direction they were going.

She watched Gideon's worn-out boots tread the ground in front of her, and it took two of her steps to keep up with each long stride. Still smiling, she smeared her hand down her arm as raindrops rinsed her skin. The trees blew helplessly in the breeze. The slender branches rocked and swayed.

It was not long before rain fell in heavy sheets, and Lonnie found herself huddled beside Gideon under the shelter of a steep boulder. The stone rose tall amongst the black oaks and curved over to form a roof.

She pulled her knees to her chest and sighed. Her soaked dress clung to her legs, and she tugged at it in a vain attempt to reshape the fabric. When that failed, she leaned her head back against the stone and closed her eyes. Her throat was hot, and she swallowed the sour taste in her mouth. A drop slipped down her cheek, and she brushed it away.

"You all right?" Gideon asked, his voice no more than a murmur.

She stared out into the pelting rain. Her skin felt hot and cold at the same time. Through burning eyes, she glanced at her husband. "I think so. I just feel...funny."

He studied her for a moment without speaking. "I'm soaked through. How 'bout you?" He seemed to study his hands, where lingering drops of water pooled and dripped down his forearms.

"Pretty much."

A bolt of lightning split the darkened sky, and they startled in unison.

Gideon cleared his throat. "Wish this rain would stop." He ran a soaked sleeve over his dripping brow, then caught the water that trickled down the side of his face.

Lonnie nestled against the rock. Their arms touched. Too tired to move away, she let her eyes fall closed.

As if sensing her weakness, Gideon spoke up. "We'll rest awhile. Doesn't look like we'll be movin' on anytime soon."

Eyes still closed, she nodded softly and listened as he fidgeted with his things. He rustled for a minute or two, then she heard the melancholy hum of his mandolin over the rain.

Although wet and uncomfortable, Lonnie rested her cheek against her shoulder. The sound of Gideon's voice whispering a song she did not know lulled her. His elbow gently bumped her side as he plucked the strings on his mandolin. He sang in a soft, throaty whisper, filling her with a surprising amount of peace. Even if she had the strength to join in, she wouldn't. She didn't like the idea of him hearing her sing. Songs were so much more than words put together to music. Singing was for showing joy.

It was something she'd only ever done with Aunt Sarah. Something her pa clearly overlooked when he had forced her on that stage. Besides, she didn't like the melancholy songs she heard now and again. Life could be rotten enough. She didn't see the point of putting heartache to music. She'd never voice that to Gideon. He wouldn't understand.

Her head nodded to the side, and her cheek rested against Gideon's shoulder. Too tired to move, she fell asleep.

When she woke, the rain had stopped and the damp forest held a musty scent. Gideon hadn't moved from her side. She lifted her head from his shoulder, and her cheek cooled. She glanced into his face to see if he had minded, but he seemed to be studying the rain-blackened trees; the stony set to his features revealed nothing. The trees seemed to stretch their limbs higher to the sky, as if to thank God for the long cool drink. Birds called out in cheerful song.

"We've lost several hours." Gideon stood and brushed the leaves from his pants.

Lonnie wondered if they would make camp before long. The last thing she wanted to do was walk through the night, but when Gideon stretched in the filtered sunlight and tossed his pack over his shoulders, she forced herself from her nest.

Her stomach growled, and she longed for a bowl of stew and a plate of steaming cornbread drenched in butter. Her mouth watered, and she chided herself for her daydreams. Besides, the O'Riley cupboards had been nearly bare. They hadn't packed much food since that wouldn't have been right. Lonnie pulled a cold slice of bread from the pack and broke it in half, fighting the urge to hang on to the larger piece. They ate in silence as they walked along, her feet falling in sync behind his, their rhythmic footsteps just a touch apart.

Thirteen

G ideon peered at the log cabin. Wind pulled smoke from the chimney, sweeping it to the east.

"You think anybody's home?" Lonnie fiddled with the buttons on her sweater, trying to slide them into place.

"Hope so." He took a deep breath, then stepped out of the trees. Leaves crunched as she followed behind. He stopped when the front door opened. A young man emerged.

The man hooked his thumbs in his pockets. "You folks lookin' for something?" He leaned against the doorjamb and crossed one foot over the other. Gideon studied him and realized he was near to his own age, but the man looked superior, standing up on his own porch, able to run a stranger off his property with the slightest inclination.

Squaring his shoulders, Gideon chose his words carefully. "Yessir." He tugged his floppy hat away from his unruly hair, then suddenly thought the wiser of it. "We were wondering... Well, my wife and I were wondering if perhaps...we could have...um, borrow a bite of food." He cleared his throat. "You see, we've come down from Rocky Knob, and we've been travelin' for a couple days."

The man narrowed his gaze. "Borrow a bite of food, huh?" He glanced into his cabin and puffed his cheeks.

Gideon shifted.

"Don't know about *borrow*." The man motioned to someone inside, then turned his attention back to Gideon. "But I sure could give you some. We got a bit to spare. You wanna come in?" His hand spread flat against the door, and it creaked open until it thudded into the wall.

When Lonnie's face brightened, Gideon struggled to reply. "We… we better be movin' on, mister. We don't have much time to linger." Pride fed his words. He hadn't even wanted to stop, but the gnawing in his stomach had made his feet slow when he first spotted the cabin.

"You runnin' from something?" the man asked.

"No sir, just in a hurry, that's all." It wasn't entirely the truth, but it was close enough. He didn't care to spend too many more nights beneath the stars. The sooner they got to Stuart, the sooner he could find work and, if luck was on his side, a warm place to sleep.

The young man glanced between them, a curious expression on his face. Finally, he smiled. "Name's Jonathan. You are welcome to some food, but I sure wish you'd come in and rest a spell. My wife can cook up a mighty fine pot of beans, and we've got fresh venison."

"Gid, we could rest a bit, couldn't we?" Lonnie's voice was for his ears alone.

The thought of such a meal warmed him, but Gideon shook his head.

Jonathan shrugged. "Well, can you hold on just a bit while I go and fetch somethin'?"

Gideon glanced at Lonnie, then nodded. "That'd be fine. We sure do appreciate it."

Leaving the door open, Jonathan disappeared inside.

A woman's voice drifted out.

Tilting his head, Gideon strained to listen. When the lace curtain slid aside, a young woman peeked through the glass. He blinked but didn't avert his gaze.

Jonathan returned with a handful of brown eggs and a tin can. "Beans." He lifted the offering. "Take these." His boots pounded the steps.

Cradling the eggs as best he could, Gideon passed them to Lonnie, who clutched them delicately. He pressed the tin can to his chest. The beans were still warm and fragrant with the smell of molasses and pepper.

"Sorry it's not more." Jonathan pulled another tin from the crook of his elbow. "Here's applesauce. My wife insisted you take it."

He handed the can to Lonnie, followed by a spoon, and she dipped it into the apple mush. The bent spoon clanged inside the can. After a few bites, Lonnie offered the rest to Gideon.

He felt Lonnie's frown on him, and when he looked at her, he saw something more in her eyes. Hurt. Gideon shifted. It was just like a woman to be difficult. The sooner she realized he had her best interest in mind, the better.

He ate quickly, then glanced at the window. "Tell your wife she's got the best applesauce I've ever tasted."

Jonathan grinned. "I'll tell her."

Still savoring the taste on his tongue, Gideon tipped his hat. "Guess we'll be on our way now. Sure do appreciate you and your wife's generosity."

"Sure you won't stay for supper?" Jonathan tossed a thumb toward his house.

It pained Gideon to turn down such an offer. The more the man asked, the more tempting the idea became. "We should really be movin' on." His eyes flicked to the window.

Jonathan accepted the empty can. "Suit yourself." He turned when his wife appeared in the doorway.

Her blond hair, slicked back in a tight and shiny bun, spoke of a fresh bath. She smoothed the apron that covered her well-worn dress and smiled, showing a tidy row of white teeth.

"Ma'am." Gideon tapped the brim of his hat, sending a spatter of moisture up and away. He studied her pretty face longer than he should have, then dropped his gaze. For an instant, he wished he had taken the man up on his offer to stay for supper. Lonnie cleared her throat. He looked at her and wished he hadn't when he saw the pain that flitted through her brown eyes. Gideon waved good-bye to Jonathan and walked off.

Lonnie walked behind him. "Sure was nice of them to give us fresh eggs." She spoke softly, and when he didn't respond, she sighed. "I'm surprised you didn't want to go in. I half expected you to change your mind." Her tone pierced him.

Gideon pinned her with his gaze. She returned his stare. Not much got past her. He'd have to keep that in mind.

Her shoulders seemed heavier, but Gideon refused to let it dampen his spirits. Turning, he glanced past Lonnie to the porch and licked the sweet taste of applesauce from his lips.

They walked for several hours, and he couldn't help but notice that Lonnie didn't say a word. When they stopped to make camp that night, Gideon gathered scraps of wood, a few dry twigs, and a handful of crisp oak leaves. It wasn't cold, but he couldn't shake the thought of fried eggs. As he knelt before his makeshift firepit, Lonnie spread out the bedroll. She curled onto her side and closed her eyes.

Gideon pulled the small pan from his pack and set it near the flames. He sat back on his haunches. "We gonna have these eggs tonight?"

Lonnie shrugged. "I've lost my appetite." She didn't look at him. "That food didn't sit right on my stomach."

After the look she'd given him earlier, he was certain there was more to it. A muscle clenched in his jaw. Using his fingertips, he twirled two eggs across his open palm, willing himself not to crush the delicate shells under the weight of his irritation. "Suit yourself," he mumbled into the fire.

"We could have them for breakfast."

Gideon drew in a slow steady breath. "Sure, that'd be fine." He carefully wrapped the eggs and tucked the precious bundle in the pack. They might break, and it would have all been a waste. He shook his head.

Lonnie stretched out her legs and crossed her ankles. She placed a tender hand on her stomach and closed her eyes. Gideon studied her pale face. He had noticed that her steps had slowed, and her breathing sounded strained as they walked.

His stomach grumbled, and he worked his way through what remained of the beans. He cleaned the last cold bite out before realizing he should have rationed them. But the comfort of a full stomach had blurred his judgment. His spoon clanged when he dropped it into the empty tin. Gnawing on the inside of his cheek, Gideon glanced at Lonnie. With her eyes closed, she seemed more at peace than she had in days. Annoyed with himself, and still hungry, he worked his jaw and stared into the flames.

Lonnie blinked against the early morning light. She sat up slowly and glanced down at Gideon, whose face rested atop his outstretched arm. Careful not to disturb him, she rose and checked the fire. She stirred the ashes with a brittle stick and, blowing on the last remaining embers, managed to revive it.

With her husband still snoring, she snatched up the water jug to fill in the creek. She didn't know how Gideon managed to find water nearly every day, but she counted it a blessing. She pulled his shirt from the pack and shook out his dirty socks. Stacking her own things on top, she carried the bundle to the water's edge, where she dunked Gideon's shirt below the chilly surface before slapping it against a rock. Dunking and scrubbing alternately, she took care to turn the fabric to clean it all over. Her hands were red and numb by the time she finished, and spotting a sunny cluster of bushes downstream, she laid the wet shirt out to dry.

She smiled to herself and, with a song on her heart, made quick work of the rest of his clothes. When she finished with Gideon's things, she turned to her own, content at the sight of the fresh, clean clothes in the sun. By the time she was finished, she smelled eggs cooking. Her empty stomach spurred her to finish the task. She rinsed her last stocking and neatly tossed it onto the bush before clutching her skirt and scrambling up the bank to get back to camp.

Gideon sat on a rock, his back to her, staring blankly into the flames.

"I see you made breakfast," she said, wiping her cold, damp hands on her skirt.

He nodded so softly she hardly noticed the motion. His flannel shirt hung open, allowing the thin undershirt to peek out. He stared at the fire, his eyes as blank as his expression.

"There's a fork in the bottom of the pack." She bent and opened the leather flap. "I grabbed it when I took the pan."

"No need," he said with a faint shake of his head. "I found it."

"Oh." Lonnie glanced at the fire and saw the pan. Then she looked at Gideon. Her mouth fell in a silent gasp, and her eyes widened. "You... *ate* them?"

Gideon stuck up his lower lip and dipped his chin in a single nod.

Lonnie drew in a shaky breath, then let it out.

His eyes met hers. "You said you weren't hungry, so I ate them." His tone was not apologetic. "I didn't know you would want any. Seems to me you can't make up your mind lately."

Lonnie opened her mouth to speak, then closed it. When tears stung the backs of her eyes, she glanced up at the canopy of trees overhead and blinked into the cool air. Her stomach groaned.

Gideon's gaze, still pinned to the flames, never wavered.

He didn't move. She picked up the pan, resisting the urge to smack the stupid look off his face. She dropped it in the dirt by his boots. "Don't for one *minute* think I'm gonna clean up after you."

She strode down to the creek and, as she collected his things, wished she'd laid them under a flock of birds. She wadded everything into a heap, not bothering to fold it. She willed her heart to harden. To ice over so she wouldn't have to hurt anymore. But when her vision blurred, she knew it was useless to try.

Fourteen

Lonnie tugged on her pack. It seemed heavier than usual, and with each step she took, the damp socks hanging from the top strap padded behind her, a muted taunt. All the laundry had dried, and she had tucked it away. *But those darn socks.* Her shoulders slumped forward as she trudged along. Her stomach knotted, and she tried not to think about food. When her shoelace unraveled, Lonnie hobbled along and tugged it into place without stopping. She stumbled but kept her footing. With a grunt, she heaved the pack higher and bent beneath the weight of it.

The land rose, and Gideon's boots stomped out a rhythm that was anything but joyful.

He had the energy of a stallion. Lonnie felt more like a tired mule. She struggled up the steep grade, slipping more than once on the loose soil. She caught hold of a branch and tried to pull herself along, but her grip shook and she stumbled just the same.

Gideon glanced at her, and she straightened. "C'mon', Lonnie. I want to get over this hill before it rains. We need to hurry."

Disheartened, she looked up at the sky, where a tumble of gray clouds inched closer. She said a silent prayer, then dug the toes of her boots into the dirt and scaled the hill with surprising speed. When she reached the top, she collapsed at Gideon's feet.

God, I don't know if I can go on.

Gideon grabbed hold of her arm and tugged her up. When he released her, she rubbed the tender skin. She fought the urge to glare at him and, with a set of her jaw, remembered God's promise.

His eye is on the sparrow.

The words touched her heart but did not fill it as they once had. She did her best to cling to the promise as she walked on. The wind shifted, slowing the clouds' approach, and relief washed over her when Gideon announced they would make camp early.

The first hint of dusk settled around a clearing along the trail. Lonnie untied the bedroll, and as soon as her head hit the soft mat, sleep beckoned. With her eyes closed, she listened to Gideon rustle about. Before long, flames crackled and popped beside her, and she sighed as their warmth spread through her thin sweater.

She shuffled through the pack and lifted a small cube wrapped in cheesecloth. She looked pleadingly at Gideon.

"I was hoping to save that. It's the only piece of pork we've got."

Lonnie turned the package in her hand, and Gideon sighed.

"I s'pose there's no sense trying to make it last. I'm starvin'."

"My thoughts exactly." She tugged the pan from the pack. Gideon pulled a knife from his pocket, flicked it open, and sliced the meat into thin pieces. She ledged the pan on a rock near the flames, and Lonnie knew it wouldn't be long before the smells of pork filled the air. It was nearly the last of their food.

Gideon scrambled to his feet.

Lonnie jolted upright. "What is it?" she whispered.

"I dunno. Thought I heard somebody." He crouched beside her.

A twig snapped.

He pulled his rifle close. "Who's there?" He lifted the butt of the gun to his shoulder.

"Don't be alarmed." A man stepped forward, hands aloft, palms lit by the light of the fire.

Gideon's shoulder slumped, but he did not lower the gun.

The man drew closer, pushing a cart in front of him.

"Name's Bert." He glanced from Lonnie to Gideon. "And unless you're a man of the law or a preacher, I come bringin' white whiskey." His lips parted, revealing a snaggle-toothed grin.

Lonnie grimaced.

A faint chuckle escaped Gideon's lips.

Lonnie bristled even as her heart sank.

"Per-cise-ly," Bert pronounced.

Gideon lowered his rifle until the butt of it sat on the toe of his boot. "Settle on down."

The stout man lowered the handles of his cart. He tugged off his sun-faded hat and tossed it in the cart. He ran a hand through dark, matted hair.

"Live around here?" Gideon perched on the edge of a small log and shook the pan.

"You could say that." Bert rested stubby hands on a tree trunk of a waist. He raised a jug, and it caught the light of the fire. The glazed crock glistened.

Gideon's eyes flickered, and he yanked his shirttails loose. Bert settled himself on the ground, closer to Lonnie's makeshift seat than she liked.

Gideon motioned toward the fire. "Care for something to eat? We've got a pan of salted pork frying up here." He shook the skillet again, and the meat danced across the sizzling iron.

Bert shook his head. "Naw, I got food." He motioned toward his cart. "Sure do appreciate you letting me share in your fire." His jug rested between his feet, and he tapped on the cork, his fingernail so worn down it almost didn't exist. "Can I offer you a drink?" He uncorked it with a hollow *thump*.

Firelight danced across Gideon's collarbone. "Sure." Gideon moistened his lips and tugged his top button free. Lonnie watched as his demeanor changed from the quiet man he had been to another person altogether. A person she didn't care to know. A man too much like her pa.

Turning to Lonnie, Bert smirked. "What about you?" He slid the jug toward Gideon.

"I'm sorry." Gideon's finger hooked through the crook of the roughly formed crock, and after lifting it to his lips, he swallowed with a satisfied sigh. "My name's Gideon and this…" His eyes failed to meet hers. "This here is…Lonnie."

She fiddled with a dry leaf. *Just "Lonnie." Not "Lonnie, my wife"?* She crushed the leaf, and the pieces fell.

"Right. How 'bout you?"

She looked up. "No, thank you."

Gideon tipped the jug back and held it to his lips longer than before. His Adam's apple bobbed and rose.

Take it easy, Gid. She pulled her legs up and rested her chin on her knees. *This is…uh, Lonnie. Just Lonnie. Plain, little, old, slow Lonnie.*

The pan hissed. Using the edge of his shirt, Gideon pulled it away from the flame. He and Lonnie shared the meat, burning both fingers and tongues, but she was too hungry to care.

"You play that thing?" Bert mumbled. The words were nearly inde-cipherable with his mouth half full of the bread he'd unwrapped from a handkerchief.

Gideon flicked his head toward the mandolin peeking out of its sack and nodded.

"Let's hear, then." Bert licked his thumb.

Rising, Gideon stepped toward the shadows and returned with his instrument. The oiled wood gleamed mahogany in the firelight.

"You sing, little lady?"

"I—"

"She doesn't like to sing for people," Gideon said softly. His eyes nearly found hers over the flames.

"Don't sing for people?" Bert licked the tip of his pinkie.

But Lonnie was too distracted by Gideon to respond. How did he know? She'd never told him as much. Realizing Bert was still watching her, Lonnie struggled to find the words. "I prefer not to."

"Shy, then, eh?" Bert poked a stubby finger into her side, and Lonnie nearly yelped.

A muscle flexed in Gideon's jaw.

The color rose in her cheeks, and she inched farther away. Gideon twisted the keys of his mandolin, his broad hand dwarfing the small spruce neck. Sour notes sharpened.

Bert rubbed his palms together hastily. "All right, then. Whatcha got?"

With a slow, seemingly measured breath, Gideon began. He played softly, his gaze fixed on the ground at Lonnie's feet. Bert studied her, and trying to ignore the chill it gave her, Lonnie stared at the smolder-ing coals. As Bert chattered about making moonshine, Gideon seemed to listen halfheartedly. The jug passed from man to man, Bert pausing only long enough to swig. When he slid closer to Lonnie, Gideon drank heavily—his face shadowed, eyes filled with an emotion she couldn't pin down. Lonnie crossed her ankles and folded her hands in her lap. Anything to become as small as possible.

If only she could disappear completely. She nearly got up and walked away when Bert elbowed her, his arm lingering against her side, but it would do little good to wander around in the coal-black night.

At a joke she hadn't paid attention to, Bert elbowed her again. Lonnie gulped. She felt Gideon watching her. When she glanced at him, his attention shifted to Bert. A glint of anger passed through his green eyes.

The reaction surprised her. He seemed to have read her thoughts, for Gideon shifted all his attention to the instrument he clutched to his chest.

Bert rose and slapped his knee. Spinning, he danced toward the shadows, hooting and hollering loud enough to startle a family of birds nestled down for the night.

Then he came back toward Lonnie. His hand gripped her arm, and in one swift motion, he pulled her to her feet. His fingers dug into her flesh, and Lonnie planted her feet to keep from being pulled into him. He swung his other arm around her, his grip painfully tight.

The music silenced.

Gideon gripped Bert behind the neck and pulled him back. The drunk man opened his eyes to half-mast. Gideon's other hand found Lonnie's wrist. His fingers were firm but trembling.

"Aw, come on. Just havin' some fun with the little lady."

"Get out of here, Lonnie." Gideon's voice was so low it startled her.

Without argument, she reached for the pan and carried it to the water's edge. Moonlight lit her path. Glancing back, she saw Gideon release Bert and shove him toward his cart. She couldn't hear his words, but his meaning was clear.

Needing to busy her hands, she plunged the skillet into the creek. Relief washed through her as she scrubbed the cast-iron pan in the dark, frigid water. And despite her best efforts, hope burned in her heart. Perhaps he cared after all. If he cared even a little, it was a start. And in time, it could grow. Moonlight carried her shadow forward as Lonnie returned to camp. She found Gideon lying on his back, hands folded behind his head, feet crossed.

"Thank you." She sat down softly beside him. "I'm glad you saw…" Her voice trailed off when he let out a sigh, his annoyance clear.

"Don't ever make me do that again," he said gruffly.

Her eyebrows fell.

"You should be more careful." His voice, void of emotion, was as cold as the air that seeped through her stockings. "You could have been hurt." His throat worked.

She fiddled with a tattered corner of the bedroll. "You should pick better company, then." Her tone came out as cool as his.

"I do just fine." Moonshine reeked on his breath.

"You could have told him I was your wife." Lonnie blinked up at the star-studded sky. "But I suppose you try and not think about that, right?" Her voice faltered, and she chided herself for caring.

"I do well enough to get by."

His words pierced her, and setting her jaw, Lonnie lay down, lest she give him the satisfaction of seeing. She pulled her knees into her chest. "This marriage wasn't my idea," she whispered. Her heart, having clung to the frailest thread of hope, now broke as the thread severed. She closed her eyes, the mat rough against her cheek. *Twenty-five.* Her count was climbing. Gideon rolled to his side, facing away. She had no Bible, though, and suddenly wished she knew all the psalms by heart.

Fifteen

Lonnie awoke shivering. A rock poked into the cold bedroll beneath her, and she fumbled for the blanket. When her hand grazed nothing but air, she sat up and pushed her unruly hair from her face. She found herself staring at the cold, gray ashes of last night's fire.

Having abandoned the bedroll sometime in the night, Gideon slept on the other side of the fire. His knees were pulled into his chest. His shoulders and boots stuck out from under the tangled blanket.

"Gideon."

His hand swatted at a fly.

"Gideon," she said louder.

He stirred and lifted his head, and when his glazed eyes found her, he struggled to stand. "What's the matter?" He stumbled over to her. With one hand covering an eye, he squinted through the other.

"I ain't feelin' so good." She wished she had a better answer. She ached. Her feet tingled and her skin crawled. With the tips of her ears as cold as her toes, everything in between was chilled through. "Could we stay here for the day and rest? I don't know if I can go on."

He hovered over her, his eyes roving. "What's wrong with you?"

"I don't know."

A frown creased his lips and he lowered his hand. "No." His voice was sharp—final.

After eating several handfuls, Gideon picked enough blackberries from the prickly bush to fill his palm, then slid them into his pocket. He massaged the ridge between his eyes. His head throbbed, and he could not get his vision into focus. A berry ran down the inside of his pants leg and struck the ground. He pulled the berries out and found the hole. He slid the plump fruit into a handkerchief and shifted the bundle into the other pocket but didn't bother to pick up the one he had dropped.

He ran his fingers through tangled hair and tried to set it in the right direction. He glanced at Lonnie. Her unbound hair fell to one side, unruly in the morning dew. A bare shoulder peeked out where her dress had slid down, and her left stocking sank around her ankle. Nearly a week on the trail and the dark circles under her large brown eyes mirrored the shadows in her cheeks.

He straightened his collar and crossed his arms over his chest. At least he was wearing a clean shirt.

Gideon turned and took off. Lonnie fumbled the last things into her pack.

"I'm coming," she called, as if he had questioned whether she was.

He glanced behind him. She was yanking a loose shoelace into place.

Gideon kicked at a clump of dirt and waited for her to catch up.

"How long till we get to Stuart?" she asked, already breathless.

When he noticed the frailty in her walk, worry inched its way into his heart. "Few more days, I expect." He blinked and stuffed any concern aside.

"Then we'll find a little piece of land?" Her voice was uncertain.

"That's the plan," he said, ignoring her skepticism. He had everything under control, but it was just like a woman to doubt that. He knew from experience.

He heard her scurry behind him, and although his strides were long, he quickened his pace. With an eye on the sky, he watched a cluster of thunderclouds approach. "Hurry," he mumbled.

She panted behind him, but he made no attempt to slow down.

By late afternoon, rain pelted them.

Though he knew he should stop, Gideon didn't. He was sick of caring if he was pushing her too far. He strode forward as fast as he could. Despite the slippery mud, he kept up a demanding pace.

Lonnie struggled behind him but never complained.

He honestly expected her to. Women were predictable that way. He knew what to expect. Until the day he married Lonnie Sawyer. He hadn't asked for this. Any of it.

The rain fell harder. Gideon tugged his hat lower, so the wide brim sheltered his face from the sting. He glanced over his shoulder. Lonnie's wet hair clung to her cheeks. She pushed it out of her eyes and blinked into the downpour. Her drenched dress clung lifelessly to her skin, leaving bare arms and legs with no protection from the tiny pellets.

A twinge of guilt struck him. *You should stop. Give her time to throw on a shawl or sweater.* Gideon let the rain drown out the inner voice—a voice he'd rather not listen to. The more he pushed down his pity, the easier it became.

"Gid," Lonnie moaned.

When he heard her feet slide in the mud, he halted and turned around. She struggled to stand.

"Can you get up?" He brushed strands of hair from his forehead.

"I'm trying." Her voice was thick. Rain dripped from her nose and ears, sliding in tiny rivers down her cheeks.

He paced back to her. Reaching down, he lifted her by the arm. Lonnie's wet skin slipped from his grip, and he struggled to catch her. When she was steady, he moved on.

The slick mud taunted his boots, and he slipped twice. All he wanted was to get away from it all. Why did women always have to try to ruin his life? First his ma. And then Cassie.

Now Lonnie. He just needed to get to Stuart. He wanted a warm bed and a hot meal. And here he was, carting Lonnie the whole way. Somewhere in the back of his mind he knew a husband was supposed to take care of a wife. Protect her. But right now, with the rain beating down on his back, hardly a coin to his name, and Stuart still days away, having to shoulder Lonnie's frailties was beginning to grate on his nerves.

He climbed over a fallen log, and hard bark scraped his legs through his pants. Landing on the other side, his heels dug into wet earth. He held on to the log, suddenly at the top of a deep ravine. He waited for Lonnie to pull herself over. She straddled the fallen tree. With her stockings limp, her bare calves rubbed across the surface. She tried to hold herself up, but her boots dangled above the ground. Her eyes met his, hopelessness carved through her features. His pulse pounded through his veins, and he gritted his teeth.

He reached toward her, and when her hand clamped around his forearm, the muscle flexed, and he helped her over. She let go and, after brushing pieces of bark from her legs, examined the fresh scratches.

Guilt slowed his heart, but he turned away. Gideon chewed the inside of his lip as he considered the best way to get down. Lonnie bumped against him, panting.

"Are you sure this is safe in the rain?" she asked, practically pleading.

He started down. "It's fine. Look." He tilted his face to the sky. "It's stopping." He reached out a hand, but his stiff fingers lacked compassion. "If I can do it, you can." His heartless words fell like rocks, visibly crushing what was left of her spirit.

Drenched leaves slipped from under his boots as he made his way down with carefully placed footsteps. At the bottom, he turned. Lonnie clung to trees, stepping sideways on the water-soaked hillside. Mud caked her shoes and dirt streaked her legs.

He waved her forward. "You've got it," he hollered.

She looked at him wide-eyed.

Gideon swallowed. She was following him trustingly, and he was making her suffer. But like a candle in a midnight wind, images of the life he could have had blew out the flame of his concern. "C'mon. You're almost there."

She swiped her hand across her lashes, and as she stepped forward, the drenched hillside clung to her feet. She slid and her ankle jerked, twisting to the side. Lonnie gasped and, falling to her knees, righted herself. She crawled to a stand but took only one step, and her foot sank.

She shrieked.

Her body lurched forward, and she tumbled down. The pack slipped off her arm and tumbled into a murky puddle.

Gideon snatched the pack out of the puddle and tossed it to drier ground. He grabbed hold of Lonnie's arm and pulled her toward him. Her feet skidded in the mud.

"Please don't." Her hand held his wrist.

"Get up."

Her feet fought with the ground as she tried to stand, and when he released his grip, she fell back into the mud.

Gideon took hold of her arm and tried to tug her up. "Look at what you've done. Get up!" He shook her, making her head bob forward and back.

Her face twisted as she cried.

"Stop it." He ground out the words.

Her chin hit her chest, and her shoulders shook with sobs.

Gideon drew in a sharp breath. Something burned like bitter acid in his soul—neither satisfying nor yielding.

The rain slowed, individual drops striking the top of her drenched head. Her crying turned to a whimper. His fingertips smeared mud along her face as he gripped her jaw until it was still.

Lonnie looked at him, her eyes round.

Anger pulsed through his veins, and even as the battle raged inside him, Gideon forced himself to loosen his grip.

Chin trembling, she wriggled her wrist free. His fingerprints lingered on her ivory skin.

"You have no idea what you have put me through."

Her gaze moved past him as if he were no longer there. When she glanced at the sky, he could almost hear the prayers that filled her heart. Gideon tilted his gaze as if he could see them floating upward. Lonnie had God on her side. That much he knew. Thunder shattered the murky silence—a confirmation.

Gideon grabbed the pack and flung it open. Water had pooled through the opening, soaking the inside of the oilcloth. The bread was no more than mush. He squeezed it in his hand and walked toward Lonnie. She scooted herself back, and he slapped the soaked bread on the ground in front of her.

"Look at what you've done!"

"This has to stop." She laid a hand on his boot, her fingers slowly sliding to his leg. "Please. I won't go on like this." She pressed her cheek to his shin, eyes closing. She mumbled something he could not make out.

Gideon clenched his jaw, hating the way she made him feel like the villain. He shook his leg to release her, but she didn't let go. He shook his leg again, harder this time. His balance slipped, and before he could catch himself, his foot caught the bottom of her chin. Even over the noise of his struggle, he heard the sound of her jawbone against his boot as he slipped to the ground.

She fell back with a shriek.

Gideon caught himself and stood. He smeared muddy hands on his pants and struggled to keep his footing. Something hard smacked against the back of his head. Pain seared through his skull as he fell forward.

"Don't move," a deep voice boomed behind him.

Gideon fell in the mud and rolled to his side.

Click.

He recognized the familiar sound of a shotgun and froze.

Sixteen

"Don't move, young man. Don't even scratch."

Lonnie lifted her head and pushed back a tangle of hair. An old man stood before her, shoulders squared, shotgun aimed at Gideon.

The man's voice was gruff but soft. "Miss, are you all right?"

She spat out a mouthful of blood. Her gaze lifted as high as his plaid coat, and she nodded.

Fear filled Gideon's eyes, and Lonnie felt her body relax, more grateful than she could express for the sudden change in power.

Gideon swallowed. "This is none of your business."

The old man chuckled grimly. "It looks like it just became my business." He lifted the gun slightly. "Now I've got an idea to introduce this here buckshot to you. What says I shouldn't?"

When Lonnie tried to stand, the old man made his way toward her, shotgun still aimed at Gideon. He crouched beside her and lifted her arm over his shoulder. She noticed the sweet smell of pipe tobacco as she clung to him. He pulled her to her feet and held her steady. Her throat thickened with relief.

For the first time in weeks—no, in her life—she felt the steady strength of a kind man.

He tucked the gun under his arm, pulled a handkerchief from his coat pocket, and handed it to her. She took the folded square and dabbed at her mouth, smearing streaks of mud and blood into the white fabric.

Gideon sat a few feet away, his forehead pressed to his knees. He held the back of his head with his hands, no doubt seeing stars. Lonnie felt a surge of satisfaction.

The old man tossed his head toward Gideon. "All right, you. Get up. Let's go."

Gideon glared at him. "I ain't goin' nowhere."

"Suit yourself." He shrugged and held Lonnie steady. "But you're not staying here with this little lady." He stepped away without waiting for Gideon to respond. "Come along, missy. Let's get you home to my wife. She'll have you fixed up in no time."

Lonnie's feet moved slowly, but she pressed her cheek to the plaid shoulder. The deliverance she'd prayed for. She'd never expected an angel could smell of pipe tobacco and carry a shotgun, but never had she been more grateful to someone as she was right then. She needed no further answer, and with her eyes on the horizon, they walked past Gideon. She hoped he wouldn't follow.

Her escort's steps slowed to match hers, and she peered up into a wrinkled face half shielded by a coat collar.

She scarcely noticed Gideon's footsteps behind them. Glancing over her shoulder, Lonnie watched him snatch up the pack, his shoulders slumped. He looked around the ground in clear confusion. And when realization dawned, Lonnie blinked up at the man who clutched two guns beneath his arm.

Her eyebrows knit together. With a smile in his gray-blue eyes, he dipped his head. "My name is Jebediah Bennett. Most folks call me Jeb."

When she tried to smile, her jaw ached. "My name is Lonnie Sawyer. Uh, I mean Lonnie…O'Riley." She said the last word flatly.

He chuckled. "Just married?"

Reluctantly, she nodded and looked into a pair of kind, knowing eyes set deep among years of wrinkles. She stared at Jebediah, fearing that if she glanced away, her angel might disappear.

"Who's that fella with you?" He flicked his head back. "He your husband?" Gray eyebrows pinched together.

Lonnie stared at the trail. "That's Gideon. We got married a few weeks ago and have been heading toward Stuart."

The older man stopped, giving her a moment to catch her breath. He lifted his face and stood silent for several moments. He looked down at Lonnie, his eyes tight, almost apologetic. Then, turning, he faced Gideon, his voice stern. "I'll take that pack there, young man."

One eyebrow lifted as Gideon let the pack slide off his shoulder.

Jebediah loosened his grip on Lonnie's arm. "This little lady's all tuckered out, and we're headin' uphill a good ways. She's not gonna make it on her own."

Lonnie's heart skipped a beat, and she stared up at him.

But Jebediah continued. "My back ain't much for carrying." His eyes flashed over Lonnie. "Though I don't think she could weigh more than a few pounds. Who's been feedin' her?"

Gideon set his jaw. "We've been doing fine, sir."

Jebediah grunted. "I'd have to be dumber'n a sack of rocks to believe that." He pulled Lonnie's arm from his neck.

"No, I can walk just fine." She forced a weak smile and started uphill. Jebediah fell in step beside her. She heard Gideon lumber along. Lonnie slipped, but Jebediah was quick to grab her elbow. He held it as they walked on. When her head grew so light she had to pause, Lonnie felt Jebediah's arm around her waist.

"Are you all right?"

"Fine." She set her gaze on the trail ahead. She was not about to let Gideon carry her. He'd probably just toss her into the bushes the first chance he got. With a fire under her feet, she strode on. Her jaw ached, and blinking, she fought to keep the world in focus. Jebediah spoke to her again, his voice distant. She swayed. Jebediah barked an order, and Lonnie blinked again, certain he wasn't speaking to her. She felt an arm slide behind her knees, and in a *whoosh* of breath, she was lifted off the ground.

The arms were too long to be Jebediah's, and the breathing in her ear too familiar. Her skin crawled at Gideon's touch, but her head spun and a wave of nausea rose in her stomach. She swallowed the taste and forced herself to take one deep breath after another. All the days of walking and climbing seemed to flood her limbs, and her eyelids fluttered closed. She forced them open when they stepped into a small clearing. The light blinded her and played with the unease in her stomach. With each jolting step, Gideon's chest heaved. The bounce of his step made her eyes close once more, and her head fell limp against his rigid chest.

The rain only misted now, making it easier for Gideon to keep his footing. Lonnie grew heavier by the minute. He was tired too. Did no one care? Still, he wasn't about to let some crusty hobo cart off his wife. They'd been doin' just fine until the old man had appeared out of nowhere with his stupid shotgun and perfect aim. When the back of

Gideon's head throbbed, he bristled as he eyed Jebediah, who trudged a few paces ahead. When the man looked at him again, Gideon tried to appear contrite. Whatever that looked like.

When Jebediah rolled his eyes, Gideon knew the old man would need more convincing than that.

His frustration rose afresh, and he forced himself to snuff it out. He knew all too well where that took him. They all did. He glanced again at Jebediah, who was watching his every move.

With Lonnie's eyes closed and her cheek pressed to his shoulder, Gideon felt his throat burn. When she stirred, he shifted her weight, knowing that if she woke, her heartbeat would quicken against his chest. He couldn't blame her.

The metal barrel that bobbed from the crook of Jebediah's elbow gleamed in the sunlight—a silent warning with each bouncing step. Gideon studied the old man, still stunned that he had crept up on them. *Crazy old goat.* Gideon's eyes instinctively narrowed.

"We're almost there. How you holding out, little lady?" A tiny waterfall trickled off the brim of Jebediah's hat when he turned.

Gideon slowed, trying to maintain his distance. "She's asleep."

The man looked at her kindly. Gideon cringed at the marks that tainted her skin.

"Well, we're almost home."

Fighting the urge to turn and carry Lonnie away, Gideon put one foot in front of the other. As much as it pained him to follow Jebediah, he didn't seem to have much of a choice. Gideon lowered his chin and peered at his wife, her eyes closed in long-needed slumber. The red scrape on her chin scarcely concealed a forming bruise. A muscle pulsed in his jaw.

How far would you have gone?

His footsteps slowed.

A groan rose in the back of his throat, and he swallowed it away lest he frighten her. He felt worse with every step and cringed when Lonnie tightened her grip and her mouth brushed against his coat. Her breathing was faint and steady.

"There's home," Jebediah called, tearing Gideon from his thoughts.

They stepped into a yard that framed the largest house Gideon had ever seen. Whitewashed boards rose two stories, ending in a peaked roof with uniform shingles. *Hmph. Some hobo.*

"Elsie!" Jebediah hollered. "We've got company."

The screen door squeaked open. "Afternoon, folks." A round-faced woman stepped onto the porch, her hands resting on thick hips wrapped in a red apron. "What do we have here?" She offered Gideon a warm smile as she came down the steps. Then her gaze shifted. "Lord a mercy," she whispered. Slanted eyes, the color of a copper pot, narrowed beneath soft eyelids. "What happened to her?"

Gideon swallowed.

"She had a rough tumble down a hill." Jebediah motioned Gideon toward the house, a warning in the old man's eyes.

"Well, I'd say so. Get her inside before it starts pourin' again." She hurried toward the porch, and her shoes padded up the steps. Gideon followed close behind.

Elsie shoved the kettle onto the stove and tightened her apron strings. "We need to get her cleaned up." She waved Gideon forward and led him through the kitchen and into the front parlor.

At Elsie's bidding, Gideon laid Lonnie on a floral print sofa and stepped back. The older woman sank to her knees and smoothed a plump hand over Lonnie's muddy forehead.

"What's her name?"

"Lonnie, ma'am."

"She doesn't look so well. How far did she fall?"

"Not far," Jebediah muttered behind him.

Elsie cupped Lonnie's chin and gently moved her head from side to side. Her fingertips smoothed over the scrapes. Elsie spoke to her husband, but her eyes nailed Gideon into place. "Jeb, get the soap, will ya? And I'll sponge her down a bit."

Gideon shifted.

Elsie lowered her ear to Lonnie's chest, then pressed a thumb to her wrist. She stared at the grandfather clock. "There's somethin' more," she murmured as seconds ticked by.

"She hasn't been feeling well lately." Gideon knelt beside her.

"For how long?"

He stared into the old woman's face. "Few days. Few weeks, maybe."

"Hmm."

"She's seemed tired lately and sleepin' a whole lot." He fiddled with the cuff of his shirt even as shame burned his ears. "You see, we've been travelin' by foot and she's had a rough time keeping up."

Elsie sat back on her heels. "Why didn't you stop and rest?"

"We've been trying to get to Stuart." The pendulum above his head swung from side to side as if to taunt him. "We're in sort of a hurry."

"I see." Her tone said otherwise.

Gideon's fingertips grazed the fabric of the couch near Lonnie's hand.

Elsie looked up at him. "Why don't you head out and see if Jebediah needs any help. I'll sit with Lonnie, see if I can't get her to stir." She smiled down at Lonnie. "I hope you'll both stay for supper."

A warm hand pushed hair away from her face, and Lonnie felt her cheek wedged against something soft. Someone spoke her name, the voice too sweet to be Jebediah's or Gideon's. Lonnie opened her eyes and flinched.

"Shh."

A pair of soft eyes cradled her face. "Didn't mean to startle you, Lonnie." An old woman sat beside her. "My name's Elsie. I'm Jebediah's wife."

Lonnie's body complained when she sat up. Elsie tucked a pillow behind her back, and Lonnie sank into it. She swallowed, and her mouth was as dry as sand.

"Can I get you anything?"

"A drink of water?" Her voice came out raspy, and Lonnie cleared her throat.

Elsie patted her hand. "I'll be right back." She disappeared, and Lonnie blinked, taking the room in. She peered down at the sofa where her hand rested on a thick, floral print.

When Elsie returned with a small cup, she sat beside Lonnie. "Can I get you anything else? Are you hungry?"

Lonnie shook her head. She sipped the water, and it cooled her mouth. "Thank you," she said, staring into the cup.

The woman smoothed Lonnie's hair off her shoulder, and she gave her arm a gentle squeeze. "You had a rough go of it, I'd say."

Lonnie nodded when emotion welled in the back of her throat, followed by another wave of nausea.

"Sure I can't get you anything else?" Elsie's eyes widened when Lonnie pressed her fingertips to her mouth. "Sure you're all right?"

"I think so." Lonnie forced her hand into her lap, but her stomach still churned.

Ducking her head, Elsie peered into her face. "Honey, you don't need to be frightened. I'm here to help you."

"I fear I'm gonna be sick."

A cool hand pressed against Lonnie's cheek.

"You're a bit pale." Elsie rushed off, and within a minute's time, she returned with a bowl of warm water. A plate was tucked in her other hand. She set it in Lonnie's lap, and Lonnie peered down at a slice of buttered bread. Elsie lifted a damp cloth and dabbed the side of Lonnie's face.

Lonnie winced.

"Sorry, dear."

The sofa was soft, and Lonnie wanted to close her eyes again. She pressed her head to the back of the cushion and sighed. Her body seemed to melt. She lifted the bread to her mouth and took a small nibble. Her nostrils flared, and the food turned sour in her mouth. It must have shown in her face, for Elsie jumped up again and rushed back with a metal bowl. Lonnie held the bowl to her chest and forced herself to take slow, steady breaths.

Elsie's eyebrows fell as she studied Lonnie. "How long have you been feelin' this way?"

"Few days. Maybe a week." Lonnie clutched the bowl tighter and pressed a hand to her ribs where her stomach complained.

"Is it possible that you are...?"

Lonnie's chin trembled, and she turned her face to the side. Elsie took hold of her hand. Lonnie's shoulders shook in a silent sob. She blinked her dry eyes and stared at the far wall. "It's possible."

"Have you had any other signs?" When Lonnie nodded, Elsie

squeezed her hand. "A baby is a blessing." Her tone was encouraging, and when Lonnie looked into Elsie's face, she saw nothing but kindness.

"For some."

Elsie tucked a strand of hair behind Lonnie's ear. "But not for you?" The soft words, void of judgment, made Lonnie tighten her grip on Elsie's hand as if never to let go.

"I don't see how a baby could help anything."

With a slow, shaky sigh, Elsie wrapped another hand around Lonnie's. "How about this? You rest awhile. Got a nice bed upstairs with your name on it." Her smile was warm. "I've got a broth simmering on the stove, and I'll bring you some if you feel up to eating. You and your husband are welcome to stay the night. Give you a chance to rest up a bit." She gave Lonnie a reassuring squeeze. "And when you're feelin' a little better, we'll move on to the next step."

Telling Gideon. Lonnie gulped, but unable to resist Elsie's offer, she nodded.

Seventeen

Looking for Jebediah was no use. The man had vanished. Gideon had been walking in circles for the last half hour, and after trying the barn once more, he gave up and strode back to the house. He rapped lightly on the door with his knuckles. Elsie's face appeared behind the glass, and she opened it.

"Just sent your wife upstairs for a lie-down." She motioned for him to come in. "I was going to bring her up a bowl of broth." She spoke over her shoulder, apron strings bouncing as she scooted through the kitchen.

"Mind if I...?"

Elsie studied him a heartbeat and then handed him the bowl. Her tone tightened. "Door on the left."

Gideon found it easily and, after slipping into the bedroom, saw that Lonnie was asleep. The collar of a fresh nightgown brushed against her cheek. Elsie bustled in behind him, a pitcher of steaming water in her hand. She poured the water into the washbasin and stuck her finger in. She ducked out, then returned, a tin can in the crook of her elbow. She lifted the lid and pulled out a dark glass bottle. Tipping several droplets onto a clean rag, she gently touched the scrape on Lonnie's face.

She looked to Gideon. "Fetch me when she wakes up."

He set the bowl on the nightstand and pulled a chair closer to the bed. Elsie stepped out, leaving the door cracked.

As Gideon watched Lonnie sleep, he rubbed his hands back and forth on his pants. The broth steamed on the nightstand.

He glanced to her hands. They were clean now—no mud in the creases of her palm or caked beneath her fingernails. He lifted his eyes to the washbasin, and his gaze fell on a glass of water on the nightstand, half full. He crossed his arms over his chest and watched her. Elsie bustled about below, pots and pans clattering. When the grandfather clock chimed from the parlor, Lonnie's eyes opened slowly, and, blinking, she peered up at the ceiling. When she turned and saw him, fear flooded her eyes.

"It's all right." He straightened. "Everything's going to be all right." He didn't want to be a monster. He swallowed, hoping someday she would forgive him for it. But with his dreams for the future suddenly collapsed around him, Gideon didn't know what to do. He hadn't asked for this. Any of it.

Lonnie's chest collapsed as she finally let out a breath. She swallowed, and her head settled back onto the pillow.

"I brought you something to eat. Are you hungry?" Gideon gestured toward the bowl of broth.

At her nod, he lifted the bowl from the nightstand and balanced it on his knees. He hesitated, clutching the spoon. Should he feed her, or just give her the bowl and leave? When Lonnie didn't move, Gideon scooted forward. He tipped the spoon down and then lifted it to her mouth.

Her face registered surprise, and he halted. Several droplets struck her nightgown.

"I suppose you could do this yourself."

She nodded slowly, confusion thick in her brown eyes.

Heat swept over the back of his neck. "Sorry." He handed her the bowl.

She took it but made no move to eat.

He glanced at the dresser drawer that was still slightly open. His gaze traced the lace at her collarbone—bright white like everything else in this house seemed to be. "Should…should I fetch something else?"

"I'm not really hungry. Thank you." Her voice was even, void of emotion.

He suddenly wished he could read her thoughts. "Well, I suppose I'll leave you." He stood, the chair skidding back awkwardly.

She peered up at him. "Gideon? What are the odds you could just sit still for a minute?"

When she motioned with her head toward the chair, he sat. His knees bumped against the bed. She handed him the bowl, and he placed it on the nightstand. She folded her hands in her lap and seemed to study them. When she didn't speak, Gideon cleared his throat. She looked up at him, her eyes glossy.

Something stirred in his chest.

"There's something I need to tell you."

He leaned forward and rested his forearms on his knees. "I'm listening," he said dumbly. Staring at the floor, he tugged at his still-damp shirt and shifted his boots. When he forced his eyes to meet Lonnie's face, he felt every moment of his shameful actions. He didn't know what to make of that.

"There's… I mean, I suspect…" She drew in a shaky sigh and didn't look at him. "I'm thinkin' I might have a baby on the way."

He blinked rapidly. He tried to swallow, but his mouth could do nothing but hang open. A strange sound slipped from his throat. "A...a baby?"

"It's possible." She pressed her hand to her collarbone.

Possible? He groaned. Stupid man. He pressed his forehead to his interlocked fingers and slammed his eyes shut. This wasn't happening. It couldn't be. No baby...not him.

"Gideon?"

"I... I..." He stood and left the room.

He didn't need this. Ever. A sickening churned in his gut as he stomped down the stairs and through the house.

Gideon slipped out the door and stood on the back porch. The air was dimming, and glancing up at the gray sky, he could only guess that the sun would set within the hour. He slid his hat into place. Jebediah was leading a cow into the barn. Gideon surveyed the lay of the farm as he waited for Jebediah to return. When the man appeared, Gideon strode in that direction.

"How's that little wife of yours?" Jebediah asked.

"Fine."

"She better be." Jebediah pointed to the woodpile. "See that?"

"Yessir."

"Get choppin'."

"All of it? I don't know if—"

"I wasn't asking." Jebediah held out a pair of work gloves, his face hard.

Gideon took the gloves before Jebediah could beat him over the head with them.

"When you're finished, you can go check on Lonnie."

Nodding, Gideon strode off. He didn't want to think about Lonnie just now. He studied the woodpile. Larger pieces lay about, waiting for an ax blade. He glanced from the mess to Jebediah.

"In there." Jebediah pointed to the barn. "Hangin' by the door."

Gideon stepped inside the barn, nabbed the ax, and yanked the rickety door closed. He glanced around, but Jebediah was gone. Gritting his teeth, Gideon pounded a chunk of wood on the chopping block, steadied it, and stepped back. Squaring his shoulders, he adjusted his grip, then heaved the ax over his head. In one broad swing, he brought it down with all his might. Two halves spiraled into the yard. He reached for another chunk. Bending made his head hurt. He rubbed at the lump. A baby on the way. He ran his hand over his eyes. *You gotta be kidding me.*

"Jebediah got you hard at work?"

At the sound of Elsie's voice, Gideon straightened. "Yes ma'am."

A pan in one hand, she strode across the yard and disappeared into the barn. His shoulders settled, and he let his troubles slip from the front of his mind even as blood pumped through his veins. Overcome with the urge to break something, he lifted the ax and brought it down, splitting the piece into two halves with one smooth blow. He had split dozens of pieces by the time Elsie stepped back out. She set the pan full of milk down and pushed against the heavy barn door. It creaked closed.

"Need a hand?" Gideon panted.

"Naw. This old door has acted this way for years." She pushed harder, and the latch finally fell into place. Elsie picked up the pan and walked back to the porch. "Come on inside when you get hungry."

"Yes ma'am." Gideon glanced around for Jebediah and doubted the old man would like to find him sitting at the table. Maybe later. His stomach grumbled, but he wasn't about to cross Jebediah any more than he already had. Gideon tried the barn door. Tilting to one side, it creaked open when he pulled on it. He pressed against it, and the wood complained. He ran a callused hand along the hinges and eyed the repairs that needed to be done. The Bennetts needed help with more than just the woodpile. Gideon chewed the inside of his cheek and made a note to look at the door again tomorrow. Not for Jebediah. For Elsie. He'd work on it before he and Lonnie left.

He didn't know how Lonnie would react when he told her they had to keep moving, but she needed to understand. They couldn't stay here. Jebediah's armload of wood confirmed Gideon's worry. Winter wouldn't wait for him to find work. It certainly wouldn't wait for him to find a home. And he was about to become his pa. A man with too many mouths to feed.

The burden hung around his neck like a millstone.

It took all his restraint to keep from kicking the door closed.

Returning to the woodpile, Gideon split another piece. The ax felt right in his hand. He glanced around for Jebediah, but the man was nowhere in sight. For a moment, he looked up at the bedroom window, where Lonnie lay resting. He turned back to his work. He couldn't think about that right now. He pushed his thoughts to the wind and felt his muscles and mind relax as one. He bent and lifted a large round piece. It took all his strength to settle it on the chopping block. He flung off his flannel shirt and tossed it on the stack. Sweat dampened his undershirt to his skin. As the land grew darker, he continued to split wood. Just when his sore shoulders warned him to stop, Jebediah appeared. Pieces were scattered everywhere. Gideon began to stack them, making a show of taking great care. Jebediah would probably spit in his soup if he didn't.

"Not bad." The man crossed his arms over his chest and studied Gideon's work.

Gideon rubbed the scruff of his jaw and almost smiled.

"Just finished up the rest of the chores. Let's head inside."

Gideon snagged the edge of a flannel sleeve and stuffed his arms through. He folded down the collar, then worked the buttons into place as he followed Jebediah to the porch. He froze when he caught his image in the cracked mirror that hung from a rusted nail. He tousled his hair, but it was no use. He needed a bath.

When they finished washing hands and faces, Jebediah pitched the foggy water into the yard and set the empty bucket in place. Gideon ran a dry cloth behind his neck. As he watched the old man, he thought about asking him why he hadn't just run him off with that shotgun of his.

Gideon cringed at the sight Jebediah had stumbled upon. The beast he had seen. Though he'd tried to trample it, his guilt surfaced.

"I've been wondering something." The words came out weak. "Earlier, I mean. About what you saw and all."

Jebediah's face shadowed.

"I didn't mean to…I don't know what came over me—"

"That so?" Jebediah replied, his voice flat.

"What I mean to say is…I'm sorry."

Silver eyebrows shot up. "Sorry? To me?" He grunted. "I'm not the one you were flingin' about." His gray eyes hardened.

"No sir." Gideon hung his head.

"But if in fact you are sorry, you might tell the person who needs to hear it." Jebediah drew in a deep breath and let it out slowly. His gaze filtered over the farm. "There's a lesson to be learned in this."

"Yessir." Gideon rubbed his sore shoulder, exhausted from sweating off his frustration. His guilt.

A pair of gray eyes followed the movement. "But you ain't learned it yet."

"Sir?"

"You've got a ways to go, boy, if you think you deserve that little lady upstairs."

Dropping his gaze, Gideon stared at his tattered boots and shifted his feet. He stuffed his hands in his pockets.

"I hope you'll get there, though. For her sake."

When Gideon didn't answer, Jebediah reached for the door. He motioned with his head for Gideon to follow. "Come on. I smell supper."

Elsie slid cups onto the table and spun around. Her eyes flicked from Gideon's muddy boots to his disheveled hair. "I see you've been working hard this afternoon."

"Yes ma'am." Lifting his head, Gideon listened for signs that Lonnie was up and about.

"Have a seat." Jebediah handed him a glass of cold tea.

Gideon accepted it and stepped toward the table. The kitchen, nearly the size of his pa's entire house, was nothing like the one he'd grown up in. Lace curtains framed glass-paned windows, and pots of herbs and flowers lined the sills. The floor was smooth and well polished. Nothing like back home where a boy got splinters in his bare feet just from crossing it.

When Elsie brought him a plate of food, Gideon lifted his elbows. "Thank you." He stared at the mound of beans, still steaming and topped with a biscuit. She placed a bowl of hot broth beside it. It was all he could do to wait for Jebediah to say grace, and he accepted another serving as soon as he cleaned his plate. He set down his empty glass and wiped his mouth. "How's Lonnie?"

"She's doin' just fine." Elsie's face took on a warm glow. "She's been resting real good all day. That poor girl was plumb tuckered out." She rose from the table and grabbed Gideon's glass, shaking it as an offer for more.

"No, thank you."

"I was gonna bring her another bowl of broth. Would you mind takin' it up to her while I wash the dishes?" She tapped her ladle on the side of the pot.

"Yes...yes ma'am." Gideon fought the reservation in his voice.

"And Gideon." Elsie's eyes were kind. "I spoke to Jebediah, and we both hope you'll stay on for a few days. No sense in rushin' off."

Jebediah's face was hard, but he tipped his head in agreement.

Uncertain of what to say, Gideon nodded. Would a few more days make a difference? Possibly. But with Jebediah breathing down his neck and watching his every move, Gideon doubted he had a choice.

Eighteen

Lonnie nibbled on the end of a slice of cold toast. It tasted better now that she had rested. She hadn't eaten much the last few days and knew it was taking its toll. A knock at the door drew her attention. Gideon stepped in, and she tried to mask her surprise.

His eyes fell to her stomach, as if it would have grown in the few hours he'd been gone. She swallowed her toast and wiped her mouth. He sat across from her and ran his palms across his pants. Her appetite gone, Lonnie set the toast on the plate beside her. Instead of looking at him, she brushed crumbs from her fingertips.

When he sat there in silence, she knew she would be the one to speak first.

"You look troubled."

He shook his head. "I'm fine. Just...just worried about you, that's all."

She doubted that was the truth. Her heart still aching, she tucked it behind a stone wall. "I'll be all right."

He ran his hands across his pants again, clearly stalling.

Lonnie fiddled with a chip in the plate. She broke off a piece of bread and forced herself to take a bite. She chewed slowly, waiting.

"Lonnie," he began, her name weak on his lips. He looked around the room. "I...I need you to know that I'm...sorry."

"Sorry?"

He let out a quick *whoosh* of air. "For hurting you."

"Which time?" When he winced, she knew her words had the effect she'd intended.

"Um..." His palms swished together. Color crept up his neck. "For today. For earlier." His eyes fell to the bruises on her arm, and she yanked her sleeve down. "You have every right to be angry with me. And you don't have to accept my apology. I know that." He paused. "You didn't deserve that. No one deserved that."

Tears stung the backs of her eyes. He had turned on her as no husband should ever turn on his wife. But she was hardly a wife. She was just the woman he was forced to marry. And now she was carrying a child he didn't want. Yet here he sat, apologizing. He was her husband, and she had promised to stick by him in front of the church and in front of God. Lonnie did not take those vows lightly. *One more chance. God, do I have the strength for one more chance?* She looked to the darkening window and fiddled with the edge of the quilt. In her mind's eye all she saw was his anger from earlier. "Go away, Gideon."

Gideon O'Riley knew little of what he had done to her. He couldn't. He would never be on the receiving end of someone's anger the way she had. Someone she could never fight off, no matter how hard she tried. Did he understand that? understand that she would stay despite what he had done?

A few compliments and a handful of smiles, and she'd sold her future for the hope that she could be loved. Afterward, he'd left her that day with hardly a word. Now she would pay the price. Lonnie pressed her fingertips to her eyes. *Lonnie, what have you done?* She heard Gideon stand. Without speaking, he lifted the creaking chair, and it thudded into the corner. He stepped out and shut the door softly behind him. Lonnie pushed the plate away and lay down. Draping an arm over her eyes, she tried to shut out the remaining light. Tried to shut out her life.

Nineteen

Gideon ducked into the kitchen, a bucket of fresh water in his hand. At the table, Lonnie and Elsie fell silent. "Afternoon." He set the bucket down and turned to go.

"Thank you, Gideon." Elsie rose. "Haven't hardly seen you all day."

"Jebediah's kept me pretty busy." He'd woken before sunrise and, having skipped breakfast, accepted the bowl of soup she poured for him. He ate in the doorway. He was tired and wanted to sit, but he feared that if he got too close, Lonnie would burst into tears, or kick him in the shin, or whatever it was that women did when they were mad. Gideon took a bite of soft potato and chewed as Elsie used the water to fill the kettle.

"Can I get you anything else, Gideon?"

"No ma'am. Thank you."

He'd spent a better part of the day working for Jebediah and hadn't expected to see Lonnie sipping tea at the table. She wore a clean dress, and her freshly combed hair curtained over one shoulder. He ate his soup quickly, then excused himself. He looked around for Jebediah. Surely there were more chores to be done. He'd do anything to be free of the kitchen.

At Jebediah's request, Gideon made sure the cow had fresh hay and water before he went to fetch the slop bucket. The metal handle dug into his hand as he carried it across the yard and dumped the day-old contents into the pigpen. He heard the back door close and looked up to see Elsie leading Lonnie to the chicken coop. They emerged not a minute later with half a dozen brown eggs tucked in a basket on Elsie's arm. Lonnie's steps were slow, but he was glad to see her up and about.

The sun had long since arced across the sky, so Gideon turned his attention back to his work. He tugged on the barn door. As it creaked open, he thought of fixing it then and there, but it would have to wait until tomorrow.

Gideon smoothed his knuckles across his brow. Lonnie seemed to enjoy Elsie's company. A warm bed with soft sheets was a stark contrast to the rutted ground and damp nights. It would pain her to leave.

They could not stay though. They'd head out tomorrow. Shadows crept toward the house in slow strides as evening neared. By the time he'd filled the kindling box and swept the back porch, Gideon smelled fish frying and realized where Jebediah had been all afternoon. He cursed under his breath, struck with the notion of the old man sneaking off to fish while he labored.

With supper smelling as good as it did, he tried to push his troubles from mind. Besides, deep down he knew the truth—a few chores were nothing in comparison to what Jebediah and Elsie had done for Lonnie. For what they had protected her from. When his frustrations came back to mind, Gideon flexed his hands. He still couldn't believe that he had pushed Lonnie as far as he had. He hated what his life had become, but he hadn't known he was capable of that kind of anger. It would get better once they got to Stuart. When they were settled and had a little money, his burdens would be easier to shoulder. The sooner they got on the road, the better.

When Gideon sat beside Lonnie at the supper table, he struggled to join in the conversation. He pushed a slice of cornbread around his plate. The Bennetts had no need for him and Lonnie hanging around, being in the way. They needed their space. Had a routine. Two more mouths to feed would only burden the couple. Still lost in thought, Gideon nodded to himself. He and Lonnie had imposed long enough, and he had no desire to overstay their welcome.

When Lonnie laughed softly at one of Jebediah's jokes, Gideon glanced around the table. Rosy-cheeked, Jebediah chuckled and slapped his napkin on his knee. The three of them seemed to have everything figured out. Gideon didn't know what they needed him for. He could be gone in the morning and no one would care. He tipped his head at the thought. Then again, Lonnie could run back home and complain of how he got her with child and then left her. Gideon grimaced at the thought of Joel Sawyer on his trail. No, that would never do. Whether he wanted to or not, he'd have to take responsibility for his family.

The thought sobered Gideon, fueling the fire under his feet. He would have to find work soon. And a house. He could not offer his family much, not in eight months, but there would be a roof over their heads. Maybe in a few years, when the baby got older, he would have to build Lonnie something finer. Gideon flexed his jaw. Through his own blood and sweat, he would spend the rest of his days repaying an unseen debt. Apparently God hadn't been satisfied with his sacrifices already. With his fingertips, Gideon turned his glass in a slow circle on the table. *Figures.*

"Something on your mind, son?" Jebediah asked, his voice even.

"Well," Gideon said slowly, leaning back in his chair. He had eaten more than his share of fried fish and creamed corn. Elsie placed a cup of dark coffee in front of him, and Gideon took a sip to settle his mind. "We'll be on our way tomorrow. Lonnie and I sure do appreciate your generosity."

Lonnie's mouth stilled, and her fork touched her plate. Gideon chewed his cheek.

Jebediah drizzled honey into his coffee, slowly. "Well, we'll be sorry to see you go. Elsie and I sure have enjoyed your company. You were quite a help around the farm." A muscle tensed beneath his gray stubble, and he glanced at Elsie.

Even as he tried to interpret the motion, Gideon nodded. "It was hardly enough to repay you. And with the way you took care of Lonnie, it was the least I could do." The words felt flat on his lips. They didn't sound as sincere as he'd hoped.

Jebediah nodded once.

Satisfied, Gideon turned to the apple pie Elsie slid in front of him.

When supper was over, Lonnie helped Elsie wash dishes, and Jebediah invited Gideon out to the back porch for a smoke. With a wrinkled and weathered hand, Jebediah stuck a twig in the flames of the kitchen stove, then held it to his pipe until a trickle of smoke curled upward. He handed the makeshift match to Gideon. As Gideon stepped through the door, he shielded it from the cold night breeze, his corncob pipe dangling from his lips. The sweet smell of tobacco wafted toward him, and he shook out the tiny flame, tossing the charred remains into the dirt.

They settled down on the top step, and Gideon rested his elbows on his knees.

Jebediah cupped the end of his pipe with his palm and two fingers. "Well, son. Havin' a baby's about the best thing that can happen to a man."

Gideon glanced at Jebediah. His aged face was half lit by the kitchen light.

Jebediah's words mumbled around the mouthpiece. "Gettin' married, workin' hard, and havin' babies is what turns boys into men." He blew a puff of smoke. "It's what makes life what it is." His gaze pierced Gideon.

Swallowing, Gideon studied the step beneath his boots.

Jebediah slid the pipe from his lips, and his speech became clear as glass. "A man takes care of himself first when he is young. When he gets married, he comes second." He motioned with his pipe as if a man's entire life spread before him.

Gideon blew out a puff of smoke.

"When a man has a baby, he comes third."

Third. Exhausted, Gideon lowered his head between his shoulders, his smoldering pipe forgotten in his hand. Did Jebediah have to talk *all* the time? It made a body think too much, and Gideon was in no mood for that. Besides, he hadn't even learned to put Lonnie first. How was he going to be a father? Men lived up and down the mountain—some lousy fathers and husbands. Was Jebediah insinuating that he was one of those men? that he was like Joel Sawyer? Annoyed, Gideon chewed the end of his pipe.

Smoke trickled into the cool night air, the tobacco having lost its comfort. Whatever it was Lonnie needed from him, he had nothing more to give.

Twenty

Gideon used Jebediah's pliers to bend the rusty hinge back. He struck the flat end with a hammer. The *clang* of metal rang loud and clear through the silent morning. He lifted the old hinge up to his eye. Satisfied, he polished it on the hem of his shirt and held the metal piece to the door.

"Looks about right," he mumbled to himself. He was all alone in the barn. The morning milking was done, and Jebediah trudged back and forth with armfuls of freshly cut white pine. Gideon shook his head. *Crazy old man.*

Morning light hadn't touched the cold floor when Gideon had crawled out of bed that morning. He'd slipped out to start the day, leaving Lonnie in the dim, still quiet.

It had taken all his strength and most of his patience to take down the barn door, and now the weather-beaten wood lay across two sawhorses like a patient on a city doctor's table. He circled the slab of wood, picked up a file, and smoothed away rotted and rough splinters where the hinge had sat. Then, with a worn piece of sandpaper, he made a fresh spot for it to rest.

When he opened and closed the hinge, an obnoxious *squeak* begged for oil. He dipped his hand into a can of grease and massaged it into the rusted crevices. He noticed the layer of black grime under his fingernails and in the cracks of his broad palm and knew he'd have to scrub up good to be clean enough for Elsie's breakfast table.

He worked the grease in until the hinge opened and closed like a well-read book. Gideon wiped his oily hand on the rag dangling from the back of his pants, then ran his still-greasy finger under his nose to stifle a sneeze.

"Food's on," Jebediah said behind him.

Gideon glanced up from his work. The bright morning sun outlined Jebediah's husky figure—a black form in the doorless frame.

"I'll be there in a minute."

Jebediah stepped in. His hand swished as he slid it over sanded wood. "You did a fine job. This old door has been falling down for years. It's a shame I wasn't able to get around to it sooner."

Gideon shrugged. "It's the least I can do before Lonnie and I leave this afternoon."

Jebediah was silent for a moment. "I see. She doin' better?"

Suddenly fascinated by the hinge in his hand, Gideon dropped his head in a half nod.

"Well, I'm gonna get washed up. Elsie's got hotcakes and fried ham on the table. Don't be long."

After setting the hinge down, Gideon wiped his fingers on the rag too greasy to do any good. "I'm done for now." His stomach howled for breakfast, and he could finish up later. Besides, the cold barn made him long for Elsie's warm kitchen.

They walked to the house in silence. Gideon plunged his hands into the bucket on the back porch and rubbed icy water up his forearms and on his face. His teeth chattered as he reached for the towel. Jebediah held the door, and Gideon stepped into the kitchen.

Lonnie slid a handful of steaming hotcakes into a basket. "Freezin'?" She almost sounded pleased with the idea.

The heat from the kitchen made his cheeks tingle. "It's a good bit colder this morning than it's been lately."

"Tends to get cool fast down here," Jebediah said. "Bein' wedged up against the mountain like this, we get a lot of mornin' shade from one side and evenin' shade from the other."

Gideon watched Lonnie pour a spoonful of batter on the hot griddle, his mind on anything but shade.

"Sit." Lonnie offered him a faint smile, and he saw that it was genuine.

Gideon pressed his worries to the back of his mind, and when she settled into the seat next to him, he smelled the scent of soap on her skin. He found himself staring.

Jebediah cleared his throat.

"Gideon." Lonnie gently squeezed his hand.

"Huh?"

"We're gonna pray," she whispered.

He quickly dropped his head, and even as Jebediah blessed the food, his cheeks grew warm.

"Well." Elsie squeezed his hand and opened her eyes. "There's apple butter, and I got maple syrup warming on the back of the stove." She rose and returned quickly with a small copper pot. "Everyone help themselves. Don't be shy, now." She squeezed Lonnie's shoulder.

Gideon did as he was ordered and piled a stack of warm hotcakes onto his plate and smeared them with a knifeful of butter. He lifted the lid away from the cast-iron skillet and paused long enough for Lonnie to help herself to some fried ham. After everyone had taken their share, he stabbed the crispy meat with his fork and loaded up his plate.

He pulled his hands away from his food just long enough for Elsie to drizzle a pool of syrup over the hotcakes. "Thanks." Wasting no time, he crammed the warm, sticky goodness into his mouth. "This food sure is fine, ma'am." He chewed and swallowed, knowing his mouth was fuller than it should have been. "It'll do us good to set out on a full stomach. Not like last time, huh, Lonnie?"

Lonnie lifted her eyes.

His jaw slowed.

"Gid." Lonnie's voice was small. She glanced around the table, as if gathering her strength. "Miss Elsie and Jebediah have invited us to stay on a little longer. They think it would be good for me to keep to one spot for a while. Just until I get my strength back up."

Jebediah nodded his consent. "Makes no sense to rush off."

Gideon gulped, nearly choking on his food.

"I would like to stay." Lonnie faced him, her eyes eager.

Jebediah cut in. "Gideon, you ain't got nowhere to go." He rested his elbows on each side of his plate.

His food turning to ash in his mouth, Gideon washed it down with lukewarm coffee. He eyed each person at the table. They could have spoken up about this sooner, not mere hours before he was ready to leave. Suddenly annoyed, he struggled to find his voice. "Sir, with all due respect, I know just where we're headed."

Jebediah leaned forward. "And where might that be?"

Gideon kept his voice as cool as he could manage. "We were headed for Stuart. Few more days and I reckon we'll be there. Lonnie and I planned on getting us a little piece of land to build a house..."

A smile broke out beneath Jebediah's silver mustache. "I'd say you got a little off track somewhere. You gotta backtrack a day and stop following the ridgeline." He tossed a thumb over his shoulder and Gideon followed it with his eyes but only found a hand-stitched sampler hanging where Stuart apparently sat. "You ain't far though. Just head on down the mountain."

"How far did we come?" Gideon leaned forward.

"Well, you came a nice little way from Rocky Knob. Ain't that where you came from?"

Hiding his frustration took some effort. "But we walked for days and days."

"Might have been walkin' in circles."

Gideon glanced at Lonnie. Shame soured his gut. Most men of twenty-two would have traveled farther than their own front door before this. "So let me get this straight. We went the wrong way?"

Jebediah nodded.

Leaning back in his chair, Gideon sighed.

"We don't have anywhere else to go," Lonnie said. She folded her hands in front of her as if the matter were that simple to resolve.

"But we do." Gideon rose, strode to where his jacket hung by the door, and yanked out the newspaper clipping. He held it out for Jebediah.

The man took it, and his eyes scanned the small scrap. "Hmph."

"What?"

"This paper's two months old."

Gideon snatched it up and checked the date. Sure enough. "Doesn't mean that it's not—"

"My neighbor was just in Stuart three weeks ago. Banks are done and two more shops have gone up since then. He said men flooded the area after they posted this. Hotel filled up after a few days. Some of them were sleepin' in tents on the outskirts of town. Hardly a job to be found." He tugged at his beard. "There will be again, mind you. Once things settle down." He folded the scrap and handed it back to Gideon. "But I wouldn't be rushin' in there any time soon."

Gideon collapsed in his chair. "You mean…" At the defeat he heard in his voice, he fell silent. Every eye was on him, and his ears burned hot. Clenching his jaw, he looked up at Jebediah and forced his tone steady. "Then where are we exactly?"

"Not much of a town to speak of. Folks call this Fancy Gap. Nice little community. Got a church a few miles up the way and a few other odds and ends. That's about it. We head down the mountain to Mount Airy now and again. That's where the railroad comes through."

Jaw clenched, Gideon processed his words. "So if we stay, what's in it for you?"

Jebediah laughed. "You got yourself an untrusting husband here, Lonnie. And a businessman, I see." He tipped a tin mug to his lips. "Nothin' in life's free, is it, son?"

"No sir." But Gideon had a feeling Jebediah was teasing him.

Jebediah seemed to collect his thoughts a moment, then cleared his throat. "We aren't spring chickens anymore. You know as well as I do that me and Elsie can't keep this farm goin' much longer." He fiddled with the handle of his coffee cup, but his gaze was strong. "We need help. We need young hands and strong backs that can keep this place runnin'. And you need a place to stay." He tapped the table between them. "Come spring, there's corn to plant and the garden to seed. All summer, there's enough to keep busy feedin' the livestock. The grass in the meadow will need to be felled for winter hay, and what little wheat we seed will have to be harvested and shocked." He sank back in his chair as if the thought of all that work drained him. He turned to Lonnie. "How does a roof over your head and a warm bed sound to you? Three hot meals every day?"

She moistened her lips. "That'd be right nice, sir."

Gideon glanced out the window to where the path disappeared into the trees. All he wanted was to hightail it out of here. *Where you going, Gid? In more circles?* He sighed. Lonnie was going to have a baby in the spring. He had no land and no money. No house and not even a tool to his name to build it with. His heart raced faster than his thoughts.

He eyed Jebediah. Doubt made him hesitate, but the man's offer was better than any his family had given him. With his gaze still settled on the man across from him, he patted his hand on the table. "You got yourself a deal."

Lonnie straightened, her face brightening.

Gideon did not mirror her enthusiasm. "I mean to *earn* my keep."

Sliding his coffee cup aside, Jebediah leaned back in his chair and grinned. "Don't worry. I'll make sure that you do."

Twenty-One

The massive door clanged against the frame, and Gideon leaned under the weight of it. Jebediah, who had been watching with his arms crossed, stepped forward and held it steady. Gideon grunted as he searched his pocket for the peg. His hand fumbled for the metal piece, and he stuffed it in his mouth just as the door slid to the side.

"Easy." Sweat trickled down his spine. He hammered the peg into place and knelt. The door slipped.

Jebediah braced himself. "I got it… I got it."

With three quick blows, Gideon pounded the peg all the way through and sat back on his heels. Quickly, he hammered the other.

"Whew." Jebediah stepped to the side. With a touch of his hand, the door opened and closed smoothly. He grinned. "Nice work." Jebediah handed him a pair of leather gloves and signaled to the ax hanging on the wall.

Gideon squeezed a tight muscle in his shoulder and didn't say a word.

"Can you stack it by the porch?"

"Over there?" Gideon pointed to the house.

"Yep, I like to keep wood close to the house during winter." Jebediah slid his thumbs beneath brown suspenders. "We can keep that stocked when the weather's good, and when it snows, it will be easy to fill the woodbox."

It took Gideon a few breaths to gauge the distance from the woodblock to the porch. Thirty paces—at least. Easily a day's worth of work. "Got a wheelbarrow?"

"Well, I got one, but it's busted." Then in a thoughtful voice he added, "You know? That's something else you could do." Jebediah glanced around.

Gideon rolled his eyes. *Of course.*

He tugged the gloves from his back pocket and grabbed his first armful of wood. He carried small loads across the yard, starting a new stack against the side of the porch. He rolled a large piece of maple away from the chopping block. With an intricate grain, it was too precious to turn into firewood. He lined up the wood in neat rows, determined to stack only once. In the short time he had known Jebediah, he could tell that if the man was not satisfied, he'd have to start the job over.

Grumbling, Gideon went back for another load. He'd long since lost count. Then an idea hit him. He tore off his gloves to give his sweaty hands a breather, then found Jebediah in the barn. "Where's that wheelbarrow of yours?"

Jebediah was stooped over, his mule's hoof in his open palm. "It's around back. You gonna fix it now?" He spoke without looking up.

"Yep. Figured I could use it."

Jebediah grunted, and Gideon took it as a dismissal. He found the broken wheelbarrow behind the barn. Weeds hid the handles from sight, and cobwebs had stitched the rusted metal to the side of the building. After dumping out murky water and a collection of bugs, Gideon wheeled it over to the barn.

It took a few tries, but he finally wrenched the broken handle free. Eying the stub, he tossed it against the woodpile and hunted the work area for something that would fit just as well. He found a straight piece of oak on the far side of the barn and, after peeling off the bark, used his pocketknife to roughly sketch out its new shape.

By the time he had the wood smoothed and sanded, his thumb ached, and the call for dinner pulled his tired feet home under a high sun. He devoured his share of cold sandwiches, washing it down with a glass of milk, then hurried back to the barn. He shaped the handle to the curves of his palm, cradling it every so often to ensure a comfortable fit. The light dimmed in the barn, and nearly finished, Gideon moved closer to the window. When it looked near enough to the real thing, he attached it to the wheelbarrow and wheeled it out to show Jebediah.

"So, what do you think? This will make life a little easier around here now." The wheel creaked to a stop at Jebediah's feet, and Gideon blew dust from his hands.

"Looks good." Jebediah fingered the handle. "But that ain't my wheelbarrow." He stepped closer. "It belongs to Gus, my neighbor. He let me borrow it when mine broke, but I somehow busted the handle off of it."

Gideon stared at him, and Jebediah offered a lopsided grin.

"Thanks for fixing it." His tone was apologetic. "I've been meaning to get around to that. After supper, why don't you take it over to him, seeing how you're the one who patched it up and all? I'm sure he'd be pleased to thank you himself."

Words eluded him. Gideon glanced down at the new handle, freshly sanded and snugly fit. "This isn't yours." It wasn't a question. Heat crawled along the back of his neck.

Jebediah shook his head. "Mine's the one with the hole in it. It's around here somewhere. The rain finally rusted it clear through last year. It's still good for haulin' wood, though. Just not much good for smaller stuff."

Biting his cheek so hard it nearly bled, Gideon scarcely heard Elsie call them in for supper.

The candles had long since been snuffed out, and the scent of smoke faded. Lonnie pulled her pillow closer as she listened to Gideon's steady breathing. His stiff back was to her, and he didn't move, not even when she brushed her hand along his shoulder. He'd sat on the parlor sofa after supper, tuning his mandolin. He played a melancholy tune and began another, but after a few strums, he strode upstairs with hardly a word. The instrument now leaned against the chair. Moonlight glinted on the body.

Lonnie kept her voice soft. "Are you awake?"

A brief moment passed until he grunted.

"You tired?"

Another grunt.

"You worked real hard today." She stared at the ceiling, searching the darkness for words to assign to her thoughts. Words Gideon would welcome and respond to.

He rolled to face her. She did the same and pulled her knees up between them. His eyes glistened, and even in the darkness she knew he was watching her.

"Do you mind staying?" She held her breath for an answer.

Gideon blinked. The sheets rustled as he folded his arms over his chest. "I don't know." He hesitated. "I s'pose not. Not exactly what I had in mind, though." The pillow rustled as he shook his head. "Any job would be easier than working for Jebediah. The man hardly lets me sit down all day."

"He got you workin' hard?"

"Hard? He's makin' me do *everything* around here." Gideon lowered his voice, his tone sarcastic. "He's gonna work me to death, I think."

Lonnie bit her lip to keep a smile from forming. "Maybe tomorrow will be better."

If his spirits didn't lift, she feared he'd set his sights on the trail before the first frost hit.

She prayed the possibility away. Her hand fell to her stomach. This was a good home. A home where God came first and where drunken anger didn't shake the walls worse than the autumn winds. This was a home to bring life into.

"Maybe," Gideon mumbled, finally responding. He rolled onto his back and slid his hands beneath his head, bumping Lonnie in the nose with his elbow. "Oh, I'm sorry." Sitting up, he leaned over her.

Lonnie giggled and rubbed her nose. "It's all right." She stopped laughing and watched him swallow. Gideon cleared his throat and lay back down.

The minutes ticked by on the grandfather clock in the parlor beneath them, but Lonnie could not fall asleep. She listened as the gait of Gideon's breath slowed. She waited, letting the quickening of her heart beat away the time.

"Gideon...I..." She let out her breath, uncertain how to say it. "If you don't want this baby, I need to know now." She wasn't about to raise a child the way she had been raised. If Gideon didn't want anything to do with the baby, then he didn't want anything to do with her. She wasn't going to stick around to watch her child suffer for it.

His breathing was slow, steady, and she knew he was asleep. Sighing, Lonnie rolled onto her side, wishing the answer didn't have to wait until tomorrow.

At the sound of voices, Lonnie shuffled to the window and peered out. Gideon leaned into the weight of a wheelbarrow loaded to the brim with wood. She watched him make several passes, his feet lumbering over dewy grass. His hair stood off kilter, and with his face down, his head hung low between his shoulder blades.

She changed into her calico work dress and tied an apron around her waist. She threw on her shawl before hurrying down the stairs.

Elsie knelt in front of the stove, piercing the coals with a metal poker. "Mornin'!"

"Good morning."

"Coffee or tea?"

"Tea, please, but may I get it?" Hopefully it would soothe her stomach, which constantly felt unsettled. She filled the copper kettle and settled it near the percolator on the cast-iron stove, then pulled four tin cups from the cupboard. Just as quick, Elsie snatched two up by the handles and put them away. She went to her hutch, and pulled out two china teacups. She held them up, and Lonnie smiled.

When the water in the percolator bubbled dark and rich, Lonnie filled the tin mugs.

"How does Jebediah like his coffee?"

"Just cream."

Lonnie dropped a spoonful of sugar into Gideon's, then splashed cream into both. "I'll take these out." She pushed her back against the screen door.

"Take these." Elsie handed her a bowl of dried apples, and Lonnie nestled it in the crook of her arm before slipping out into the crisp morning air.

Gideon stomped around the side of the barn, and when his eyes found her, he turned toward the house. After climbing the four steps in two long strides, he tugged off his leather gloves. He took the cup from her and slid his hands around the warm tin. He looked down at her.

She watched him take small sips, and as her mind tossed and turned, she remembered her question from the night before. She needed his answer, but instead of speaking, she held the bowl of dried apples out, and he took a fistful, cramming nearly all of them into his mouth. He chewed in silence, his eyes unfocused. His jaw was dusted with a sandy beard, and hair the color of gingerbread stuck out from beneath his hat.

She arched an eyebrow. "You need a haircut."

His fingers swished over his chin, then tugged at the patch beneath his lip. "And a shave."

She smirked, then shook her head. "Jeb gotcha workin' hard this morning?"

When green eyes flicked to hers over the rim of his cup, she cleared her throat, struggling to remember what she had come out here to say.

"Always." His voice echoed inside the tin, and he took another sip. "There's lots to do around here."

Her gaze roved the yard, from the fine house to the large barn. The Bennetts were better off than any family she knew. It was a wonder they lived way up here in the Blue Ridge Mountains. They could sell this farm and live in town—maybe even a city. Somewhere where they didn't have to trek for miles to buy supplies. Buy a real fine house and never have to worry about keeping up with the animals or climbing up and down the hill in their old age.

"Why do you think they live around here?" She turned to Gideon only to discover that he was watching her.

He squinted. "It's hard to leave these mountains, I suppose." He tossed the last drop of coffee mixed with grounds into the dry grass, then ran his hand up a weatherworn porch post. "Bet this was his pa's house." He studied the wood as if seeing the man's history etched into the faded paint. "Jebediah probably lived here his whole life." Gideon circled his hand around the post, then moved it back down. Lonnie followed the movement.

As if drawn from a memory, he cleared his throat. "I suppose if a man has lived in these mountains his whole life, he becomes a part of the land. If this is where your pa was born and died, I suppose it will be where you were born and hope to die."

"But not you?"

"Me?"

"You left Rocky Knob. Your home."

"That wasn't home." His voice held years of heartache.

She leaned against the post. The bowl was empty, so she shifted it to her other arm. "Gideon, there's something I need to tell you."

His eyes widened slightly. "Can't think of what else it could be." Sarcasm ran thick in his words.

She let out a breath. "Don't be dramatic. I just need you to know something." She chewed her bottom lip a moment. "It's about the baby." She straightened. "If you don't want anything to do with our child, I'm not going to force you." She tipped the bowl, letting the crumbs fall into the dirt. "But I won't stay around for you to torment either one of us." She touched her apron, and understanding registered in his features.

Lifting his chin, he looked across the yard. His thumb hooked into his belt loop. "All right, then."

"All right, I'm leaving, or all right, I'm staying?"

"I'm not going to torment the baby." His eyes found hers. "Just know that."

But she didn't know. "We'll see, then."

"Fair enough." He thumped his palm against the post. When Jebediah came into view, Gideon tossed his head in the direction of the gray-haired man. "I should get back to work." He hesitated, then softened his voice. "I won't torment the baby." He stared at the empty space between them. "It doesn't mean I'm going to love it."

She fiddled with the end of her braid. "And you don't think that's the same thing?"

"Obviously not." He glanced down at her apron, then back to her face. "Or we wouldn't be in this mess, would we?"

Hot chills covered her cheeks. "I'll give you until the baby's born to figure it out. Not a day longer."

Just then, Jebediah climbed the porch steps.

Lonnie handed Jebediah his coffee, certain his first sip would be a cold one. Jebediah downed it in a few short swigs with nary a complaint. Without a word, he cupped Gideon on the shoulder and walked away.

As if he had more to say, Gideon twisted the side of his mouth. After a moment's hesitation, he turned and followed Jebediah's silent request.

Lonnie watched him go.

Twenty-Two

H ow's it going?"

Gideon looked up from his work as Jebediah stepped into the doorway of the stuffy barn. "Almost done," he panted and thrust the pitchfork forward. His shirt clung to his damp skin as he tossed hay into the mule's stall. He ran his sleeve against his face and glanced at Jebediah. A second pitchfork stood against the wall, near enough for the old man to touch, but Jebediah simply stood there, arms crossed, watching.

Scrape. Grunt. *Scrape.* The rhythm broke the silence, and Gideon braved a glance at Jebediah when the man didn't budge.

"After you've got that finished, Elsie wants us to bring out the wash pot. Tomorrow's wash day." Without waiting for a reply, Jebediah began rummaging in a toolbox.

Gideon leaned the fork against the wall. He had no problem working for his keep. What he didn't like was some fella taking advantage of that. Sweat slid down the bridge of his nose and stung his eyes. "Yes, master," he muttered under his breath. He smeared the back of his glove across his face.

Metal clanged as Jebediah dug through the trunk of tools. He pulled out a can of nails and stood. His hammer hung at his belt. "I'm gonna replace a few clapboards out there. Holler when you're done, and we'll get the pot."

Gideon nodded without looking up. Soon he heard Jebediah outside and flinched when the wall shook beneath the man's hammer. Wood creaked and snapped. Gideon stepped away for fear the whole building would come crashing down.

A slit of light appeared, and Jebediah lowered the sun-rotted piece. Gideon blinked against the brightness. Within moments, another board splintered and came down, illuminating the gloomy barn as if it were high noon. Gideon peered through the gap as Jebediah stripped out a third and then a fourth. A cool breeze brushed his face.

So the man can work after all.

The racket made it nearly impossible to focus, but Gideon turned back to his task. Sugar, the old work mule, watched him with clouded brown eyes. She blinked slowly—unconcerned with the stranger in her stall.

"How's that for you, girl?"

She tipped back large ears, lowered her face, and sniffed. Her nostrils flared, blowing pieces of hay toward his shoe.

"Smells good, don't it? Well, you're lucky to have it." He chuckled, knowing he sounded just like his father. He smoothed the last of the hay, then went to see how Jebediah was coming along.

With his mouth full of nails, Jebediah pursed his lips in a focused frown. "Hold that side up." The nails rose and fell as he mumbled.

The fresh wood vibrated under Gideon's hand as Jebediah pounded it into place. The older man worked his way down the length of the board, pulling a nail from his lips every few hand widths. Gideon stepped aside and admired the job as Jebediah tugged a nail from his clenched mouth and, with a few loud blows, secured the first piece in place.

"Few more to go," Jebediah grunted.

Gideon's arms shook as he struggled to balance an awkward piece, and he wished he could be the one to swing the hammer. Instead, he did as told, and when they finished, Jebediah *let* him put away the tools.

Jebediah slapped Gideon on the back. "Let's go get the wash pot."

Gritting his teeth, Gideon nodded and stuck the can of nails in the crook of his arm as he reached for the hammer. He stuffed them on a high shelf, then followed Jebediah into the yard.

With practiced precision, Jebediah laid twigs then wood in a ring of blackened stones. Above that loomed an iron tripod with a hook hanging from the center. Together, they heaved the heavy pot onto the hook, where it rested just above the stones.

"Time to fill 'er up." Jebediah elbowed Gideon in the side, then, bending, snatched up two buckets. "Then all Elsie'll have to do is light it and our job will be done."

Gideon sucked in a breath and held it until his lungs burned. His job would never be done. Not if Jebediah had anything to say about it. The lump on the back of his head had turned to a dull ache over the last several days. Gideon rubbed it again.

Jebediah handed him the buckets, and a metal handle dug into Gideon's chest. Gideon eyed him. "Ain't you gonna help?"

Jebediah fiddled with his fire. "You can't carry two buckets at the same time?"

With his jaw clenched, Gideon ground out the words. "Yessir, I can."

"Well, then, good."

Dismissed, Gideon started toward the creek but froze within a few steps. He spun around. "I just been thinkin'." He squared his shoulders when his voice faltered. "I've been doin' an awful lot of work around here—"

"Thought that was *your* idea."

"Yessir, it was. But…" Gideon rubbed the back of his neck. "Well… you ain't been doin' much."

The wrinkles in Jebediah's forehead lifted. "Is that so?"

"Well, yes. I mean…no sir."

"Well, which is it? Yes or no?" Jebediah folded his arms in front of him, his stance widening. " 'Cause the way I saw it, you were gonna earn your keep around here. Isn't that what we agreed on?"

"I've been earnin' twice my keep." Gideon held his ground. It was high time Jebediah stopped making a sport out of punishing him. Gideon gritted his teeth. He'd told Lonnie he was sorry. Wasn't that enough? Elsie had moved on. Lonnie too. Sort of. Gideon's gaze faltered. What else did this fuddy-duddy want?

"That so?" Jebediah's thick, rough fingers lifted the buckets from Gideon's grasp. "Why don't you go inside and take the afternoon off. You must be *plumb* tuckered out. *I'll* fill the wash pot." He started away. "Maybe you could do some mendin' on the parlor sofa."

"What did you say?" Gideon strode after him.

Jebediah spoke without turning around. "You heard me." A breeze picked up and filled out the sides of his plaid coat.

Gideon lifted his chest even as he quickened his steps. "What is your problem, old man?"

Jebediah froze. He turned slowly. "Pardon?"

Stepping forward, Gideon thrust a finger into the man's chest. "You heard me."

Jebediah tossed the buckets aside, and they clanged against the ground. A handle snapped free. In one long swing, he grabbed hold of Gideon's shirt and yanked him forward. Gideon's feet skidded in the dirt as his face neared Jebediah's. "You listen to me, son." Gray eyes blazed. "You have no idea how lucky you are that I didn't shoot you like a dog." He spat out the last words.

Gideon pulled himself away and stumbled back. His fingers curved into fists, but he knew he could never strike Jebediah.

"Do you hear me, boy?" Jebediah's eyes narrowed. "You better watch yourself—actin' all high and mighty." He tossed his head toward the house. "You got a wife up there who's too good for you. This," he said waving his arms around the farm, "this ain't nothing. You're *lucky* to be where you're at."

Gideon gulped.

"'Cause right about now—oh, I don't know, Gideon, use your imagination. Where do you think you would be?" He reached for the nearest bucket. "Where would Lonnie be?"

Gideon winced even as he tried to stomach his anger.

"If you're scared of a little hard work, then you best be movin' on. 'Round here, a man earns his keep. My pa and I built this farm out of nothing." Color crept into Jebediah's face. "I've run it without you my entire life, and I can do it again." Steely eyes hardened. "I don't need a sorry boy cryin' all day about doin' a few chores. I'd rather do 'em myself." He drew in a heavy breath. "Don't convince yourself that you're doin' me any favors, Gideon. Look around you."

Gideon blinked.

Jebediah snagged the broken handle of the second bucket and tucked it into the crook of his arm. "This ain't nothing"—his voice rose, and he nodded to the bucket under his arm—"to what you'd be doin' right now if you got what you deserved back there." His throat broadened as he swallowed. "Don't make me wish I'd done it." He strode off toward the well.

Gideon stormed toward the house. He tore open the screen door, and it slammed closed behind him. The kitchen was empty, and he let out the breath he'd been holding. Climbing the stairs two at a time, he ducked into the bedroom and kicked the door shut.

He sat on the bed and dropped his head in his hands. Who was Jebediah Bennett to judge him? Gideon pinched the bridge of his nose. Standing, he looked around the room. Enough was enough. He grabbed his pack from the bottom of the wardrobe and yanked open the top dresser drawer. With quick hands, he crammed his things into the pack, not sure if he grabbed it all or not. He just needed enough. Enough to get to Stuart and start over.

Footsteps sounded on the other side of the door. He grabbed his mandolin, slung the strap across his chest, and glanced around for his hat. What he did with his life was nobody's business.

The door creaked open, and Lonnie peeked her head around. "Gideon?" Her eyes seemed to take it all in at once.

"I'm done."

"Done with what?" she asked slowly, but he could see that she knew.

"You know this is for the best." The words came out strained, and not wanting to stand around and chat, he brushed past her.

"Gideon!"

He stomped from the room. Lonnie trailed behind him, her footsteps lighter than his dogged stride. After looking around for his coat, he thrust his hat over his hair and yanked the door open.

Her fingers grazed his sleeve. "Where are you going, Gid?"

"Does it matter?" Outside, he saw Jebediah hauling water from the well. The sun blinded him, and Gideon turned in the opposite direction. His lengthy strides barreled him through the yard, and he disappeared into the forest.

Elsie darted in from the front porch, broom still in hand. "Was that Gideon who just stormed out of here?"

Lonnie ran to the back door and pulled it open, but Gideon was nowhere in sight. "I don't know what happened."

Elsie's shoulder brushed hers.

Lonnie's fingers clung to the wire screen. "He had everything he owned." The words scarcely slipped out.

Jebediah strode up the steps, and his husky voice filtered through the mesh. "I set him off. I'm sorry, Lonnie." Jebediah shook his head. "But what that boy needs is a trip out to the woodshed."

Lonnie searched Jebediah's face. "Are you going after him?"

"Only if I can bring a switch." He glanced in the direction Gideon had gone. "He's gonna do whatever he wants. No matter what any of us say." He tugged on his beard. "That boy's got more than a few lessons yet to learn."

Chilled, Lonnie folded her arms in front of her. She studied the path, where it curved out of sight, and thought of the man who had charged through its scattered leaves. "All right, then." She looked from Jebediah to Elsie, her resolve sinking in. "It's better this way. If he comes back, fine." She thought of the life forming inside her. "If he's the kind of man who'd rather be gone, then we're both better off." But her heart throbbed as she spoke.

Twenty-Three

Gideon cursed the sky as he trudged down the hillside. The moonless dark made it impossible to see the trail. He stormed through a low stream and soaked his boots. Coming up on the other side, he paused to catch his breath. He folded up his shirt collar, the night air piercing the fabric, and thrust his hands in his pockets.

His damp feet were turning numb. *Some idea this was.*

He had no idea what time it was. His stomach growled, but his pockets were empty. If he were at the Bennetts', supper would be long over, and he'd be asleep with Lonnie at his side. Her face flashed through his mind, and he smeared his hand across his eyes, hoping it would erase the image. But it was too late. His chest had filled with a sense of longing, and even as he cursed himself a fool, Gideon trudged on.

He wondered if Lonnie was thinking about him. Wondered if she would wait up, clinging to hope. When dawn broke, would she still wait for him? Gideon slowed his pace and thought about the woman he was walking away from. He nearly stopped when her face filled his mind once more. She had to be wondering about him. She was his wife.

Anger had driven him away. Pride was keeping him here. When his feet could carry him no more, Gideon found a place to rest. But sleep was uneasy.

He set out the next morning with a heavy heart. By late afternoon, without a bite of food in his stomach, he felt queasy and had to rest. Leaning against a tree, he saw a blackberry bush and quickly plucked withered berries. He didn't care that the thorns poked and scratched his hands.

He ate hungrily, yet food could not fill his void.

Gideon sank back on his heels and looked up at the noon sky. *Go home, Gid.* He surveyed the land around him but, deep down, wasn't sure what he wanted. His heart and mind wrestled over a broken compass.

He'd never been good at sorting through his feelings, but he knew one thing: he wanted to go home. Even if he didn't know where that was. He wanted to go to Stuart, but he suddenly felt empty without Lonnie by his side.

"Do you want to do this or not?" he said aloud to himself. Going back meant apologizing. Perhaps more. Gideon licked dried berry juice from his thumb as he mulled over the notion. Was it in him to change?

He wiped stained hands on his pants and turned back toward the Bennett farm. His steps felt lighter. He'd figure it out along the way. His chest lifted as he drew in the first deep breath he could remember.

"Well, looky here," a familiar voice sneered.

Gideon turned. A pair of beady eyes locked with his, and a stout hand lifted in greeting.

"If it ain't ol' Gideon," Bert said. A group of men loomed a few paces behind him.

One of them moved into the fringe of his vision, and Gideon took a step sideways.

Bert glanced around greedily. "Where's that pretty li'l wife of yers? What was her name? Lydia. No, Bonnie."

Gideon squared his jaw. "She ain't here."

Bert grunted.

"Who's this?" A man stood head and shoulders over Bert. His eyes narrowed.

"Just an old friend." Bert grinned.

The tall man stepped forward, his words directed at Bert. "Well, I don't think we should be socializing with nobody."

"Don't worry." Bert drew out the words. "Gid's a good fella." But his eyes said otherwise.

Gideon knew better than to get on a man's bad side twice, so he blurted out the first thing he could think of. "It's good to see you again. Whatcha doin' around here?"

A man with dark curly hair cut in. "This here's our territory." He was as short and stocky as Bert and had his cap pulled so low Gideon could hardly see his eyes.

"That would make you a trespasser," another said.

Gideon gnawed the inside of his lip and glanced from one face to the other. "Trespasser?" He glanced around. At the bottom of the wooded hill, a shanty was tucked against the mountain. "I didn't realize anybody owned this land. If you point me in the right direction, I'll be outa here as quick as I can."

A chorus of chuckles filtered through the men. "It ain't our land. It's our *territory*," the tall man said.

Remembering Bert's jug of moonshine, Gideon scanned a row of brush. The men in front of him shifted. Gideon took an involuntary step back. Though he couldn't see it, he was certain their still was only a few yards away. Narrowed eyes and clamped jaws bespoke it.

"Well...I didn't mean any harm, if that's what you're gettin' at." He took another step back. Lonnie was waiting for him.

"Don't trouble yourself. I know you're trustworthy. Come on and join us for a spell." Bert waved Gideon over. "You look like you could use a drink."

Gideon hesitated. He hovered between his past and his future.

Bert motioned toward the bushes with his head. His eyes dared Gideon to decline.

Slowly, Gideon nodded. He followed the men up a small hill, dense with trees and heavy shrubs.

Bert pointed. "There she is."

Through the foliage, Gideon spotted a half-shielded metal pot.

"Drops of golden liquid." Bert settled himself down on a rock next to his still. "Ain't nothin' finer in this world."

Gideon nodded. The smell was overwhelming, and his mouth watered. He tried to swallow it away, but when Bert lifted a clear jar—pure moonshine sloshing behind the glass—his feet pulled him forward.

Bert motioned to the still. The big pot, capped with a lid, seemed to be made of solid copper. A small hose poked out and curved down into a simple green jar, then, as if the hose couldn't make up its mind, it bobbed out, running down into a galvanized pot.

Bert held up the offering.

Gideon hesitated. Battled. And when his heart lost, he reached for it.

With a chuckle, Bert drew it back. "Ain't you gonna pay first?"

Pay? Gideon patted his pocket. "I don't have any money."

Bert set the jar beside him. "Aw, shucks."

Even as he spoke, Gideon detested the desperation in his own voice. "I could pay you next time I see you." *Just walk away.*

Bert shook his head. "I've been burned enough times by that promise."

His men laughed.

Heat splintered along Gideon's neck. He took a few steps back and folded his arms across his chest. He wanted to leave.

Bert took a swig, his eyes keen, focused. Gideon's mouth watered, and he fought the urge, knowing his escape had already been granted. His thumb found his ring finger. The metal was cold to the touch.

Bert followed the movement.

Shutting off all his thoughts, Gideon slid the metal from his finger.

A subtle nod was enough for him to hand it out. Bert took it and studied it a moment, displeasure in his face. Gideon knew it wasn't worth much. But surely it was worth enough.

Bert butted the quart jar onto his knee. "All right."

Gideon stared at his ring in the man's palm. Shame coursed through him, like the hot liquid itself. His fingers itched for the glass, and he forced his eyes away from the only thing Lonnie had ever given him. "Are you sure?"

Bert rolled his eyes and thrust the drink toward Gideon.

The jar was cool in his hand—the glass icy smooth—but the liquid burned as it slid down his throat. Instead of feeling satisfaction, guilt settled into the pit of his stomach.

"Somethin' wrong?"

"You know what? I changed my mind." He held out the jar. "Keep it."

Bert made a face, his annoyance clear. After hesitating a moment, he snatched the drink back. "Suit yerself."

When Gideon didn't move, Bert blinked up at him. "You can leave now."

"I'll take that ring back."

Bert grunted. His men laughed. "I don't think so." Bert slid the ring inside his coat. He stood. His men hovered. "Deal's a deal."

Grinding his teeth, Gideon snatched up his hat. He stormed

forward, and his shoulder smacked Bert's. In an instant, the men were around him, arms shoving him this way and that, coats flapping open. Gideon shoved his way free.

"Let him go," Bert growled. "He's not worth our time."

Gideon crashed through the brush and jogged down the hill until he spotted the trail. He panted but didn't slow. It wasn't until he'd put half a mile between him and them that he hunched over and caught his breath. His mouth curved in a smile. He slipped his hand into his pocket and pulled out the chain of a silver watch. He had a mind to get a lot farther from Bert's men before it was missed. He tossed the watch from one hand to the other, then slid it back out of sight. There was no need to worry, really. It wasn't like they knew where he was staying. He threw a glance over his shoulder to the quiet forest behind him. The watch would fetch a pretty penny, but he had a better use for it.

Twenty-Four

Shlap. Lonnie threw the damp sheet across the clothesline, then rose on her tiptoes to smooth it across the tight rope. She nabbed a wooden pin from her apron pocket, determined to keep the late afternoon breeze from claiming her laundry.

She bent and tugged two pillowcases from the wicker basket, the wet fabric chilling her already cold hands. After pinning them into place, she stepped back. She was out of room on her line, and fortunately out of laundry.

A light wind caught the sheet, pushing damp fabric against her bare legs. Lonnie tugged her skirt down toward her ankles and shivered. Leaves rustled overhead, and several spiraled to the ground. She wrapped her arms around herself. October hovered on the horizon, and as if the seasons belonged in the churner's hand, summer had quickly changed to fall.

Lonnie doubted Gideon had much to protect him from the cold. She had tried not to think of him all day, but he crept into her mind more often than she could count. Her gaze lifted to the edge of the yard, shadowed by thick stands of trees. How she longed to see him coming into the yard with regret written across his features. Lonnie crouched down and lifted the empty basket to her hip.

But she knew better. What made her think he would apologize?

Sliding the basket onto the porch, she clenched her hands at her sides in frustration. She glanced over her shoulder to the path that disappeared around the bend. Gideon. Surly and russet haired. She shook her head.

She was glad he was gone.

He could walk right off a cliff for all she cared.

Yet she stood on her tiptoes and scanned the tree line. She laced her fingers together, still damp from her chore. Again, the breeze rose, running its cool hand against her freshly hung sheets. Another glance at the empty space between a pair of oaks and Lonnie dropped her eyes to the grass.

The taste of liquor clung to his lips as Gideon walked through the shady trees. He was glad he'd just had the one sip. In fact, he wished he hadn't had any at all.

His loose shoelace whipped against the dirt, and Gideon knelt, taking care to straighten the cuff of his pants leg before standing. He'd looked back more than a dozen times but knew that no one was on his tail. He forced his shoulders to relax and strode onward. To his surprise, his hand felt naked without the ring. The thought made Lonnie's face come to mind.

When his stomach growled, he longed for a plate of Elsie's cooking.

She would have started supper by now, and Jebediah would be busy with the evening chores, and Lonnie…

Gideon pulled his hat off and ran a hand through his hair. What would Lonnie be doing? He closed his eyes.

Would she be waiting for him?

Twenty-Five

A low evening star seemed to taunt Lonnie as she glanced toward the trees again. With her feet wedged on each side of the churn, her hand slowly moved the staff up and down. The land seemed to dim before her eyes. Her feet shifted silently on the wood porch. Each glance felt as foolish as the last, but…

She strained to listen.

The soft *thud* of footsteps forced her hand still. The staff never struck down as she hovered on the edge of her stool.

The screen squeaked, and Jebediah stepped out. Rising, Lonnie wiped her hands on her apron and blinked into the gray light. She saw Gideon's hat bob. Then his shoulders. He lifted his head. His face.

She moved back, retreating through the doorway.

Seconds ticked away like hours as Gideon walked toward the porch. Her hand trembled on the handle of the screen door.

He glanced at her, and something in his eyes made her swallow hard. His shoulders slumped when he ducked his head again.

"Gideon," Jebediah said calmly.

Gideon tipped his chin up, but his eyes locked with Lonnie's.

She stared into a suntanned face hidden behind the shadow of a beard, took in the smattering of freckles across his nose. She bit her bottom lip as a battle took place in her heart.

Jebediah stepped back. "I'll just leave you two alone for a bit," he whispered, brushing past her. His gray eyes were as hard as ice. "Holler if you need me."

Lonnie knew he would not go far.

Gideon scaled the porch steps as the screen slammed closed. She slid the latch into place. His face looked pained as he squinted down at her through the wire mesh.

"You came home," she whispered.

He sucked in a chestful of air. "Yeah." His gaze swept over her. "I don't know what I was thinking."

His breath was thick with moonshine.

She pursed her lips and stared at the space between them. He pulled on the latch. It didn't budge.

His eyelids fell to half-mast. "Ain't you gonna let me in?"

Lonnie pressed her tongue against the inside of her cheek.

He grunted and crossed his arms over his chest.

"Where were you?"

With a slight shake of his head, he shrugged. "Nowhere."

"I see." She knew false regret when she saw it. Gideon's frame blocked out a coal-black sky. The air nipped at her bare arms, and she noticed he did not have a coat.

Still, words did not come. The last thread holding them together—weighed down by silence and disappointment—felt frayed. Breathing was suddenly a struggle as anger and sorrow bubbled inside her.

Jebediah's heavy coat hung on a peg next to the door. Lonnie pulled it down and opened the screen just enough to push it through. Gideon stared at her offering, blinking slowly. A muscle flexed in his jaw as he reached for the flannel. His fingers grazed hers.

The screen slammed.

"What am I supposed to do with this?"

"Good night, Gideon." Her throat burned.

His eyes narrowed. "What?"

"I said good night." Reaching back, she fumbled for the door.

"You gotta be kidding." He leaned forward, the scent of his breath piercing her heart. "*I'm sorry.* How many times do I have to say it?"

It took all her strength not to cry when she looked at him. His pleading eyes disappeared as she shut the door.

"Lonnie!" he yelled, his voice muted. The screen door squeaked open.

She jammed the lock into place, and when his hand slammed against the door, she jumped back. Her trembling fingertips flew to her lips, and she stepped away. Gideon called her name again. The door shook when he kicked it, and the screen rattled so hard she feared he would tear it from the frame.

Then silence.

"Please, Lonnie." His voice was broken.

Though he could not see her, she shook her head and stepped away.

Jebediah stomped in. "What's going on?"

Tears came. "Just leave him," she whispered. "If he's gone in the morning, then he's gone and that's that."

Gideon stepped in front of the window. "Lonnie." His voice was muffled behind the glass. His eyebrows lifted in surrender, and Lonnie clasped her hands together, hating the sound of her name on his lips.

He pressed his palm against the window, leaving a dirty handprint.

She backed out of the kitchen and ran up the stairs. Gideon's voice trailed after her. She threw herself down on the bed and sobbed. *Oh God, what do I do?*

"Lonnie!"

She jumped. He was below her window. She slid off the bed and fell to the floor. She trembled as she crawled out the bedroom door, desperate to flee his voice. Huddling in the hallway, she barely noticed Elsie at the bottom of the stairs, her mouth open. Lonnie looked away, too embarrassed for words. Elsie stood silent as Gideon clamored around the outside of the house, making more noise than any man should.

Finally, Elsie spoke, her voice impossibly calm. "I'm sorry, Lonnie." She twisted a damp tea towel in her hands. "You don't deserve this. No woman does."

"Well, life doesn't always happen the way we'd like." Lonnie stared at the papered wall in front of her. The faded print was as worn as her spirit.

"No. It doesn't." Elsie climbed the steps and sank down next to her. "But you gotta keep fightin' the good fight." She rested a soft hand on Lonnie's knee.

"I don't know what that is anymore."

"You did what you had to do."

Tears stung Lonnie's eyes. "Then why do I feel so terrible?"

Elsie sighed. "Because Gideon hurt you. I know this ain't the first time either." The back of her finger traced Lonnie's jaw, where the bruise had faded. Elsie dropped her hand and took Lonnie's. "The best way for him to deal with that is to make *you* feel like you are the one who is hurting *him*. If he turns your troubles on you, then he can act like nothing is really ever his fault."

Lonnie leaned her head against the wall and stared at the ceiling.

"Really, what that man needs is a good whuppin'." Elsie half smiled. "I'm sure Jebediah would volunteer."

Lonnie rested her chin on her knees. "Jeb's gonna have to stand in line, then."

Elsie's smile filled out. She pressed her shoulder to the wall, and her face sobered. "God is in control. He has you in the palm of His hand." Elsie's grip tightened as if to drive her words deep.

"I'm so afraid. I don't know what to do."

"Well, know you are always welcome here." Elsie's other hand moved in a slow circle on Lonnie's back. "Seems like God placed an impossible fate before you, doesn't it?"

"I don't know why." Lonnie lowered her head as the rhythmic motion calmed her. "I don't mean to complain, but haven't I had enough yet?" Her voice felt small. "All my life it's felt like I've been drowning—barely keeping my head above water."

Elsie let out a slow sigh. Gently, she kissed the side of Lonnie's head. "Fear not: for I have redeemed thee, I have called thee by thy name; thou art mine." The words came out no more than a whisper.

Lonnie nodded softly. She knew the passage well.

Elsie pressed her cheek to the top of Lonnie's head. "When thou passest through the waters, I will be with thee; and through the rivers, they shall not overflow thee." Her voice was soft. Soothing.

Lonnie sniffed when her emotions threatened to spill over again. She whispered the last few words. "When thou walkest through the fire, thou shalt not be burned."

Pulling her knees up, she pressed her palms to her sore eyes and sniffed. God was here. He'd always been here. And He wasn't going to leave her.

A star blinked from the window. Lonnie lay in the middle of the hall with her back curled up against the cold wall. She waited and listened. Elsie stayed by her side, round fingers gently combing through Lonnie's hair.

Lonnie sat up and brushed her hair away from her cheeks, which were sticky with dried tears. She glanced down the hall and stared out the tiny window as the sun glinted in the glory of its own reflection. All she could hear was silence. Morning.

Her heart sank and rose in the same instant. *Gideon.* Lonnie scrambled to her feet and tiptoed down the stairs, her black gingham dress crumpled and dusty from the hallway. Her bare feet hardly made a sound as she crossed the cold kitchen floor. She stopped just short of the window and peered out. The glass fogged in front of her face, and Lonnie smeared it with her wrist. She scanned the porch steps but saw no sign of Gideon.

He was gone. The feeling struck her like a hammer on an anvil.

Pressing her forehead to her arm, she squeezed her eyes shut and gripped the door handle. A reassurance, low in her gut, lifted warm and sure, pulsing through her veins like her own blood; wherever Gideon was, God was by his side. And His promises were at hand.

Lonnie lifted her eyes, and after unlatching the door, she pushed it open. Something blocked the doorway, so she pushed harder.

"Hey!"

She froze, seeing a pair of unlaced boots. Two legs slid out of sight, and Gideon's face appeared in the crack of the doorway.

The warmth left her limbs, concentrating in her heart. "Gideon?"

"Well, it ain't no 'coon," he grumbled, scratching his head. He crawled to his feet and wiped his face with his sleeve. He eyed her grumpily.

She could not think of what to say. "It was a cold night," she blurted.

Gideon shrugged. "Not any colder than the night before. At least this time I had a jacket." He stood slowly. One hand was pressed to the wall, the other to the side of his head.

Jebediah shuffled into the kitchen. "Mornin'." He brushed past Lonnie and opened the door wider.

Gideon glanced at her, his expression torn.

"You stayin', son?" The older man stepped onto the porch, and the screen slammed closed behind him.

Gideon dropped his eyes. "Yessir. If...if it's all right with you. " His eyes nearly lifted to Lonnie's face.

Leaning back on his heels, Jebediah studied him. He glanced at Lonnie, his expression soft, as if to ask permission.

She nodded slowly, bewildered and stunned.

Jebediah stepped closer to Gideon and thrust a finger into his chest. "I don't ever want to see you like that again." His jaw clamped shut. "No liquor. Not one drop. You hear?"

Gideon nodded.

Jebediah tilted his head to the side and kept his finger pinned into place. "Or else don't bother comin' back next time. Lonnie might be your wife by law, but the way I see it, she's my responsibility until you prove your worth. If that means keepin' you around a lot longer, so be it."

Gideon lowered his face. "Yessir."

Jebediah stepped back, and Gideon reached for the door.

"What do you think you're doing?"

"Sir?"

"I don't want you in my house right now. Besides, you stink." Jebediah made a face that matched his words. "I need to decide what to do with you. In the meantime"—he tossed his hand toward the yard—"go...kill a chicken or something."

Twenty-Six

Gideon stared at the quiet house and flicked up the collar of his coat. Lonnie was still avoiding him. Not just for a morning. Not even for a day.

Two weeks.

For two weeks, she'd kept her eyes down and her answers short. Though he'd tried to speak with her here and there, he hadn't gotten more out of her than "yes" and "no" since his return. *And why should she care what you have to say?* Gideon wiped his hands on his pants and glanced around the yard. With the barn door shut and latched for the evening, he headed toward the house with more than supper on his mind.

He couldn't figure out what was wrong with Lonnie. If she noticed his missing ring, she didn't say as much. A few days ago, he thought he'd surprise her with the pocket watch. A peace offering of sorts. When she'd asked him where he got it, he struggled to answer. When he finally told her, she flung the watch at his head. He caught the trinket just in time, the metal clasp digging into his palm.

Women. Hardest creatures in the world to please.

Elsie looked up when he stomped into the kitchen. She shoved a piece of wood into the stove and slammed the heavy lid.

His gaze flickered over the kitchen. There was evidence of his wife's hand everywhere. As if of its own accord, his chest lifted.

Elsie pulled out a cutting board. "Lonnie ducked into the cellar a moment ago. She'll be right back."

"Oh."

Jebediah stormed in, newspaper tucked under his arm.

Gideon made a show of rubbing his hands together. "I'm gonna wash up a bit." Before anyone could speak, he stepped onto the porch, only to stare at the wash bucket. Elsie and Jebediah chatted away inside, and with them paying him no mind, Gideon slipped away.

He walked around the house to the cellar, not surprised to see the door closed. Lonnie knew better than to leave it open for a raccoon or a fox to make its home among Elsie's abundant stores. Gideon lifted the door and started down the ladder, suddenly wishing he knew what to say.

"Gid?" His name lifted from below, a trace of surprise in Lonnie's voice. She held up a lantern, casting a soft light across her face. "What are you doing here?"

He made sure to shut the door before descending the last two rungs. The still air, heavy with the smell of herbs, seemed to swallow him up. "Elsie said you were down here. Thought you might need a hand." He ducked when a spider's web tickled his forehead.

She stacked bars of roughly cut soap on wooden slats.

"What are you doing?"

"Setting these to cure. I offered to make soap for Elsie." She looked at him, clearly bewildered. "They need to set for a couple weeks before we can use it."

"That's right."

"Didn't know you were a master soap maker." A smile carried on her voice.

"I have my secrets."

She rolled her eyes and continued stacking her soap. Gideon moved to her side, and she looked up at him. "Do you need something?"

Gideon pressed a hand to the earthen wall, the soil cool to his palm. "I just thought that you might have something to say to me."

Silence settled between them for several moments. "And what gave you that impression?" She didn't look up.

He fingered a damp root in the wall. "Oh, I dunno," he said dumbly, then cleared his throat. Talking to girls had always been easy. Until Lonnie. "It's just that you haven't said more than a few words lately, and I figured I'd clear the air."

She kept her eyes on her work. "Clear the air of what?"

"Well, er…of any problems."

She let out a soft grunt. "That so?" She straightened another row of soap, and her eyes finally met his. "Where would you like to begin?"

"I…uh, wanted to make sure you knew that I was sorry. For leaving like that."

"I know you're sorry."

"You do?"

She drew in a slow breath. "You said you were."

"Right." He scratched his head. "So then why are you still mad at me?"

"Didn't know I was mad."

"Is this your way of saying you like me, then?"

"Hardly." Lonnie wiped her hands on her apron. "Gideon." She shifted her weight. "I'm not mad at you. And I appreciate that you're sorry. Really, I do. But…" Her eyes scanned the earth ceiling. Lantern light danced across her face. "It's like that story from the Bible." She lifted a basket from the ground and slid the handle over the crook of her arm. "When is a thief no longer a thief?"

"I dunno." He tugged at the patch of hair beneath his lip. "When they stop stealin', I suppose."

"Not quite." She fingered the handle of the basket. "It says they're no longer a thief when they stop stealin' and do something useful for others. Like plant a field and give food to the poor."

"You want me to plant a field?"

"This is why I don't talk to you." She moved to leave.

"Wait." He touched her elbow, then pulled back. "I want to understand." He rubbed his hands together. "Really, I do."

Her face softened. "When you say you're sorry for all that you've done, that's nice and all, but it will mean more to me when the change runs deeper than that."

"Deeper."

She nodded. "Bein' sorry is just not enough." She picked up a jar of green beans and tucked it in her basket. Her eyes scanned the shelf, and she pulled several potatoes from a low crate. Gideon watched her movements as if from a distance, a destination he could never reach.

Couldn't, or didn't want to?

In an instant, he wondered if he could undo all the damage he had done. Perhaps in time. But did he want to? His eyes fell to her stomach. Another mouth to feed. That's all a baby was. Wasn't that the way his ma had put it? Wasn't that what he was to his family? He watched Lonnie work, her movements slow. Why should his new family be any different? Whether or not Lonnie saw this child as a good thing, he saw it for what it was.

Lonnie crouched, her knees jutting up against her dress. Her braid fell over her shoulder. He suddenly wanted to feel the end curled around his finger. Gideon found himself unable to look away. The lantern light flickered.

Did he want her to hate him? He deserved it. After all he'd done, there was no question about it. The severity of the situation struck him, and he tugged at his hair. Surely there had to be some way to smooth this over. Some way to buy himself time until she could better understand what was truly at hand. Maybe it was just Lonnie Sawyer. But she was awful pretty. And when she looked at him with that glint in her eyes, like she knew something about him that he did not, he felt drawn to her in the strangest of ways. He had no name for what she evoked in him. But he had never experienced it before. The feeling belonged to her and her alone.

He stared at her. His chances were running out—if they weren't already gone.

With her hand on the ladder, Lonnie started up. One push on the door and the cellar would fill with light. She would step outside, and he'd still be standing there with his mouth half open. His eyes caught her every move.

"Lonnie," he whispered.

"Hmm," she hummed as she continued to climb. She took hold of the latch and lifted.

"Lonnie, wait." In as much time as it took for him to speak, he climbed the ladder. The old wood creaked beneath their weight.

The cellar door slammed closed. "Gid, what are you doing?"

He slid one arm around her and grabbed the ladder with the other. With his feet one rung below hers, their faces nearly touched.

"Gid—" Her braid slid from her shoulder when she turned to face him.

The wicker basket poked him in the ribs, and in one final attempt to make any sense out of his actions, he kissed her.

Her lips moved beneath his. "Gid, what are you doing?"

He pulled back.

Still wrapped in his grasp, she made no move to climb away. Her calmness stunned him, and she simply stared, confusion etched in her face.

"I'm sorry." Gideon lowered his head and climbed down. *You fool.*

The ladder became Lonnie's again.

"Don't let me keep you." He thrust his hands into his pockets, barely able to look at her. He heard her hesitate, but without a word, she released a sigh, climbed into the sunlight, and was gone.

Sinking against the ladder, Gideon dropped his head in his hands. What was he thinking? She didn't love him. And why should she? He didn't love her. Gideon snatched the lantern up and extinguished the light.

Twenty-Seven

Lonnie's hem brushed along dried leaves as she scavenged for chestnuts. Crouched in the underbrush at her side, Gideon blew on his hands, and puffs of white air escaped through his fingers. He rubbed his palms together, but by the look on his face, he found no relief from the cold October morning. He shifted his legs, head low, and seemed to study something in the distance.

Lonnie peered past a dead spruce, the brittle needles copper. Less than a stone's throw away, a hog dropped his face to the ground and rummaged through fallen leaves. They hadn't come to hunt, but Gideon watched it.

"Hey, whatcha doin' over there?" Jebediah stood and tossed a handful of nuts into a bag. "You takin' a break or something?"

"He's just cold," Lonnie teased. She slid her sack forward.

Gideon nabbed a chestnut. "I was thinkin' how I wished I had a gun."

Jebediah followed his line of sight, then his gray mustache tilted upward. "Hungry?"

"Not exactly."

Clearly unconvinced, Jebediah chuckled.

Lonnie leaned forward, and her knees dug into the cold, wet ground, dampening her dress. Beside her, Gideon picked up three nuts, rolled them around his palm, then dropped them into the sack at her side.

"Are you doing that on purpose?"

"Sorry?" He looked up, half distracted.

"Yours is nearly empty." She clutched the rough fabric of her sack and made a show of its heft.

His eyebrows fell.

When she motioned to the empty, limp bag behind him, she couldn't help but let out a laugh. "You've been doing it for the last half hour. Not that it bothers me, mind you." An icy wind tickled her cheeks, and she brushed wisps of hair away from her face. "But I do feel a little guilty taking all the credit."

"Oh." He shook his head, then glanced around.

"Gathering nuts must not be your favorite chore."

His mouth tipped up on one side, green eyes softening as he studied her. "No, I wouldn't say that it is." He snatched the empty bag from behind him and tossed several nuts inside. "I'm more of a field planter."

She elbowed him.

He smirked.

Lonnie gathered up her own handful and added them to his pitiful stash. When surprise registered in his face, she blushed. "Only seems fair."

The other half of his grin filled out, softening the face of stone she'd come to know. "Does this mean I get a second chance?"

"Second?" She clicked her tongue. "I think it would be more like chance number twelve."

He winced and his smile faltered.

"Chance for what?" she added, seeing that for once he was *trying* to make an effort. "To prove that you're not a total brute?"

He stared at the ground a moment. "I haven't done a good job of being anything else, I s'pose." His face was pained.

For a moment, hope stirred inside her. Then her eyes moved to his hand. Her heart seemed to slow.

As soon as his smile dented his cheeks, it faded. Pressing a palm to the tree, he pushed himself to a stand. Lonnie glanced up at him and blinked into the low sun, unable to speak.

"Lonnie." His hair caught the light that filtered through the trees. He flexed his fist and then tucked his hand just out of sight. Hiding his bare ring finger. "For what it's worth…" His voice fell to a near whisper. "I didn't mean to hurt you." He glanced down at her as if to say something more. Instead, he motioned to a nearby spot. "I think there's more over here." He strode off.

Shoulders back, Lonnie slowly worked her way around the base of the tree. Leaves clung to her skirt. When her eyes stung, she blinked quickly. *It's just a ring. Just a token,* she told herself. But the ache still ran deep. And judging by the guilt etched in Gideon's features, she almost believed him. Almost.

Though she could not see Jebediah and Elsie, she heard their voices and knew they were gathering just beyond a stand of young oaks. More than once her name floated by on the breeze, spoken in Elsie's tender voice. Lonnie was curious to know what the older couple thought of them, but in truth, she knew, for with each passing day, the Bennetts continued to welcome them. Lonnie had never found two kinder souls.

Her fingers rummaged through twigs and brittle leaves. Little by little, the rough sack filled out.

"You about done?" Gideon asked from behind.

Her eyes didn't meet his. "I'd say so." She sank back on her heels. She started to stand, her legs stiff and nearly numb.

When she wobbled, Gideon cupped her elbow, only to pull away just as quickly. He heaved his bag over his shoulder, and the small nuts clicked against his back. Her feet tingled as the feeling returned. With a soft grunt, she dragged her bag away from the tree. The heavy load left a trail in the dirt. She gripped the coarse fabric, intending to swing it up to her shoulder as Gideon had done. But before she could, he wrapped his hand just below hers. Surprised, Lonnie watched as he ducked one shoulder, swinging the bag up in the same motion.

Her lips rounded in silent surprise. "I can carry it."

He blinked down at her. "This bag's heavier than you. Besides, you shouldn't be carryin' things like this." His gaze flicked to the middle of her apron, his expression guarded.

"We better meet up with Jeb and Elsie," she blurted out and motioned to where she'd heard them.

She spotted Elsie a few paces off, raking fingers through a pile of leaves.

"You two are done already?" Elsie tipped her face back, eyes dancing between them. Without looking down, she dropped a few nuts into her sack.

Gideon let the bags fall off his shoulder and jingle to the ground. He opened the mouth of one. "I'd bet between us all we have five bushels just this morning. With four dollars a bushel they're takin', that's a good bit of money." He tapped the arithmetic out on his fingers, but the sum never formed on his lips. He cleared his throat, the skin beneath his freckles reddening. Lonnie pretended not to notice.

"Where's Jebediah?" he asked, changing the subject.

Elsie pointed to a shallow bank. "He took off in that direction. That man's like a wild turkey the way he hunts these woods for chestnuts."

"If I'm a turkey," Jebediah said, stepping out from behind a tree, "then that must make you a 'coon, 'cause I bet you like 'em just as much as I do." He pushed his patched-up wheelbarrow, loaded with Elsie's galvanized washtub full of golden-brown nuts.

With her hands on her hips, Elsie shook her head. "Come on, let's go home and roast some of these." She patted Lonnie's arm. "We'll see if your baby likes its first chestnut."

Lonnie dropped her gaze to her belly, amazed at how quickly it was growing. When she realized Gideon was watching her, she simply smoothed the fabric. His words from the other day echoed in her mind...
It doesn't mean I'll love it.

With a few grunts, Jebediah turned his wheelbarrow and started for home. Elsie fell in step with him. Gideon stood beside her, as if waiting. Lonnie strode forward, their elbows bumping. His pace fell in sync with her own. Lonnie was careful not to rush. She could only begin to guess the weight of the sacks that burdened his back. Neither of them spoke. Lonnie didn't know what to say. Not after the way Gideon had acted in the cellar. She could still feel his lips against hers, see the determination in his eyes before he'd kissed her. As if something had awakened inside of him. Something that ran deeper than desire.

Lord, let it be so.

Twenty-Eight

Gideon tossed the chisel to the floor with a muffled *thud*. He ran his hand across the wood. Rough and misshapen. Nowhere near smooth enough. He picked up a piece of sandpaper, and it *swished* as he passed it across the surface. His tongue stuck to the corner of his mouth in concentration. He wasn't much for numbers and letters, but he knew how to work wood. Measuring sticks and fractions got lost inside his head. The breadth of his hand, the length of his arm, and a picky eye served as sufficient tools.

He smoothed his thumb along the red maple. Not there yet. He was doing this project only out of necessity, but it should still be done well. Gideon twisted his mouth to the side and picked up his chisel.

He heard voices from the house and looked through the barn doorway in time to see Lonnie crossing the yard. She had a lunchpail in one hand and a cup in the other. Her dress was taut across her waist as she swung the pail back and forth. Her lips moved as if in song. Jumping up, he slid the heavy piece behind a stack of old crates and yanked a canvas over the top. He darted away and plunked down on a stool. His heart pounded as he picked up his pocketknife and dug into a soft piece of spruce.

He looked up from his work when she strode in. "Whatcha got there?" He set his whittling down, hoping his act was enough to distract her.

"Your dinner." Lonnie slid the offering onto the workbench.

Gideon knew Jebediah was inside eating his own dinner. There was no need for Lonnie to pack him a lunch. He watched as she arranged the food in front of him. Elsie could have hollered for him when it was ready, and he would have come. The corner of his mouth turned up.

Lonnie tucked her hands behind her back. Now in her third month, the calico pinched and puckered at her waist, and each night she labored over the workings of a new dress while loosening the seams in her old ones. Gideon realized just how quickly time passed. Was spring really just around the corner? Lost in thought, he forgot he was still staring. "What did you bring me?" He reached for the pail.

"Elsie's rabbit stew. Thanks to you." She smiled. "Cornbread, milk, and"—using two fingers, she lifted the corner of a cloth with dramatic movements—"a slice of fried apple pie."

He couldn't help but grin. "Sounds like a feast."

He unwrapped the cornbread first and licked apple butter off his fingers. He took a bite and washed it down with sweet milk. "Good," he said, lifting the golden square. He took another bite and realized Lonnie was not eating. "Aren't you hungry?"

She shook her head. "I ate inside with Elsie. We waited for you to come, but the time must have gotten away from you." She scrunched up her freckled nose and rubbed at an itch. Gideon pulled his handkerchief from his pocket to offer her.

"No, thanks," she said. "Just the cold, that's all."

Without bothering to fold it, he stuffed the white cloth back in his pocket, then propped a foot on the stool rung.

Lonnie pinched wood shavings between her fingers. "Elsie says there's a wedding comin' up."

The last of the cornbread vanished inside his mouth. "Did you want to go?" he mumbled and brushed his hands together.

She shrugged as if it didn't matter. "I'd like to. It'd be nice to meet some of the folks around here."

He wasn't much for getting dressed up. Hated the idea of a stiff shirt and tie. But Lonnie's eyes were bright, and he had a mind to show her that there was indeed a civilized bone in his body. Gideon lifted a spoonful of stew to his lips and stilled, his eyes on his wife. "Then we'll go."

Surprise registered in her face. "Elsie said it's in a few days." Her voice brightened.

"All right." He watched her and realized they were truly speaking again. He suddenly felt compelled to say more. "Do you want to sit down?"

When she nodded, he snatched a short stool from the corner, then steadied it as she sat. Her knees poked up, revealing a hole in her stocking. He realized he was staring again—a habit he'd developed around her. He cleared his throat and turned his attention back to his food.

He tipped the bowl to his lips and drank the broth. "That was good. Thank you."

"You're welcome." She reached for the bowl, but he tucked it inside the pail along with the rest of his dirty dishes.

"You don't need to clean up after me. I can take this inside."

"I don't mind." She reached for the pail. "I'm not exactly bedridden." Her eyes sparkled.

His mouth tipped in a lopsided grin. "Then thank you."

She hooked her finger beneath the pail handle, and their hands touched. He watched her for a reaction. Her eyes were warm—the sight trickling through his every limb. He swallowed, suddenly realizing the effect he had on her. His mind drifted to the day Jebediah had found him. Had he really been that monster? Gideon studied his boots as shame made his cheeks tingle.

She touched his arm, drawing him from his thoughts. "What are you thinking?"

He lifted his gaze. After all that, here she stood.

The realization baffled him, but he forced his brow to unfold. "Nothing." He glanced to the open doorway, where tiny specks of white floated down. "Lonnie." He pointed. "Look."

Her chin brushed her shoulder when she peered behind her. He heard her gasp. "Would you look at that?"

"C'mon. It's too cold for you out here." He grabbed his jacket off the workbench and, with her still seated on the little stool, draped it over her shoulders.

"Won't you be cold?" she asked, even as she slipped her fingertips into the flannel-lined pockets.

"Nah. I'm fine. Let's go inside." Without thinking, he held his hand out to her.

She hesitated, blinking quickly. She slipped her hand inside his, and he helped her stand. He released her fingers as gently as he could, but the foreign sensation lingered on his skin. They walked back to the house side by side, and when their arms brushed, Gideon offered her more space. He had no idea how to act around her anymore.

It wasn't in him to follow through. Never had been. How could he make this time different? The scent of cinnamon lifted from her flour-dusted apron when she stepped too close. He gulped at the thought of failing.

Snow fell in a whisper around them, and the November breeze tousled his cotton shirt, but Gideon felt none of it. He opened the door for Lonnie, and they stepped into the warm kitchen, fragrant with the scent of fried apple pie.

Elsie dropped diced carrots into a pot and wiped her hands on her apron. "Well, aren't you a pair, all bundled up."

"Gid sure ain't." Lonnie squeezed his arm. "Go and sit by the fire."

He enjoyed her touch too much to argue.

Jebediah burst in. "Wanna lend me a hand?" he panted. "These wives of ours want to take a bath again. I got the washtub set up in your room already. I just need help haulin' water *upstairs*."

Lonnie ducked her head. "I'm sorry. I don't have to—"

"Jebediah Bennett!" Elsie shook her wooden spoon at him, but her eyes sparkled with mischief. "How dare you. Lonnie is our guest."

Jebediah chuckled. "Now, now. Don't get your feathers all ruffled. I was just teasin' her. Really, Lonnie, I don't mind." With his palms up, he backed onto the porch. "You were probably used to takin' a bath every Saturday, before church back home."

Lonnie nodded, and Jebediah smiled. Gideon watched the exchange, knowing full well the Bennetts did not attend church. It was too far for them to walk, and they had no wagon.

"Are you sure?" Lonnie asked again.

The old man tipped Elsie's chin. "I just like to get my wife all fired up sometimes."

Elsie stopped stirring to put her hands on her hips, and broth dripped from her wooden spoon onto her apron. It took only one look from Elsie and, still grinning, Jebediah left. Lonnie handed Gideon his jacket, and he followed the older man outside.

Jebediah's gray beard grazed his plaid collar. "You know I don't really mind, right?"

"I know."

They strode shoulder to shoulder, and Jebediah flicked his thumb back to the house. "That's what women are for, I suppose. Keeping us busy."

"Always needin' something."

"Who you foolin'?"

"Sir?"

"I've watched you with her lately. I'd say you don't mind half as much as you're lettin' on."

Gideon's throat worked. He glanced toward the house, feeling colder, and knew it wasn't just the loss of the fire.

Twenty-Nine

A lone fiddle played as a crisp breeze swept into the old barn. The preacher turned toward the groom, the smile on his wrinkled face a clear symbol that he was pleased with the match. The music faded.

Lonnie's hand rested beside Gideon's, their fingers almost touching. She blinked back tears. She tilted her gaze to the heavy beams supporting the barn roof and willed her eyes to dry. Sniffling, she savored the sweet smell of straw that filled the giant building. The bride, wearing a dress the color of creamy columbine, stood beside her groom, her smile radiant as she looked into the face of the man she loved. Lonnie wiped her nose with her handkerchief.

She saw joy. Pure, unbridled joy in the young woman's face.

Lonnie remembered the morning she had given Gideon her own vow. Her tears had not been happy. She wiggled her fingers absent-mindedly. His head dipped, hand hesitating against hers, before he clasped his hands in front of him and leaned forward. Lonnie folded her hands in her lap, and the tin ring warmed. She did not need to look at Gideon's hand to know his was long gone. The ache in her chest grew, and she turned her attention back to the wedding. How lucky to be so full of joy on one's wedding day. Her chest burned as she drew in a ragged breath and fought to hold her emotions in check.

Hanging his head, Gideon's back lifted as he sighed. Lonnie wished she could read his mind. Wished she could better understand the man who sat beside her.

When the bride's mother dabbed her nose with a lace-edged handkerchief, the sight made Lonnie think of her own mother, and she tore her gaze away. An ache rose deep in her chest. Brushing her wrist against her stomach, she heaved out a shaky sigh.

What she wouldn't give to see her ma. Hear her voice. How she longed to visit with her aunt Sarah. Whisper her deepest desires.

She longed to be loved.

Lonnie inched closer to Gideon. He didn't budge, and his shoulder warmed hers. A tear slipped from her cheek, and Lonnie hurried to wipe it away. Gideon traced slow circles on the back of his hand.

The preacher closed a thick Bible and prayed a benediction for the happy couple. Folks clapped and cheered when he finished. Lonnie offered her applause, while Gideon clapped slowly, as if distracted. Lonnie spotted a young woman eying her husband and felt a flush in her cheeks. She braved a glance into Gideon's face, but he stared straight ahead, eyes wide, as if in another world completely.

Lonnie gently touched his arm, and he looked at her, his expression full of pain. Something she saw there made her breath catch. But before she could speak, chair legs scraped the plank floor. Women bustled to the food tables, slicing pies and stirring beans. The men cleared away dozens of mismatched chairs, moving them against the walls. Soon the music began. Lonnie stood beside Gideon in line for dinner. The boy behind her tapped his feet to the music, and turning, Lonnie smiled at him.

Tables draped in red gingham cloths were covered with bowls of creamed corn, dill pickles, and platters of ham. Lonnie also spotted plates of biscuits, a crock of potato salad, and fried cabbage. Gideon cut two slices of bread, smearing his with apple butter and the other with blackberry jam—Lonnie's favorite.

"Thank you." She took her plate and forced herself to pass by a dozen pies. She glanced up at the broad black coat in front of her and watched as the groom's father shoved a cookie in his mouth.

Gideon did the same, and when he saw Lonnie watching him, he shrugged and grinned. He chewed quickly. "It's more food than a man can fit on his plate."

A spotted dog poked his nose out from beneath the table, eyes large and golden. Gideon slipped a piece of ham beneath the checked cloth, where it vanished. He cleared his throat, and Lonnie shook her head. They made their way over to the Bennetts' picnic blanket, spread out beside a dozen others on the plank floor of the giant barn.

Gideon rolled a piece of ham and took a bite, then sipped his cider and shivered. "It's cold." Setting his plate aside, he blew on his hands.

Lonnie broke off a piece of biscuit. "Put your gloves on."

"I can't eat with my gloves on." He flashed her an impish smirk.

Lonnie soaked in the sight. "I will go and get you a fork. Anyone else need anything?"

Jebediah lifted a fried chicken leg. "A napkin would do me good."

"I'll be right back." She ducked into the line long enough to snag what she needed, and when she returned, Jebediah was busy licking his fingers. She tossed him the napkin, then handed Gideon the fork. "You're a lot of work, you know that?"

His smile bloomed into a grin. Her breath caught. She sat down, closer than she needed to, and tried to think of something to say that would keep him smiling.

A man behind her cleared his throat. "Excuse me, are you Gideon?"

They turned in unison, and Lonnie glanced up at a bearded man who balanced a tow-headed girl on his hip.

Gideon wiped his mouth. "Yep, why?"

The man tipped his head toward the makeshift stage. "Wanna play for a bit? A man over there said he heard you a time or two in Rocky Knob. Said you played the mandolin real good." He shifted the long-legged girl to his other side. "And I need a break."

"Good?" Gideon lifted his eyebrows and glanced into the crowd, and Lonnie followed his gaze in search of the familiar face. "Well, I don't know about that." His tone was humble.

Lonnie elbowed him. "C'mon, Gid. Play."

"I don't have my mandolin." He shrugged it off.

The man slapped a friendly hand on Gideon's shoulder. "You can borrow mine. I'm plumb tuckered out up there." He shook his head. "It's gonna be a long day, and I could use a bite of food."

Gideon looked at Lonnie. "Do you mind?" He licked his fingers, and she thrust a napkin into his hand.

"Not one bit."

He tried to fight a smile but failed. "Just a few songs?"

With a laugh, she pushed against his chest, urging him toward the music. "Go. They're waiting!"

Gideon felt the crowd swallow him up. He brushed past people he didn't know, faces he'd never seen before. He spotted a stout fellow in the corner, the man's thick arm around a dark-haired girl. His heart froze. Was it Bert? But when the man tipped his chin and lifted his face, thick eyebrows and broad-set eyes declared him a complete stranger.

Gideon sighed in relief, grateful Bert wasn't around. As he walked past, he felt the girl watching him. A glance confirmed his suspicions. Gideon ducked his head and walked on, leaving the couple behind him as he neared the stage. A few short months ago, he would have paid attention, but he felt no pull to the girl or what she might have to offer.

The realization lifted an unseen weight off his shoulders.

He'd gotten more than one stare from a girl that afternoon, yet he cared nothing for the glances he'd received or the dimpled smiles meant for him alone.

There was only one girl whose gaze he hoped to capture.

And he'd left her sitting on a plaid blanket in the center of the barn.

The man lunged onto the stage, Gideon right behind. He handed Gideon a mandolin and scratched his dark hair. "It's nothin' special, but it stays in tune."

"Looks nicer than mine." Gideon rubbed his thumb along the spruce top.

The man chuckled. "I'll be back in a few songs. Hey, I appreciate this." He set the little girl down, then held her hand as they walked away through the crowd. Gideon quick-checked the tune.

"What can you play?" A stout blond looked up even as he tucked his fiddle beneath his chin.

"Anything you want." Gideon pulled up a crate and slid it between his legs. He held the mandolin snug in his lap, the feel of wood familiar against his chest. "You pick. I'll just follow along."

"If you say so." The fiddler smirked. "That's Tom Parson on the banjo over there. Just thought I'd warn ya." The bow stretched across the strings. "*Good* luck."

Gideon's mouth parted, but he slammed it shut. He glanced at Tom, who held his banjo ready, and it struck Gideon just what kind of lick this would be. He stretched his fingers, wishing he'd had the chance to warm them up. The crowd cheered at the fiddler's teasing.

The stout blond leaned forward, and his bow slowed, then silenced. Vibrations hovered among the rafters. Gideon sucked in a deep breath.

As if tipping his sword in a duel, Tom dipped his hat. Gideon nodded, and the duel began. Tom started, and Gideon followed just as fast. The mandolin trailed the banjo—nine plucks from each. The crowd cheered louder. They played quicker. Gideon's stiff fingers struggled, but as his hand softened to the instrument, he felt a fighting chance inside him.

The song quickened. Stubby fingers twanged the banjo so quick, Tom's cap fell off, and Gideon took no care to hide his pleasure. The faster they played, the louder the crowd yelled. A boy in the front let out a shrill whistle, and Gideon felt the vibration of a chuckle in his chest, though the sound was lost in the roaring room. A wave of clapping kept the tempo ever quickening until finally, to the crowd's clear dismay, Tom threw up his hands. Exhausted, Gideon lowered his head and clapped in honor of his opponent.

"How did you learn to play like that?" Tom yelled from across the stage.

Gideon shrugged off the compliment. "You wore me out!" he hollered. "No wonder your other man needed a break!"

They played a few more songs, most of which Gideon knew. Those he didn't were easy to pick up. After a final waltz, the band stopped for a rest, and Gideon gladly returned the instrument to its owner.

"Here." Tom set his banjo aside and waved Gideon to the back corner of the stage. He tipped a bottle of whiskey to an empty glass. "You earned this." He held the glass to Gideon, amber liquid sloshing against the sides. Tom's smile was genuine.

"I—uh…" Gideon stared at the offering as his heart picked up its pace. The liquid stilled.

Tom's eyebrows knit together.

"No, thanks." Gideon blurted out, stunned by the sound of his own voice.

"No problem." Tom downed the glass in one shot, then clapped Gideon on the back. "Good job, man. That was fun."

"Yessir," Gideon said, his heart suddenly lighter.

As the band shared a celebratory drink, Gideon strode off in search of Lonnie. His stomach growled and he remembered his half-eaten supper, but as he pushed his way through the thick crowd, he had to pause for handshakes.

"That was amazing," a tall man said.

"Where are you from?" a croaky voice asked.

Gideon just shook their hands. "Thank you" was all he could get out. His head spun. He needed to find Lonnie. Finally, he spotted her with Elsie, curled up on the blanket, her dark shawl draped over her body. Several pieces of golden straw stuck to her hair. Her face was peaceful, and her wrist lay gently across her belly.

"How long has she been asleep?" Gideon knelt beside her, his voice barely audible over the hubbub around him.

"Not long, but I don't know how she can sleep with all this racket." Elsie handed Gideon a stack of cookies wrapped in his napkin. "I'm going to go find Jebediah. We need to get her home." She disappeared into the crowd.

Gideon leaned against a bale of hay, and as he ate his cookies, he watched the commotion. When the music began again, dancers found their partners, and a few men on the outskirts jigged alone. An awkward display of knees and elbows. Gideon recognized one too many drinks in their faces. The lusty taste of liquor filled his mind, but a smile tugged at his mouth, and he glanced down at Lonnie.

He pulled a piece of straw from her hair, smoothing his fingertips across limp curls—something he would never have dared had she been awake. Her hair was silk to his skin. She shifted beneath her shawl. He grinned. With his head clear and heart light, he knew no bottle or jug would have made this day any better.

Thirty

Gideon blinked into the light that filtered through the curtains, spilling across the floor. He sat and shook his head, stunned to see the sun so high. He'd never slept in this late, but by the time his head hit the pillow the night before, it had seemed morning was already itching to rise. He glanced to his side, only to find the bed empty. He rose and coveted the warm covers even as he dressed and lumbered downstairs.

Pots clanged and dishes clattered into place at the table. He combed fingers through his hair but knew it wouldn't improve his appearance. Still standing in the entryway, he rubbed his knuckles against his jaw and watched Lonnie and Elsie prepare breakfast. Batter dripped down the side of the skillet, and there was a broken eggshell on the floor. It looked more like chaos than anything else.

"Mornin'." Lifting onto the pads of her feet, Lonnie reached for a stack of plates and spun toward the table. "You must be hungry."

Gideon yawned. "Starv-ing."

"Breakfast is almost ready." She pointed to his chair. Her striped apron caught the air as she turned again. Her hair was freshly combed and plaited. A few tendrils scattered around her face. Gideon remembered the feel of it in his hands.

He rubbed the back of his neck. "I better do the chores first."

Lonnie cleared her throat even as Jebediah pushed his way into the kitchen, a pail of milk in his right hand.

Gideon straightened.

"Those girls don't wait for sleepyheads like you who were out too late." Jebediah scooted the bucket off to the side.

Elsie clicked her tongue. "Let the poor man have two minutes without having a chore or fence to build or whatever else you make him do."

"I second that." Chuckling, Gideon sat. He propped his elbows on the table and dropped his face in his hands. He rubbed his palms against burning eyes.

A sting struck his arm, and Gideon glanced up.

"Elbows?" Elsie propped her hands on her hip, wooden spoon hovering. Her eyes sparkled.

"Sorry." He rubbed his arm.

When Lonnie sat next to him, her cheeks were rosy from the stove. Gideon's stomach growled as he waited for Jebediah to bless the food, and he hardly had enough time to lift his fork before Elsie filled his plate with hotcakes. He drizzled maple syrup on top and helped himself to the stewed apples Lonnie pushed his way.

"You know what we're going to do today?" Jebediah asked, draping one arm over his chair.

Gideon shook his head and stirred a bite of hotcake into his syrup, then stuffed it in his mouth.

"I wanna take a load of stuff to trade."

"All the way to town?" Gideon lifted his eyes from his plate.

"Naw, Mount Airy's too far. I just stop around at the neighbors'. Folks this far out are always willin' to trade with one another."

Gideon wiped his mouth, then dropped his napkin in his lap. "What are we gonna trade?"

"Well, chestnuts for a start. Some folks can't gather their own, and we might unload a whole bushel." Jebediah sipped his coffee. "Elsie's got half a dozen jars of apple butter and a couple pounds of butter." He shrugged. "Then again, we might not be able to trade anything, but it's worth a shot. You never know when you got something that someone else might need, and likewise." After rising from the table, he pulled an enamel pitcher down from the shelf above the stove, then tugged a leather pouch out by its strings. "And I'll bring this." Coins jingled when he shook the sack. "Ol' Red Pickler up the way always has a good wheat crop. He usually sells me a few sacks of flour. Maybe I'll be able to talk him into more. We'll see."

"Can I come along?" Lonnie asked, her face full of hope.

Reluctantly, Gideon looked at her. "Might be better if you stay here. It's cold out there today, and who knows how long we'll be gone."

Her smile faded. Why did he have to blurt that out? Gideon finished his meal in a few bites.

"Well, ladies. We thank you for the food." Jebediah dumped his plate in the washtub, then slid his hat over silver hair.

Gideon's chair scraped across wood planks as he stood.

"I'll get some food together for later." Elsie sliced through a loaf of bread.

Jebediah patted his stomach, his expression pained.

"You'll be hungry later." Elsie moved the lunchpail in front of her and wrapped the bread, then a few pieces of cheese.

"She's right, Jeb." Gideon put on his jacket and pulled his floppy hat down over his hair. It insisted on curling around his ears this morning. He licked his fingertips, combing it down.

Lonnie was clearing away plates at the table. Grabbing the stack from her, he carried the dishes to the washtub. "I didn't mean to say no just like that. It's cold out there today, but you'd be more than welcome to come, Lonnie. If you want to."

Her face softened. "I would. But I should really stay. There's so much to do. I don't want to leave it all on Elsie." Lonnie's cheek brushed his shoulder. "Thank you, though."

The sentiment took him off guard as Gideon looked down on hair the color of chestnuts. "You're welcome."

"Afternoon, Jebediah. Who's this young fella with you?" Black skirts swayed as a gray-haired woman stepped onto her porch.

Jebediah stopped, and Sugar halted. The cart burdening her sloped back stilled, and Jebediah lifted a worn canvas, revealing his goods. "Afternoon, Mrs. Krause." He pulled off his hat. "This is Gideon. He and his wife are staying with us for a spell."

"Ma'am." Gideon tipped his hat to the woman on the porch.

"Look at all this!" She moved several furs aside, and her breath caught. "I got a quart of honey I could part with if that's Elsie's apple butter I see." She smiled, eyes crinkling, and smoothed a strand of wiry hair.

"Yes ma'am, it sure is." Jebediah pulled out the jar. "Last one. I parted with five others this afternoon. I'm outa chestnuts too, but I've still got a half pound of fresh butter, if you're interested."

The woman turned the jar in her hand. "This should do it, but let me fetch that honey."

She rushed inside, and while they waited, Gideon kicked around a pile of leaves. "'Staying with us for a spell,' huh?"

Jebediah glanced at him. "I smoothed over the rough parts."

Gideon half smiled. "I appreciate that." The winter breeze tickled his face, inching its chill beneath the collar of his coat.

The older man chuckled. "'Sides, wouldn't want to scare the neighbors." He winked. "Can't let on that I let any ol' riffraff onto the farm."

Chuckling, Gideon stuffed his hands into his pocket. "I take it you're not talking about Lonnie."

Jebediah grinned.

The door squeaked open and the woman returned. "Here y'are."

The jars passed hands, and Jebediah dropped the honey into the cart. He tipped his hat and patted Sugar on the hind end. "We'll be gettin' a move on. Sun's setting and we got two more stops to make."

"Take care, boys. It was good seeing you, and say hello to Elsie for me."

Jebediah waved his good-bye.

"This is Odis's place," he said a little ways down the worn path. "He lost his wife recently, and I'd like to pay him a visit." Jebediah pulled off his hat and turned it in his hands, his eyes staring into the setting sun. "Wouldn't be surprised if he has a few letters for me as well. Odis gets to town twice as often as I do and is always willing to pick up the mail." Jebediah stepped toward the rickety cabin. "Head on to the last stop, and I'll catch up."

Eager to get home, Gideon nodded. He turned and tugged on Sugar's line. The mule followed with slow steps. They didn't go far, and after knocking on a heavy, oak door, he introduced himself to the family inside. They had no need for trading, but Gideon accepted a stack of warm cookies and was on his way again.

Still brushing crumbs from his jacket, he hurried to the fork where Jebediah had asked him to wait. Thoughts of a warm fire quickened his tired feet. "Almost home." He patted the mule's scruffy neck.

A stray sound caught his attention, and Gideon peered over his shoulder. He didn't see anything and lowered his head and tugged on Sugar's line. "Get on up!"

The mule leaned into her load.

Leaves crunching made his hand tighten around the rope. "Jebediah?"

Then he heard footsteps—too many to be one man.

Before Gideon could react, three men emerged. A muscle in Gideon's shoulder flexed. He recognized them all.

"Hiya!" Bert called, stepping onto the path. "Ain't seen you in a while." His voice dripped with sarcasm.

Bert hurried toward him. Gideon willed his voice steady. "Evenin', fellas." He flicked the brim of his floppy hat and watched as they formed a half circle around him. He hated the way his heart jumped. He glanced from one scruffy face to the next. Each man looked as if he hadn't slept in days. Hadn't bathed in twice as many.

"Fancy meetin' you here." Bert licked his teeth.

Pulse racing, Gideon kept Sugar's lead rope tight as he pulled her closer. Her front hoof stumbled, but she kept her footing.

Bert flicked his head to the two others, and their formation tightened. Everywhere Gideon looked, he saw one of them watching him.

"You in some kind of hurry?" Bert placed a stubby hand on Sugar's back, making her step sideways. Her thick coat shuddered beneath his fingers.

"Just wanna head home and get this cart unloaded before sunset."

Bert slid his hand down the lead rope, and Gideon's grip braced against the tension. "Sun's settin'. You ain't gonna make it." He patted an empty coat pocket. "Might as well sit a spell with us."

Gideon eyed the grimy fingers. "Thanks, but if it's all the same, I'll be gettin' home." He tried to step away, but Bert held the rope tight.

A taller man spoke up. "Hey, don't he owe you somethin'?"

Gideon drew in a slow breath.

"I'd say so." Bert circled him. His eyes flicked to Gideon's pockets. His eyebrows shot up, and Gideon knew he was waiting.

"I don't have it," Gideon said, his voice defeated.

Bert scratched his head. "Then it looks like we've got a bit of a problem." Bert glanced to the cart, tracing his gaze along Jebediah's pile of goods. "Betcha got enough there to make up the difference." His eyes lifted to Gideon's face. "Don't ya?"

Gideon's blood thinned. His hands itched to yank Bert up by his shirt collar. This wasn't Jebediah's debt to pay.

Bert's eyes dropped to the cart.

Gideon tightened his grip. The rope burned his palm.

"That's fine cargo you got there."

Squaring his shoulders, Gideon glanced at the other men. He could take one, *maybe* two. But not three.

As if he'd heard his thoughts, Bert smiled up at him. He reached beneath the furs, and Gideon gritted his teeth as glass jars clanged together.

A dirt-creased hand flicked the fur back into place. "This looks like enough to feed a coupl'a men for a few weeks. How much you'd say a cartload like this is worth?" Glancing over his shoulder, Bert smiled at his men, and they chuckled.

Outnumbered, Gideon knew that putting up a fight would do little good. "A lot less than a watch." Though he doubted by much.

Bert looked up at him.

"I still have it."

Anger flashed in Bert's eyes. "You better." He rubbed his jaw. "And I know you'll get it to me. Right?"

Gideon nodded once.

"And then some." He glared at Gideon. "Let's call it interest." One of his men chuckled. "But what do we do in the meantime?" Bert motioned to the men behind him. "Boys, got any ideas?"

As Gideon stared down the man in front of him, he wished he'd never met Bert.

He forced himself to inhale.

One of Bert's men coughed, and Gideon shifted his stance. He couldn't keep all of them in his line of sight at the same time.

"I'll get it back to you. You have my word." He would pay the debt. Not Jebediah.

A sharp laugh escaped Bert, and he glared at Gideon. "A lot of good your word is worth."

Grimacing, Gideon shook his head. "I will get it to you."

"Which reminds me." Bert hooked his thumb in his belt loop. "That ring you traded." He stuck up his lower lip. "The man I sold it to said it was hardly worth the two pennies."

Gideon sucked in a slow breath through his teeth at the thought of his ring holding so little value. Even to him. Bert motioned with his hand, and the nearest man stepped in the path. His chest bumped Gideon's shoulder. Gideon tugged on the rope and stepped into the underbrush. He would cut through the woods if he had to. Anything to get away from them.

Months ago, he would have put up a fight—thrown a few curses their way—and paid the consequences if need be. But now, knowing who waited for him, he had no desire for trouble, and the second reaction that came to mind was little like the first. He prayed. That's what Lonnie would have done.

Footsteps followed.

Dropping his head, he leaned into the weight of the mule, urging her to hurry. A plaid coat stepped into his line of sight just up ahead, and Gideon lifted his gaze to see Jebediah standing a dozen paces away, his face sober, gray eyes hard.

"Let him go," Bert muttered.

Gideon glanced over his shoulder and saw the trio had stopped at Bert's command.

"We'll meet again." Bert nodded slowly.

With a toss of his head, Gideon motioned for Jebediah to walk on. The older man complied. As they rounded the bend, Gideon slapped Sugar harder than he liked. She and her cart lunged forward.

"Sorry you had to see that."

"I was starting to get worried about you." Jebediah adjusted the furs that had shifted out of place and slid a handful of letters beneath the canvas. "When I didn't find you waiting, I decided to come look for you." He glanced back in the direction they'd come. "Everything all right?"

"Just an old friend," Gideon muttered, not caring that disdain leaked into his voice.

The old man eyed him. "So I see."

Marching home through the fading light proved to be difficult, and Gideon kept his eyes to the ground, glad for Jebediah's calming presence. Remembering the prayer he had said, he glanced at his hands, where the mule's lead rope had worn a red mark. Did God expect a thank-you? He wasn't sure and, keeping his head down, hoped that what he did not know how to say would be seen in his heart. He was grateful. His thumb touched his empty ring finger, and he wished there was something he could do to prove it.

Thirty-One

Lonnie let the door close softly behind her and stepped onto the porch. She watched Gideon raise the ax high above his head. With a grunt, he brought it down. A shudder coursed through her as wood splintered and flew. He grabbed another wedge of pine and centered it. When he glanced at her, his expression tore at her heart. *Crash.* Another piece shattered in half. There was no need for him to chop wood. There was enough to last the winter and then some. Lonnie swallowed. He'd been like this for days.

She tightened her shawl and skidded the toe of her boot across the frosty step. No sense in stalling. With a cup of coffee that nearly burned her hand, she strode toward Gideon. She passed spent vines in the garden. They were gnarled and brown, their fruits and vegetables having been canned and tucked in Elsie's cellar.

She sat on an upturned log, and her feet dangled just above the ground. Gideon leaned the ax against the chopping block and sat beside her. His shoulder pressed warm against hers, and to Lonnie's surprise, he made no effort to move away. He pulled off his hat and turned it in his hands.

Gideon leaned forward and rested his elbows on his knees. With his hat pinched between his fingers, the brim nearly touched the mud. "We kill the hog tomorrow."

"Is that so?" she said softly, hoping he would say more. Lonnie realized that come springtime, half a dozen piglets would be running around the pen. "He's not gonna see his babies."

"No, I suppose he won't."

Her eyebrows fell. "It's a shame."

His voice was soft. "It's a part of life." He flipped his palms up as if to emphasize the insignificance in it.

Lonnie watched as he pulled at a sliver of wood and peeled it off. A few seconds passed, and he flicked it into the mud.

She sighed. Soon she would feel the child inside her kick and squirm. Lonnie wondered if she would still be making good on her promise. *I'll give you until the baby's born. Not a day longer.* Had her words struck a chord in him?

He was changing. She saw it in tiny strides each day. Perhaps one day it would bloom into something more. She took in the shapes of his face, uncertain how that made her feel. *Who are you fooling, Lonnie?* She knew just how it made her feel. Lying by his side at night was becoming natural. More than that. It was the only way she could imagine her life.

His brow creased as he studied the pig in the distance, its dirty snout rummaging through the muck.

"A penny for your thoughts."

He peered down at her. "I don't want to talk about money."

She nearly laughed. "I was teasing you."

He hung his head.

"Gideon, is everything all right?"

His head bobbed in a nod, but he didn't look up at her.

She touched his arm briefly, then pulled back. "What's the matter?"

He ran his hand over his face. "Everything, it seems."

"What do you mean?"

When he looked down at her, he searched her face. Her cheeks warmed beneath his determination. "It's all such a mess."

"What's a mess? Gideon, I don't understand."

"What I'm trying to say is that I wish things had been different."

"How so?" Her voice sounded small to her ears.

"I wish I had been more." His Adam's apple bobbed. "I wish things had begun different. Much different."

She let her fingers rest beside his, overlapping ever so slightly. "I do too." She watched the hog push his snout through a pile of scraps. "But in a way I don't."

His eyebrows pinched together.

"There are so many regrets. But not everything is something I would take back." She smoothed her thumb along the band of her apron that covered her rounding belly.

He followed the movement. "No?"

She shook her head, wishing with all her heart that he might one day feel the same.

His chest lifted, sorrow heavy in his sigh. "I should get back to work."

Gideon lowered his head as he trudged away. She deserved more than he had to give. Gideon shook his head. Had? Or was willing?

He was never meant to be a father. Nothing about him suggested he could raise a child. *Not even Lonnie's?* He glanced back to where she sat, dark boots crossed. He wondered what the baby might look like.

Emotion thickened his throat when he imagined a baby with large brown eyes. Just like its mama.

He picked up his ax and carried it toward the edge of the yard. That morning Jebediah had mentioned a fallen branch blocking the path. Perhaps he could have it cleared by sundown.

His boots stomped through the wilting layer of snow. He wondered if Lonnie had gone inside but didn't look back. What was he so afraid of? He shifted the ax from one fist to the other. He knew the answer.

He wasn't worthy of Lonnie...or their child. Not with his demons chasing him.

Once he returned the pocket watch to Bert, he'd be able to shake the chains of his earlier life. Nearing the path that meandered from the Bennetts' farm, Gideon spotted the fallen branch. It lay like a dead man in the snow. He heard the door close and glanced back to see that Lonnie was gone.

Using the side of his boot, he kicked at the hefty branch, but it didn't budge. He set to work, his arms weary from an afternoon of wielding the ax, but he kept a steady pace. The sound of steel striking wood filled the silent forest, echoing from mountaintop to mountaintop. When he finished, Gideon went back for the wheelbarrow, loaded the smallest portions into the rusted metal bin, and headed back toward the farm. When he brought back the last load, he spotted Jebediah in the doorway of the barn, wiping his hands on a rag.

With a grunt, Gideon dumped the last of the gnarled wood beside the chopping block, pausing only long enough to rub his arm along his temple before he trudged toward the barn. Jebediah had disappeared, and stepping into the warm building, Gideon inhaled the dry scent of animals and feed. The humble smell calmed him.

"Looks like you got the path cleared," Jebediah said without looking up from his work. Using stout fingers, he smeared grease into a large trap.

"Yessir." Exhausted, Gideon pulled up a stool, then thought the better of it. "Need a hand?"

"Naw. Just making use of the last hour of daylight." Jebediah clamped the lid on the can of grease and swiped the grungy rag over his hands. He slid a stool from beneath the workbench, and the rickety wood creaked as he settled down. They sat without speaking for several moments.

Gideon threw words around in his mind but couldn't think of how to begin.

"Somethin' eatin' you, son?" Jebediah spoke without looking up.

Gideon fiddled with the edge of his thumbnail.

Tipping his face up, Jebediah looked to the doorway. The house lay a stone's throw beyond. "That Lonnie of yours is quite a lady. It's been a right fine pleasure having her."

"She is." That was one thing he knew for sure. Yet he was nowhere near to deserving her.

"I'm starting to get used to the idea of you bumming around as well."

When Gideon looked up, Jebediah smiled and he saw that he was teasing.

"You've been working hard, and I sure do appreciate it."

"Thank you, sir."

Jebediah glanced at him, his gray beard brushing his coat. "Can't believe there's gonna be a little one 'round before we know it."

Gideon grunted. "Me neither." He glanced out to the house and imagined his child playing inside with Lonnie. She would take the baby for walks in the woods. His baby would have pieces of him, whether he was willing to give more of himself or not. Stabbing the toe of his boot against the plank floor, Gideon suddenly wished he had more to give.

He wished he were a better man.

"You ready?" Jebediah straightened, and steely eyes danced with curiosity.

"No."

"Neither was I." The older man's gaze faltered.

"You had children?"

Heavy eyelids, wrinkled with age, blinked. "A girl." Jebediah rested an elbow on the worktable behind him. "Many years ago. Probably before you were even born."

Gideon felt his mouth open.

"She died when she was three." Jebediah smoothed his thumb over a knot in the worktable. "Fever took her."

"I'm sorry."

Jebediah ducked his head and seemed to gather himself before speaking. "Don't be. It was hard at first, especially for Elsie. She was real young then. Fever almost got her too."

Gideon could think of nothing to say. But something inside him began to ache. The Bennetts deserved better than that.

Deep lines etched across Jebediah's forehead. "God always has a plan, though. Whether we're privy to it or not."

"Can't say I agree."

"Didn't say you had to."

Gideon glanced at him.

"Life's short, Gid." He plopped his heel on the lowest rung. The stool creaked its age. "It's too short to be wastin' time worrying. Too short to be wastin' time runnin'."

"I'm not runnin'."

"You've been runnin' since the moment I met you. Before that, I'd reckon." He squeezed Gideon's shoulder. "I'd say the sooner you stop and face whatever it is that's chasin' you, the sooner you'll see how much time you're wastin'."

Gideon dipped his head.

Jebediah lowered his face, forcing Gideon to meet his gaze. "I can tell you've been thinkin' about it. It's time to get off the fence, Gideon. It's yer pride and nothin' more."

Crossing his arms over his chest, Gideon chewed the inside of his cheek. Finally, he nodded slowly. Jebediah spoke the truth and nothing less.

"I know you've been itching to get you and Lonnie on your way, but that baby'll be here before you know it. If you want to know what's good for Lonnie...if you know what's good for that little one...I hope you'll stick around here a little longer." With a weary sigh, Jebediah rose. His movements were slow as he lifted the stool back into place. "Just want you to know you're welcome."

Thirty-Two

The air hung heavy with the smell of smoking pork as Gideon walked past the kitchen window, a load of fragrant cedar pressed to his chest. He spotted Lonnie through the glass. She was focused on the bowl of batter she was whisking. Her hair was coiled at the nape of her neck, still damp from the bath she'd taken. The empty tub sat waiting for him, but with Lonnie fully occupied, Gideon quietly set the wood down and strode to the barn, hoping to get a little more work done on his project before suppertime.

He pulled the heavy piece from its hiding place, picked up a square of sandpaper, and started where he had left off. Every few minutes, he ran his hand across the wood. Wherever he felt a spot that was not to his satisfaction, he sanded it some more. Though it was going slower than he liked, the cradle was taking shape. His baby was going to sleep in this cradle. Lonnie would sit barefoot and rock it with her toes. He'd built it large enough to last the baby through the first year. Kneeling, he eyed one edge and ran his thumb across the silken wood. It had to be perfect.

He hummed a tune as he worked. He blew a puff of dust from the edge, the intricate grain a slowly developing mystery. Just last week Elsie had whispered that Lonnie's birthday was in a few days. The twenty-first of January. Gideon hadn't been able to hide his surprise. It pained him as much now as it had then that he'd never thought to learn her birthday. He touched the smooth wood. He hadn't planned on completing his project so soon, but he didn't want to pass up on the opportunity to surprise her. A few more days after that and the gift would be ready to oil. He hoped she wouldn't mind that it would not be finished.

He was certain that Lonnie was in the parlor this very moment, knitting the booties she'd been working on all week. Nearly every afternoon he found her with a different type of needle in her hand. She was always making something out of yarn. When she wasn't doing that, she spent the quiet evening hours writing letters home. How long was it now that they'd been at the Bennetts'? Gideon shook his head. He'd lost track of the months.

When shadows stretched across the yard, Gideon knew he had lingered too long. He moved the hefty gift out of sight, swept up his mess, and put away Jebediah's tools. Wiping his hands together, he glanced around to make certain everything was in its place—the cradle tucked safely out of sight.

He stepped out into the cold night air. Snow crunched under his boots. He latched the barn door and rattled the handle. One glance at the dim sky and he was certain it would snow again during the night. After checking the woodbox, he glanced around the farm. All seemed well.

After dropping his hat on the washstand, he rolled up his sleeves and filled the pitcher with cold water. Elsie always set out a hot pitcher before supper, and Gideon glanced in the window, wondering if he'd kept the others waiting.

"Wait!" Lonnie pushed the door open with her hip, a pail of water pressed to her chest. "I had this warming near the stove for you." Water sloshed over the edge as she lowered the pail down at his feet.

"You didn't have to do that."

"Now you won't have to come in and stand next to the stove after washin' up." She wiped her hands on her apron. Fir boughs hung on the door behind her, hints of dried needles catching in her hair. Gideon fought the urge to smooth them away.

"Thank you." He took his eyes off her only long enough to pick up the pail.

"Hurry or it will get cold." Her fingertips fumbled the side of the bucket as if trying to help him.

Gideon stared at her. Lonnie stared back. It took him a moment to remember what he was doing. *Wash. Right.* He splashed his face and ran a soft rag over his neck. With her still watching, he cracked a smile. "Are you checking to see if I get behind my ears?" Water dripped from his face.

"Maybe." She held a towel out to him. "It would be a first, I bet."

He laughed out the words. "Are you saying somethin'?" He slid his hands back into the water, enjoying the way his fingers thawed. Then Gideon rubbed water up and down his forearms, chagrined by the dingy tint to the water. He shook his hands at the bucket, and droplets flew. "Do I have time for a real bath before supper?"

She placed her knuckles on her hips and tilted her head to the side. "Plenty."

"All right, then. I'll put some water on the stove."

"Already been done." Lonnie smiled and opened the screen door. She disappeared before Gideon could say anything.

He stepped into the warm kitchen.

"Water's ready." With a hot pad, Lonnie clutched the kettle away from herself, and Gideon followed, carrying a hefty pot. He struggled to see the steps with the bulky pot in front of him and nearly tripped twice.

"Let me get the door." She pounded up the stairs, nearly knocking him down. Between her belly and his jutted elbows, it took careful maneuvering for her to squeeze by. As she smashed him against the top of the railing, the smell of dried cedar boughs filled the hallway.

"Sorry!" She slid into the bedroom and held the door. He squeezed past.

She poured the kettle of water into the tub, and steam rose. It took them several trips to fill the washtub, then Lonnie left him to his bath. He heard every click of her shoes as she strode down the hall. The water barely hit his calf when he climbed in. He splashed water up and down his arms, feeling the tension melt away. He scrubbed his face and took extra care to wash behind his ears.

A knock came through the door. "It's me," Lonnie called. "I've got the scissors. Holler for me when you're done."

"Scissors?"

"For your haircut. And I don't want to hear any excuses." A smile carried on her voice.

He chuckled. Pressing the rag to the top of his head, he closed his eyes and water dripped down his face and chest. He sat there until his bath turned cold and the smell of roasted pork wafted from downstairs.

Gideon dried off and shuffled through the dresser drawer until he found a clean shirt. He put it on and checked his appearance in the mirror. He ran his hand through hair that hadn't been cut in months. He dumped out his bath water and put the tub away, then went in search of his wife.

"Lonnie's gonna cut my hair. Have you seen her?"

Elsie glanced up from the pot she was stirring. Her eyebrows rose. "She went to fetch a stool."

Gideon ducked outside in time to see Lonnie struggling across the yard. Snow fell in soft flakes around her. He jogged out, took the stool, and carried it back to the house. "You shouldn't lift things like this."

Her cheeks colored, and a smile was his only answer. She grabbed the broom as they passed through the kitchen. Gideon set the stool in the center of their bedroom, and Lonnie leaned the broom against the wall, then pulled a small pair of scissors from her apron pocket. "I have been waiting for this for a long time."

"Is it that bad?" He tossed his hand through his hair, swiping what few snowflakes remained.

"Shirt." She pointed to the bed.

He made quick work of the buttons and tossed it onto the bed before sitting.

She ran the comb through his wet locks, and Gideon tried to sit still. "Don't cut me," he murmured.

Her words were near his ear. "I'll try not to."

Gideon held his neck steady as she tugged at his hair. *Snip, snip.* Autumn-colored curls fell to the floor.

He glanced at the mess around his feet. "You're sure you ain't cuttin' too much now?"

"Will you just hush and let me work?" She forced his head up. "I'm good at this, trust me."

His pa had once told him to never trust a woman who said "Trust me." Gideon sighed and looked ahead.

Her hand stroked through his hair in rhythm with the comb. The soft pull made Gideon's eyes flutter closed, but every bit of his consciousness was on the fingers touching his hair. As she made her way from side to side, her belly brushed against his back. He wondered what it would be like to run his hand over the fabric of her dress.

"Hold still," she whispered and then placed fingertips on each side of his head, steadying it.

He swallowed. "Sorry."

She breathed softly as she worked in silence. His head felt light when she smoothed the strands behind each ear.

"How's it going back there?" His voice came out dry and raspy. He cleared his throat but couldn't bring himself to open his eyes. "Does it look good?"

"Uh-huh," she murmured. "All done." She grazed the strands at the base of his head.

Lonnie brushed the fallen crescents off his shoulders. "Just a moment. Close your eyes." She touched his temples.

He did as told and felt her fingers gently smooth over his nose and brush at his cheeks. His heart pounded. He licked his lips and reminded himself to breathe. But when Lonnie leaned in and blew on his forehead, he forgot what he was supposed to remember.

"Open your eyes," she said, and he looked up at her. She clutched a hand mirror to her chest and stepped behind him before reaching it around.

"What do you think?"

Gideon stared at his reflection, scarcely recognizing himself. "You did a fine job." He turned his head from side to side.

"You look very handsome."

He caught her watching him in the mirror. "Thanks," he said sheepishly.

Thirty-Three

Finished sweeping, Gideon leaned the broom against the wall. He spotted a slow shadow moving along the edge of the property. He narrowed his gaze. A black coat flickered between the trees. Chills pricked along Gideon's shoulders, but in a blink, he realized it was Gus, Jebediah's neighbor. Gideon pressed his hand to his chest and let out a slow breath. Still, the debt tainting his name gnawed at him, and as he watched Gus stride out of sight, he knew Bert and his cohorts were coming for him.

He vowed to get the watch back to Bert. And then some. Bert's words echoed in his mind. The man expected more than just a watch. Gideon shook his head. He scarcely had two pennies to rub together.

Gideon stepped away from the window. He had no way of making money. He worked for food and board. Nothing more. And rightly so. Jebediah and Elsie gave freely of all they had. As he put the broom away, he knew he had to think of something.

The smells of roasted pork and hot gravy pulled Gideon into the kitchen. He sat beside Lonnie as Jebediah blessed the food, then his hands followed hers. She took a biscuit, and he took one too. With each platter that passed his way, he made certain she'd taken her share before helping himself to any. Lonnie's laughter rang in unison with Elsie's when Jebediah told a joke. Gideon glanced at his wife and couldn't help smiling along. He found it impossible to pull his gaze from her cheery face.

When Elsie began to pick the rest of the meat from the bone, Gideon leaned back in his chair and smoothed his hands down his stomach. "You feed us too well." He stretched, stepped to the woodbox, and found a thin shard. Crouching in front of the stove, he held the sliver to the flames until it caught. He lit his pipe, then handed the small flame over to Jebediah, who followed him into the parlor and lit his own.

Lonnie sat at the writing desk and scribbled away on another letter. Gideon cupped his pipe between his thumb and forefinger and watched his wife. She reached behind her and rubbed her lower back. The tin ring on her finger clicked against the wooden chair.

She turned and looked at him, catching his stare. "Promise me you will get this to the post office soon?"

He cleared his throat. "I will do it soon as I can." Mount Airy was more than fifteen miles away, and there was rarely a day that he had that kind of time. But something in him made him want to get it there.

Her mouth moved in a silent thank-you. She tucked the letter aside and moved to the rocking chair. Gideon set his pipe on the mantel and reached for his mandolin. He began to tune the eight strings, and before he finished, Lonnie offered up a request.

"I don't know that one." Gideon shifted the instrument into place.

"It's an old, old hymn."

He clutched the mandolin to his chest. "Why don't you start singin' it and I'll catch on?"

She fiddled with the edge of her apron. Finally, she nodded softly.

"All right." She crossed her ankles and set the rocker in motion. She drew in a measured breath, then let it out slowly. Her voice began small, the first words barely more than a whisper.

Gideon moved his hand to the fret board as he listened. He felt his mouth tip in a half smile. She was singing. For him.

Her voice grew louder, more sure. The melody unfolded in Gideon's mind, and his hands moved out of instinct as he began to play softly. Quietly, Elsie joined in. Jebediah leaned back against the sofa, arms folded over his chest, and closed his eyes. His head nodded in rhythm. Elsie chose the next song, and together they sang into the night. Elsie's soprano was pleasant. Lonnie's was smooth, but just like the spruce beneath his hands, it had the slightest grain. Gideon couldn't take his eyes from Lonnie's face. She seemed to stare at the fire, her expression serene.

The last song ended, the vibrations quieting. It wasn't until the grandfather clock chimed nine that Lonnie blinked as if coming back from a faraway place. When her eyes met Gideon's, she smiled sheepishly.

Elsie reached over and patted Lonnie's knee. "That was lovely, dear. You should sing more often."

Gideon set his instrument aside and, leaning forward, rubbed his palms together. "I second that."

Lonnie blushed and he winked.

Jebediah glanced over his shoulder at the clock. "Is it that late? I should have been in bed a good hour ago. We've got an early start tomorrow."

"And I have a special breakfast planned for someone's birthday." Elsie said.

Lonnie's rocker stilled. "Oh, Elsie. You don't have to do that for me."

"Fiddlesticks. It's something to celebrate."

"Sure is," Gideon added.

The color in her cheeks deepened.

Gideon smiled. Rising, he offered Lonnie his arm. She hesitated briefly before taking it. They walked up the stairs without speaking, and by the time Gideon had unbuttoned his shirt, Lonnie was crawling beneath the covers. He slid in beside her but could not shut his eyes. Lonnie rolled to her side, and her breathing slowed. Lifting his head, Gideon saw that she was already asleep.

He turned toward her, his hand resting on the mattress between them, the tip of her braid near enough to touch. Ever so softly, he grazed the silken strands with his thumb. He was not the least bit tired, so he rose and made careful to tuck the blankets gently around Lonnie. With the snow falling harder now, no moonlight slipped in through the window, and he could scarcely make out her sleeping form. Gideon stepped from the room and moved down the stairs as quietly as he could. With Lonnie's birthday only a few hours away, his surprise had to be finished.

A bright morning glinted against her face, and Lonnie opened her eyes. She was eighteen today, old enough to be on her own. If she were home, she'd be packing for her aunt Sarah's. Those dreams seemed like a lifetime ago. Lonnie rolled onto her side only to see that Gideon was gone. Her brows knit together. From the kitchen, she heard stove lids clanging. Lonnie climbed out of bed and dressed quickly. She shivered her way to the wall, grabbed her shawl from the wooden peg, and with a quick peek out the window, went in search of Gideon.

She stopped when she saw Elsie in the kitchen. "Good morning."

"Happy birthday." Elsie closed the stove door. "You look mighty cheerful. Bet that husband of yours is still asleep."

"He's not up already?"

"Haven't seen him." Elsie licked the end of a spoon before tossing it in the washtub. "And I've been up since Jebediah left to check his traps."

Lonnie chewed her lip and stepped to the window. "I'll be right back," she murmured against the cold glass. She stepped outside and tightened her shawl as she peered through falling snow, awash with the brightness of day. The barn door was sealed shut, and no fresh footprints forged a path in that direction.

A dull pain caught hold of her lower back, and with a soft moan, she massaged it. She pressed a hand beneath her stomach, which seemed to get bigger each day, and gave it a little lift, trying to make both her and the baby more comfortable.

She decided to try the barn anyway. Her boots sank in the deep snow that crept above her ankles and moistened her stockings. She lifted her dress until the hem brushed her knees. Lonnie reached the barn, gripped the icy latch, and struggled to tug the door open. She blinked into the darkness. Her mouth parted, a small gasp slipping out.

Leaning against the workbench sat Gideon, his chin to his chest. An elbow was propped up on the milk stool, and his other arm draped across a large cradle. A piece of sandpaper lay just inches from his relaxed hand.

Lonnie touched her fingertips to her heart.

Gideon lifted his head, and when she stepped closer, his eyes opened.

"Lonnie?" He blinked up at her.

She crouched beside him. "You were gone, so I came to find you."

He glanced from her to the cradle and jumped up. "What are you doing here? You weren't supposed to see this until your birthday."

"It is my birthday." She couldn't hide the smile in her voice.

His brows pinched together. "But it's not your birthday in the *barn*." He broadened his stance. "You can't see this yet."

"Did you make this...?" She stepped around him. Kneeling next to the cradle, she smoothed her hand along the side. "It's beautiful."

His voice was soft behind her. "It's for you—and the baby."

"The baby," she whispered and looked up at him, tears blurring her vision.

His hands were dusty as he pressed them together. "Do you like it?"

Lonnie nodded, unable to speak.

"I...I've been working on it for a little while now."

"When did you find the time?"

"Here and there." He sank beside her and, with a broad hand, set the cradle to rocking. "I figured every baby needs a place to sleep."

The ache rose in her heart, and she pushed it down, hoping that perhaps he saw their baby as more than a burden.

"Lonnie, I...I want you to know that I regret so many of the things I've done. Especially the things I've done to you." His hand moved to her jaw, the skin smooth beneath his thumb.

Her throat tightened.

"If I could change the past, I would." He stood.

She peered up at him. He would never have married her. Is that what she saw in his eyes?

"If I could go back and be the man you deserved, I would."

Hope filtered into her heart. "And you think it's too late?" She started to rise, needing him to know it wasn't.

He glanced away with a sheen in his eyes. With him still standing above her, she expected him to turn and walk out as he'd always done. His shoulders sank and rose, his face pensive. When he looked down on her, she saw the same hope reflected in his eyes. He held out his hand, and Lonnie studied the lines of his palm. Tentatively, she reached up and took it.

Thirty-Four

The ink pen scratched across the page as Lonnie sat in the upstairs rocker and scribbled a last few words to her aunt. She'd already written her ma, and the letter was sealed and ready to be delivered the next time someone made it into town. Finished, Lonnie read her words again. They were a bittersweet reminder of how much she missed her family. She felt a tremble in her chin when she envisioned her aunt holding this very page one day.

"Knock, knock." Gideon nudged the door open with his boot. He carried the gift she'd discovered nearly two weeks ago. It was now stained and oiled and ready to be brought in.

When he shouldered past the door, she tossed her letter to the bed and nearly jumped up.

"Where do you want this?" he grunted, arms taut from the weight of the hefty piece.

She pushed a pile of books out of the corner and stepped back. "Here, please." She wiped dust from her hands, her joy nearly bubbling over.

Stooping, Gideon lowered the heavy piece into place. "Is this good?" He straightened and shook out his wrist. The cradle rocked from side to side, and he steadied it.

"Perfect." Lonnie smoothed her hand over the oiled wood.

"I'm just glad you like it." He ran his thumb along a blotch of stain.

Lonnie wrinkled her nose. "Sorry. You shouldn't have let me do that part."

"You were very adamant." His voice was serious, but when she looked into his face, she saw a smile edge his eyes.

"It's just beautiful," she said breathlessly.

Gideon brushed dust from his shoulder. "I'm just glad you like it."

"To think"—she perched on the edge of the rocker, surprisingly tired—"soon a baby will sleep here. Our little baby." She watched Gideon for a response.

He stared down at the cradle as if unable to speak.

Her smile faltered.

Kneeling beside his gift, he touched the wood with a gentle hand, and the cradle rocked from side to side. "Pretty amazing." His voice was soft.

Her chest lifted. "Truly?"

His nod was brief, but when he glanced up at her, something filled his eyes that she'd never seen before. The emotion nearly knocked her from her seat. Lonnie slid down and crouched beside him. "Gideon." Her throat was so tight, she could hardly squeeze out the word.

"I don't know if it's in me to be—"

"Shh." She touched his arm. "Don't say it. This…" Her hand slid down to his and she held on tight. "This is enough."

His eyes were pained, and his lips parted as if to protest.

"Believe me." Bending forward, she kissed his hand.

His throat worked, eyes wide.

"This is enough." She was more thankful than she could express.

Gideon's gaze dropped to her belly. His fingers twitched as his hand slid forward, finally pausing on his knee. Lonnie held her breath, and chills covered her skin like a morning frost as she waited.

Seconds ticked by, but he didn't move his callused hand to her gingham dress.

Green eyes scanned her face, and he cleared his throat. "A name." His Adam's apple bobbed. "Does the baby have a name?"

"I've thought of a few." Lonnie fiddled with the hem of her dress, tugging on a loose thread. "I was hoping to give our baby a name that means something."

"Means something?" His forehead wrinkled. "You mean like… George Washington?"

"No." She smiled. "Not like that. A name that means something special, like the name of a past relative. Or a Bible name."

"Bible name," he repeated.

"*You* have a Bible name."

Still crouched beside her, he seemed to ponder her words a moment. "Well…is *Lonnie* a Bible name?" He looked up at her with eyes as wondering and unknowing as a child's.

She chuckled. "I'm afraid not."

He blinked. "I suppose you'd have to pick one for a boy and one for a girl, since there's no knowing."

"That would be wise."

He sat quietly for a moment and pressed his knuckles to the floor. "I like the name Jacob. My pawpaw's name was Jacob."

With the tip of her finger, she traced a line of grain in the maple. "That's a good name."

Slowly, he rose and wiped dust from his pants. "I better get back to work." She felt his fingertips brush her shoulder, and he was gone.

Lonnie didn't move. She replayed his words in her mind, hope building inside her. Were her prayers being answered? Tilting her face to the ceiling, she closed her eyes. *Please, Lord, let it be so.* Reaching, she pushed the cradle into motion.

Where there was only smooth maple, Lonnie pictured cozy blankets knit from the softest wool and a tiny face peeking out at her. As a little girl, she had never imagined being a mother, but now that she was almost one, she could not wait to hold her precious child in her arms and—

A kick!

Lonnie gasped. She placed a hand where life had made its presence known, and smiled. It was not the first time she had felt the baby, but each small kick and wiggle filled her with joy. She closed her eyes and tried to imagine whether it was a hand or foot that pressed against her, but as quickly as the baby moved, it stilled, and she felt a different sensation. It started low in her back, then worked forward and down. Her breath halted, and she clutched the rocker beside her. The horrible grip tightened, as if her insides were a rag being wrung out.

"Gideon!" she cried, even as her vision blurred. Then the pain released its hold and her body relaxed. She sank back and tilted her face to the ceiling that seemed to sway with every beat of her racing pulse.

Elsie stormed up the stairs and stopped in the open doorway, her wrinkled features etched with fear. "He's outside. What's the matter?"

"I don't know." Elsie's face blurred as tears pooled in Lonnie's eyes.

Elsie dropped to her side and pulled her into an embrace. "Shh, shh," she whispered and ran a soothing hand down Lonnie's back. "Was it the baby?"

Lonnie nodded and swallowed. "I don't know what it was."

A cool hand covered her stomach, sliding from side to side. "Might have been a birth pain. How do you feel now?"

"A little tender, but it doesn't hurt like it did before. Is the baby gonna be all right?"

"Should be. I wish I knew more about this than I do." Elsie rose. "Do you want me to have Gid fetch Aunt Orla?"

Lonnie wiped her forehead. "Who?"

Elsie smoothed Lonnie's hair away from her face and tucked it into her braid as only a mother could. "She's the midwife. Gideon could leave and have her back here in no time."

The pain was gone. Lonnie stared at the empty cradle, knowing it was much too soon to be thinking about the baby coming. "I feel better now."

"If you're not in pain anymore, maybe everything is fine." Elsie paused, and Lonnie knew she had more to say. "It may happen from time to time, but if it's severe or if…" She hesitated. "If there was blood…"

Lonnie felt her eyes widen.

"You check." Elsie patted her hand. "I'll heat some tea. I have something that should soothe your muscles a bit, and then you can lie down and rest. I want you off your feet for the rest of the day." Elsie bustled from the room.

As Lonnie changed into her nightgown, her hands trembled with fear. When she saw that all was well, she closed her eyes and nearly fell as relief washed through her.

When Elsie returned with a cup, her mouth was drawn in a tight line. "So?"

"Nothing."

"Praise the Lord. That's a good sign." She handed Lonnie the tea. "Now drink this and don't get out of bed. Do you want me to send Gid just in case?"

Lonnie sipped the hot brew. "I feel better now."

"Well…" Elsie lifted her eyebrows. "If it happens again, you tell me."

"I promise I will." Lonnie took another sip.

"Try and rest a bit."

"Yes ma'am."

Elsie straightened the blankets and tucked them under Lonnie's elbow. She fluffed the pillow and made sure there was an extra covering, then checked that the window was closed snug. She turned to leave. "Are you sure you don't want me to—"

Lonnie nodded but willed her cup not to shake between her hands. "I am."

Thirty-Five

A tumble of clouds blocked out the last of the sunlight as Lonnie waddled down the path to the henhouse in search of eggs. Wrapping her arms around her chest, she shivered and wished she'd grabbed more than a shawl. Gideon waved as she passed the barn. Lonnie waved back, feeling a stirring inside that seemed to intensify with each passing day. She ducked through the small doorway and into the room where half a dozen hens roamed. They flapped out of her way when she checked the roosting boxes. She found only two eggs, but considering the cold weather, that was good. When the stubborn door wouldn't close right, she pushed it shut with a grunt. The wind stung her cheeks, and she clutched her hair before it could whip about.

Gideon set down a loaded wheelbarrow to wave again as Lonnie passed back by. Her shoes scurried along, barely grazing the snow as she headed to the house. She nearly tripped when Gideon flashed her a disarming smile.

The door slammed as she panted into the kitchen. Elsie looked up and eyed Lonnie curiously.

"Here are the eggs." Lonnie set them near the cutting board. "Supper's smelling good. What can I help you do?" She rubbed her hands together over the stove.

Elsie waved a flour-covered hand in the air. "Just sit and chat with me." She brushed away a gray lock and tucked it behind her ear, leaving a white streak across her wrinkled cheek. Her copper eyes sparkled with mischief.

Curious, Lonnie did as told, but before she had pulled out a chair, she spotted a small stack of mail in the center of the table. Her name, written in her ma's scratchy hand, sat on top. Lonnie gasped.

"Thought you'd be surprised." Elsie wiped her palms on her apron. "Jebediah picked those up weeks ago. Found them in a nook in the barn just now." She shook her head. "Somethin' about having been in a hurry." Elsie let out a fond laugh. "That man."

"It's been months since I first wrote my folks." Lonnie pulled out a chair and wasted no time tearing into the envelope. "I was beginning to wonder if we'd ever get word."

"I bet they miss you something terrible," Elsie said. Her voice held a hint of sorrow.

Lonnie unfolded the page to find that a letter from her aunt was tucked inside. Her chest swelled. She read through the letters quickly, knowing full well she'd read them again and again over the coming weeks. By the time Elsie had set three loaves to rise, Lonnie was folding the pages and sliding them back into the torn envelope.

She pulled the rest of the stack closer and saw that one was for Gideon. His ma's name was written in careful print in the corner. Another letter was also addressed to him—the penmanship graceful, methodical. There was no other name on the envelope. Lonnie felt the thin parcel and fought the urge to hold it up to the light.

"Somethin' wrong?" Elsie asked.

Lonnie glanced up to see that the woman had stopped working. "Nothing." She cleared her throat. "I was just thinking that I should go show Gideon."

Elsie kneaded another mound of dough in silence. Staring into the yard, Lonnie watched Gideon stride toward the house, burdened with an armload of firewood. His breath blew white as smoke. The wind whipped at his open coat.

She rose, pinched a piece of dough from Elsie's board, and chewed the sweet dough as she flung on her shawl. Outside, the wind nipped at her cheeks, and she shivered. A few snowflakes fluttered down. She blinked up at a dark and ominous sky. She clutched Gideon's letters to her chest and walked toward him. Her gait was slow and awkward.

"Whatcha got there?"

She held them out, the wind trying to tug them from her grasp. "Letters from home." She smiled.

Gideon tugged off his work gloves. "That so?" He took them from her, and his eyebrows pinched together as he read the first envelope. "Jebediah had these weeks ago." He shook his head, a grin warming his scruffy jaw. "Crazy old goat," he muttered. He flipped to the second letter. His smile faded as his eyes scanned over his name written in the flowery script. "Hmm." Moistening his lips, Gideon continued to study it.

Her curiosity heightened, Lonnie stepped closer and touched his arm. "Something wrong?"

He blinked down at the envelope, turning it over. It was blank.

"It doesn't say who it's from," she offered, hoping to make sense of the shift in his demeanor. The wind stirred her hair, and with cold fingers, she brushed the thin strands from her face. The snow seemed to fall quicker.

"No, it doesn't," he said softly, almost inaudibly. He studied her, his expression strangely urgent. As if finally noticing the rising storm, Gideon motioned to the barn. "Follow me." They hurried under the eaves, and he pulled the door open. He waited until she ducked into the doorway and then stood beside her, his back to the jamb. The light was dimming.

"What would you say"—his eyes found hers; his gaze was so intense Lonnie couldn't look away—"if I were to say this might have meant something to me at one time in my life?" He held the letter out, and it seemed to fill the space between them.

Lonnie swallowed, uncertain of how to respond. The wind tugged at her skirt, flapping it around her legs.

"But not anymore." His forehead crinkled as he looked down at the envelope. "I don't know who it's from." With his chin to his chest, his voice was soft. "I'm sorry to say it could be from a handful of girls." His hair danced in the rising breeze, and he nodded. "I have no desire to open it." He moved closer to her and held the letter out. Evening light moved across his face. "Because I…I have you."

She drew in a slow breath, which she held until it burned. "Me?" she finally whispered.

He nodded.

She took the letter.

"I don't want to be that man anymore." He touched her elbow. "For your sake." His lashes fell. "For the baby's."

Her heart throbbed. With the future shining in his eyes and his past in her hand, Lonnie felt torn. "No going back?" She eyed him, needing to be certain.

He shook his head. "No going back."

A smile bubbled up inside her, and Lonnie held out the envelope. "Then I don't want to look back."

He took it from her and seemed to study her a moment before he tore the letter in two. He tore it again, and with a sigh that seemed to lighten his heart, Gideon tossed the pieces to the wind. They landed haphazardly in the snow, only to stir out of sight. He pulled her farther into the barn, farther into the warmth. "I'm just sorry it took me so long to see what I had." The back of his hand brushed against her stomach, and he turned his wrist to let his fingers graze the gingham that covered her round belly.

Lonnie's eyelids faltered and her head went light. Her mouth parted to speak, but he shook his head.

"Please, let me say this." He drew in a deep breath and forced his eyes to meet hers. "I failed you so many times, beginning the night I walked you home." He hung his head as if the guilt from that night punched the air from his chest. "I hurt you. I never should have done that." His voice thinned, and when he looked at her in such agony, words failed her. "Oh, Lonnie. I did so many things."

His plaid coat fell open, inviting her in. Her forehead pressed to his chest. "Gid."

He groaned and stepped back, peering into her face. "That night when we made camp and we met…" His throat thickened. "The time with Bert—when I should have done more." He paused, shaking his head slowly, eyebrows clamped together. "I've been so unworthy. I'm so sorry." He cupped the sides of her head, pressing his lips to her hair.

"I forgive you." Her eyes searched his, and when his face didn't brighten, her cool palm found his cheek. "But perhaps it's more than my forgiveness that you need."

Thirty-Six

Checking the last trap, Gideon saw that it was empty. With a pair of rabbits already slung over his shoulder, it was just as well. His thoughts turned to the evening before. The letter he'd torn. The look in his wife's eyes when he answered a question she never should have had to ask. For the first time in a long time, Gideon's heart soared. With Lonnie by his side, the future suddenly looked bright. And a baby on the way—someone to call him Papa. He still wasn't sure what to make of that, but he was realizing it wasn't a burden.

What did it matter if there was another mouth to feed? By the sweat of his own back, he'd see the child cared for. Wasn't that what his pa had done for him? Whether he'd taken the time to appreciate it or not? Nearing the creek, Gideon scaled the bank, his steps steady in the fresh snow. He heaved a slow, heavy sigh. The world had a different light to it now. Jebediah's words rang in his mind as they often had the last few months.

When a man has a baby, he comes third.

Was he ready for that? Crouching, Gideon dipped his hand in the icy water. With Lonnie's heart in the balance, it was time to step up. He was determined to never risk her again. He should have lost her already.

By some unseen mercy, he hadn't. So why did he suddenly feel so uneasy? With quick knife work, he cleaned the rabbits, then rinsed his blade in the water.

Gideon knew the baby would be born under the Bennetts' roof. He'd heard the invitation from Elsie's lips. And as for Jebediah, the old man had made it clear. More than once. Gideon's legs were stiff when he stood, but he was eager to get home. With the limp feet in his grip, he lunged up the bank. His damp hands chilled in the morning air. The sky was clear overhead, last night's storm having blown past before dawn. The land stood bright in its whiteness. Almost blinding. Branches glittered beneath their collection of new snow, and the crisp air was perfectly still. He glanced around, and a nagging feeling tugged at his conscience. Gideon shook his head, trying to toss it off.

Rounding the bend, he spotted the house, nearly invisible in its white surroundings. When he strode into the yard, Lonnie was on the porch, a hand shielding her eyes. She set a basket of laundry at her feet, and her belly seemed even bigger in the morning light. Gideon's chest swelled, and he fought against the melancholy that threatened to sink in.

He made his way toward her. "How ya feelin'?" he asked, chagrined when he realized it was for the first time.

"Fine, mostly." Something in her eyes made him doubt her words. She must have sensed it. "Well, a little achy. But not all the time."

"Is that normal?"

"Maybe. I'm not really sure."

A tremor mixed with the unsettled feeling already in his gut. "I want you to take good care of yourself. Will you do that for me?"

She nodded, and he saw that he had pleased her.

"I better get these to Elsie." He held up the pair of rabbits. "I'll wash up and be back in a few minutes."

Lonnie picked up her basket, perched it awkwardly on her hip, and walked toward the clothesline. Gideon scaled the porch steps in two strides. At the table, Elsie and Jebediah looked up when he came in. Their conversation clipped to an abrupt end.

"Talkin' about me again, Jeb?" Gideon chuckled and glanced to Elsie. "Don't believe a word he says."

Her small eyes were warm, and when she tilted her teacup to her lips, a smile flashed behind the white porcelain.

"Never you mind what he says." Elsie motioned to Jebediah. "I still like you."

"Now, now." Jebediah leaned an elbow back on his chair. "You're gonna get me into trouble, woman." He looked to Gideon, fondness in his wrinkled face. Gideon knew he had a friend in Jebediah. No, he had much more than that.

But why that was, he couldn't begin to guess. Never once had he deserved the man's kindness. Never once did he deserve his mercy.

Gideon left the rabbits for Elsie and went upstairs to wash. He unbuttoned his soiled shirt and tossed it on the edge of the bed. The water in the basin was cold, but he scrubbed his arms, then ran a wet hand over his face. He dried his forehead and cheeks on a rough towel. He moved to the dresser and dug through his things before he spotted a clean shirt at the bottom. After shaking out the wrinkles, Gideon slid one arm in and then the other. He pushed the top button into place when something caught the sunlight that came in through the window. His hands stilled.

He reached in and pulled out Bert's pocket watch. He hated the feel of it in his hand. Hated everything it reminded him of. He'd shoved it into the drawer, where it had fallen to the bottom. Why had he been so stupid? He thought of Bert's men and the way they spoke of Lonnie.

His shoulders tensed at the thought of them coming around looking for him. If they were to find him…

No. He couldn't let that happen. He set the watch on top of the dresser and grabbed his coat. He put it on and folded the collar down, catching Lonnie's faint scent from the flannel. He knew he would never forget the way she'd looked at him the night before. Or the promise he'd made her. No looking back.

He picked up the watch again, and a muscle worked in his jaw. With hesitant fingers, he opened it. Having been neglected all these months, the hands stood motionless. He closed the watch—the remnant of his old life that he did not want around. He'd promised Bert it would be returned. Gideon glanced out the window where the morning sun burned through the treetops. It was time to make good on that promise.

Thirty-Seven

Gideon looked behind him and made sure no one was around. He stepped past the stove and paused. His eyes found the enamel pitcher. With one more glance around the kitchen, he pulled the pitcher down and felt inside. His fingertips nabbed the pouch of coins. Gideon slipped it inside his pocket soundlessly, though guilt made his hand shake.

"You're only borrowing it," he murmured to himself.

If Bert crossed his path, Gideon needed some insurance. *And then I'm done.* No more Bert. No more former life. He patted his coat where the pocket watch nestled against his chest.

Once he got to town, he would trade the skins he had cut and cleaned—products of his own hard work. Any money he might borrow from Jebediah's stash would be fully returned. Gideon patted his pocket. The coins jingled softly. There was no need to worry.

The air was gray when Lonnie opened her eyes, the sheets beside her cold. A piece of paper lay on Gideon's pillow, and she struggled to sit up.

She tipped the words to the early morning light and tried to make out his crooked scrawl.

On an errand. Be home soon.

Her eyebrows knit together. Clatter from the kitchen drew her out of bed. She dressed slowly and made her way down the stairs.

Elsie sat at the table, paring knife in hand. She lifted an apple from a bucket at her feet. "Mornin'."

"Did you see Gideon leave?"

"I thought he was sleeping in."

"No. He left a note that said he had an errand to run but that he would be home soon. Do you have any idea what it could be?"

"No." A coil of red, wrinkled apple skin dropped onto the table. "But if he said he'd be home soon, then he'll be home before you know it. How about a cup of tea?"

"I'll get it." Lonnie pulled two cups from the cupboard.

With Gideon gone, the house was strangely quiet.

"What are you making?"

"Applesauce." Elsie plopped a core in a bowl. "These apples have seen better days."

Lonnie poured the tea, then helped Elsie with the task. When Lonnie paused to rub her lower back, Elsie followed the movement.

"How are you feeling?" she asked.

Lonnie picked up another apple and sliced it in half. "Pretty good." She shrugged. "I'm not really sure what I'm supposed to feel like."

Elsie smiled. "I wish I could be more help. I know some about this, but…" She studied Lonnie. "Well, it's been years. Mind you, I won't tell you how many." She plucked a leaf from an apple, her expression soft.

Lonnie moved to the stockpot and dumped in a handful of slices. "I bet you were a wonderful mother."

Elsie pursed her lips when a mixture of emotion passed through her copper eyes. "Thank you." A coil of red skin fell into her lap. "I wish I could have…" She set the apple on the cutting board but made no move to slice it. "I wish I could have had more time."

Lonnie pressed her cheek to Elsie's shoulder. "I'm so sorry," she whispered.

Elsie pressed her cheek to the top of Lonnie's head, and they stayed that way for several moments. "Look at me," Elsie finally said. She dabbed at her eyes with the hem of her apron. "Carryin' on in the middle of the day when there's work to be done." She pushed her knife through the apple.

"You have to be the strongest woman I know," Lonnie said.

Elsie rose and tipped her chin. "Why, thank you. I never get through a day on my own."

Knowing what she meant, Lonnie smiled. "It shows. I hope to have your faith one day."

Elsie stirred the softening apples with her longest spoon. She tapped the wooden handle on the edge of the pot. "I'd say you've got your share of faith, little missy." Her eyes sparkled. "I'd say you're doin' a right fine job."

The side of Lonnie's mouth turned up. She drew in a deep breath, and with an ache still in her back, she rubbed it again.

"Why don't you rest for a bit? There's nothing left to do but keep an eye on the pot."

When Elsie ducked outside to fetch jars from the cellar, Lonnie moved to the parlor and settled herself on the sofa. She unlaced her boots, freed her swollen feet, and stretched tired ankles before tucking her feet beneath her.

With her knitting basket in her lap, she pulled out a tiny cap she'd been working on. Her tongue found the hollow of her cheek as she concentrated on each yellow loop. She hummed a nameless tune in rhythm with the gentle click of her needles. Her eyes lifted to the window, her thoughts on Gideon. She wished he'd given her a chance to say good-bye. With a prayer on her heart, she reminded herself he'd most certainly be home for dinner at noon.

After a row was complete, she shifted in her seat. A few moments later, she shifted again. Was there no comfortable position? Lonnie set the knitting in her lap long enough to knead her aching muscles. She let out a weary sigh and stretched her neck from side to side.

Her needles found where they left off, and the clicking began once more. Her slightly swollen fingers tingled, making it difficult to work with accuracy. She scrutinized a row of tiny loops; the yellow yarn weaved in and out in a crooked pattern, and Lonnie grunted as she tugged the yarn loose. A second attempt only produced the same result. Dropping her work in her lap, she leaned her head against the back of the sofa and closed her eyes. *This is hopeless.*

She laid her knitting basket on the floor and scooted it out of the way. The baby's cap would have to wait until she got a little rest. She slid a pillow beneath her head, propped her feet on the sofa, and closed her eyes, allowing the quiet of the morning to lull her to sleep. It wasn't until a chunk of wood clanged into the stove that Lonnie's eyes fluttered open. She rolled onto her side and peered into the kitchen, but all she could see was the table. The door creaked shut. She glanced to the window, where the midday sun shone bright. The smell of cinnamon and apples pulled her from her nest and carried her into the kitchen, where she stood in the doorway and yawned.

"Have a good nap?" Elsie popped a loaf of bread out of a pan.

Lonnie ran her fingers across her eyes and nodded. "Gideon home?"

"Afraid not." Elsie eyed her curiously. "Are you feelin' all right?"

She stared out the window, wishing he would appear on the pathway. She knew her words sounded distant. "A little drowsy, but I feel fine."

"Hmm." A touch from Elsie brought Lonnie's attention back to the kitchen. "Why don't you have a seat?" She stirred the mush bubbling on the back of the stove. "You can keep me company."

"I should lend you a hand." Lonnie moved forward. Her steps were slow. "I've been feeling sluggish lately. I'm exhausted every day. I don't know how I'm going to manage for another few months."

Elsie nodded. "Little ones will do that to a mother. But spring's about here. The baby won't be long after."

Lonnie gasped. The child inside her moved, and she placed Elsie's pudgy hand against her dress.

Elsie's mouth parted. "Oh. What a dear." Her gaze softened on the empty space between them. "I can't believe how quickly the baby's grown."

"Me neither." She felt her stomach, stunned at how much baby could fit inside her. She started to set the table, and by the time she folded the last napkin, her aching back forced her up the stairs, where she sank into the mattress with a soft moan. Tucking her hands beneath her cheek, she closed her eyes. *Be safe, Gideon.* A prayer lifted from her heart. The stirring of worry grew.

Thirty-Eight

Gideon whistled as he walked, and although it made the solitude pass easier, his steps were slow in the fresh snow. One glance at the lifting sun and he knew he was not making good time. All the same, he would be there soon. He sighed, feeling the sun higher on the horizon than he liked. He knew it wouldn't be a bad idea to keep an eye out for a place to stay. Just in case.

He stuffed his hands into his pockets. It was a tight fit with his gloves on, but some habits never faded. After a dozen more paces, he slung his pack off his shoulder. Long before daybreak, he'd stuffed the rest of yesterday's bread in the bottom, followed by a jar of cider. It wasn't much, but he planned on being home before sunset. He tore off a chunk of bread before tossing his pack back into place.

Gideon crammed the bread in his mouth as he glanced behind him. His were the only tracks except for those of a deer and a few birds. He was completely alone. He shook his head, hoping this wasn't as crazy as it felt. But he remembered Bert, and he quickened his pace. He wasn't about to let that man anywhere near Lonnie.

That was all he needed to know.

When the trail split, he slowed. He was certain he remembered where Bert's camp was, but Gideon kept to the path toward town. On the way back, once he had enough money to cover his debt, he'd veer toward the right and hopefully find Bert. Patting his coat pocket, he felt the coin pouch, certain he would have no need of it.

Lonnie pressed her hand to her throat, but her skin was cool. She leaned against the pillows and laid her hand on her forehead, but her skin held no hint of a fever. Then why did she feel so terrible? She blinked up at the ceiling. It had to be something different. Crossing her arms over her stomach, she rolled onto her side and let her eyes fall closed, but even in the darkness of her mind, the room spun.

Was that Elsie calling her?

Lonnie sat up, and her feet fell to the floor like lead weights. She grunted to a standing position and shuffled to the door. Every step was an effort as she descended the stairs. Halfway down, Lonnie paused, placed her palm to the wall, and, fearing she would faint, sank onto the step behind her. Even as she dropped her head into her hands, she fought to keep her eyes open. *Come on, Lonnie.* With a groan, she forced herself to stand and took one weary step after another.

As she crossed the parlor, a faint pain struck low in her back. It started slow at first, then pulsed deeper. She sucked in a shaky breath and let it out slowly as the pain released its grip. She stood motionless for several minutes, and her breathing steadied. She straightened, surprised at how quickly the pain had come and gone.

"That you, Lonnie?"

She turned to see Elsie with her head in the cabinet under the stairs.

The older woman sat back and frowned even as she pulled a cobweb from her tidy bun. "What have I gotten myself into?" She brushed the dust off her apron and struggled to her feet.

"What are you doing down there?"

Elsie closed the cabinet door. "Oh, I had some baby things from long ago. I know I saved them…" Her voice trailed off as she glanced around the parlor. "I just can't remember where." She smoothed a hand over her hair and seemed lost in thought. "It will come to me. I've gotten forgetful over the years. Sometimes it just takes a moment or two for my mind to find itself again."

"Can I help? I'm good at findin' things." Lonnie straightened a stack of books on the end table and, using the edge of her apron, wiped a volume of poetry clean of dust. "I had four brothers and sisters. Someone was always losin' something if they weren't losin' each other." A bead of sweat trickled down her temple. She brushed it away but caught wise eyes following the motion. Lonnie picked up the broom and started sweeping.

"You feelin' all right?"

Lonnie fanned herself with her hand. "I'm just a little warm. It feels hot in here for some reason." The sun sank lower in the window. She wished Gideon would come home.

"I've got a good fire going." Elsie hurried to open a window. "Figured the men will need it when they come in." A gust of cool air filled the parlor, and Lonnie closed her eyes, finding comfort in Elsie's confidence. Gideon would be home soon. If only she knew why he'd left in the first place.

"It's a cold one out there today," Elsie murmured against the glass. She turned and studied Lonnie. "Have you had any pains?"

"Some. But not much."

Elsie pursed her lips together. "Well, no sense in overdoing it, then. Why don't you go have a lie down?"

"I'm fine, really. I don't want to be a burden." Lonnie felt Elsie's eyes on her as she worked her way to the back porch. "Besides, I've been resting all morning."

Elsie seemed hesitant to let her go. "Promise me you'll take it easy now."

Lonnie smiled over her shoulder, thankful for Elsie's help. "I will." She stepped out and breathed in the cool air. She kept one hand on the broom and placed the other on the side of her stomach. Her child moved beneath her fingers. Lonnie circled her belly, trying to feel it all at once. "Hello there, little one. Are ya getting antsy?" She waddled to the edge of the porch. "You're just like your pa. Be patient now. You've got a while yet."

Her words were light, but closing her eyes, she sent a desperate plea heavenward, praying that her child was in no hurry to meet the world. Willow scraped across weatherworn pine as she started on the top step.

She did not come out here often. Most everybody used the back door; it was the fastest way into the kitchen and the most likely place to find Elsie. As she took the beauty in, Lonnie allowed her thoughts to drift. One thing circled in her mind these days—what she would name the baby. Picking a name for a girl had proved to be easier than choosing one for a boy. *Maddy* and *Sarah* were her favorites, and while she tossed around a few names for a son, she could only narrow it down to two. She favored the name *Adam,* but when Gideon suggested *Jacob,* it stuck with her.

Through the window, she spotted Elsie scrubbing at the glass until it shone. Lonnie moved the broom over the boards.

Her body warmed, and Lonnie caught hold of her stomach just as it tightened. An unwelcome sensation shifted through her, and her eyes widened. She dropped the broom against the house and did her best to hurry through the parlor and up the stairs. Even as the bedroom door slammed behind her, she yanked at the folds of her apron and skirts.

Elsie's footsteps pounded behind her, but Lonnie screamed her name regardless.

The bedroom door burst open. "Heavens, child! You scared me half to death."

"It's serious." Lonnie stumbled sideways and caught herself on the brass headboard.

Elsie's face paled. "What do you mean?"

Lonnie closed her eyes. "There's blood."

"How much?" Elsie stepped closer.

"Not much." How much was enough? Lonnie's hands trembled as she clutched them to her chest. "My baby," she mouthed.

"Has this happened before?"

"No." She hadn't felt pain like that ever. Was it enough to draw the baby out of her? take away the life she had been growing? Her and Gideon's child. Her voice trembled when she spoke. "Elsie, what does this mean?" The longer it took Elsie to reply, the smaller the hope in Lonnie's heart became.

"I'm not too sure. I've been to plenty of births, but I ain't too keen on the beforehand stuff."

A tear slipped down Lonnie's cheek, and she smeared it away. "How will I know what to do?"

Elsie shook her head. "Time. That's my guess. The more time, the better."

"My time's comin', isn't it, Elsie?" Lonnie turned away, not wanting a response. The clock on the wall ticked away the seconds. Seconds that her baby was still alive and safe. *God,* Lonnie cried in her heart. *Keep this child safe. Just a little longer. Please, God. Don't take my baby away from me now.*

She watched Elsie's face change from concern to sorrow. "We should fetch the midwife."

"Gideon." The word slipped out in a whimper.

"I know." Elsie moved to her side and slid an arm around her shoulders. "That baby's not comin' just yet, and Gideon'll be home before you know it." Elsie squeezed her hand, her face urgent. "I'll go tell Jebediah right now. It shouldn't take long to fetch her. In the meantime, I want you in that bed. I'll be back in just a minute." She released Lonnie and hurried from the room. Lonnie stood motionless in the center. She could do nothing but listen to the pendulum on the grandfather clock below tick slowly from side to side.

Thirty-Nine

Elsie had hardly been gone two minutes when Lonnie peered out the bedroom window and saw Jebediah stride across the yard, his pace quick. Within a few hours, his shadow would fall on the midwife's door, and they would be back as soon as they could. The thought of summoning the woman sent a shudder of fear through Lonnie. Her fingertips grazed the glass. *Where are you, Gideon? Come home.*

She bent over and struggled out of her wool stockings. With a gasp, her body arched up. A dull cramp seized the muscles low in her stomach, nearly taking her breath away. She massaged the tender spot, and although the pain eased, it did not fade completely. Her cheeks tingled as she struggled to stand upright. She held her belly in one hand and pushed against the bed with the other. With a groan, she reached for her shoes. "Uh!" The spasm pierced her again. Lonnie bit back a yelp and lay against the pillows. With her feet still on the floor, she stared at the ceiling.

Delay this, God.

Though she tried to keep herself calm, a squeal escaped her lips. The ceiling faded to a blur, and she rested the back of her hand over her eyes. It took the last of her strength, but Lonnie slipped her feet under the cool sheets and sighed into the feather pillow. *Perhaps if I just rest.* If she could sleep, the baby would not be able to go anywhere. Lonnie pulled the quilts over her body and closed her eyes. She steadied her breathing and forced herself to relax. *Just hold on, little one.*

She lay that way for several minutes and then shifted. Was there no way to get comfortable? Lonnie rolled onto her side and clutched Gideon's pillow to her chest. She blinked up at the window. *Where are you, Gideon?* She pressed her nose to his pillow. Squeezing her eyes tight, she sent up a quick prayer for him.

Elsie tapped on the door and bustled back in. "How are you faring?"

"Fine," Lonnie said softly.

Elsie smoothed her hair away from her face. "Jeb should be back before nightfall." She lifted her face to the window. "And hopefully Gideon will be home before then." Her hand stilled. "His note didn't say anything about—"

"No. Just that he would be home soon." Lonnie squeezed his pillow tighter.

The quilt was cool when Elsie tucked it beneath Lonnie's chin. "You just rest now. I'll keep an eye out for both our husbands."

Lonnie closed her eyes and tried to read what her body was telling her. The ache had faded, but sometimes it rose again. A tightening that she couldn't describe. She forced her breathing steady and tried to count the weeks she'd been carrying the baby. A pain began, and she opened her eyes. The pain intensified. She gasped. "Elsie," she said weakly. The dull ache rose into a burning, and Lonnie's breath cut off short. When it passed, she struggled to sit up. "Elsie!" she called as loudly as she could, but her throat was tight.

Footsteps sounded on the stairs. "Are you all right?"

Lonnie flung back the sheets to see that her nightgown was wet.

"Mercy. Have you had more pains?"

Lonnie's hair tumbled from her unraveling braid when she shook her head. "It's been hurting and I don't know what to do!" She tried to stand, but Elsie stopped her.

"How close together?"

"I don't know," she cried.

"I need you to keep still. No walkin' around." Elsie tightened her grip on Lonnie's elbow. "This baby might be comin' whether we want it to or not."

"Is the baby going to die?"

Lonnie's words hung in the air, unanswered. She whimpered.

Elsie tightened her grip on her arm. "We will do everything we can. And the midwife will be here soon."

Lonnie struggled to stand. Another pain came. It grew and grew. Just when she thought it was going to stretch her body to the limits, it faded away. Overwhelmed, Lonnie leaned her cheek against Elsie's shoulder. She needed Gideon.

"Was that another one?"

Lonnie nodded, fearing the worst when Elsie's face darkened.

The older woman touched trembling fingers to her lips, then lowered her hand, shoulders square. "I'm here. I'm not going to leave you, and Orla will be her soon."

"Will she know what to do?"

Elsie pursed her lips and sank onto the bed. Her hand was cool when she took hold of Lonnie's, and her eyes slid closed. Lonnie tried not to cry, but she could not help it. Elsie's fingers trembled as she prayed, and Lonnie felt air leave her chest as if she'd been struck with a blow.

They both knew the truth. It was too soon.

Forty

Gideon thrust his hand into his pocket yet again and grinned. He had spent less than two hours in town, and even in his rush, he had delivered Lonnie's letters and sold his entire bundle of furs. Cold coins jingled against his fingers. He now had two and a half dollars to his name. Not much, but it was a start all the same. Soon his debt would be paid.

He drew in a chestful of chilly mountain air as he neared the spot where he'd seen Bert's still. Slowing, Gideon dusted the remains of his dinner off his coat and swiped a hand across his mouth.

A tune he recognized floated on the breeze, and as Gideon came around the bend, he saw a small shanty, the same one he'd spotted the day he'd been to Bert's still. Gideon glanced around, realizing it wasn't far off. An old man sat on a rickety porch, carving knife in hand. The gray-haired man sat hunched over, clearly engrossed in his work. His hat tipped forward, blocking out the late afternoon sun. Not wanting to startle him, Gideon took a cautious step closer.

He looked up when Gideon approached. "Don't even think about robbin' me. I ain't got a dime." The old man snatched up a cane and poked at the ground near Gideon's feet.

Gideon's hands flew up. "I wasn't going to rob you, sir. I'm just passin' through."

The man grumbled something about young uns and tipped his hat back. "Few folks come up this way." He glared at Gideon, his stick held in front of him. "Unless they're lookin' for somethin'."

And he was.

"See that trail?" the old man mumbled without looking up.

Gideon nodded.

"It ends here. Anyone who passes on is askin' for nothin' but trouble."

Gideon studied the trail of footprints in the snow that disappeared into thick brush. He took a step forward and tipped his hat.

The man eyed Gideon. "Don't say I didn't warn ya."

Gideon stepped into the trees. He climbed for several minutes. A branch snagged on his coat, and he pushed it away. Ducking beneath the branches of a laurel bush, he stepped into a small clearing. A firepit held nothing but gray ashes, smoke trailing skyward in a flag of surrender. Men didn't often leave their stills unattended. It struck him as odd. Gideon glanced around at the empty place when the silence gave him an eerie feel. Where had they gone?

"Drink this now. It will ease the pain a bit." Elsie tipped the steaming cup to Lonnie's lips. "Just tiny sips now."

Lonnie swallowed and panted for breath before sinking into the pillow. The clock in the parlor chimed twice.

Elsie said nothing of Jebediah, and Lonnie feared that the midwife might have already been called away.

Through a veil of tears, Lonnie looked up. "Gideon?"

"I know, honey. I know." A cool cloth touched her cheek. "He will be here as soon as he can."

Frustration burned the back of her throat. Lonnie stared at the window. Another spasm found her, and she curled onto her side, gripping the brass headboard with white knuckles. "Elsie," she groaned and felt hair being pressed away from her face. The cool cloth smoothed down her cheek, and when the pain subsided, the room brightened as Elsie flung back the curtains.

With her face near the window, the woman stared into the yard and sighed. She turned back and took Lonnie's hand. "You are doing so well. It will be over soon."

Lonnie's chin trembled as fear wrapped its hands around her. Her carrying time was over too soon. Would the baby be strong enough? She stared up at the ceiling as if to find the answer written there.

"It will be over before you know it," Elsie whispered again. Words meant to soothe fell like daggers to Lonnie's heart.

A door slammed below. Elsie rushed out of the room, then returned just as quick. "They're here," she breathed.

"This little thing?" a cool voice drawled.

Lonnie's eyelids fluttered open.

A wrinkled face hovered above her, and a pair of sunken eyes peered through wire-rimmed spectacles. The old woman frowned. "She don't look a day past thirteen."

"This is Aunt Orla." Elsie patted Lonnie's arm.

Lonnie moaned.

Orla placed a hand low on Lonnie's stomach. "Hmm," she mumbled and raised silver eyebrows. "Baby's comin', that's for sure."

Reluctantly, Lonnie bobbed her head.

"How old are you?" Orla pulled off her spectacles.

"Eighteen."

"Well, that ain't too young at all." She picked up her doctor's bag and dropped it on the bed. "I've seen 'em younger."

"How will the baby be?" Elsie's voice trembled. "Is it too soon?"

Orla bumped Lonnie's leg as she sat. "How long you been carryin'?"

Lonnie glanced from one face to the other. "Over seven months."

Orla inched her bag onto the nightstand. "Don't you trouble yourself about it. I've seen them come out as soon and be fine. You're doin' all right now, you just sit tight."

Lonnie sank into the pillows and watched Orla take out a bottle of auburn liquid and set it on the nightstand. "Apple brandy," she said to Elsie, before pulling out a pair of scissors and a ball of heavy string. "See that these get boiled." She held the offerings out to Elsie, who hurried away.

Lonnie rolled onto her side and cried out, and Orla held her hand and spoke in hushed tones. When it ended, the hunched woman straightened the blanket and looked up as Elsie strode in. "How often is the pain comin' on?"

"It was every few minutes." Elsie set a handful of candlesticks on the dresser. "But now it seems to come quicker."

The wrinkles around Orla's mouth puckered.

Lonnie studied her face, hoping to get the answers she needed. The flesh beneath Orla's high cheekbones was sunken, and the clear wisdom shining through her eyes comforted Lonnie.

As if reading her thoughts, Orla adjusted her spectacles. "I've delivered more babies than I can count. I'm gonna take real good care of you." She rolled up the sleeves of her black dress and came around to the end of the bed. "You started those things boiling?"

Elsie bobbed her gray bun.

"Where's your husband?"

Lonnie felt Orla studying her. "Gid's gone today...should be back tonight or—" She squealed and gripped the sheets. Her heart thudded away the seconds, and when the pain finally passed, she peered up. "Is the baby coming *now*?" she panted.

"Well, let's see. Try and sit tight a bit, Lonnie. I'm going to check you over."

With her mouth pursed, Orla pulled a tube from her bag. She placed the small metal end in her ear, then slid the broad end over Lonnie's round stomach. The metal was cool against Lonnie's skin. Orla sat quiet as she listened. "You still got some time to go. Just hang in there." She removed a pair of small bottles from her bag before bustling to light another candle.

When Lonnie's chin trembled, a thin, rough hand squeezed hers. "You're doin' a fine job, li'l missy." Orla reached into her bag. "Don't worry, dear. There ain't no city doctor who knows what he's doing more than I do. I been catchin' babies for years."

Forty-One

Leaving the clearing, Gideon held his fingers to his mouth and blew warm air on them. It took him several minutes to trace his snowy trail back the way he had come. He spotted the shanty and strode toward it. He hoped the old man could give him the information he needed. Gideon rounded the tiny house.

Still in the same spot, the man looked up when Gideon approached. "What's your business, anyway?"

Gideon hitched his pack up higher. "I need to repay a debt."

The old man ran his knife through a soft piece of wood. "You ain't the first man to say that 'round here." A pair of small brown eyes searched Gideon's.

"I believe it."

"You gonna stand 'round waitin' all evenin'?"

"If that's what it takes." Gideon crouched against a tree and propped his forearm on his knee. The snow had already soaked through the hem of his pants. He peered up into the old face. "I'm ready to be free of this."

"So I see." The man pulled a pipe from his pocket and stuck it in the crook of his mouth, where it dangled, no match in sight.

Silence settled between them. Gideon opened his pack and broke off another piece of bread. His stomach rumbled as he chewed the dry crust. One glance at the changing sky and he frowned. Even if Bert returned by nightfall and he was able to set off for home, he wouldn't get far in the dark. Gideon hung his head in frustration, but there was no changing it.

He suddenly wished he'd left a better note for Lonnie. Worse, he wished he'd told her where he was going. But it was too late now. Glancing up at the sky, he knew his dry blanket would be no match for the layer of clouds lining the gray sky. He had passed an empty trapper's cabin on his way down and hoped to get that far before sunset.

"Any idea when they'll be back?"

The old man shrugged a bony shoulder, the arms beneath his dingy shirt wiry. "They went out lookin' for some fella. Heard 'em grumblin' about it as they passed by."

Gideon blinked up at him. His food turned to ash in his mouth.

"Someone's always owin' those boys money." The man pulled the pipe from his lips. "Ain't right the way they bully around this mountain." The breeze stirred the silver hair that grazed his shoulders.

Something inside Gideon turned ice cold. He rose as blood pulsed through his veins. If what this man said was true…if it was him they were looking for…

Gideon snatched up his pack and, without so much as a good-bye, darted from the clearing. A cold breeze crept beneath his thick layers of clothing with a boldness he did not like. The trail rose toward home—toward Lonnie—and his feet quickened as if a fire had been lit under his boots.

Elsie rushed in with an oil lamp just as the first candle flame burned down to a puddle of wax. "How is she?"

"She's as brave as they come." Orla smoothed her hand over Lonnie's stomach.

Lonnie could hardly hear over her own groans. She swiped at a bead of sweat, and Orla stuffed rags beneath her back.

"This is too much blood for my likin'," Orla murmured. Elsie knelt beside the bed, and the hunched woman shook her head. "I don't like this. Not one bit."

Nausea rose in Lonnie's stomach, and she tried to sit up. She cried out.

"I know it's hard, but try and stay calm. The baby needs you to relax."

"What's happening?" Elsie's voice was sharp.

Using the back of her hand, Orla pressed her spectacles farther up her nose.

Lonnie's chin fell to her chest and she grunted. Her jaw shook and her lips turned numb.

"You're a brave girl." Orla squeezed her hand. "Just breathe now and try to stay calm."

Despite Orla's caution, a squeal slipped from Lonnie's throat, and she sank into the mattress. Elsie slipped a wet rag inside Lonnie's sweaty palm, and she barely had time to clutch it before more pain seized her. This time, it struck her body harder than she'd ever felt before. Lonnie screamed. When the throbbing subsided, the crushed fabric fell to the floor.

"It hurts!" Lonnie cried, not caring if she looked like a fool. "It hurts so bad!"

Orla's voice rose stern. "You're gonna have to stay calm, Lonnie. This is almost over." She wiped her wrinkled forehead with the crease of her elbow. "You are so close."

"How close?" Lonnie grunted.

Wrinkled eyes blinked quickly. "I can see the baby." Her voice held a surprising tremor.

Orla's words slapped sense into Lonnie's heart, and she gritted her teeth.

"That's it!" The old woman had Elsie slide her arm behind Lonnie and help her sit up.

With her heels braced against the footboard, Lonnie gave her child every piece of strength she had left.

"Good girl!" Orla leaned over the brass bars.

Lonnie rested between surges, and each time the pain came, Orla promised her that the end was in sight. Lonnie groaned, and her fingernails dug into her palm through thin sheets. Then suddenly, she felt a burst of relief. Elsie's hands flew to her mouth, and Lonnie sank back—head spinning, chest heaving. She tossed her head to the side and gasped for breath, but there was no air to be had in the hot room.

Orla jabbered tensely to Elsie as they rushed about. Lonnie tried to lift her eyes to see her baby, but she was too weak. Moments ticked by like hours, and Lonnie forced her ears to be her eyes.

The room fell silent. Not a whisper. No cry.

Lonnie lifted her head. A hand squeezed her shoulder, and Elsie knelt beside her. "It's over, sweetheart. It's all over. You did so good." She kissed her forehead—her arms empty, her eyes full of tears.

"Where's the baby?"

"Elsie, I'm gonna need your help," Orla called.

Lonnie watched in agony as defeat darkened Orla's face. She wrapped the baby in a blanket, then handed the bundle to Elsie.

No, Lonnie mouthed soundlessly.

Orla pushed her spectacles up and glanced through the wire frames, her mouth taut.

"Can't you do something?" Lonnie cried as Elsie stepped closer. The bundle scarcely filled the crook of her arm. It was too small.

"I'm so sorry, Lonnie. The baby's gone." Orla's voice thinned. "Been gone for some time."

Her eyelids slammed closed, and Lonnie gasped for breath. "My baby," she moaned tearlessly. Her heart rampaged inside her chest as if to crush itself against her bones. She covered her face with her arm, and just as she did, another pain flexed its angry muscles inside her. "What's happening?" She choked the words out through her tears. Her stomach tightened, then burned.

"Lonnie?"

When she grabbed Elsie's hand, the older woman helped her sit up. After several seconds, the pain subsided, and Lonnie realized Elsie was handing her the tiniest bundle of a baby.

"No," Lonnie moaned at the sight of Elsie's crumpled face.

"A girl." Elsie tipped the baby, and Lonnie peered into the face of her child.

The lump in her throat choked her. *A girl?* Her hand shook as she pulled a flap of fabric away from a little nose, two eyes, and the tiniest mouth. Her fingers trembled against her baby's cool, dusky forehead. Lonnie brushed a tear from her eyes, too overwhelmed to piece together the whole truth, yet too certain of her loss to keep control.

"I'm so sorry," Elsie murmured.

Turning her soul and her body over to her grief, Lonnie sank against the mattress and shook with sobs. She lay that way for several minutes. Without warning, pain tightened around her belly. She cried out.

"Is this normal?" she heard Elsie exclaim. "Should she be feeling so much pain after the baby is born?"

Lonnie caught hold of Elsie's hand and squeezed. Death could take her now. She held her baby in her arms and prayed that heaven would summon her as well.

Orla's voice drew near. "I thought this might be..." She peered at Lonnie through her spectacles. "I didn't say anything. I didn't want to overwhelm you from the start."

"What do you mean?" Elsie insisted. She shook her head so fiercely, her bun tumbled out of place.

Orla glanced at Elsie and motioned toward the bundle. Elsie stepped forward, her hands grazing the blanket, and instinctively Lonnie tightened her grip. Orla peered down at Lonnie and squeezed her ankle in reassurance. "Give the baby to Elsie now, love." Orla's face was grave, but hope glinted in her old eyes. "There's another one comin'."

Forty-Two

Panting, Gideon clambered up the steep slope. Snow drenched his pants and slid inside his boots, but he struggled forward and, with a last grunt, scaled the top of the slope. He saw his footprints from that morning and felt a surge of relief that he was on the right path.

He straightened and hurried on as much as the deep snow would allow. The sun had vanished behind the trees. The light was gray. Ducking his head against an icy wind, Gideon strode forward, his heart thundering in his chest. But each footstep seemed harder than the last. Frustrated, a growl rose in his chest. He lost his footing and stumbled. His hands struck the snow, and he caught himself. The sleeves of his coat grew wet as he struggled to stand. Despite the cold, sweat dampened the fabric between his shoulder blades. He needed to get home to Lonnie. He needed to know she was all right. He took a few more steps, and when exhaustion poured through him, he pressed his palms to his knees, panting. The land was darkening. Night would be upon him within minutes.

He spotted a cabin—no more than a shanty—in the distance, amazed that he had traveled so far in an hour. He could rest there. Lie down, even if only for a little while. Head off well before sunrise.

Gideon ran his damp temple against his shoulder and trudged toward it even as exhaustion poured through his every limb.

There was no time to grieve. Pain held no fear for her anymore. A spasm came, and even as it tore her in two, Lonnie determined that this child would know its mother.

"This one will be quick." Aunt Orla's eyes danced alive, her voice drawing Lonnie's gaze forward.

Hope. She saw hope in the woman's face.

Lonnie clung to her words. Elsie lit another lamp and set it on the nightstand, illuminating the room.

Without Orla even speaking, Elsie picked up a blanket and held it ready. Orla's hip knocked a bottle from the table, and without bothering to pick it up, she shoved a stack of clean rags onto the bed. A curl of silver hair slid from her bun, and Lonnie stared at her, trying to believe that this moment was truly happening.

A rag fumbled from Orla's hand, and she gripped Lonnie's knee. "Here it is."

All pain faded away.

And with her eyes closed, Lonnie saw only one face—the face of her daughter. She fought with everything she had. She bit her cheek to keep from giving a voice to a fresh wave of agony. She heard gasps, and it was over.

Orla flipped the baby over and, using her finger, cleared its mouth. She pulled back and the baby gurgled, then let out a wail. Lonnie lifted her head.

"It's a boy." Orla grinned.

Lonnie peered into the tiny face of her child. His crumpled forehead was the most beautiful sight she had ever seen.

Elsie wrapped them in a hug. "He's beautiful."

"He's alive," Lonnie said breathlessly. Her fingertip grazed a tiny fist. She looked up into Elsie's face.

Orla grabbed a length of clean fabric and helped Lonnie sit. She fashioned a snug sling around the tiny baby and, after tying it over Lonnie's shoulder, buttoned the nightgown over them both. The velvet head pressed to her chest made Lonnie gasp in wonder.

"He's weak." Orla knotted the fabric. "He needs to stay this way until he gets stronger."

Lonnie slid her hand beneath the warm bundle. "How weak is he?"

"He's very small. These next few days will be the most important. You keep that baby pressed up against you like that to keep him warm." A soft smile lit her face. "He will be able to hear your heartbeat. Babies like that, especially when they're first born." She stroked his cheek with the back of her gnarled finger. "He will hardly have to move, even to nurse. The more you keep him still and warm, the better. He's got a little growing to do. Growing that was meant to be done inside of you."

Lonnie nodded. "I will." She glanced down at her son when his cries tapered off. "I think he's falling asleep."

"Good. He will be like that for a while."

"Is he hungry now?"

"Not yet." Orla pulled her doctor's bag off the nightstand. "First thing is to get a few herbs into him. Best to brew a tea." She pulled out a tiny satchel and handed it to Elsie, who hurried out of the room. Orla rooted in her bag and removed a small glass bottle. With steady hands, she put a drop of liquid in each of the baby's eyes and rubbed gently. "That should do it."

Elsie returned with a steaming cup. "This might need to steep another minute."

"Did you put sugar in it?" With her earpiece in place, Orla pressed the other end of the tube to the baby's chest.

"No. I didn't think about it. Should I fetch some?" Elsie started toward the door.

"It would be a good idea. Makes it go down easier." Orla's eyes seemed to stare at nothing. Finally, she lowered the earpiece, draping the contraption around her neck. "Heart sounds strong and he's breathing well." She smiled. "That's very good."

After a minute, Elsie returned with a bowl and sprinkled sugar into the tea.

Orla set the steaming cup aside and saw to Lonnie's needs. She shoved soiled rags to the floor. "So, Lonnie, what are you going to name him?"

Lonnie looked down at the tiny face and saw her husband's image. "His name's Jacob."

"That's a fine choice."

Lonnie cleared her throat. "The girl…," she whispered and sad eyes turned toward her. "I want her name to be Sarah."

"Every baby needs a name." Elsie's words were strained.

When she was finally finished, Orla pulled the sheets up over both Lonnie and the baby. "Even those that don't make it." Heartache laced her words. She washed her hands near the window, then picked up the teacup and sat on the edge of the bed. She dipped her finger in the tea and forced Jacob's tiny lips apart. "He'll take it. You can keep going."

She held the cup out for Lonnie. Lonnie dipped her finger in the warm brew, and the baby's mouth sucked. "He's drinking it." Her heart soared at the sight of a perfect, breathing baby—but the tiny bundle nestled in Gideon's crib wrenched her heart in two.

Orla drew her from her thoughts. "Good. Try and get him to take a little more. Then you can nurse." She left the bedside and murmured to Elsie, who, after a brief hang of her shoulders, lifted the baby from the cradle.

Lonnie sniffed. "Just once more?"

Elsie ducked her head. "Of course." She carried the tiny bundle over. It was difficult with Jacob strapped to her body, but Lonnie took her daughter and held them both close. One was warm and full of life. The other wasn't.

"You two remember each other, don't you?" Lonnie whispered. Her throat was so tight it was almost impossible to speak. "You knew each other so well. Remember all that time you were together inside of me?" She envied Jacob for having known Sarah. "You are a lucky boy." She kissed his head, then her daughter's. Her skin was cold against her lips. "How I love you." Her chin quavered. *How your pa will love you. Oh, Gideon.* How she needed him. How they all did.

Elsie reached for the baby, and Lonnie tightened her grip.

Pulling back, Elsie stepped away, her face apologetic.

A cool hand landed on Lonnie's arm. "We best take care of it directly," Orla said soberly. "She's with Jesus."

Just then Jacob started to fuss and squirm.

"He might be hungry. You could try feeding him now." Orla's voice was soft, and her eyes were sad as she unwound a length of thread.

Lonnie tightened her grip, but Jacob's fussing rose, and tears blurred her vision as Elsie reached for her daughter.

"It's hard." Elsie kissed the top of Lonnie's head. "Believe me, I know."

Lonnie nodded, unable to speak, and with a tender hand, Elsie reached forward. Gritting her teeth, Lonnie forced herself to loosen her grasp.

Orla opened the door and whispered something to Elsie about a box. Elsie swept the baby from the room.

Pinching her eyes shut, Lonnie clung to Jacob and wept.

Forty-Three

Lonnie woke to the sound of Elsie tiptoeing into her bedroom, a tray rattling in her hand. "I brought you something to eat," she said softly, kneeling near the bed. "How is he doing?"

"Still sleeping."

Elsie kissed the tip of her finger, then touched Jacob's tiny ear. "He is precious." Her eyes looked as if she'd been crying. "I have never been so worried. I checked on the two of you all night long."

"You did?"

"You slept for hours. I kept adjusting your pillows to keep you propped up. I didn't want you rolling over." Elsie moved the tray to the bed. There was a plate of hotcakes with a pat of melting butter.

"Do you feel like eating?" Elsie asked.

Lonnie nibbled on a piece of pork sausage. Slowly, she reached for her fork. She found it tricky to get her arms around the sleeping baby without bumping him. "He's so fragile."

"He is, but you're doing a fine job. Jacob is lucky to have a mama who cares so much about him."

When Lonnie struggled to pick up her teacup, Elsie turned the handle so it faced her. "You just eat up. I want you to get your strength back."

Lonnie licked syrup off her thumb. "I will."

"I figured you might be starving."

"Mmm hmm," Lonnie mumbled into her teacup. She wiped her mouth, her voice soft as the words trailed off. She pulled the blanket away from Jacob's down-covered head and studied him. "He has hair everywhere."

"That will fade. That little boy has a lot of growing to do. It will all come in time. Soon he will be as chubby as any baby. Why don't I fetch his cap?"

Lonnie pointed to the dresser, and Elsie rummaged through the top drawer, finally finding it.

"It doesn't fit very well." Lonnie adjusted the cap from side to side. She took a small bite of hotcake.

Elsie moved a sack of soiled rags into the hallway and stacked two enamel bowls that once held hot water.

As carefully as she could, Lonnie smeared syrup on her hotcakes. Elsie slid the cradle closer to the wall, but then her trembling hands stopped. The smile faded from the old woman's face, and sorrow—the ache Lonnie had tried to keep pressed down—rose in her own heart.

Elsie smoothed the fair wood. "It's hard to be happy."

Lonnie swallowed and, even as she tightened her hold on Jacob, yearned for the little girl who should have been asleep in her cradle. Her throat burned.

Eyes watering, Elsie coughed, then sniffed. "Somehow I want to get you changed and put fresh sheets on the bed."

"All right." Lonnie fought the quaver in her voice. But within a few minutes, she was sitting under the window, and she rocked Jacob gently as Elsie stripped the bed and set it to rights with fresh sheets and clean blankets.

"Now, about your nightgown."

Lonnie tried to work the buttons loose and then finally gave in to Elsie's help. By the time she had wiggled out of it, Elsie had filled the basin with warm water. Jacob didn't even stir, and Lonnie was washed and back in bed, blankets nestled around both her and baby. "Any sign of Gideon?"

"I've kept an ear out for him all morning. But nothing." With the mound of bedding clutched in her grasp, Elsie backed into the hallway. "I will get these things washed. I'll be back to check on you later. Oh." She stilled. "I cut up some fabric for diapers. They aren't hemmed yet, but they will do the trick for now." She turned to leave.

"Elsie?"

The older woman halted. "Yes, dear."

"Whatever happened with…"

Elsie smiled softly, her eyes sad. "Jebediah built a little box last night."

"Is he going to bury her?"

"Ground's pretty frozen," she whispered. "But it's such a small box. He's gonna try."

Fire licked the back of her throat, and Lonnie pinched her eyes shut as she kissed Jacob's head. She wished Gideon were here. She looked to the window, but the curtains were still closed. "Would you?"

Elsie flung back the curtains and let in the light. "Now you can watch him come home."

Gideon recognized the fork in the trail and followed the path as it veered left past two small oaks. As the sky brightened, he kept up his brisk pace. If he didn't slow, he'd be home within a few hours. Like a fool, he'd slept later than he meant to, and with morning light spilling through the shanty window, he had coaxed his sore muscles out into the chilly sunlight.

When his shoelace unraveled, Gideon crouched to tie it. His fingers were stiff, nearly frozen.

"Well, looky here," a voice bellowed.

He did not need to look up to know who stood there. Gideon tucked the lace into place. He hated knowing that they were so close to his home, but he kept his fear in check as he slowly rose.

"If it ain't Gideon O'Riley." Bert stared from beneath a broken straw hat. Shadows struck his face in odd places. "What brings you out this way?"

"Lookin' for you, matter of fact." Gideon glanced at the other men. There were four now.

Bert flailed a hand. "Gordy." He motioned with his head toward Gideon.

The large man rushed forward. His potbelly hung over his pants, stretching his suspenders to the limit.

Gideon took a few steps back and yanked the pocket watch from his coat. He forced his eyes away from arms as thick as aspen trunks.

Gordy glanced at Bert. At Bert's nod, he took the pocket watch.

"And the rest?" Bert asked flatly.

"I have that too," Gideon said.

Bert announced a sum that would nearly buy another watch.

Gideon's mouth parted. "You've got to be—"

"It's called interest, Gideon. And I am a businessman. Of course, we could get our payment another way."

His own money would never suffice. Swallowing his agony, Gideon reached in his pocket and withdrew Jebediah's pouch. Loosening the strings, he began gathering up coins when his fingertips struck paper.

Blood drained from his face.

This was supposed to be a coin pouch. Clutching several coins in his palm, Gideon withdrew his hand, careful to keep its true contents concealed. But when he stuffed the jingling pouch back in his pocket, an evil longing flashed in Bert's eyes. Stepping forward, Gideon dropped all of his earnings plus Jebediah's money into Bert's outstretched hand.

Bert made a show of counting the coins. He pocketed them. When he glanced up, the look in his eyes made Gideon take a step backward. His hand clutched over Jebediah's pouch.

"A deal's a deal," Gideon said.

"That so?" Bert patted his upper pocket where the watch now resided. "How do I know you're not gonna pull that funny business again?" His face darkened, and Bert flicked his head toward Gideon. The men closed in.

Gideon glanced from one man to the other and knew that his only chance was to run fast. If he could catch them by surprise, tear through the shrubs to his left, he might be able to lose them.

Before he could change his mind, Gideon darted off.

He stole only steps before an arm clamped around his throat and a man's weight struck his back. Another foot clipped his, and he landed on his stomach in the snow. Strong hands gripped him. Gideon tried to toss them off, even managing to kick one in the knee before his face struck the snow. He blew out icy gasps.

Three sets of arms flipped him onto his back, and Gideon stared up at a cloudless sky until Bert leaned over and sneered down. The man pulled a flask from his coat pocket and swigged. "Looks like you ain't goin' nowhere." Droplets of auburn liquor fell from his lips as he spoke.

Gideon felt the veins in his neck bulge as he fought to free himself. "Get 'im to his feet."

A pair of iron arms jerked him off the ground.

"You thought you were pretty smooth, huh?" Bert took another drink. "Well, it's time you had a taste of your own medicine."

A dense arm draped around Gideon's neck, holding it fast, and the man behind him chuckled. The others yanked his wrists behind his back, and Gideon glared at Bert even as he fought against the grip around his neck.

Bert paced in front of him. "Say, Gid, how's that little wife of yers?"

Gideon spat.

Bert moistened his lips. "She sure was a pretty li'l thing…" A shrill whistle escaped his teeth.

Gideon clenched his jaw and tried to lunge forward. A searing pain wrenched through his arm. His vision blurred when the vise around his throat tightened.

"Think you're goin' somewhere?" Reeking breath sneered in his ear, but the grip loosened.

"Like I was sayin'." Bert rolled his eyes. "Lonnie…" His smile returned. "By the way, I hear congratulations will soon be in order."

"How did you…" Gideon thrust his shoulders forward, and a fiery pain shot through his back.

"Struck a nerve there?" Bert smoothed his palms together, an evil glint in his eye. "I have my sources. It didn't take a genius to figure out where you've been staying."

"If you ever come near—" Gideon bit his tongue when a fist struck his side. He doubled over, spitting blood into the snow.

Bert scratched his jaw. "You know…it's customary for the father to be around at birthin's…"

Gideon pulled all three men forward before they dug their heels in and yanked him back.

"So I've been thinking. When the time comes, somebody better send for me—"

Three sets of arms couldn't hold him.

Gideon rammed into Bert's chest, knocking him down. He put all his strength into a single punch, knowing it would be his last. And just as Bert cried out, hands snagged Gideon, and he slid backward, still kicking. Bert shrank back, blood dripping from his nose.

Blow after blow, the men found different places to strike Gideon's body. He tried to cover his face, but it was no use. His vision blurred, and his head throbbed with a pain he likened to death. Someone grabbed him by the hair and hoisted him up until he stared Bert straight in the eyes.

"Good knowing ya."

A pair of fists pounded Gideon's ears, and he went limp. The only thing he could feel over the cold and pain was the realization that he couldn't get to Lonnie.

Someone shook him.

Through one swollen eye, Gideon looked up to see Bert standing over him, a flask in his hand. He took one final swig, light glinting on shiny metal, then Bert tipped the flask upside-down and poured the rest of the liquid on Gideon's face. Bert chuckled, his expression dark. "Hey, we got any more?"

"You ain't wastin' it on him," a voice said.

"Just bring it here!"

Gideon tried to twist free, but pain pierced his body, paralyzing him. Warm blood trickled down his temple and into his hair.

Bert took the jug and uncorked it. "Hold him."

An arm wrapped around Gideon's head, holding him still, while a greasy finger pried his mouth open. Gideon bit down.

"I said hold him!" Bert shouted when the man yelped.

"He bit me!"

"Someone else help!" Bert growled.

Merciless hands held him down, and Gideon gasped for breath as Bert poured moonshine into his mouth. He coughed and choked, sputtering liquor down his chin. When he managed to tip his head to the side, the liquid oozed down his neck, soaking his shirt. The cold air stung his skin, and Gideon shivered, his lips trembling.

"Keep holding him," Bert demanded, shaking the jug.

"What are you doing?" one man asked.

"Let's just call this a little insurance, huh?" The last of the moonshine dripped from the jug, and Bert corked it. "Leave him."

Gideon hit the snow with a grunt, and by the time he managed to lift his head, they were gone.

Forty-Four

L onnie could not stay awake. She drifted in and out of sleep all day. Each time Jacob woke to nurse, she struggled to keep her eyes open. She was all the more grateful for Elsie's help.

When she looked at Jacob sleeping, her heart lightened. His little cheek pressed against her chest, making his rosebud lips pucker. Tiny legs and arms were tucked cozily in the blanket, and Lonnie took care to move him as little as possible. She tried to do all that Aunt Orla had instructed, knowing with all her heart that nothing could be better than this.

If only Gideon were here. She looked to the window but saw only the reflection of the late afternoon sun. Both breakfast and dinner had come and gone without him.

Elsie had brought Lonnie a plate of biscuits and ham, and as Lonnie nibbled on everything in front of her, Elsie looked on. She waited for Lonnie to down a glass of cold milk, then whisked away the tray. Lonnie realized it had been several hours since Jacob had nursed, and she positioned him. She was getting better at it now and rocked him gently until he woke. "There you are, my sweet boy."

Lonnie spoke softly to Jacob as Elsie bustled in and out of the room.

Elsie returned with a stack of clean linens. "Being a mother comes so natural to you. You are doing wonderful."

A flap of Jacob's blanket fell in front of his mouth, and she brushed it away. While Jacob clung to her, snug in his sling, Sarah was nestled in her tiny box. "And to think"—her voice faltered—"Gideon doesn't even know yet."

Elsie lifted her head, her eyes filled with sorrow. Lonnie drew in a short breath, her heart breaking anew.

Gideon should have been home by now.

When Jacob drooped against her chest, asleep, Lonnie turned her heart toward her blessings, knowing it was the only way she would get through another day. She kissed the top of his head, inhaling his scent.

A knock came at the bedroom door, and Lonnie hurried to straighten her nightgown. Elsie waited before answering.

Jebediah stepped quietly around the door. "How's he doing?"

"Fine." Lonnie tilted Jacob's face up for him to see. The tiny newborn grunted and stretched a wobbly, thin arm above the sling. Jebediah pulled up a chair and sat.

"He's a handsome fella." He leaned forward and grazed Jacob's blanket with a rough finger. "Boy, he looks like Gid."

Lonnie grinned. "He sure does."

Jebediah fiddled with his mustache, eyes on the floor. "Lonnie, I get the strange feeling that somethin's the matter." His eyes narrowed when they met hers, and he shook his head. "Wherever he went, it shouldn't have taken Gid this long to come home. Now, don't get alarmed, mind you." He wiped his palms on his knees. "I would just feel better if I went lookin' for him."

Lonnie gripped a handful of sheets. What if Gideon didn't want to be found? Her heart throbbed. Forcing away the fear, she clung to the hope that something had delayed him. Clung to the hope that he would make good on his promise to never go back to the man he had been.

When uncertainty deepened the wrinkles of Jebediah's forehead, Lonnie shifted her gaze to the wall. "I would feel so much better if you did."

Elsie touched her husband's shoulder. "Are you thinking of leaving now? It'll be dark soon."

"If Gid's in trouble, *he'll* be out there. I have to go."

He rose, and Lonnie caught him by the hand. "Thank you, Jebediah. This means the world to me."

He cleared his throat, but the words came out choked anyway. "That little fella's got a papa out there somewhere, and there's a reason he ain't home. I'll find him. I will."

Gideon rolled onto his back and peered up at an orange sky. He blinked several times, trying to recall where he was, but it wasn't until he sat up that the ache in his side reminded him of what had happened. Pain seared through his skull, blurring his vision, and Gideon blinked furiously, trying to focus. He groaned as he struggled to stand. Bert's men were strong, and their blows did not fall lightly.

He had wasted enough time. After scrambling to his feet, he swayed and the forest spun. He clutched his head, and his fingers touched dry blood. Gideon grimaced, his stomach churning. His ribs cried out in pain as he brushed snow off his clothes. But it did little good—he was soaked to the skin. He looked around and found his hat lying in the snow, trampled and crushed. His pack was not too far off, its contents strewn about. Gideon spotted the last of his food, now ruined, and grabbed his few belongings.

He stuffed his things into the pack. Sitting back on his heels, he scanned the empty ground. His heart quickened. Yanking the pack back open, he thrust his hand inside. Frantic, his fingers groped one pocket, then the other.

His search proved useless. The money pouch was gone.

He lowered his head and closed his eyes, willing this to be a bad dream. He began to shake. From cold or fury, he didn't know. With a deep breath, he rose to his feet. Afternoon had come and gone, and now the first stars announced the last minutes of light. Gideon growled, startling a bird nearby.

How long had he been lying there? He had no answers, only a name that stirred his heart into action: Lonnie.

He stumbled forward and clutched his aching head. The first stars seemed to trade places with the cold, wet ground, and Gideon fell forward into the slush. He coughed, making his ribs ache more, and a spatter of blood appeared against the stark white. He gasped against the pain and struggled to his knees. He wiped his mouth with the back of his hand. *Home.*

His arms shook as he pushed himself up, but as he tried to stand, his vision blurred and the forest darkened, then went black.

Forty-Five

Gideon felt himself drift in and out of consciousness. His body shook uncontrollably, and pulling his coat tighter didn't help. *I should light a fire.* Teeth chattering, he didn't know how to begin. One thought ran into the other.

He struggled to move and felt something cold and hard against his head. That's right. He was in the shanty. He couldn't remember why he'd searched for the shanty, but with his clothes still damp from the snow, Gideon was thankful he'd found it. The air bit through his wet coat, but the small room was dry and the four walls blocked the worst of the winter wind. How many hours had he been lying here?

A breeze whistled through the crack above his head. Opening one swollen eye, Gideon glanced up at the moonlight that slivered through. *Lonnie.* She would be worried about him. Or had she been with him? His muscles worked as he tried to lift his head. No. She was home safe.

Jebediah's voice came to mind. As if the man were calling him by name.

Gideon's swollen lip flinched. If there was anyone who would protect Lonnie, it was Jebediah. He knew the man would do anything for her. The peace of that knowledge seemed to warm him through, and the shaking began to subside. Gideon relaxed deeper, his cheek pressed to the rough wood. Sleep called to him, luring him away from the pain.

The door creaked open. A rush of icy air followed. Thick hands rolled him onto his back.

Gideon flinched.

"Wasn't going to shoot you, if that's what you're thinking." Jebediah's voice filled the shanty. He took hold of Gideon's coat and shook him. "But I'm mighty tempted."

Gideon opened one swollen eye. "Jeb?" He looked around the shack, then back at Jebediah. "I…" The cold returned, and his lips trembled. He tried to speak again, but Jebediah stopped him.

"Let's get you home. You're half frozen."

Slowly, Gideon sat up and his feet fell like lead to the wood-plank floor. He stared at the wall and made no effort to move. Instead, he glanced up at Jebediah.

Jebediah squinted at him, as if to study him.

He felt his good eye widen, but the focus didn't sharpen.

Jebediah shook his head and grabbed his arm. "I've been up most of the night lookin' for you. Let's go." He shifted the grip on his gun. "What happened to you?"

Gideon stared at the broken window, where a sliver of the full moon peeked through.

Jebediah grunted and yanked Gideon to standing. Pain shot through him.

Catching hold of Gideon's shirt, Jebediah pushed him through the door. "Let's go. I ain't gonna sit around here all night while you find your brain." The rotting door barely held onto the frame when Jebediah slammed it closed.

He raised his lantern, and light glinted across the gray-white ground.

The light bounced from one snow-covered tree to the next. Gideon swayed.

His head pounded. He took a few shaky steps down the path and paused. But when a firm hand pressed his back, he trudged on. He touched his bloody lip and winced at the sting. He slid fingers inside his jacket and felt the spot where several ribs cried out in pain. What had he done? Jebediah lifted the lantern up just as a deer bounded into the darkness.

When Jebediah mumbled under his breath, Gideon did not have to turn around to see the look on the old man's face. He couldn't blame him. How would he explain the missing money? He didn't want to imagine what Lonnie would think. Gideon searched for the right words, but his swollen lips never moved.

Their footsteps tromped forward.

"There's, uh," Gideon started. "There's something I need to tell you." His throat fought the taste of sour blood when he swallowed.

"I'm listening," Jebediah said sharply.

Gideon wrung his hands. "Before I left, I..." He slowed, but Jebediah nudged him. "What I mean to say is that I borrowed, no, I took... wait." He slammed his eyes shut, then winced. "I took your pouch of coins. Well, at least that's what I thought it was. I didn't realize..." He braved a glance at Jebediah. The old man's face was stone. "I only borrowed it in case I needed it, but I was going to pay you back." He was only making a mess of the truth, and Gideon knew he looked like the liar and thief he was.

"I don't care about your excuses." Jebediah's gun glinted in the moonlight where it dangled at his side. "You have more to worry about than stealing my money."

When Gideon slowed, Jebediah shoved him forward.

"You have a wife at home who's been waiting on you, and you've been off—" He sniffed.

Gideon grimaced.

If only there was some way he could explain. But he dropped his head, knowing his past had come back to haunt him. He had no way to defend himself.

Forty-Six

When a tear dropped and landed on the windowsill, Lonnie wiped its trail away with the edge of her nightgown. Jacob slumbered against her, still snuggled safely in his sling. She peered down through the glass at Elsie, who knelt inside the tiny picket fence. In the bleak light of dawn, the gray-haired woman struck at the frozen ground with a hand spade.

Scrape. Scrape.

Lonnie winced at the sound of steel hitting unyielding earth. She glanced away. *Oh, Elsie.* But even as tears blurred her vision, she forced herself to watch.

Elsie tossed the spade aside and thrashed at the ground with her hands. She paused and pushed wild hair away from her face. Her mouth twisted in despair. On the ground beside her sat the tiny box. With her throat on fire, Lonnie touched the cold glass.

The box was so small. Too small.

Lonnie pressed her forehead to the window, careful not to bump her son. A pine box. That was all she had left of her daughter. Her head spun. In clear defeat, Elsie pressed her cheek to the earth. Lonnie's vision clouded, and she choked on the tears that spilled forth. Beside the small hole stood a weather-beaten cross that had seen many winters, and Lonnie knew Elsie mourned for more than one little girl.

God, why? She held her burning throat. Sarah's life was taken before it ever began. There would be no ribbons or bows or sticky fingers to wipe after baking. No warm sun on a little girl's hair. When her sobs began to stir Jacob, Lonnie forced herself to step away from the window. She sank into the rocking chair and leaned her head back. Her feet rose and fell. The chair rocked, and she stared at the wall, unable to get the image of the tiny box out of her mind. It was too small to be a coffin. Too final to hold her daughter inside.

Everything was familiar—gnarled oaks, snow-cloaked rocks, the curve of the trail. Gideon was almost home. He was exhausted, and the sunrise hurt his eyes. He felt sick with hunger. As much as he looked forward to a hot meal and bath, there was one thing he feared. One thing he dreaded.

Lonnie would not be waiting for him on the porch steps and waving as he once imagined.

She would want to know what had taken him so long. Gideon watched the puff of breath in front of his face. All he could say was the truth. And the liquor that reeked from his skin and clothes? That wasn't his fault. They'd done it to him…right after they stole his bag of money. *The bag of money that you stole first?* Gideon groaned, and even as he lifted his eyes to the treetops, he prayed Lonnie would believe him.

Jebediah called his name.

Gideon slowed and looked into a pair of eyes softened by an emotion he couldn't read.

Jebediah glanced away. "I've got something I have to tell you." He cleared his throat. "It's about the baby." The sorrow in his face pulled Gideon's feet forward.

Jebediah ran his hand over the back of his neck. "The baby was born." His voice trembled.

Air left Gideon's lungs. "What?"

"The baby. It was born."

He stepped forward. "Is the baby…all right?"

With a lift of his brows, Jebediah nodded. "He seems to be doing just fine."

Gideon stumbled toward home. "It's too early. How did it happen?" His breath came in short bursts. Then he froze. "Wait. You said…he?"

"He." But Jebediah's voice cracked.

Gideon placed his hands to his head. "What is it?" he pleaded. The cry echoed softly through the still forest.

With bright morning light hitting Jebediah's wrinkled features, his mouth opened in silent despair.

"What's wrong with the baby?" Gideon grabbed Jebediah's shoulder. "Did something happen to Lonnie?"

"No. Lonnie's fine. She's safe," Jebediah whispered, his voice hoarse and scratchy, and when tears glinted in his eyes, Gideon's stomach lurched.

"Did my child—?"

"There were two." Jebediah looked away and stared at the ground.

"Two?" Gideon fell to his knees as if he'd taken a blow to the chest.

"Two." Jebediah stepped closer and knelt in front of him. "A boy." He kept his eyes on the snow. "And a girl."

With his fists on the frozen ground, Gideon pressed his head to his forearms. "What happened?" he said in a small voice that blew cold against the snow.

"The girl. She, uh." Jebediah's voice cracked. "She didn't make it."

"Didn't make it?" The words charred in his throat. "And Lonnie?"

"She's well. Healthy and strong."

Air filled his lungs even as tears burned his eyes. "The boy?"

"He's hangin' on. He's a strong fella."

Gideon sat back on his heels and wiped his sleeve across his eyes. "When?"

"Yesterday. Not too far apart. Lonnie had a rough time of it, but she was so brave. She's doin' good now. Elsie's watching over her. And that baby—"

"Tell me." Gideon lifted his gaze in earnest.

"He's a fighter. He's clinging to his mama, and he's gettin' stronger by the minute."

Gideon swallowed, but the lump in his throat would not go down. "Did she name him?" *Did she name her?*

"Jacob." Jebediah squeezed Gideon's arm. "Your son's name is Jacob."

Even as he spoke the words, Gideon's heart burned as it tore in two. "The girl?" *Was she beautiful? Did she look like her mother?*

"Sarah."

Gideon's eyelids fell. In an instant, he saw what would have been. A little girl with freckles. A warm hand inside his. Butterflies and bedtime stories. With slow, impossible movements, he turned his head and wept.

Forty-Seven

E lsie wandered in from the cold, gray curls feathered around her forehead and cheeks streaked with dried tears. She sank on Lonnie's bed, and without a word, she wrapped cold fingers around Lonnie's hand and prayed for the little girl who was with Jesus. Lonnie caught a tear that slipped from the end of her nose and sniffed as Elsie added words for the men. "Lord, bring them home safe." With their hands clasped atop Elsie's damp, muddy skirt, she whispered a soft amen.

Elsie opened her eyes and smoothed her thumb across her cheeks. "Are you hungry?"

Lonnie brushed a kiss to Jacob's temple. She didn't want to admit it, but her stomach knotted with hunger, and she nodded. "What can I help you do?"

"Not a thing." Elsie flashed her a muted smile and sniffed. "I have a pot of soup on the stove that'll be done in a bit. In the meantime, there's some cookies to nibble on."

She disappeared down the hall, and Lonnie flashed her gaze to the window. Scolding herself for being so anxious, she turned her attention to Jacob. She found it easy to disappear in the joy of his presence. She bounced him gently. His purring slowed, and with awkward movements, he stretched and opened his eyes.

"Hello there, my sweetheart." She grazed her thumb across a velvet-soft ear and down his wee nose. "Aren't you precious?" She tilted him toward the window so the sun could touch his skin as Elsie had suggested. "You are such a wee thing. You will have to get lots of rest and drink all your good milk to get healthy and strong. Then"—she lifted his hand to kiss tiny fingers—"you can play with your pa, and he can hold you in his arms."

Elsie returned with a plate of cookies and a glass of milk. Lonnie nibbled on a cookie.

Elsie took a bite of one and brushed the crumbs from her gray dress.

Lonnie adjusted Jacob, then lifted her chin. "Did you hear that?"

Elsie arched her neck toward the doorway and placed a finger to her lips, eyes wide. Neither of them made a sound, yet noise came from somewhere.

The back door opened. It closed.

"Jebediah." Elsie jumped up and squeezed Lonnie's knee. "You sit tight."

Lonnie leaned forward, willing her heart to cease pounding. When voices lifted from below, she placed a hand to her heart. Only one man spoke with Elsie. And it was not her husband.

Jacob whimpered, and she scooted him around until he was in position to nurse. When he quieted, she leaned toward the door. Frustration crawled like hot fingers up her neck and cheeks.

Finally, Elsie returned, her face somber.

"Gideon?" Lonnie's mouth hung open.

Elsie's gaze whipped to the hall. "Jebediah found him."

Lonnie released her breath. "He's home?"

"Yes."

Footsteps trudged into the doorway, and Gideon stopped just shy of the room. Lonnie gasped. Blood was caked in the creases of his lips and beneath his nose. A bruise high on his cheekbone fanned into cuts and scrapes that reached his forehead.

Her hand flew to her mouth. "Gideon!"

He stared at the floor.

Elsie cleared her throat. "Jebediah found him. He was in a pretty bad way."

"What happened?"

Gideon looked up. His face was heavy with guilt, but his eyes softened when they landed on the bundle against Lonnie's chest.

"Is that…?" He hesitated, then took the few short steps forward. Kneeling, he reached out but pulled his hand away.

Lonnie moved the blanket from Jacob's face and tilted him toward his father.

Gideon's eyes danced over the face of his baby. "He's…," he choked. "He's my son."

She looked down on the man she missed more than words could say. "Yes." They were a family now.

With his face full of longing and wonderment, Gideon wrapped his arms around her, and fresh tears sprang to her eyes when he gently pressed her head to his shoulder. Lonnie sighed, her eyes pinched shut— savoring his essence—then she pulled away.

She blinked up at him. "Have…have you been drinking?"

He leaned back, his face suddenly ashen. "No. I mean, I can explain."

Elsie stepped forward. "I'm sorry, Gideon, but she needs to know the whole truth."

"What whole truth?" Lonnie glanced from one face to the other, the scent of corn liquor making her stomach churn. "You've been gone for two days. What happened? Who did this to you?"

Pain seared through Gideon's eyes. "I didn't mean for it to happen."

"Gid—"

"I didn't tell you, Lonnie," Elsie interrupted. "Jebediah discovered it just yesterday—"

Gideon lifted a hand. "Lonnie," he began. "What she's trying to say is that I took their money."

Lonnie's jaw fell.

His eyebrows dropped in clear agony. "Lonnie, please trust me. I would not lie to you." He wrapped her hand in his cold palm. "The watch...I was trying to find Bert. But he wasn't alone." Gideon's gaze faltered. "He took the money from me. I promise I was going to give it back." His voice thickened.

She clutched the sheets in one hand, bracing her heart against her rising pulse.

"It's all just a misunderstanding. And this"—he tugged at his soiled shirt—"isn't what it looks like either. It was those..." He rose. "Bert poured it—"

"Stop!" Lonnie snapped. "Just stop." She placed a hand to the pounding beneath her nightgown.

Hands still raised, Gideon stepped back. His lips parted, eyes pained.

"Why?" Lonnie moaned.

Elsie touched Gideon's elbow. "Maybe this isn't a good time. Let's get you cleaned up, and you can talk about this later."

"No." Lonnie closed her eyes. "Leave." Her finger pointed to the door—a sword tipped to an enemy's heart. Her eyes narrowed. "Go. And don't come back."

As if a hammer had struck his lungs, Gideon slumped. "But I—"

"Go!" she screamed, covering Jacob's head with her hand. He woke anyway and started to fuss.

"Come on, Gideon." Elsie motioned him toward the hallway. "Let's leave her alone."

His eyes remained fixed on Lonnie. But with a gentle pull on his arm, Elsie coaxed him from the room. His agonized face disappeared.

He spoke. "Elsie, I—"

"How dare you!" Lonnie screamed even as she choked on tears. "You left me!"

Jacob's cries rose, and she rocked him from side to side, but he wouldn't be soothed. Tilting her face to the ceiling, she struggled for breath. *Why, God?* She wept, her shaking body jostling her son. She heard Elsie and Gideon murmuring at the top of the stairs. Why was he still here?

Her words came out like poison, hurting not only the one they were spoken to but the one whose heart they came from.

No going back? she had asked.

His promise resounded in her heart. *No going back.* But it had been a lie.

"Don't ever come near me!" she screamed, knowing the daggers of her anger would pierce him. "I never want to see you again!"

Jacob wailed louder, and she did not have the strength to soothe his cries. She tucked her chin to her chest and wept against his head.

Forty-Eight

Lonnie listened. Every stomp of Gideon's boots brought the end nearer.

She sat on Elsie's bed with the door closed. She couldn't be in the same room with her husband as he packed his things. Obeying her wishes. She tilted her head toward the noise that leaked beneath the bedroom door. Dresser drawers opened, then closed. The bed squeaked. Boards creaked under his feet. Lonnie placed her fingertips to her lips. Every sound tore her apart.

He was leaving. And she had told him to go.

A lighter pair of steps walked down the hallway, stopping between the bedrooms. Elsie spoke softly, and Gideon responded, his voice deep and rumbling. Lonnie lowered her face, her resolve thinning. She placed a protective hand on Jacob's silken head. No. It had to be this way. It was better for her son.

War raged in her heart.

Gideon was still so close. All she had to do was run out of the room and tell him she was sorry. And he would stay.

She clutched the quilt to keep herself from leaping off the bed.

As Ma would have done? Lonnie gritted her teeth. She couldn't be that woman. Remembering the sight of Gideon's blood-caked face and the reek of moonshine, she owed it to Jacob to see this through.

She heard Gideon speak her name, and when her resolve faltered, Lonnie gripped the quilt tighter. *Leave.* Her heart wrenched as if the life were bleeding out of it. *Just leave.* This waiting was too much to bear.

Footsteps pounded across the floor, steps too heavy to be Elsie's and too determined to be Jebediah's. *Oh, Gideon.* Her head spun.

The door slammed.

Lonnie jumped and slid toward the end of the bed. She clutched Jacob close so she wouldn't bump him. Heavy steps paced the length of the hallway, then descended the stairs. The pounding of her heart mimicked his dogged stride. In the middle of the room, her feet froze in place.

The front door opened, sending a waft of cold air up the stairs. The door downstairs slammed. She hurried into her bedroom, and her hand flew to her mouth. All of his things were gone. She flung the wardrobe door open and gazed at the emptiness. Everything. Lonnie stumbled toward the window. There, in the snowy yard, stood her husband. The man whose deception was the blade that cut the last cord of hope between them. *Or had it been your anger?* Lonnie shook her head. She had a right to be angry.

When she had needed Gideon the most, he had failed her.

There was nothing else to be done.

The man below turned in a slow circle, as if studying the yard one final time. Lonnie touched the cold glass and bit her lip to keep from calling his name.

He turned toward an unpainted cross, the young wood golden. Lonnie's breath caught. His shoulders slumped, and he placed a hand to his head. Then, in a few strides, he scaled the tiny fence and stood inches from the mound of black earth. Dropping to one knee, he placed a hand on the wood.

Lonnie cursed her tears for obscuring her sight.

She swiped at the moisture with her sleeve as Gideon hung his head, and she coughed at the knot of tears in her throat. Finally, he rose and ran his hand over his eyes, then turned toward her window.

Their gazes locked.

Then, with slow, labored steps, Gideon walked away—his few belongings, a little food, and Lonnie's heart stowed in his bag.

She turned so Jacob could face the glass. *Open your eyes.* His tiny lashes remained pressed to his cheeks. Lonnie could not hold back her tears any longer. Her son had never seen his father.

And now he was gone.

She stared at the trail of snowy footsteps, wishing she knew his course. Where would he go? Lonnie sank away from the window and faced the room. She would have no way of finding out. No way of ever knowing.

"Lonnie," Elsie called through the door. It opened, and the older woman wrapped both mother and child in a gentle embrace. "He's gone," she whispered softly. Meant as an encouragement, the words sliced into Lonnie's heart.

"Elsie, what did I do?" She buried her cheek in Elsie's soft shoulder and wept. "I don't know what to do now."

Elsie rocked her gently. "You did what you had to."

"I'll never see him again."

She lifted Lonnie's chin. "Nothing in life is final."

Frayed beyond repair, the last thread of her strength severed. Her body shook with sobs. "He's gone," she moaned. "Elsie, he's gone." Her breath came in short gasps. Elsie kissed the top of her head and offered a tight hug before finally releasing her.

"I'll come check on you in a little while." She slipped out the door.

Lonnie sent one last hopeless glance out the window, then she loosened the curtains and let them fall. The room dimmed. That would be the last time he'd look up at her window. Never again would she see him cross the yard.

She moved to the bed, knowing she'd jostled Jacob too much already. Something caught her foot, and Lonnie stumbled forward but righted herself against the wall. Her ankle smarted, and she rubbed it against her calf. She spun around to see Jacob's heavy cradle swaying.

"Oh," she moaned at the reminder of the man she loved. She wanted to lay Jacob in the cradle his father had made. Maybe then the two would be close. Lonnie tucked her chin to her chest and looked down on her sleeping son. It would be weeks before he could sleep away the afternoons in his cradle.

Kneeling, she touched the smooth wood and imagined Gideon's hands working along every grain and sanded knot. She sniffed and wiped her eyes with her shoulder. The cradle stilled. She slipped one foot inside, and then the other. As she sank down, her nightgown puffed around her knees. She fit between the four low walls, but when she tucked her knees up, Jacob began to fuss.

"I'm sorry, baby. All you want to do is sleep and here I am moving ya all over." Instinctively, she rocked her hips from side to side, and the cradle swayed. Lonnie closed her eyes. "Shh," she hummed. "Sleep, my precious baby. Sleep."

Jacob's fussing turned to a whimper, and soon he was wailing.

"Oh, my love." Lonnie smoothed the back of her hand down his velvet cheek. "Don't cry." Tears burned her eyes as a helpless hand waved against her chest, his tiny mouth searching.

But Lonnie had no strength.

Sitting in the cradle built by the man they both desperately needed, mother and child clung to each other and cried.

How far did he have to go? How far to take him from his misery? Gideon knew the only place for that was with Lonnie. He dropped his head in his hands and leaned against a broad pine. He wasn't much for crying, but this day, after seeing his son, his Lonnie, and his Sarah for the final time, he could not control himself. *What have I done? How have I messed up so many times?*

Lonnie did not want him anymore.

He had taken her when she was not his to take. She had loved him when he did not deserve her love. But she could only take so much disappointment. She could only be let down so many times. Gideon lifted his face to the patches of blue sky overhead. Lonnie needed no more heartache. It was best that he leave. *For her sake.* And before he could hurt Jacob too.

He pressed onward and trudged down the well-worn path. He had no idea where he was going, but he didn't care. Wherever he ended up would be good enough for him. Just as long as it was far enough away that he could not hurt Lonnie again.

Gideon pressed his hand to his eyes. He had gotten only a glimpse of his precious son. Would it be enough to last him a lifetime? And Sarah. He had never even seen her little face. A tear dripped down his wrist. Jebediah, Elsie, Lonnie…they would all insist Sarah was with the Lord. Gideon ran his hand down his face. *And you? Do you believe that?* His heart throbbed at anything less. He tipped his head to the sky, knowing he'd disregarded God for far too long. Gideon blinked into the brightness and wondered if God saw him.

He'll be a better Father than I ever could.

Forty-Nine

Gideon pulled the scrap of paper from his back pocket and read the scribbled words again: *T. Jemson, apple orchard.*

When he had stopped in Stuart in search of work, the storekeeper had handed him this name and pointed him in the right direction. Gideon had walked all day and now stood in front of a whitewashed sign with *Jemson* written in peeling green paint.

He turned off the main road, following the path that led through a row of apple trees. Their bare limbs, though blanketed in frost, seemed to whisper a call for warmer days. As Gideon walked on, he spotted a pair of buildings in the distance. A large rustic shed stood nearer than the two-story house, which was painted the same crisp white as the sign. Made of rough-hewn boards, the shed's slanted roof sloped down to the back. Several missing boards left gaping holes, and as Gideon drew closer to the large open door, he saw tools and worn barrels stacked and piled high.

He thrust his hands in his pockets and studied the main house. *You have to do this.* Just as he bolstered his resolve, a man neared, then slowed.

"Afternoon." Gideon tipped his hat and shifted his pack.

The man eyed him as he lifted a weathered hand in welcome. "Afternoon, young man. Can I help you?"

"Yessir." Gideon cleared his throat. "I'm lookin' for work and was wondering if there was need for another hired hand."

The man clicked his teeth. "I'm sorry, son, but my crew is off this time of year. They'll be back come July. I hire most of my men for the three and a half months come the start of harvest. Come back then, and we'll see what we can do." He pulled a small pouch from his pocket and tucked a pinch of chewing tobacco inside his cheek.

Gideon knew of nowhere else to go. "Sir," he began.

"Call me Jemson. Tal Jemson."

"Yes, Mr. Jemson. You see…" He glanced at the shed. "I need work real bad. Isn't there anything I can do for you now?" Rotting boards begged to be replaced, and Gideon's hand itched for a hammer and nails. "I'm good at just about anything. If you give me a job, you won't be sorry."

Tal Jemson shook his head. "Like I said, son, apple pickin' don't start for several more months. There's nothing to be done."

"Nothing." Gideon bit his lip. "Well, what do you do in the meantime?"

The man chuckled and sent a shot of dark liquid into the snow. "What's your name, son?" He licked his bottom lip clean.

"Gideon O'Riley."

"How old are you?"

"Twenty-two, sir."

"Well, Gideon who's twenty-two, I got me enough to keep busy." He motioned with his thumb toward the orchard. "There's pruning and irrigating, and I keep the wild animals away from my fields best I can. But like I said, it's not enough work to keep anyone on this time of year. There's just me and my oldest son, and we stay busy enough. We're a small outfit, and honestly, I just can't afford the help right now." He squinted when the sun broke through a patch of clouds, hitting the stubble along his jaw. "Come back in the summer."

"Sir," Gideon blurted. He pulled off his hat and turned it around in his hands. "I'll work for half—"

Tal's eyebrows shot up.

"—half of what you pay your men."

"You kiddin' me?"

Gideon hiked his pack higher on his back. "No sir."

Tal stared at him, and it was then that he seemed to notice the bruise on Gideon's cheekbone for the first time. Instinctively, Gideon ducked his head, then forced himself to meet the man in the eyes. A silent moment passed, and Gideon waited for the questions, but Tal let out a soft chuckle. His face turned serious.

"I pay my foreman four dollars a week. Pickers get two and a half dollars a week, and whoever is up to the task of driving the loads to town gets 'em another dollar." He folded his arms across his chest. "Half of that ain't much, son. Are you sure?" His eyes narrowed. "Where you from, anyway?"

"Different places." Gideon straightened his stance. "I'm a hard worker, though. If you just give me a chance, I'll prove it to you." He glanced over his shoulder. "I could start by fixing that roof over there. And if it's prunin' time like you said, I could help you. I don't know much about apples, but I'm willing to learn."

Tal stared at the small pouch that was still in his hand before cramming it into his coat pocket. He took his time to tuck the laces out of sight. "My missus is about to put supper on. If you're to stay on and help, you might as well join us at table. Hope you like fried chicken."

Gideon let out the breath he'd been holding. "That'd be fine, sir."

"I'll show you where the workers' quarters are, and you can wash up." He waved him around the back of the house, where a small shack hid between stands of apple trees. The angled roof sloped sharply, finally ending where a tiny stovepipe jutted out.

Tal pointed. "No need to fight for which bunk you want. Make yourself at home. There's a washbasin and ladle in there somewhere— you'll find it. Water's just over there."

Gideon followed the length of Tal's arm.

"Supper's on in ten. The missus expects clean hands and faces at her table. I'll tell her you're here, and she'll set an extra place for you." He gave Gideon a slight nod—a dismissal.

Inside, the workers' shack was dark, dusty, and cold. Gideon dropped his heavy pack to the plank floor and stepped toward the only window. He swung the wood shutter up and propped a small stick underneath to keep it aloft. The little light that passed through revealed six beds, two bunks against the longest wall and another set butted up against the other. Gideon sat down on the nearest bed. He twisted his neck from side to side and gave his stiff muscles a firm squeeze.

A spider crept along a small table with uneven legs, and beside that was a chair with an upside-down washbasin on the seat. Gideon flipped the basin over and blew away the cobwebs that had settled around its metal rim. A bucket hung just inside the door, and he pulled out the metal ladle, tossing it on the table before toting the bucket to the well. He thought of Lonnie in Elsie's cheery kitchen and let his eyes fall closed for the briefest of moments.

After washing his face and neck, Gideon knew he was as present-able for supper as he would ever be. He stepped out into the early eve-ning light, and he paused and examined the house. He finally decided to knock on the back door instead of the front. A petite and slender woman came to the door when he tapped on it.

"Gideon?"

"Yes ma'am." He removed his hat.

"I'm Mrs. Jemson. Come on in. Tal said we'd be expecting you." Her smile touched her eyes, and she held the door open for Gideon. "You sure were a surprise to us, but we're glad to have you." She smoothed her red hair and patted a neat bun at the nape of her neck.

Gideon's cheeks warmed. "Thank you, ma'am." He stepped into a kitchen thick with the aroma of batter and grease. He moistened his lips.

"You sit here." Mrs. Jemson pointed to a bench stretching the length of the table.

When he sat, two young boys barreled into the kitchen. They pushed and shoved their way onto the bench, and it was not until all four shiny shoes hid beneath the tablecloth that they seemed to notice Gideon.

A red-haired boy creased his forehead. "Who are you?"

"I'm Gideon." He propped his fists on the table.

The little boy mimicked the action. "I'm Jimmy, and I'm eight." He elbowed his little brother, who sat to his left. "This is Carl. He's only six."

The youngest boy narrowed his eyes and opened his mouth, revealing two missing front teeth. "Thix and a half!"

Mrs. Jemson placed a hot pad in the center of the table. "You'll soon find that these two are a handful."

Footfalls echoed, and Gideon glanced up when a younger version of Tal filled the doorway.

"Who's a handful?"

Mrs. Jemson looked up at the young man looming behind her. "Owen. This is Gideon. He has come to work for your father."

Owen stepped into the kitchen. "Why?"

Mrs. Jemson's voice sharpened. "I believe he's discussed the details with your father."

Gideon extended a hand, and Owen hesitated before shaking it briefly. The young man plunked into a chair opposite him. His eyes stayed on Gideon.

The back door slammed, and Tal entered the kitchen. He wiped his hands on the front of his overalls, then kissed his wife on the cheek.

"Supper's about on. Have a seat." She heaved a heavy pan of golden fried chicken over to the table, and Tal followed behind her with a bowl of steaming mashed potatoes.

He cleared his throat when he sat. "We'll say grace now."

Gideon bowed his head and folded his hands along with the others. When the meal was blessed, he helped himself to a chicken thigh at Mrs. Jemson's urging.

"So"—Tal dropped a ladleful of creamy potatoes in the center of his plate—"you got any family around here?" He lifted the bowl toward Gideon.

Gideon fingered the handle of the ladle. The truth would sound strange, but he did not want to hide anything—not anymore. "Yessir." He helped himself to mashed potatoes. "I've got a wife. And, as of a few days ago, a new baby boy."

Every head lifted.

Mrs. Jemson raised her eyebrows, and Tal's jaw paused midchew.

Gideon felt the heat rise in his neck. "I know it sounds strange, but it's true." He pushed food around his plate. "I figured I could send my earnings to them. My wife needs the money more than me."

Tal dabbed at his mouth with a brown-and-white-checked napkin. "Well, I'll be. If you don't mind my askin', what brings you here?"

He glanced at his wife. "I mean, don't you want to be with your family?"

Gideon took a sip of sweet tea. "Yessir, but right now that just ain't gonna happen. But I promise you"—his eyes met Tal's—"it won't change how hard I'm gonna work." He dropped his gaze to the table, his voice soft. "And if it's all the same, without bein' rude or nothing, I'd like to not talk about it." He tugged at a lock of his hair. "Still a sore subject."

"By all means," Mrs. Jemson declared. "Ain't none of our business. Have another biscuit, Gideon. And please, help yourself to some jam." She lifted a napkin from a steaming basket, and the yeasty smell warmed him through.

"Thank you, ma'am."

Tal smiled at his wife and chuckled. "Well, Gideon—can I call you Gid?"

"Most folks do."

"All right. Tomorrow we start bright and early." He motioned with his head toward the window. "You can count yourself pretty lucky. I usually have the men cookin' their own meals outside the bunkhouse, but seein' as there's only you, you can join us. Sound all right?"

"Sounds good, sir. I sure appreciate it."

When supper was over, Gideon excused himself. He wanted to impose on the Jemson family as little as possible. He carelessly chose a bed, and before the sun had even sunk behind the trees, he climbed into the cold bunk, wrapped his arms over his chest, and thought of his family.

An icy breeze seeped through the cracks in the wall, and the trees outside swished in a rising wind, humming a lullaby that neither comforted nor soothed.

Fifty

Gideon stood outside the apple shed as Owen walked toward him, the young man's head tucked low into the folds of his coat collar. Gideon shivered. A thick fog covered the farm, and the gray mist grazed cool and moist against whatever skin wasn't covered.

"It's a cold one."

Owen smiled. "Sure is." He extended a chapped hand. "We ain't met proper, I suppose."

They shook hands. "Suppose not."

"It's cold as the dickens, but Pa'll have my hide if I don't help you, so let's get to it." Owen stepped into the shed and, without ceremony, Gideon followed. The air inside was as cold as the yard, but it smelled like sweet apples and sawdust.

Owen hissed through his teeth, "It's freezin'!" A shudder rumbled through his shoulders. "If I remember right, we have some shingles around here somewhere." He lifted the corner of a stained canvas, and a waterfall of dried apple leaves tumbled to the ground. A stack of crates filled with tools poked out from beneath, and Owen moved to raise the other corner of the stiff, sleeping canvas.

"Here they are." He tossed the canvas back, and together they rolled it up. "Pa split these last year, but we never got much further. A couple of the hands came down with somethin'—I can't remember what it was. Anyway, they couldn't work for a couple of weeks and it set us back. Long story short"—he picked up a handful of shingles—"here they are."

Gideon lifted a smooth shingle and turned it in his hand. "I suppose we ought to get on up there and strip off the old ones."

Walking across the slick roof proved to be difficult. Being a few years older and the hired hand, Gideon felt responsible to see that he took on the more dangerous position. Still, Owen's skill with a hammer was impressive, and the younger man kept up an equal pace. They spent the morning working side by side, peeling off shingles and laughing about stories from years past.

Owen chuckled. "Should have seen the look on Pa's face."

"I hope he fired him." Gideon tossed a shingle to the ground.

"Oh, you bet he did." Owen tugged on his hammer and freed a rusted nail. His laughter faded, and he wiped his nose with a gloved finger. His face sobered when he sat back on his heels. "Say, Gid, what brings you out this way? If you've got a wife and son, why don't you get a job near them? Why come so far?"

Gideon tugged on a shingle, and when it snapped in two, he tossed the pieces to the ground. "I would if I could." He set his hammer down long enough to scoot sideways, and brittle splinters scratched at his pants. "She wants nothin' to do with me."

Owen dropped his eyes. "I'm sorry—"

Gideon held up a hand. "Don't be." He snapped another shingle loose. "I wish it weren't this way. But it is. I'll send her all I earn." *Then maybe she'll know how much I love her.*

The dinner bell rattled, and Mrs. Jemson hollered through the fog. "Soup's on!"

They needed no further encouragement to climb down, and with noses inches away from steaming bowls, they made little conversation. Mrs. Jemson slid a plate of hot cornbread in front of Gideon, and he glanced up. "Thank you, ma'am."

"Looks like you boys are getting a lot done out there today. Tal will be glad when that job's done."

"I think we will too." Owen dunked his bread into the thick broth. "It's too cold out there today to be up on a roof. That job should have waited until spring. Whose idea was this, anyway?"

"Mine." Gideon smiled as he chewed. "I was just trying to convince your pa to give me work."

"Well, thanks for dragging me along." Owen licked a drop of honey off his finger and shoved the last bite of cornbread in his mouth. When spoons scraped empty bowls, he scooted his chair back. "Ready?" he asked, his mouth still half full.

Tossing down his napkin, Gideon stood. "Why not. Let's get this done and over with."

They worked until the mist cleared and a burning sunset glittered through a wall of leafless trees. It reminded Gideon of a familiar lace hem. His fingers moved together involuntarily as if remembering the feel of the fabric in his hands. His chest burned with a yearning that would never be satisfied.

The supper bell drove them indoors. Chilled through and ravenous, he ate what Mrs. Jemson placed in front of him, then said good night, wanting to use the last of the light to make his way to the bunkhouse.

He sat on his bed and stared at nothing. He made marks on the grungy floor with the heel of his boot. After pulling his mandolin from its sack, he tuned the strings and indulged in a few strums—a song not quite forming—before setting the still vibrating instrument aside. Bending over, he yanked his laces free, and two boots banged against the wall as he kicked them loose.

With a grunt, he lay down and pulled his feet onto the bed. He tugged a worn quilt over his body and shivered. He stared at the bunk overhead, and he thought about lighting his pipe but didn't have a match.

The room dimmed as day gave up its last breath. The silent sigh drew his eyes to the window.

Grateful for the darkness, Gideon let his mind wander home. Images of the people he loved danced in his mind. Taunting him. He wished he could reach out and hold them. But he could no more will them into reality than he could brace his back beneath a setting sun.

When the pain proved too sharp, he closed his eyes and begged for the mercy of sleep.

Lonnie slid the bedroom window open and peered into the damp yard. A surprise rain had washed away most of the snow, leaving the musty scent of blackened oaks and matted leaves behind. The cold stung her cheeks, and as the frigid air filled her lungs, she scanned the yard, finding it as empty as the day before. The snap of pine splitting in two no longer echoed from the chopping block, and the familiar creak of the barn door never brought Gideon into view.

She leaned against the cold window frame and pressed her temple to the trim. Her cried-out eyes did not have to search hard to find the small cross at the edge of the clearing. She swallowed and looked away.

When Jacob stirred, she bounced him gently. His tiny nose had turned rosy, and Lonnie stepped away from the window. As she paced the floor, urging him to sleep, she looked into the face of her son.

And thought of his father.

Where is he? Her heart lurched, unbridled. *Lord, keep him safe.*

The image of Gideon's battered face held fast in her mind, but it was her words that struck her afresh. Tired of replaying the horrid events, she rubbed her eyes and willed herself to think of something else—anything else. Jacob let out a soft sigh and nestled in the crook of her arm. It was hopeless. Just looking into his tiny face made her think of the man she had loved. *Still* loved. Her heart broke afresh as it did every time, and Lonnie reminded herself that this was the best way for her son.

She stopped her pacing and sank into the rocking chair with all the heaviness she felt in her being. Even if she wanted to find Gideon, she had no idea where he was. With Jacob so weak and still nursing, she could not take him with her, nor could she leave him behind. And where would she go? Where would she begin? Lonnie tightened her arms around her son. She could scour the mountainside, but he might not have even stayed in Virginia. The thought sent a fresh burst of fear through her.

She pushed the rocker forward and then tugged the curtains farther back. The room brightened.

Once again, Lonnie prayed for Gideon's safety. She prayed that he would one day find peace with God. She looked out the window. He was somewhere out there. Yet "somewhere out there" didn't feel like enough. Not when she had a lifetime to share.

Fifty-One

K eep it up, boys. We only got a little bit of daylight left!" Tal looked down through the branches of a Jonathan tree and nodded at the setting sun. "Let's get this row finished."

Gideon gathered up another armful of branches and carried the awkward load to the wagon. Yanking off his leather gloves, he let his hands cool and studied the work still to be done. He wondered how many hours it would take to prune sixteen acres. After weeks of work, he wondered how many more it would take for the ache in his chest to yield.

Owen brushed past him, his arms full. "Hey, it ain't break time."

Gideon slid his gloves back on. "At a dollar and a quarter a week, I'm entitled to a break now and then."

After tossing an armload of branches into the wagon, Owen stooped to pick up stray twigs. "I ain't gettin' paid at all, so don't tell me you need a break."

Gideon knelt and snagged a branch at his feet. "Are you sayin' that this orchard—all these fields—won't be yours someday?"

Owen chuckled and punched Gideon's shoulder. Tal jumped down from his ladder and tossed his saw into the wagon. "That's it." He stooped to help clear the ground of trimmings. "Good work, boys. Couple more days of this and we'll be finished."

After folding up the ladder, Gideon lifted it into the wagon, then climbed up. He'd pruned enough branches to last a lifetime. He wondered how Tal and Owen did it year after year.

The wagon lurched forward, and Gideon clutched the side to steady himself. "Sure is a lot of work."

The mules leaned into the weight of their load as the wagon arched over a small hill. Tal glanced back. "It's a lot of work, but it's worth it. Wait until you see the apple harvest. It's a beautiful sight." He inhaled the evening air as if it were already late summer. "The sweet scent of apples warming in the sun. Plucking ripe fruit from their stems. Sliced apples over hotcakes. Cider and pie. There ain't nothing better than harvest time."

Gideon shrugged.

The side of Tal's mouth cocked up in a grin. "It suits *you* well enough. I ain't had many men work as hard as you, and if I'm not mistaken, I'd say apple farming may be in your future."

"Not me." Gideon leaned against the back of the wagon seat and crossed his feet one over the other.

"Why not?" Owen slapped his glove against Gideon's shoe. "You could get yourself a couple of acres and start a real nice farm. Settle down, raise a family—"

Tal shot him a look.

Owen pursed his lips and fell silent. When Tal cleared his throat, Owen spoke up. "Gid, I didn't mean nothin' by it."

Gideon picked up a twig and slid it between his lips, elbows on knees. "Don't worry about it."

They traveled the rest of the ride in silence.

The wagon slowed in front of the shed, and Gideon hopped out before it stopped. Tal called after him, but he just waved. He wasn't as hungry as he had thought. The ground was a quilt of mud and snow patches, and he trudged through the muck toward the bunkhouse.

He lit a fire and sat on the ground near the small stove. The fire crackled and popped. The wind that sneaked beneath the door blew dried leaves around the dusty floor. *Settle down. Raise a family.*

There was a time when that was the last thing he'd wanted. But he had taken his blessings for granted. When he felt warm enough, Gideon pushed himself to a stand and settled down at the rickety table. He fiddled with the piece of paper Mrs. Jemson had given him. He asked for it so he could send word to Lonnie. But it had been a foolish idea. He stared at the white page. He had nothing to write.

"Knock, knock." Tal's baritone filtered through the bunkhouse door.

"Come in."

Tal stepped in, pulled his hat off, and glanced around the single room. "You've tidied things a bit." He nodded a clear approval. "Place looks good."

"Thanks," Gideon said, his mind in another place.

As if Tal noticed, he pulled out a chair and sat across from him. He rested his hand on the table and tapped his thumb as if unsure where to begin. "Somethin's eatin' you up, ain't it, son?"

Gideon drew in a slow, measured breath. He realized there was no sense in pretending, so he simply nodded.

"My guess is that it has to do with that wife and son of yours."

He nodded again. Then, like a dagger, Lonnie's words pierced his heart. *Get out!* He remembered the pain in her eyes and hung his head. *I never want to see you again!* Could he blame her?

"Well, I've got something to say to you. I don't talk about this hardly with anyone." Tal settled deeper into his chair. "But there's a time and place for everything. And if someone can learn from my mistakes, then I'd be grateful."

Gideon lifted his head.

Tal turned his face to the window, and his eyes seemed distant. Gideon understood the sight—remembrance. "Not long after Owen was born, I did somethin' stupid." He glanced at Gideon, his face somber. "Really stupid. And I almost lost everything."

Gideon ran fingertips over his mouth, his unshaven jaw scratchy.

"But I did what needed to be done. I humbled myself. And my wife, God bless her, was more woman than I deserved." He leaned back in his chair, a smile lifting his mustache. "Don't make the same mistakes I did." He tapped a fist in the center of the table. "Don't let this one get away."

"I don't want to, sir." Gideon's throat was so tight the words were barely a whisper.

"Then what're ya sittin' around here for?" His smile bloomed into a full grin.

When Gideon didn't know what to say, Tal rose, squeezed his shoulder, and reached for his hat. "Hate to lose you, son. You're one of the best workers I've had." He stepped into the gray light of dusk. "But think on it." The door closed softly.

Lost in thought, Gideon fiddled with a corner of the paper. What would Lonnie do if he were to come back? Throw him out again? The thought sickened him. He'd broken her heart once; he hated to do it all over again.

Her words stuck like knives in his gut. Had she meant them? Or had she simply been frightened, overwhelmed? Pinching his eyes shut, he tried to picture her face—a small nose dusted with freckles and brown eyes large enough to get lost in.

He placed his head in his hands. His heart ached. Eyes that seemed to peer into his soul. They had caught his attention the night he'd walked her home. Shy and quiet, her eyes lingered on anything but him. Now they condemned him to cold nights of bachelorhood and empty days spent wondering what might have been.

Tossing the blank paper aside, he pulled a crumpled envelope from his shirt pocket. He flipped it open, and Gideon thumbed over the dollar bills. He pulled several out for Jebediah, folded them, and tied a scrap of paper around the money. He scratched Jebediah's name in tiny script. He stuffed everything into the envelope, then smoothed it closed. He scribbled across the fawn-colored paper. *Lonnie O'Riley.*

His bride.

Care of Jebediah Bennett.

He didn't seal the envelope, but when he looked at the waiting sheet of paper, he had no way to begin. No way to fit his entire heart onto a single piece of paper. Reaching up, he hung his coat on a nail that stuck out of his bunk and tucked the envelope safely inside a pocket. With slow movements, he folded up his faded brown pants and dropped them on the foot of the bed. He crawled beneath his blankets and faced the wall, where the glow of the moon peeked through a crack.

When he tried to sleep, he saw Lonnie's anger-filled eyes. She hated him. *You did nothing wrong,* Gideon told himself for the hundredth time. But as always, he reminded himself of the truth. *I took that money. I did not have to take Jebediah and Elsie's money, but I did.* Lonnie need not forgive him. He didn't deserve it.

Yet he needed her. And his arms ached to hold his son.

Gideon struck the side of his fist against the wall, and the burn shot up to his elbow. He despised the solitude of the bunkhouse. It made a man think too much. With his eyes open, he saw darkness. With his eyes closed, he saw faces he was supposed to forget. Staring at the boards of the bunk overhead, he realized how agonizing his life would be without Lonnie. Work would fill his days and keep his mind occupied, but it was the silence, the sleepless nights that tormented him. This was his life, for the rest of his days, until he died. This was his existence.

Unless, of course, he changed all that.

"God," Gideon called out to the unseen listener, the name foreign on his tongue. "What am I doing?"

Silence followed.

Gideon blinked furiously, trying to remember what it was he'd seen in Lonnie. It was more than her sweetness, her goodness. He saw faith. He didn't know what it entailed, but he knew she had always believed there was something redeemable in him. Could he not think the same? *God, show me what to do.*

Sitting up, he threw his blankets off. His heart pounded in his chest, pumping blood through his veins so fast he felt his strength return. Lonnie was out there somewhere. So was his son.

Gideon ran his hands through his hair. *You're a fool.*

Did he care?

Clambering to his feet, he dressed, then snatched the envelope from his coat. He folded it in half and thrust it into his pocket. It seemed he never had a plan in life, and this time was no different. But it was too late to care.

His heart was no longer his.

He knew of only one truth: he needed his family. And he hoped they still needed him.

He didn't have the right words to make Lonnie believe him, but he knew where to find her. That alone was reason enough to try. Without her in his life, there was nothing he feared losing—not even his pride. She was more of him than the creases in his palm, the smile in his voice. She was his home, etched into his soul. And that would never change.

When first light lit the orchards and melted away the dew, Gideon confronted Tal with his request.

Tal's pleasure was clear as he clasped Gideon's forearm. "You'll be missed."

Gideon felt the truth in the man's grip.

"Part of me wishes you'd stay on through the harvest. It'd be a shame for you to not see the fruits of your labors."

"I agree, sir." Gideon ran a hand over the back of his neck. "But that fruit doesn't grow on trees."

Tal's laugh rang clear in the cool, still morning.

Gideon shook his head, smiling. If only Tal knew the power drawing him to Lonnie. The overwhelming need to hold her. His inability to imagine life any other way. When he glanced at the doorway and saw Mrs. Jemson standing there, he knew Tal understood that feeling.

"I better be off." He lifted the pack beside him. It was time to lay his offenses at the feet of those he'd hurt. He was seeking from Lonnie the same peace that was beginning to come from God—redemption that made itself known in the secret spaces of his heart where his soul had once quaked but was now awash with the blessing of mercy, the gift of truth, and the promise of peace.

Fifty-Two

Jacob pulled a finger from his mouth and laid his damp hand on Lonnie's arm. Her heart melted as she peered into the happy face of her growing son. She used the hem of her apron to wipe his chin dry and kissed the tip of his nose. The day that should have been his birthday had come and gone, and with that momentous event, Lonnie finally felt relief. Her son was out of danger.

Taking care to support his head, she lifted him from her lap and pressed him to her chest. After a few gentle pats, he let out an unapologetic burp.

"That's my boy," she cooed into his tiny ear.

Lonnie heaved both herself and the baby out of the rocking chair, trying her best not to disturb him. He rubbed his face against her shoulder, clearly ready for his nap. Clearing her throat, she searched her hidden vault of songs. It was a place she often turned when her son needed comforting.

He tipped his head back and let out an exhausted cry. She held his cheek close to her heart as she began to sing.

"Come, Thou Fount of every blessing, tune my heart to sing Thy grace; streams of mercy, never ceasing, call for songs of loudest praise. Teach me some melodious sonnet, sung by flaming tongues above. Praise the mount. I'm fixed upon it, mount of Thy redeeming love."

Jacob continued to fuss, and Lonnie pressed him to her other shoulder as she crossed the bedroom floor, bouncing him gently. His eyelids fell closed, and knowing her singing was no longer needed, she jumped to the last verse, her favorite.

Softening her voice, she sank back into the rocker.

"O that day when freed from sinning, I shall see Thy lovely face; clothed then in blood washed linen how I'll sing Thy sovereign grace; come, my Lord, no longer tarry, take my ransomed soul away; send Thine angels now to carry me to realms of endless day."

Her bare feet arched, and the chair rocked. Her eyes lifted to the window. The clear morning sky held promise for the last of May. She sighed.

The will of her heart and mind battled against the memory of a man's face.

Even as she tried to fight it, past moments filled her, and she saw golden-red hair fall to the floor. A pair of strong hands plucked the strings of a poor boy's mandolin, and the smell of cut wood and soap filled her senses as she imagined draping her arm over the man lying next to her on a brass bed.

Her feet stilled, and she turned her face from the warmth of the window only to see the memory-filled room. She blinked, fighting a battle she could not win. Lonnie shook her head. It was madness. How was one to survive a broken heart?

No. She had more than a broken heart.

She couldn't explain it, but peering into the dim future, she saw a life not fully lived. The suffocating knowledge that her numbered days would be spent away from the only man she loved made the hours pass slowly, and she found her only cheer in her son's presence.

She tried to remember that His eye was on the sparrow.

The day passed busily, but that night felt as lonely as all the others. Worse.

Lonnie climbed beneath the covers, blew out the candle, and tucked the quilt beneath her chin. Each night was crueler than the one before. Her pain did not fade. With each setting of the sun and inevitable rising of the moon, the possibility of Gideon's return dimmed. If he was traveling, he was getting farther away and she could do nothing to bring him back. For the past weeks she had wondered if there might have been an explanation for his actions. If she had given him the chance to explain…

Yet his innocence seemed unlikely. Still, she clung to the hope that perhaps he hadn't gone back on his promise. Perhaps he had truly loved her and that wretched day had been a misunderstanding. Lonnie tucked her hand beneath her chin. There was nothing she could do about it now, though. There was no distance she could run. No cry loud enough to stop him from disappearing out of her life. She would beg for the chance to hear him out—fall to her knees with a waiting apology burned to her lips—but she no longer had that chance.

Lonnie lay awake, listening to Jacob's steady breathing next to her. With no one to share the small bed, she found comfort in having him near. The grandfather clock below chimed eleven, and she closed her eyes. She had to sleep. Sleep was her only relief.

Stepping into the clearing felt familiar. Gideon paused long enough to catch his breath and long enough to take in the memories. As he stared at the moonlit frame of Jebediah's house, the emotions of his heart made his skin tingle—his family was inside. There was nothing in this moment that was missing. Nothing except Lonnie's face in his hands and his belated apology glinting in the tears of her eyes.

Gideon knew what he wanted for his life.

He wanted summer nights on the porch, sipping cool tea. He dreamed of fresh-baked apple pie cooling on the windowsill, made by his wife's hand from apples he seeded. He had a debt he was determined to repay the Bennetts. Stepping forward to what he once knew as home was the easiest thing he had done in a long time.

The back door would be locked. He knew that even before he tested the latch. No one ever used the front door, and that would be locked too. He was more than willing to face Jebediah, but at the moment, knowing Lonnie and his son were so close, he couldn't wait any longer to see them. He made his way around the side of the house and peered up to see the billow of lace curtains in spring's midnight breeze. Dropping his pack, he hurried to the barn. He tugged the ladder away from the wall and chuckled to himself. *Jebediah won't mind.*

Or would he? Jebediah had taken it upon himself to protect Lonnie. Gideon lowered the ladder, but only for a moment. What would Jebediah do when he found him? Gideon gripped a rung, pressing it against his shoulder. He would have to face the consequences, but he couldn't worry about that, not now. Right now, he had a wife who was waiting for him. *Please, Lord. Let it be.*

It took all his strength to lower the heavy ladder against the side of the house without a sound. His breath was loud in his ears as he climbed toward the window without making a sound. Gideon hesi-

tated and swallowed, then, brushing the curtains aside, peered into a
dark room.

With slow, quiet movements, he lifted one leg over and then the
other. His boot touched the hardwood floor, and he pulled himself into
the room. *What am I thinking?* Lonnie would wake and he would startle her. Suddenly unsure of what to do, he crouched down, and his shirt
grew taut over his shoulders as he pressed palms to the floor. He should
climb down and bang on the door.

But Lonnie rolled toward him, and her arm came down and gently
draped over a tiny person.

Gideon had to remind himself to breathe. He stepped as close to
the bed as he dared, then, falling to his knees, pulled back the corner of
the quilt that obstructed his view and found himself inches away from
a face that mirrored his own. A pair of rosebud lips drooped against the
softest-looking cheeks he had ever seen. With a trembling hand, he
reached forward.

"Gid?" Lonnie whispered.

He jumped and snapped his hand back. "Lonnie!"

"Gideon?" Her voice cracked. Before he could stand, she nestled
the baby out of the way and clambered off the edge of the bed.

They sank to the ground in a tangle of arms and legs.

He filled his hands with her nightgown and drew her as close as he
could.

Lonnie flung her arms around him and gripped his neck. "Oh,
Gid, you came back!"

Her skin was soft beneath his hands as he brushed her wild hair
from her face and soaked in the sight of her. "I did. I'm so sorry—"

Lonnie pressed his head into her shoulder, silencing him. Her body
shook with silent sobs.

Gideon struggled to speak, but he had no great words. He was no poet. He was simply a man who missed his wife and needed her by his side.

"I had to see you." He cupped her face in his hands. "I had to see the baby."

"Oh, the baby!" She scooped up the sleeping bundle and held him against her chest. She turned, and he saw Jacob's face. She looked back over her shoulder and smiled, and Gideon knew his expression had to be one of bewilderment and wonder.

His voice cracked as he spoke. "Can I hold him?"

She gently placed Jacob in his arms. "His head's a bit wobbly."

Gideon stepped toward the window and held Jacob to the moonlight. Tiny black lashes fanned across his pale skin. "He's perfect," he whispered. The weight of his own son in his arms was enough to fill his heart and chase away the emptiness.

"I know."

He swallowed, and when pain flashed through her eyes, he pulled her close with his other arm. "I'm sorry I was not there for you when it happened."

She nodded and wiped her palms across her eyes. Her chin trembled even as she peered up at him. "Jesus has her. She's in a good—"

"She is." Gideon kissed the top of Lonnie's head and closed his eyes when his emotions overwhelmed him. "I wish I had been here."

"Me too."

"Will you forgive me?"

Lonnie didn't speak. But when she tightened her grip on his arm and buried her face in his chest, she didn't have to.

"I was heading home," his voice cracked again. He tilted his face up, willing away the lump in his throat. "I was trying to get to you." His voice weakened. "All I wanted to do was get home. Please believe me."

She smelled of honeysuckle when he kissed the top of her head. His lips moved against her hair. "I'd gone lookin' for Bert—to pay a debt. I just didn't know what it would be."

She touched his cheekbone, where the flesh had long since healed.

"I was worried that they'd come lookin' for me. I didn't want to bring that type of trouble to you or the Bennetts." He swiped his forearm across his eyes. "I tried to fight them off, I did. I swear I did everything in my power to get to you. But I couldn't."

Lonnie covered her face.

He gripped her shoulders, willing her eyes to meet his. He needed her to see that he was telling the truth. "There were too many of them." Gideon drew her close. An ache burned in his chest as he held his family. "I love you more than anything."

She sniffed and nodded. "I know you do." She wiped her nose with the sleeve of her nightgown. "I'm so sorry."

He shook his head. "Enough with the sorrys. We're together now. Nothing can ever change that." He pulled her closer. "I'm not leaving you again, Lonnie O'Riley." A laugh lightened his voice. "I'll never give you a reason to ask me to leave. I'll sleep in the barn for the rest of my life if you want me to. But you won't be able to get rid of me."

Glistening eyes met his, and the joy of her heart confessed itself in her smile.

Footsteps sounded in the hall, and the door flung open. Gideon blinked into the light of a lantern.

"What's going on?" Jebediah's angry face froze, then his jaw fell.

Elsie stuck her head beneath her husband's arm and screamed. "Blessed be! How'd you get in here?"

Lonnie tightened her grip on Gideon. "He climbed in through the window. Scared me near to death!"

Gideon smiled down at his wife. "Hey, *you* attacked *me*," he laughed. Jacob lifted his head, and Gideon tilted him back to get a better look. "He's beautiful."

"He looks like you."

Gideon grinned. No matter which feature he admired, he saw himself. "I suppose he does."

They fell silent.

"Now what?" Lonnie asked.

Jebediah cleared his throat.

Gideon faced him. "I'm sorry, Jebediah. I never should have… I was going to replace… I mean, I *will* replace—" With a deep breath, Gideon relayed the truth of what had happened—all of it—knowing so much responsibility lay on his own shoulders. "I'll pay back every cent."

"I know you will." Jebediah stepped into the room and set his lantern on the nightstand.

Elsie looked up at Jebediah. Lantern light flecked on the lace of her nightgown.

"I'd like to tell you something, Gid." Jebediah wrapped an arm behind his wife's shoulders. "Well, Elsie and me. I was going to tell you before everything happened. But then…"

It was the first time Gideon had ever heard the man's voice falter.

Elsie wrapped an arm around Jebediah's waist and kissed his shoulder.

"This place," Jebediah said with a sweep of his arm. "The house. The land. All of it…" He paused and glanced down at Elsie, who smiled up at him. His eyes met Gideon's. "I hope you'll stay around a little longer because, well…it's yours. If you want it."

He heard Lonnie gasp.

"I ain't got no one to leave it to, and I couldn't imagine it any other way." Jebediah chuckled even as tears formed in Elsie's eyes. "Your wife is like a daughter to me, and that little boy—" His voice caught.

Jebediah stepped forward, and when Gideon extended a hand, the older man wrapped him in a crushing embrace. "You ain't too bad yourself. Well, not anymore." He chuckled, and Gideon couldn't help but grin.

"The baby!" Elsie cried.

When Jebediah jumped back, Gideon cradled a still-sleeping Jacob in his arms. He had no words to thank his friend. It seemed like a lifetime ago that the end of Jebediah's gun had pointed at his back. And Gideon could never begin to voice his gratitude for the divine intervention that had taken place that day.

"I'll take it," he whispered through a voice so tight, the words barely got out.

How did a man come so far? How did he pick himself up by his bootstraps, shake off the dregs of an old life, and have his hands filled with such blessings? Gideon hadn't done anything by his own strength, of that he was certain. And he didn't deserve one bit of it. He was humbled by the people surrounding him. He'd chased his own desires his entire life. Now that he knew what it meant to care for others more than himself, he would do everything in his power to see it through.

He prayed the Lord would keep at bay all that lay outside his own strength.

Lonnie squeezed his hand. Her soft fingers spoke the silent promise that she would always be by his side.

Gideon squeezed back and buried his face in her hair. "I'll never leave you again."

Her lips brushed the back of his hand, warming him through.

Author's Note

A special thanks to the Patrick County Historical Society for copies made, questions answered, and the deliciously thick *History of Patrick County*, one of the greatest resources I turned to for historical details on this region of the Blue Ridge Mountains.

For eagle-eyed history buffs and those who watch the sun rise and set from the Blue Ridge Mountains, it was my constant goal to ensure the historical quality of this book and to uphold the beauty and integrity of this region. It was my utmost desire to take as few liberties as possible. For any that appear, it was solely for the sake of telling Lonnie and Gideon's story.

I have been blessed by many prayers and words of encouragement during this season of my life and am humbled by the outpouring of love and enthusiasm shown by so many faithful readers and writers whom I'm blessed to call my friends. A huge, heartfelt thank-you to all of you.

If you would like to stay in touch, you can sign up at my website, www.joannebischof.com, to receive my free e-newsletter, *The Heartfelt Post*, sent out each spring and autumn. It's always a blessing to meet new readers on Facebook and Twitter, so I hope you will stop in and say hi. I would love to hear from you! Thank you for journeying the Blue Ridge Mountains with me in *Be Still My Soul*. I hope you will join me for the next leg of our adventure in *Though My Heart Is Torn*.

Readers Guide

1. What does the title, *Be Still My Soul,* signify to you? Do you feel it reflects Lonnie or Gideon? Or perhaps both?

2. Lonnie and Gideon grew up in the same hollow, yet were never well acquainted. Having only known each other from afar, how do they view each other the night of the singing? In what ways did those opinions change by the time Joel gathers them together several days later?

3. Both Lonnie and Gideon have faced difficulties growing up. Which of their difficulties are similar? How do their families differ? Whether good or bad, how did each of their home lives mold them into who they are in the beginning of the book?

4. Lonnie's aunt Sarah is very dear to her. What traits do you feel the two women share? What lessons has Lonnie learned from Sarah that support her along her journey?

5. Views of marriage in the early 1900s were much different than today, and Lonnie is faced with a difficult dilemma. When refusal to obey her father's wishes would result in consequences both physical and emotional, do you feel she has a choice to refuse Gideon—refuse her pa's demands? What would you say to encourage her during this time?

6. Jebediah and Elsie provide shelter for Lonnie and Gideon physically, spiritually, and emotionally. While the Bennetts are kind and generous, they are also wealthy. Do you feel the Bennetts would be equally as generous if they had less? What is it about their character that influences your conclusion?

7. There are many things in Gideon's life that he regrets, yet he's unsure of how to move past them. He has a difficult time owning his actions and admitting when he's wrong. What counsel would you give him? In what ways do you see him grow as the story progresses?

8. Jebediah challenges Gideon in ways the young man has never experienced. He's also patient at times when Gideon is undeserving. What does this say about Jebediah? What role does the older man play in Gideon's life over the course of the story?

9. There are many choices to make in life, but sometimes the choices of others affect us the greatest. How does this relate to Lonnie and Gideon's journey?

10. Being faced with a situation that is out of our control is difficult. Is there a purpose for these moments in life? If so, how does it shape the person enduring the hardship? How can losing everything draw us closer to the Lord?

11. The Cadence of Grace series is based on 1 Peter 5:10: "But may the God of all grace, who called us to His eternal glory by Christ Jesus, after you have suffered a while, perfect, establish, strengthen, and settle you." In *Be Still My Soul,* how does this scripture relate to Lonnie and Gideon's journey? Have you seen this scripture reflected in your own life?

12. In the final moments of the story, Gideon vows to cherish his family. He also prays that God will keep at bay all which lies outside his own strength. Do you feel a change might be coming for the O'Rileys? What do you think might be on the horizon?

Acknowledgments

When I begin to thank You, my great God, words fail me. I am so grateful You can see into my heart. It is my utmost prayer that these pages honor You.

I am immensely grateful to my parents, Mike and Janette, for allowing me to daydream and make believe from the moment I could hold a pen and paper. Your enthusiasm and support have meant the world to me.

This book wouldn't have been possible without my amazing agent, Sandra Bishop. Thank you for your enthusiasm and for championing this story from the start.

A very special thank you to my editors, Beth Adams and Shannon Marchese. Your insights and wisdom have helped shape this story and this writer. I am incredibly grateful. Also a huge thanks to the entire team at WaterBrook Multnomah Publishing Group for opening your doors to this story and for all the hard work and creativity that has made it take flight.

Thank you to Rebecca Farnbach and all those at the Temecula critique group for creating a wonderful and safe haven where writers can blossom. And I could never begin to express my gratitude for the hours poured in by Dona Watson, Beverly Nault, and Ashley Ludwig. Your advice, guidance, and encouragement helped me through the last stages of this story. Thank you for the laughs and the tears and the red pens. You are all amazing.

To the Hemet teachers who led me down the path of creating and discovery: Mrs. Drumm, Mrs. Edmundson, Mrs. Dement, Mr. James, and Mr. Rossi. This is how you live in my heart. Thank you.

And lastly, a thank-you-so-much-it-hurts to my brown-eyed husband and three brown-eyed children. This green-eyed girl is blessed to have your hearts and your smiles.

About the Author

Married to her first sweetheart, Joanne Bischof lives in the mountains of Southern California where she keeps busy making messes with their homeschooled children. When she's not weaving Appalachian romance, she's blogging about faith, writing, and the adventures of country living that bring her stories to life. *Be Still My Soul* is her first novel.

Coming Spring 2013!

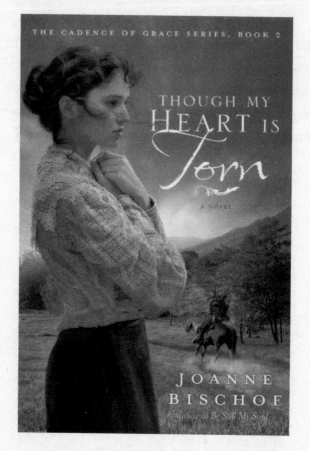

THE CADENCE OF GRACE SERIES, BOOK 2

THOUGH MY
HEART IS
Torn

A NOVEL

JOANNE
BISCHOF

Author of *Be Still My Soul*

Lonnie only ever wanted to be loved.
Now that she's won her husband's heart,
will his past destroy their happily-ever-after?

Read an excerpt from this book and
more at www.WaterBrookMultnomah.com!